BECOMING
Lottie Moon

BECOMING
Lottie Moon

EMILY HALL

To request permission, contact the author at emily@emilyhallbooks.com.

Paperback: 979-8-9886118-0-6

Ebook: 979-8-9886118-1-3

First paperback edition 2023

Cover illustration: Joel Cockrell, joellaneart.com

Cover design and layout: Emilie Haney, eahcreative.com

Author photo: Robert Jaron

Correspondence, Papers, Addresses, Articles, etc. of Lottie Moon, 1870 - 1927, Archives and Special Collections, James P. Boyce Centennial Library, The Southern Baptist Theological Seminary, Louisville, Kentucky. Reprinted by permission.

All scriptures are from the King James Version, public domain.

Printed in the United States of America

To Thomas and Violet, two of the greatest gifts I have ever received.

To my parents, Mark and Susan, my first readers and encouragers.

"Now to him who is able to do far more abundantly than all that we ask or think, according to the power at work within us, to him be glory"

— EPHESIANS 3:20-21A

CHAPTER ONE

1847 Viewmont, Virginia

S ix-year-old Lottie Moon cupped her hands around her face and pressed into the cold living room window, watching for any movement down the carriage drive of Viewmont Plantation. It was getting late, and Father wasn't supposed to return from his business trip for another day, but sometimes he came home early. And he always brought books with him to further stuff the family's library shelves. In the dark night, Lottie couldn't see much of her family's fifteen-hundred acres. Most of it sprawled behind the house, where the slaves' cabins stood beside miles of tobacco and cornfields. Lottie fixed her gaze forward. Her nose touched the window. If Father arrived soon, maybe she could hear a story from his travels before bed. One day, she would go far away and bring home stories of her adventures just like Father.

"Orianna, get away from that freezing window," Grandmother Harris bellowed from the sofa.

Lottie whirled around. Before she could correct her, her twelve-year-old sister, Orie, spoke without looking up from untying a bag of new marbles. "That's Lottie, not me."

Grandmother peered at Lottie with a puzzled look. "Oh, yes. Well, come away from there, child."

Orie dumped the marbles onto the floor while Tom, the eldest of her brothers and sisters, laid a string circle around them.

Ike, the third oldest, walked over from the fireplace and sat cross-legged beside the marble circle. "Why can't they be in a cross like normal?"

"Because I'm setting up this round, that's why." Orie glared at her brother. "Knuckle down and play or leave us alone."

Ike mumbled something about just asking a question.

Lottie heaved a sigh and pulled her heavy robe tight around her white nightgown. She obediently crossed the parlor and sat on the floor with her siblings. A crackling fire kept the large room warm as a March wind howled outside. Gilded mirrors and landscapes of the Wild West decorated the walls, along with portraits of family from the past, staring down on the current generation of Moons. The portraits hung so high, it seemed that they presided in judgment from heaven. Lottie avoided eye contact with them.

Everyone chose their shooter, and Lottie scooted toward the pile of marbles. As she bent low, she brushed away a lock of brown hair from her face. Aiming with her mouth and one eye open, Lottie flicked her yellow-swirled shooter toward the other colorful orbs. They clacked when they hit each other, then silently rolled across the soft red-patterned rug all in different directions. Lottie grinned as the swirls inside the glass spun.

Mother's silk dress rustled as she came and rested a hand on one of the high-back chairs between the cozy sofa and the smaller settee. The tips of her long silver dress brushed the rug. When she offered a bedtime story in the girls' room, Lottie scrambled up and ran toward the stairs, careful to avoid any stray marbles that might trip her and ruin her victory.

She looked back over her shoulder and saw Orie close behind her. Ike hopped from one marble to the next, collecting each one into the drawstring leather pouch. Tom calmly rose from his seat. Lottie would win for sure.

She didn't really have a reason to beat her sister and brothers to the bedroom she and Orie shared. Each of them had long ago laid claim to their favorite spots for Mother's story times, so no one was likely to steal Lottie's place. And yet, she raced up the steps and down the hall.

Lottie rushed in through the doorway and plopped down onto the braided rug near the rocker, jostling the chair's small cushion. The rug was just as thick as the one in the parlor but nowhere near as soft. Still, Mother said it was special because women who lived years ago had made it by braiding scrap fabrics together. "On their own, those scraps could never be what they are now together," Mother had said.

Her older siblings filed in. Orie lay down and settled her head on top of the extra blankets hanging neatly over the foot of her carved wooden bed. Ike sat on the floor and leaned against Orie's bed. Tom stretched across the rug and propped his head up with his fists, cushioning his elbows with a pillow.

Mother walked in carrying a book about Adoniram and Ann Judson. As she settled onto the rocker, Lottie scooted closer. She loved this story about missionaries who had sailed for India thirty-five years ago.

Mother propped the book up on her lap and read from where she'd left off last night. "'The government officials received their orders: the foreigners had to go.'" She glanced up and met the eyes of all four children. "'The young missionaries had been evangelizing and baptizing in the area for less than a year, but the message of Jesus was bringing too much change. The missionaries were not welcome any longer.'"

Lottie had heard this story several times but did not understand what the officials didn't like about Jesus. In Bible stories, he only did nice things. Jesus was harmless.

Mother's focus returned to the page. "'Men banged on the door of the small missionary home, yelling in the local language, "Open up!"'"

Mother's shout jolted Ike, and he bumped his head against Orie's footboard. Orie giggled. Mother smiled and continued.

Some of the stories Mother read at night were so boring that Lottie fell asleep right there on the floor, needing to be scooped up and carried to her bed. But she thoroughly enjoyed adventure stories like this one.

Lottie hugged her knees up to her chin as Mother shared about this couple who had rejected their boring lives and crossed vast oceans, traveled to distant lands, and blazed through dangerous jungles, even though the Judsons' relatives wanted them to do the same things their parents and grandparents did before them. What gumption they had, to go against the rules like that. If only she could escape from the ones imposed on her—like sitting still in church and behaving properly when Grandmother Harris was around. Lottie wanted a life of freedom and adventure, and she was determined to have it one day.

"'After Adoniram and Ann were banished from proclaiming God's message in India, they and their partners left, settling in the land called Burma. This is where God had called them to preach now, and this is where He would provide a harvest.'"

"Mother, where is Burna?" Ike asked.

"It's Bur-*ma*, dear, and it's east of India, near China."

"That's where Uncle James and Aunt Julia want to be missionaries!" Lottie dropped her knees and sat up straight, lifting her chin.

"That's right." Mother smiled at Lottie. "But because it upsets your grandmother, you all know not to mention it around her, right?"

She locked eyes with each of them until every head nodded.

As far back as Lottie could remember, Grandmother Harris spoke her mind whenever the adults quarreled about things. Lately, even the mention of anything unpleasant set her crying or yelling. Mother reminded the children often about which things were best left unsaid.

Mother continued reading. "'Although Ann's heart broke for the lost souls in India, she believed in the good Lord's sovereign direction and focused her prayers on the new group of people around her. She prayed, *Dispel the darkness over Burma, oh thou radiant Light of the world. May thy brilliance radiate, revealing thy goodness and might to the people of Burma. Win their hearts and make them thy favored ones.'"*

Mother closed the book. "That's a good place to end for tonight."

Tom stood and released a yawn as he stretched with both arms. He and Ike shuffled out of the room and down the hall. Lottie rubbed her eyes as she tottered over to her bed. Orie flipped over to her side and slid under the covers.

As Mother started to close the door, Orie said, "I have a question."

Orie often asked Mother questions right before bed so she would stay just a little longer.

Mother sighed quietly, crossed the room, and sat beside Orie.

"Why didn't Mr. and Mrs. Judson go somewhere nice when they had to leave India?"

Mother's dark eyebrows rose at the genuine question. "They went where they thought God wanted them to go."

"Why did he want them to go to such an awful place?"

Lottie's once-restful mind, ready for sleep, now raced with thoughts about Orie's question. The Judsons found adventure in India, but they also found danger. Would Lottie be brave enough to face danger in her adventures one day?

"Burma isn't an awful place. Although life there was challenging. Sometimes when we follow God ... he asks us to do things that aren't very easy."

Orie's brow furrowed, and she rubbed her forehead.

Every other time Mother had told them that story, she read that Mrs. Judson got a terrible disease in Burma and died. How would Mother explain that it was good that they followed God there?

"Remember our Psalm from last week?" Mother's brown eyes brightened as she leaned closer to Orie. "'He maketh me to lie down in green pastures. He leadeth me beside the still waters. Though I walk through the valley of the shadow of death, I will fear no evil for thou art with me.'"

Lottie remembered. If she had to pick a favorite Psalm, it would be that one. The green pastures and still waters made her think of Viewmont. And she liked to imagine trekking through a rocky valley full of sharp ridges and creepy shadows.

"God leads us to good things, even when the path looks scary and dangerous." Mother smiled. "We don't have to fear anything because he is always with us."

Such a mysterious answer! But it seemed to be all they were going to get for now. Mother kissed Orie and Lottie, then left the room.

Thoughts of the Judsons and Burma collided with thoughts of Uncle

James and Aunt Julia sailing to the mission field in China. After several minutes of not sleeping, she whispered, "You awake?"

Orie rolled over to face Lottie.

"Is China a hard place to live?" Lottie asked.

"Maybe," Orie answered drowsily. "Uncle James says God wants them to go there. So it probably isn't very nice."

Panic swelled in Lottie's chest. Uncle James said God wanted him to be a missionary, just like the Judsons. "Do you think Aunt Julia will die in China?"

"Grandmother won't let them go," Orie said mid-yawn. "She is much scarier than God."

Orie rolled over, and Lottie relaxed. Thanks to Grandmother, Uncle James and Aunt Julia would stay safe at home. Lottie pulled her blanket up closer to her chin and snuggled in for a good night's sleep.

But a tinge of sadness came to her heart at the thought of her aunt and uncle missing out on adventures that would never happen as long as Grandmother had a say in it.

Anna Moon peeked into the nursery to check on Sallie. She smiled as the four-year-old's tummy slowly rose and fell. Perhaps Sallie would ask hard questions like Orie someday, but for now, she was simple to manage. Anna blew a kiss and closed the door.

"Another day done, and everyone's accounted for." She sighed. "Well, almost everyone."

Edward was still in Louisiana, but he would be home by the end of next week. Although she was used to him going away to meet with his trading partners, managing five children and the Viewmont estate alone was a lot of work. She could hardly wait to see her husband's carriage coming up the road.

Stepping softly down the stairs, she wrapped her arms around the book and held it with the front cover close to her chest. The title would certainly provoke her mother, who was in the parlor by the library.

She winced when the old wood creaked beneath her. She should have known. That step always gave her children away when they tried to sneak around the house at night.

"Anna, is that you?" Mother called out.

The woman may be growing weaker, but her hearing was as sharp as ever.

"Yes, Mother. I've just put the children to bed."

"Please come here."

"I'll be right there." Anna quickened her pace down the last couple of steps and hurried past the parlor toward the library.

"I need you now!" Mother barked. "My blanket has slipped off again, and I'm freezing in this drafty room."

Her mother hadn't always barked. She'd never been overly soft or empathetic, but she usually spoke more kindly to her daughter and grandchildren. Lately, she had become demanding about the tiniest problems. And she occasionally mixed up the family's names.

Anna stopped at the parlor doorway, glanced up to the heavens, and pleaded for divine help before entering the room. As she reached down to pick up the blanket off the floor, Mother gasped.

"What is that?" She pointed to the book as if she'd just caught a child holding stolen candy.

"It's a bedtime story for the children." Anna clutched the blanket in her hand.

Before her mother could stress herself into a fit, Anna took a deep breath, laid the blanket over her mother's lap, and knelt beside her. "I loved the stories you read to me as a girl. Do you remember?"

Her eyes misted. "Yes."

After Anna's father had died when she was an infant, Mother crumbled under the sudden pressure to run the house and the business. She sold both and sent Anna's older siblings—Tom, Mary, and James—to move in with other relatives. She kept only Anna. By the time they all lived under the same roof again, Tom and Mary said they were too old for bedtime stories, but Anna enjoyed cuddling with James and Mother around a book.

"I read from the Bible and books about missionaries." Mother's eyebrows furrowed. "That was a mistake. If I hadn't read those stories, James wouldn't have developed such an obsession with missions that he wanted to leave us."

Anna set the book on the floor and pushed it under the sofa, out of sight. She would re-shelve it in the morning. She tucked the warm blanket around her mother's knees and kissed her cheek.

Anna considered trying to lift Mother off the sofa, help her up the stairs, and settle her into her own bed, which was far more comfortable to sleep in. But her mother was old and the hour was late. Forcing a journey from where she was now didn't seem worth the time and effort, not to mention the inevitable grumbling.

"James is happy he stayed here, isn't he?" Mother asked softly.

"Very happy."

"Good. There's no need for people like us to go off to China. He could easily obey God's call here. And if he had to leave home, there are more than enough heathens out West. Not to mention those wayward Christians up North, what with their spiritualism and Mormonism and other such nonsense."

"Yes, Mother." Anna had heard these justifications before. She didn't challenge them.

"If he had gone to China, he wouldn't have come home," Grandmother went on, as if trying to answer accusations that only she could hear.

Anna put a reassuring hand on Mother's shoulder. "Why don't you rest your eyes a bit? I'll be back in a few minutes with pillows."

As she left the room, her mother muttered, "I didn't stop him from marrying a Presbyterian or joining her church. And then they say they want to move to China. No one should expect a mother to stand for that. And if Anna keeps reading those stories to my grandchildren, the same thing will happen to her."

By the time Anna came back with an armload of spare pillows, Mother had fallen asleep. Anna gently tucked them behind her head and under her arms.

Why was Mother so concerned about James's happiness all of a sudden? She didn't show concern for it ten years ago when he and Julia told the family they felt called to missionary work in China. Maybe as Mother was nearing the end of her life, she regretted things in her past. If only James would come see her and assure her that all was well.

James and Julia lived in the bustling town of Scottsville, not ten miles away, but they hadn't been over, not even for supper, since New Year's. Their apothecary business kept them busy, they said. And traveling in the winter was wearisome. But James needed to visit soon, before it was too late.

Mother stirred, turned her head, then settled back into sleep. Anna's heart constricted. If Mother was approaching her last days, would a conversation with James disturb her? Then again, she wasn't at peace now.

Perhaps a simple family meal would be what they all needed. She could invite Mary and her family to join them. If no one mentioned anything about missionaries or China, they could all enjoy a peaceful time together. As long as everyone cooperated and behaved themselves, it should work.

Unfortunately, cooperating and behaving weren't strong traits in the Moon family.

CHAPTER TWO

1847

The following Sunday, Lottie carefully fastened the buttons on her navy dress with a white collar. Orie was flattening the lace on her collar when Mother walked in.

"Stop dawdling, girls." She spoke loudly without quite yelling, her attempt to keep the Sabbath holy. "Your father, brothers, and sister are all at the wagons with the servants."

Lottie lifted and looked under a bonnet on top of her dresser and *Oliver Twist* that Orie had read aloud last night. She dug through her dresser drawers. "I can't find my navy hair ribbon." Mother always said it was important for them to look their best at church. And since they sat close to the front, Lottie's hair ribbon was what most people would see when they looked at her.

"You can borrow mine." Orie handed Lottie a dark green silk ribbon.

"But this doesn't match my dress!"

Mother grabbed the ribbon. "The green looks nice with your hair." She quickly arranged it into Lottie's chestnut curls. "You should be grateful we have a church to drive to each week. Before you were born, since your father wasn't a Baptist yet, I had to hold services at home most Sundays."

Lottie had heard the stories many times. Pine Grove Baptist Church was a small country church near Viewmont that only met once a month. When Pine Grove was closed, Mother gathered the family and the slaves downstairs to listen as she read from the Word.

"You are fortunate to worship in a beautiful, brick chapel and hear from a seminary-trained pastor." Mother finished primping Lottie's hair with a gentle tug on the bow.

Lottie didn't feel fortunate. She dreaded going to church. But the carriage ride down the country roads was surely better than sitting in the parlor listening to Mother's Bible lessons.

The three of them waved goodbye to Grandmother on their way downstairs.

The rest of the family waited in the covered carriage. Mother joined Father up front. Orie hopped in the back with their siblings. Lottie stepped up and glanced behind her.

The slaves crowded in plain, open buckboard wagons. Lottie waved at Peggy in the wagon right behind the family's carriage. She smiled back. A year older than Lottie, Peggy squeezed between her parents, George and Fannie. Fannie licked her thumb, then used it to smooth down Peggy's tight curls.

"Shoulda used more bacon grease," Fannie said.

Despite her efforts, little ringlets sprang out around Peggy's braids like a halo.

Peggy put on her plain bonnet, undoubtedly to protect her hair from further attention from her mother. She grabbed the tattered, faded shawl that Lottie's mother and father had given her three Christmases ago and wrapped it around her shoulders. Back then it was thick and a rich brown color.

Mother snapped her fingers at Lottie. "Get in. Don't gawp at the servants."

Servants—that's what Mother always told her and her siblings to call them. But Lottie knew they were different than the servants in *Oliver Twist*. The servants at Viewmont weren't free, and they never would be. It wasn't fair.

Lottie climbed in and scooted across the cushioned bench next to Orie. Father snapped the reins, and they all headed for Scottsville Baptist Church.

Along the way, Father told them about the early-blooming wildflowers they passed. He grinned as he talked, handsome in his dark wool suit. Later in the spring, he would probably point out the leafy sprouts in various fields like he did last year and quiz Lottie and her siblings about what crops they would grow to be.

Mother leaned over to speak to Father. Lottie strained to hear what they said.

"After the service," Mother murmured as she rested her head on Father's shoulder, "I'd like to stop by the Disciples Church and speak to James for a moment."

If only Lottie's aunt and uncle would join the family in their pew at Scottsville Baptist. Mother and Father had helped found the church and fund the building before Lottie was born. But Uncle James had joined the Disciples of Christ. He build the pews and the pulpit for their church on Main Street. He even preached there sometimes.

"We'll wait to drive home until you walk over there and get back." Father clutched the reins in one hand and moved the other to Mother's back. "Do you need help with anything?"

"No, I've just got a question for him."

What question did Mother have that was too urgent for a letter? Maybe Lottie could walk with Mother to the Disciples' church and find out.

Uncle James and Aunt Julia didn't visit Viewmont near as often as Lottie wanted them to. Her cousins were such fun to play with, and Uncle James could turn a plain conversation into an interesting argument like no one else could. Lottie didn't fully understand a lot of the things he said, but she could tell by the way Father and Aunt Julia suddenly found great interest in their shoes or a wall ornament that they were things Uncle James wasn't supposed to say around Grandmother. Mother often shushed her brother, and Grandmother lifted her chin and threw her shoulders back as if ready for battle.

Maybe that explained why the two families went to different churches.

Aunt Julia had been a Presbyterian before she became a Disciple of Christ, and she had a lot of family who were Baptists. All that experience surely made her an expert on religious things. Lottie had once asked her why everyone fought about God and church. She told Lottie that people often fight about the things they love, especially when they see them in different ways. The only difference Lottie had noticed was that the Baptist pastor dismissed the congregation several minutes earlier than the Disciples got to leave their service.

When they reached Scottsville Baptist, everyone climbed out of the wagons and headed up the grassy hill for the church. Lottie paused before she reached the doors. The church sat higher than the rest of the town. Streets of houses, churches, and shops sprawled in every direction. Uncle James's church was on a smaller hill across from the canal basin where yawl boats and small boats went through along the James River.

Mother tapped Lottie's shoulder and cocked an eyebrow. "Time to go inside."

Lottie followed her family into the sanctuary. They walked toward their pew near the front. The slaves took the steps up to the balcony.

Lottie looked back and saw Peggy remove her bonnet and shawl as she chatted with another dark-skinned girl. The balcony was always crowded. Must be cozy on chilly mornings. But summer Sundays had everyone in the balcony sweating, the women fluttering their paper fans as fast as they could.

"It's not polite to stare," Mother whispered.

Lottie took her seat at the end of the pew between Orie and the aisle.

When the music started, Lottie stood to sing. When it stopped, she sat up straight and faced forward so she would look engaged even though the service rarely broke through the distractions in her head.

Today's sermon proved mildly interesting, though. Pastor Fox read from the Gospel of Matthew, then talked about a narrow gate that led to everlasting life and a wide gate that led to destruction. Lottie's hands became clammy when he talked about sin—the bad things that kept people from God.

"Jesus is this narrow gate." Pastor Fox flashed a tight-lipped smile so big that his eyes nearly shut behind his oval spectacles. "He is the only way to heaven. We need to forsake our sins that Jesus died to defeat."

*Amen*s murmured from the congregation.

"So let each one of us follow him faithfully. Come up now if you wish to follow Jesus." Pastor Fox invited sinners up to the altar in front of his pulpit.

Lottie's heart pounded as she stood with the congregation to sing the last song for the morning. She felt something pulling her to make her way forward and kneel at that altar as she had seen so many others do. If the pastor was right about God and sin, Lottie was guilty.

Her muscles tightened, and she was sure everyone in the room was looking at her. She jolted when Orie elbowed her and giggled, nodding toward an old man on the other side of the aisle who remained seated as his head bobbed forward and back. Lottie gripped the pew in front of her and planted her feet.

When the song ended and the congregation sat down, relief rushed over her along with something else. Regret?

Pastor Fox closed the service with a prayer of blessing. The moment he said *amen*, Mother quickly stood and scooted out of the pew. Was *she* going to the altar to repent? As Mother hurried toward the door, Lottie realized what she was up to.

Lottie gasped. "I want to go too." But before she could return the hymnal to the pew rack, Mother was halfway out the door. Lottie's stomach dropped. Her chin quivered, and tears brimmed in her eyes. Mother left without her. After that sermon, Lottie wanted to run away from the church and away from her thoughts. Now she had to stay and wait with the crowd of parishioners gathering their belongings and chatting with friends. She struggled to smile as though everything was okay.

Anna scurried down Harrison Street and around the corner to Main Street. Pastor Fox didn't usually keep them that long. He'd stretched the invitation time as if trying to draw someone to the front. The sermon was good, but no one went up to get saved today.

When she arrived at the Disciples Church, everyone was scattered across the small lawn or sitting on the large steps, exchanging recipes and stories. There were more people than usual. The church must be growing. If she didn't find James soon, she'd delay the family's journey back home and, more important, their lunch.

Thankfully, her brother was tall and not difficult to find in a crowd. She spotted him at the top of the steps with Julia, smiling sweetly under a bonnet that was adorned with a tiny sprig of white wildflowers.

She walked up to them with a smile.

"Anna!" James opened his arms for a hug. Even on a Sunday morning, his hair stuck out as though he had just been exploring a wild wood. "It's good to see you."

Anna relished his hug, then pulled away and straightened her bonnet. "Edward's back home from his Louisiana trip. I think it's high time the family all gathered for a visit. Could you all come to Viewmont sometime soon?"

"Uh, well, I—" James shifted his gaze around as if looking for an escape.

"Come on Easter Monday and stay a few days. We'll make a holiday celebration of it. I'll invite Mary over for a day too."

James and Julia silently communicated with their eyes.

"I know prolonged visits with Mother aren't always pleasant or peaceful. But she hasn't been well, and she's been asking me about you. I know she'd love to see you both."

James cocked an eyebrow. "What do you mean she hasn't been well?"

"She's been having more outbursts lately."

"Sounds like Mother to me," James said with a frown.

"She gets confused a lot too. She just ... hasn't been herself." Anna wrung her hands, praying they would understand the importance of her request.

"We'll be happy to come." Julia patted Anna's arm. "It will be good for the children to see everyone."

James cleared his throat. "We need to gather the children."

Anna gave her sister-in-law a hug. "Thank you." She embraced her brother again. "Enjoy your Sunday. See you soon!"

Anna fairly skipped back to Scottsville Baptist, where she found the family all seated in the carriage. She joined Edward and kissed his cheek. Then she looked at her other children over her shoulder. "You're all going to see your Uncle James and Aunt Julia soon!"

Everyone but Edward cheered. "So that's what you asked them. And they said yes?"

"Of course." Anna spoke more confidently than she felt.

Edward chuckled. "Should be interesting."

Back at Viewmont, Anna started planning for the big family Easter celebration. Tomorrow she would walk to Mary's house and invite her family to join them. Lottie and Orie will be happy to see Mary's son, their cousin Jimmy.

This was going to be a wonderful occasion. Surely, no one would argue while celebrating their risen Savior.

CHAPTER THREE

1847

Lottie and Orie lounged on the green velvet chairs in the library, reading their books and watching their mother through the doorway. All morning, Mother had been rushing back and forth, directing the slaves as they prepared for the visiting family. Lottie and Orie did their best to stay out of the way.

Having finished her book, Lottie crossed the room to the floor-to-ceiling mahogany bookshelves lining two adjoining walls. After returning the volume to its proper place, she ran her fingers over spines of soft cloth and cool leather. Volumes of Shakespeare's writing and other classics beckoned to her, eager to be discovered.

Father nearly collided with Mother as she hurried down the hallway in her cleaning frenzy. With a chuckle, he ducked into the library and caught a blue pamphlet from falling off the top of a small stack of books he was carrying. "Picked up a new Dickens." He held up the pamphlet, which looked like the latest issue of a serial novel.

Orie popped up from her chair and grabbed it, smiling as she gazed at the cover. "*Dombey and Son.* I can't wait to read it!"

She went back to her chair and dumped the novel she had been reading onto the floor, adding to the pile of books beside her. Within seconds, she buried her nose into the new story.

Father deposited most of the other new books onto various shelves, then tucked the last one under his arm. It was small, covered in brown leather, and had the title debossed with gold letters. *The Narrative of the Life of Frederick Douglass.*

"What's that one?" Lottie pointed to the book.

"Nothing you need to worry about." Father took it to his study. That was where he kept books that were off limits to Lottie and her siblings. Which, of course, only piqued her interest more.

Lottie crossed her arms and glared at the floor. After a moment, she lifted her gaze. Orie's nose was still buried in the new Dickens. Even without Father's secret stash, the library at Viewmont was stocked with more than enough books to satisfy any young girl's curiosity. In this cozy, intimate room, she could learn anything she wanted—except about the life of Frederick Douglass.

Lottie sauntered over to the wide window along the room's east-facing wall. Outside, her two brothers ran toward the apple orchard. A small gasp escaped her lips. As Lottie turned away from the window, Mother hurried in, blocking her from joining the boys.

Anna couldn't control what her brother would say or how Mother would respond. She couldn't control her mother's health, her husband's travel schedule, or her children's behavior. But she could make sure the house was properly cleaned and the cushions freshly fluffed.

The library was the last room to check.

When Anna walked in, she halted at the sight of Lottie and Orie. If Mother saw them surrounded by books, she'd complain that they were reading too much. "Girls, where is your needlepointing?"

Lottie and Orie exchanged wide-eyed glances.

"Needlework is a necessary skill if you plan to wear clothes all your life."

"But it's Easter Monday," Lottie whined.

Indeed. Today wasn't only a family gathering. It was a holiday—a day of rest and celebration. She glanced up to the heavens beyond the room's ceiling, asking for strength to be calm. "Has your grandmother seen you in here, piling up these books?"

Orie closed the new Dickens serial novel. "She's in the parlor, staring out the window. I asked if she'd like me to read to her, but she said no."

"Well, that was very kind of you, Orie." Anna tried to hide her shock at such a thoughtful gesture from her moody daughter. "It's very important to be kind to your grandmother and behave properly today."

"More than any other day?" Lottie cocked her head. Her large brown eyes were the same as Edward's, but the defiance glimmering in them came from Anna's side of the family.

"Yes." Anna straightened the chairs around the table across the room. "Your Aunt Julia and Uncle James will be here soon."

"Is Jimmy coming too?" Lottie squealed.

"Yes." Anna grinned as she shook dust from the curtains. "Your Aunt Mary and everyone at Mt. Ayr are joining us for Easter supper too. Go tell Fannie the library is ready for cleaning."

After the girls left the library, Anna went upstairs to check the guest rooms. She peeked into the one where her brother and sister-in-law would stay. The bed was dressed in fresh linens and covered with a quilt of green, brown, and red patchwork. The magnolia blossoms in a large crystal vase on the dresser infused the room with a sweet scent. Fannie had done a wonderful job. But the room needed one final touch.

She hurried down to the back storage room across from the dining room and filled a large basket with embroidered pillows. As she passed the front parlor with it, her mother called out, "Is the tea ready for them?"

Anna maneuvered her head to see around the pillows piled into the basket. "For whom?"

Mother gestured toward the lace-curtain-framed window. "For James and Julia. They look as though they could use some tea."

Anna walked over. James and Julia's wagon was pulling up the carriage drive. Already? She called for her daughters.

When they came running up, Anna handed the basket to Lottie. "Please put these on the guest beds. Orie, ask Peggy to bring the tea to the parlor."

Anna rushed to open the front door. Her nephews, Robert and John, hopped out of the wagon even before it came to a full stop in the carriage drive. One of the slaves ran up to gather the guests' luggage and tend to the horse. The boys raced each other toward the orchard at the side of the house.

Anna stepped out onto the wide front porch. "Welcome, welcome."

James helped Julia off the wagon, then his daughter, Sarah. "I could use a walk around the grounds." He stretched. "That journey always makes my bones stiff."

"There's plenty of space here to roam." Anna gestured to the grounds. Maybe a long walk would make him too tired to argue with their mother.

Julia gave Anna a hug. "It's good to be here."

Anna breathed easy in Julia's embrace. Julia didn't seem worried. Maybe Anna didn't need to be either.

Edward came out and vigorously shook James's hand. "It's sure good to see you two." He took Julia's hand more gently. "I don't know where the children are, but your mother is in the parlor." He led them inside.

Mother beamed when her son and daughter-in-law came in. Both went to her for a hug and a kiss, then settled onto the plush furniture.

"Ah." James sighed as he sat down. "That's mighty soft compared to a wagon bench."

Peggy walked in with a tray of tea and treats. As she silently served the guests, Edward asked about their journey, then inquired about the apothecary business in Scottsville.

"Have you considered expanding?"

"I have." James spread a pat of butter across a buttermilk biscuit. "But with the Disciples Church and running the business, it's difficult to find time to train new employees." He glanced at Mother after mentioning the church.

Heat filled Anna, and her teeth clenched. Was he testing the woman? Not wise.

"You have a business to be proud of." Mother folded her hands on her lap. At least she seemed pleased he was thriving in the occupation she'd set him up in.

James fumbled his cup and saucer as though surprised by such affirmation. "Thank you, Mother."

The children piled into the parlor and peppered Julia and James with questions and stories.

Tom shared what he'd learned in his studies about a newly named disease. "Do you know of a drug for it, Uncle James?"

Orie leaned in close as James answered, but she didn't say a word. She must have remembered Anna telling her not to ask medical questions in front of their grandmother. Shame stung Anna's heart at the thought of stifling her daughter's growth.

Ike and Lottie told Julia about their latest race up the old locust tree with John. Lottie insisted that, even while wearing a cumbersome dress, she had climbed higher and faster than her cousin. Before Ike could set the record straight, Anna announced that everyone should let Uncle James and Aunt Julia rest before supper. She led them upstairs.

Once inside the room, Julia leaned close to the magnolia blossom and inhaled its scent. "That was a kind thing your mother said about the business."

James furrowed his brow. "Yes, but she didn't say a word about our church."

What did James expect? Mother had been a committed Baptist all her life. She would never approve of James being part of another denomination, especially not Alexander Campbell's Disciples Church. Anna rolled her eyes up to heaven, pleading in silent prayer for her brother to be content and accept Mother as she was. "Please try to get along with her."

"I will. But being here brings back a lot of memories." He opened the valise sitting on the bed and started pulling clothes out of the small leather bag and hanging them in the armoire.

Julia covered a yawn with her hand. "Pardon me."

Anna smiled. "Why don't you take a little nap?"

"Good idea." James buckled the empty valise and slid it under the bed. Couldn't sit still a moment. "And I'll go for that walk."

Anna went to the kitchen to check on supper. While he was here, would James dare to unpack memories that had been tucked away long ago as willingly as he had the clothes from his bag? She prayed that a hearty walk around the grounds would settle her brother's nerves.

She passed by the dining room and paused. Fannie was carrying a large silver bowl of food to the far end of the room. Anna walked in. Cold vegetable dishes and bread baskets spread across the table, leaving spaces for the hot dishes. The center was reserved for the fried chicken, which must still be sizzling in the kitchen. Anna smiled as she surveyed the table then frowned at the bowl Fannie had just set down. Oh no. "What is that?"

Fannie pulled her hands away from the bowl immediately. She leaned down and examined the sides as if looking for grease smudges or fingerprints. The bowl was clean. She lifted her head, wrapped in a strip of cloth. "Broccoli salad, ma'am."

Heat rose in Anna's chest. "I know what broccoli salad is." She stepped closer to the bowl and pointed at one of the raisins in the dish. "What is *that*?"

Fannie flushed. Her mouth fell open, and her eyes widened. "I—I forgot ma'am. I'm sorry." She ducked her chin down and wrung her hands in front of her apron that was sprinkled with flour and splattered with oil.

Anna clenched her hands and closed her eyes. Mother hated raisins. Anna could see it now—Mother picking out raisins, one by one, piling them onto the side of her plate, shooting judgmental glances at Anna. Mother would accuse her of being thoughtless, even though Anna's mind had buzzed all day to make each detail of this supper perfectly right. Anna grabbed the silver bowl and thrust it into Fannie's hands. "Take it away."

Fannie stumbled back and fumbled the bowl, spilling half of it onto herself and the floor.

"Fannie!" Anna threw her hands in the air then propped her fists onto her hips. "Clean this immediately." She stormed out of the dining room, steaming, as Fannie wiped her brow and sniffled while scooping the broccoli back into the silver dish.

Anna's heart pounded. Her chest heaved for each shallow breath. Maybe taking a walk in the fresh air like James would calm her nerves. She grabbed the tiny silver pocket watch chained to her belt. There wasn't time. Mary and her family would be here any minute. Anna rubbed her brow, where a gnawing headache was growing.

A friendly rap on the front door caught Anna's attention. She turned around, sighed, and dropped the pocket watch to dangle at her waist. It must be Mary. She set her shoulders back, forced a smile, and went to open the door.

Lottie shrieked with delight when Cousin Jimmy finally arrived with Aunt Mary, Uncle John, and most of their eight other children. Some stayed at home with a cold. They only had to travel from Mt. Ayr, which was within walking distance, so they weren't staying the night like Uncle James's family.

Mother and Father welcomed the adults into the house, and the children raced out back.

Jimmy stopped and searched his pockets. "Wait till I show you my new top. It spins faster than any you've ever seen!" Coming up empty, he shrugged. "Musta left it in the wagon."

"Let's go get it." Lottie led Jimmy through the house rather than taking the long way around, eager to see his toy.

When they neared the parlor, Lottie's mother and Aunt Mary were talking in whispers. She put her forefinger to her lips and motioned for Jimmy to join her just outside the doorway.

"How's it going so far with James and Mother?" Aunt Mary asked.

"Fairly smooth. No quarreling yet." A spoon clanked in a cup. "We're having fried chicken tonight. I'm hoping that will put James in a good mood. Mother was pleasant to him when he arrived. But that could change at any moment."

Fried chicken! Lottie's favorite. Uncle James and Aunt Julia should definitely visit more often.

"She looks healthy," Aunt Mary said. "Are those new tonics helping?"

"I'm afraid not. She seems to be getting worse."

Jimmy's eyes widened. "Is Grandmother dying?" he whispered.

"I don't know." Panic sprouted in Lottie's gut. She couldn't imagine a world without her grandmother in it. Grandmother may have been getting crankier each year, but she had always been there.

"I'm gonna find that top." Jimmy went out the front door to the wagon.

No longer interested in the new toy, Lottie returned to the backyard with the other children until supper.

When the meal was ready, the family all crowded around the expanded table. Side dishes spread across the table, from honeyed carrots, peas in cream sauce, asparagus, stuffed eggs, and scalloped potatoes to warm rolls. Lottie took a seat next to Jimmy, near the bread basket. Mother helped Sallie arrange a napkin over her little lap. Orie giggled with the cousins sitting near her. On the far side of the table, Tom talked in low tones with Uncle James.

Grandmother sat across from Uncle James. Lottie squinted at her and studied her movements. Grandmother's hand shook slightly as she lifted her glass of water, but that was normal. She sipped the water, then set the glass down and smiled at everyone around the table. She didn't look like someone who was dying. Lottie agreed with Aunt Mary. Grandmother looked perfectly healthy.

The chatter hushed when Fannie brought in an enormous platter of golden-brown fried chicken and set it between two tall candles in the center of the table.

While Father stood and blessed the Easter meal, Jimmy reached over to Lottie and dropped the wooden top into her lap. She laughed in surprise. Father paused his prayer and raised his eyebrows at her. Lottie did her best to contain her giggles.

After Father's *amen*, Mother placed a hand over her heart. "Thank you all for coming to enjoy this meal with us. We are truly blessed to have each other and to know the risen Savior."

More *amen*s fluttered around the room, and then everyone filled their plates with food. Over the quiet sound of silverware tapping plates, Lottie heard Uncle James's conversation with Tom.

"They're in desperate need of doctors," Uncle James said while scooping more peas onto his plate. "The Chinese are exceptionally populous, and their medical infrastructure is seriously lacking. Karl Gutzlaugh writes to me about some interesting cases he's come across."

"Who's Car Goose Laugh?" Four-year-old Sallie scooted forward in her chair to reach the chicken on the far side of her plate.

Mother shushed her, then shot a withering glance at Uncle James.

"He's a wild Polishman living as if he were a Chinaman." Grandmother cut her carrots with a tight grip on her fork and knife.

"His first name is my middle name," Cousin Robert said before crunching into a drumstick.

Uncle James straightened. "You're named after him because he's a fine missionary doctor—someone to look up to." He passed the bowl of peas and cream sauce to Tom. "He's invited me again to join the mission in China."

Grandmother locked sharp eyes with Uncle James. Everyone fell silent.

Lottie's heart leapt, and she bounced in her seat. "Are you finally going?"

Mother's mouth tightened and her eyes scowled.

Uncle James smiled at Lottie. "I will one day. I'd be there now if I were free." He faced Grandmother again, and his smile turned sour.

Grandmother tossed her fork and knife onto her plate with a loud clang.

"Did everyone get the asparagus?" Mother asked with forced cheeriness. "It's fresh from—"

"You have always been free to do as you wish," Grandmother growled between gritted teeth.

Uncle James threw his arms in the air as if in disbelief. "God called me to missions work among the Chinese ten years ago, but you made us stay here."

Fire burned in Grandmother's eyes. "I supported you when you bought that dilapidated tourist attraction."

That was before Lottie was born, but Uncle James had told her stories of when he and Aunt Julia bought Monticello and made it nice just as it had been when President Thomas Jefferson lived in it. Uncle James had planted lots of mulberry trees to attract silkworms and start a silk business, but the worms never came.

Grandmother raised her voice. "When you finally sold Monticello, I gave you a place to stay here. I bought you a home in Scottsville so you could run an apothecary there. And now you preach there. Haven't I done enough for you?"

"Knowing that I am only partially obeying God is agony." Uncle James's hands slammed down on the table, making several peas roll off his plate and a few family members jolt in their seats.

Grandmother yelled, and Uncle James banged on the table. They were breaking lots of dining table rules that Lottie had been taught.

Grandmother huffed. "Hearing your only living son threaten to leave the country—that's agony."

Uncle James heaved a sigh. His shoulders slumped, and he looked at Grandmother with a face full of pity. "Mother, you thwarted us from following God's will."

"There are plenty of souls on this continent in a spiritual state just as dire as the Chinese. Can't you minister to them?" Grandmother's stern composure melted a bit. "Then at least you could come to my funeral."

Uncle James reached across the table for her hand. "Anna and Edward are doing a wonderful job of caring for you. And Mary and John live close by. If you had died while I was on the mission field, I would have mourned you deeply even if I wouldn't have been able to get back here in time for a funeral."

Grandmother's eyes misted.

"The Chinese are dying every day without knowing the Savior," Uncle James said. "Don't you want me to obey God's will and tell them about him?"

Grandmother trembled. "How could this possibly be God's will for your life if it breaks apart our family?"

Uncle James hunched over the table with his eyes shut tight as he clutched the sides of his hair. Aunt Julia laid a hand on his back. Father stared at the remaining food on his plate. Uncle John tapped his glass of iced tea. He kept his mouth closed and hidden behind his full beard. Aunt Mary straightened the napkin on her lap, barely covering her blue evening dress.

Lottie's excitement about Uncle James going to China trickled out. She sat stiff and looked around the table. Everyone looked so sad. Why did Grandmother talk about her funeral as though it was already planned? Maybe Mother was right after all.

Grandmother dabbed her eyes with her napkin, then set it on her plate of uneaten food.

Mother stood and silently held Grandmother's arm, helping her out of the chair, then out of the room.

"Finish your supper, children." Aunt Mary pushed her chair back and took Mother's empty seat. She helped Sallie who was struggling with her knife and fork.

Lottie obediently picked up a piece of room-temperature chicken. Her eyebrows squished together. If Grandmother was dying and all the adults knew it, why would none of them say it to her face? If they all knew something that important, why wouldn't they tell her?

God was important to Uncle James, so that's why he wanted to go tell the Chinese about Him. God was important to Grandmother, too, wasn't he? So why didn't Grandmother let Uncle James go to China?

Nothing made sense about that supper.

CHAPTER FOUR

1847

About a month after the disastrous Easter meal, Lottie clasped her hands close to her heart. "Please, Mother? You said when May arrived, the strawberries would be ready. Jimmy is expecting me to bring him some."

Mother smiled and gently rubbed her round belly with the new baby growing inside. "You can take one basket."

Lottie hurried inside and tied an apron around her pink cotton dress. Then she grabbed the biggest basket she could find and giggled as she ran down to the garden. She stopped at the start of a row and dug her arms into bushes of bright green leaves, picking one ripe strawberry after another. She left the still-green berries and scooted her basket farther down the row. She winced as sweat dripped into her eye. The heat of summer had arrived early.

She stood and brushed her hair away from her brow. She untied the apron and tossed it aside. It was only making her warmer, and her dress was already pink. What harm could a few strawberry stains do? She lifted her chin as a breeze mercifully cooled her face and lightened the weight of noon sun rays. The wind caught a piece of paper poking out of her apron pocket and tossed it up into the air. Lottie leaped to catch it, missed, then clutched her basket to her chest as she chased the paper up the slope from down in the garden. It fell to the ground. She picked it up and smiled at the black lines and dashes. This must have been the same apron she had worn when she was outside practicing Chinese characters from one of Uncle James's letters. He had let her borrow it when he visited at Easter.

Lottie tucked the paper into her basket and looked up. The green trees in the distance looked inviting. Maybe before hiking to Mt. Ayr, she would cool off in the stream that ran through the woods. When Orie ran from the back door, Lottie jerked her head toward the house.

Orie tore through the yard until she dropped to the ground under a locust tree and tucked her knees up to her chest. She crossed her arms over them and buried her face. Clearly, she was upset about something. There was only one way for Lottie to find out what it was. She brushed the dirt off a few big strawberries. Surely, they would cheer Orie up. She walked over to her sister.

Lottie held out her hand. "I picked these for you."

"No you didn't," Orie shot back. "Those are for you and Jimmy. I heard you talking with Mother."

"True ... but I picked them out of the basket for you," Lottie persisted. "Come on ... you love strawberries."

Orie grabbed one berry, ate it slowly, then snatched another.

Lottie sat down beside Orie. "So why are you crying out here?"

"You're just a kid. You wouldn't understand," Orie said, either unaware or unconcerned about a drop of juice falling down her chin.

"*I'm* just a kid?" Lottie disagreed, especially with such a pitiful display from her twelve-year-old sister right in front of her. "I'm only six, but I'm taking care of you and being nice and giving you my strawberries. You're the one crying for no reason."

"I do have a reason!"

"Oh?" Lottie tapped at a pebble on the ground with her boot. "What is it?" She had to lean in closer to hear her sister mumble between sniffles.

"Tom gets to learn anything he wants, but I don't."

Lottie nodded slowly. Right. Since she and Orie were little, Father and Mother had encouraged them to read and learn. But the older they got, the more she and Orie bumped into invisible limits and shifting rules. It was confusing to have a whole library in the house and be told only to read so much.

Orie unfolded a handkerchief from her pocket and wiped the juice from her chin along with her tears. "I'm going to be a doctor, too, so I wanted to learn what Tom's tutor teaches him. You know—diseases, bones, and blood."

Lottie twisted her mouth, trying to keep a disgusted grimace from showing. Science and medicine were either dull or disgusting. Still, she listened as her sister told her what happened.

Orie headed down the staircase and paused when Tom and his tutor, Nicholas, walked into the library. Her heart leapt, and her mouth fell open.

Nicholas was much younger and more handsome than any other tutor that came to Viewmont. She tip-toed over to the half-open door and quietly sat down.

Nicholas shrugged a leather satchel off his shoulder and started unloading large books onto the library table. "I just graduated from the medical school in Pennsylvania, and I brought all of my textbooks here to show you."

Tom grabbed one and flipped through it. "Capital! That's where I'm going. My uncle got his degree there too."

Orie closed her eyes to hear Nicholas better. But then she might've heard something else. Footsteps?

"Orianna, is that you hovering?" Grandmother loomed over her.

Orie jolted away from the door. "I—Grandmother, you scared me."

Grandmother may have been losing her sight, but her voice was as strong as ever. She propped both fists on her hips. "Only a girl doing something she knows she shouldn't would be scared by an old woman. You're eavesdropping, which is rude and unladylike."

"It's only Tom and Nicholas. They're discussing biology, and—"

Grandmother's eyes bulged. "*And* you're eavesdropping on matters that in no way concern you. You're going to a finishing school, not a university. Eavesdropping only disturbs Tom's education and wastes your time." She shooed Orie up and away. "Get up and busy yourself with something proper and useful. What will people think if all you do is skulk around libraries?"

Under the locust tree, Lottie's mouth hung open as Orie finished her story.

"But I *wasn't* bothering him or skulking around. I was only listening to Nicholas's lesson." Orie buried her tearful face back into her folded arms. She whispered, "I don't belong here."

Lottie scooted closer and wrapped an arm around her sister. "Are you going to tell Father?"

Orie shrugged her shoulders.

It wasn't fair that Orie was burdened by her dream to become a doctor, while Tom got a tutor to help him chase the same dream. And it wasn't fair that Tom never had to practice needlework.

Lottie sat silently and let Orie cry. After a while, Orie breathed easier and straightened her back. She reached for Lottie's basket and bit into another strawberry.

Orie pointed to the paper sticking out from under the fruit. "What's that?"

"It's Chinese." Lottie threw her shoulders back and grinned. "I've been practicing."

"Studying Latin and French aren't enough for you?" Orie pulled the paper closer to her face. "It doesn't even have letters."

"I want to study all the languages I can." Lottie popped up. "But not right now." She snatched the paper from Orie. "Betchya can't catch me!" Lottie ran down toward the garden laughing, followed by her sister, toting the basket.

They gathered a few more strawberries to replace the ones that Orie ate, then Lottie invited Orie along to walk over to Mt. Ayr to meet Jimmy.

Even though Orie didn't seem upset anymore, her story repeated in Lottie's mind throughout the afternoon. If Tom got to study and go to school to be a doctor, then Orie should too. He wasn't smarter than her. The only difference was, he was a boy.

At supper that evening, it was clear that Orie wasn't going to tell Father. She behaved too normally for him to know that anything was wrong. It was up to Lottie to bring this injustice to her father.

After supper, Lottie marched towards Father's study and slowly opened the door. One of the new kerosene lamps glowed on his desk, and his ledgers laid open. On top of them sat another book—the one about Frederick Douglass. But Father wasn't reading it. He sat back in his leather chair with his arms crossed and his chin in the air. Was he sleeping? She looked up in the direction he was facing. Maybe something was on the ceiling.

Father chuckled. "How can I help you?"

Lottie dropped her gaze and set the agenda in a businesslike manner. "It's about Orie."

"What about her?"

"She wants to be a doctor like Tom, but Grandmother won't let her."

Father laughed again. "Yes, I know Orie wants to be a doctor. And I expect many people more frightening than your grandmother will try to stop her."

"Did you know that she tried to learn about medicine and science today from Tom's tutor, but Grandmother yelled at her and made her cry? She's fine now and didn't tell you only because I shared my strawberries with her and made her feel better."

Father frowned and furrowed his brows. "How did Orie try to learn from Nicholas today?"

Lottie explained what happened. Father didn't laugh. He said it was good that Lottie told him, and he assured her that he and Mother would talk to Orie.

Then he leaned back again and clasped his hands, tapping his forefingers together. "Perhaps during Grandmother's daily naps, Tom could start teaching Orie what he learns in his lessons."

That sounded promising, but Lottie would not be pacified so easily. "I don't like it when Grandmother yells at Orie."

Father nodded knowingly. "We must be kind to Grandmother."

"Why?" They weren't the problem. Grandmother was the one who needed to be more kind.

"Because she's your elder and family, and she won't always be around. Your mother would add that Jesus was kind to those who weren't kind to him. He wants us to do the same."

Lottie bristled. "I'm not Jesus."

"That's true—you're Charlotte. If you ask him, I think God will change your heart towards Grandmother, especially if you pray for her."

Lottie stood silent and crossed her arms. She tried not to roll her eyes.

Father got up and walked to the front of his desk and leaned against it. "When it's hard for me to be kind to unkind people, I try to remember that they may feel sad as I sometimes do."

Lottie uncrossed her arms and tilted her head to the side. Grandmother did seem sad sometimes. Like when she sat in the parlor staring out the window.

Father explained in a soothing way, "Your grandmother lost two husbands."

Lottie nodded her head in solemn agreement. "Yes, that is sad." After Mother's father died, Grandmother married Captain Harris, the man who owned Viewmont. Then he died too.

"And when her first husband died, she felt scared because she had four little children and didn't know how to be in charge of the family business. She never learned arithmetic like you learn in your lessons. So she lost the business and their home. Your mother's older siblings all went to live with other relatives until Grandmother married Captain Harris and they could all live here together again. That still makes Grandmother sad to think about."

Lottie's heart stung and her mind swirled. Uncle James and Aunt Mary didn't live with their mother when they were little? She never got to meet Mother's oldest brother, Thomas, before he died, but they all must have been sad to not live together as a family. No wonder Grandmother tried to keep Uncle James close to Viewmont. They'd already spent years apart when he was young.

The Grandmother that Father just told Lottie about sounded like a different person. Before Grandmother became so unwell, she talked about business as though she knew everything. It was hard to imagine her ever feeling scared about that, but Lottie would try if that would help her be more kind to Grandmother.

A few days later, the family relaxed together in the parlor for the evening. Lottie played pat-a-cake with Sallie on the rug while her older siblings played dominos at a round table. Mother and Grandmother wove thread and needle in and out of the fabric stretched over their embroidery hoops. Father sat in a chair and read the newspaper. He flipped to the next page in such a huff that he jostled the side table next to him and the kerosene lamp on top of it.

Mother gasped. She dropped her hoop onto the floor and clutched her pregnant belly.

In an instant, Father caught the lamp and steadied it. He wiped his forehead with his free hand, locked eyes with Mother, and chuckled. "Sorry, Anna. I was flipping to the next page too quickly."

Mother pursed her lips. The corner of her mouth twitched as if a playful smile was right under the surface. "Must be a riveting article."

Father picked up the fallen hoop and handed it to Mother. "Indeed—an editorial on the economy of abolition. I'll save this one for Orie."

Mother leaned forward as her eyebrow arched. "Which paper is that?"

"The *Richmond Enquirer*—nothing radical."

Lottie looked up at the commotion and met Grandmother's eyes. Her hoop rested in her lap. Her thin lips crinkled into a soft smile. "You're very patient and kind with little ones, Lottie."

Lottie smiled back. "What are you making?"

"It's a surprise." Grandmother glanced at Mother's round belly. She dropped her embroidery work into the basket next to the sofa, clutched the armrest, and slowly lifted herself up. "I'm going to bed. My headache won't seem to relent tonight."

"It must be the heat," Mother said as she tugged her needle through the fabric. "Would you like more iced tea?"

"No, just a kiss from my grandchildren before I go up."

The children walked over and lined up to kiss Grandmother goodnight.

Father lowered his newspaper. "A good night's sleep will carry you through till the cool of the morning. Then all will be well."

Mother set her hoop on the table next to the lamp and offered her arm to Grandmother. Mother winked at Father. "Try not to burn the house down."

Before they left the room, Grandmother turned back and rubbed her head. "I'll return soon for another story, children."

Lottie and her siblings exchanged puzzled looks. Grandmother hadn't been telling them stories that night.

The next morning, Grandmother didn't appear at the breakfast table. As

Lottie munched her apple butter toast, Fannie headed toward the stairs with a tray of tea and toast as she sometimes did when Grandmother couldn't muster the energy to come down. If Grandmother stayed in her room all morning, Lottie might be able to skip her needlepointing and read outside. Her heart raced as book titles whirled through her mind. Which one would she choose?

A scream rang from upstairs, making Lottie drop her toast. Fannie. Mother sprang up from the table and bolted out of the room. Lottie's plans flew from her mind.

All the children around the table looked anxiously at Father. His eyebrows drew close together, and his lips were pursed. "Finish your breakfast." He gathered up the newspaper that had slipped out of his hands during the scream.

No one said a word. Tom and Ike poked their forks at the eggs and ham on their plates. Orie's spoon jingled against the jam jar as she scooped a dollop. She dropped it onto the table next to her biscuit while staring out toward the hall.

A moment later, Mother sobbed past the doorway with her face in her hands. Father slid his chair away from the table and marched after her. Lottie's heart pounded in her ears. Something big had happened upstairs when Fannie brought the breakfast tray to Grandmother.

Lottie put her fork down and silently made eye contact with each of her older siblings. Did they know what was wrong? Sallie started to cry, as if she sensed something was wrong even though she was too young to know what it could be.

Father came back into the dining room and sank into his chair. He sighed and rubbed his brow. "I'm sorry, children. Your grandmother is with God now. It appears she died in her sleep."

Tears started in Lottie's eyes as Father said the words. Her cheeks burned. Only a few moments ago, she'd been relieved that Grandmother wasn't around for the morning, even excited at the hope of getting to read outside. Now, she wouldn't be around at all ever again. Lottie's gut felt hollow.

The next day, the slaves covered all the mirrors with black cloth. No light reflected around the house. Mother wore her pearl bracelet, and the whole family dressed in black. Then people started to come. More family, friends, and visitors filled Viewmont's parlors than Lottie had ever seen.

Lottie sat quietly on a wooden chair in the parlor near the front window. She tugged at her collar, trying to release the heat trapped in her wool dress. The winter dress was the only clean black one Fannie could find for her. She scooted her chair closer to the window and flattened her clammy hand against the cool glass. Rain misted all morning, and clouds like a gray fleece blanket stretched across the sky, blocking the afternoon sun.

Even with the oil lamps lit, the parlor wasn't much brighter. Everyone was either crying or offering a handkerchief to someone crying. Lottie had already cried for two days and couldn't muster any more tears. So she pulled a handkerchief from her dress pocket and crossed the room, carefully scooting around uncles, cousins, and church members, over to the sofa where Uncle James sat hunched over his knees with clasped hands pressed against his forehead as though he was praying. Aunt Mary sat next to him with an arm around his shoulders.

Lottie silently held out her offering of comfort. Uncle James lowered his hands and raised his face to hers. Heat flashed across her cheeks. She should've stayed in her chair, for no handkerchief could ease the pain in his eyes. His bottom lip quivered as though he might say something, but words never came out. Fresh tears fell down his face, and he dropped his gaze back to the floor.

Aunt Mary took Lottie's handkerchief and set it on Uncle James's knee. "Thank you, dear. He will be fine. We all will be." Her voice cracked.

Would they? It was unsettling to see the adults fall apart at the same time like that. What if they never stopped crying?

She returned to her chair by the window. Scattered around the room, Orie and Ike sat quietly holding small plates and nibbling on sliced meat and fruit next to their long-faced relatives.

Ever since Lottie overheard Mother and Aunt Mary at Easter, she knew Grandmother was dying. But it still felt sudden when it finally happened. No one was with Grandmother when she died. No one got to say goodbye. Maybe that's why everyone was so sad.

Father maneuvered around a clump of cousins and sat in the empty chair on the other side of the window. "Have you eaten?"

Lottie shrugged. "Not since the bacon this morning."

"Your mother took Sallie to get some food. You should join them in the dining room." He patted her back then stood up and smiled at her. "I saw a whole platter of strawberry scones and clotted cream in there."

Lottie smiled back at him. Talking about normal things like food made the grief in the room feel a little less heavy. Father waded back into the crowd and stopped when he encountered Uncle John. Lottie got up to find Mother and the scones.

That evening, Father, Uncle James, and other men in the family carried Grandmother's coffin up the hill where Captain Harris and Father's parents were buried. The rain had stopped, but that didn't brighten the dreary funeral service. Standing beside her family, Lottie bowed her head and folded her hands in front of her. They prayed with Pastor Fox, then left three field hands to shovel dirt into Grandmother's grave.

As everyone trudged back to the house, Lottie looked down at her dress, now covered in bits of grass and dirt. Raindrops soaked the hem. Perhaps Mother would consider it too dirty to wear tomorrow and let her choose a lighter summer dress. Walking outside in the rain-cooled air was a relief from the stuffy house, but listening to Psalms, singing hymns, and praying at the funeral service did nothing to console her hurting heart. Grandmother was gone. Lottie said goodnight before she died but never got to say goodbye.

When the last visiting mourners finally left the next day, the house felt quiet. Lottie paced the length of the library with Sallie following close behind her. Her older siblings sat around. Ike slumped in his chair, his eyelids drooping.

Father wandered in, stopped, and looked around the room. "You children need some sunshine. Go spend the morning in the garden."

Obediently, they moved outside. Lottie squinted at the world around her. Spring was alive with singing birds and blooming flowers. The grass looked fresh and bright after yesterday's rain. Lottie's spirits lifted, but she was still exhausted from being sad with groups of other sad people for three whole days.

Sallie, however, perked up right away. She padded through rows of strawberry plants and flowers, singing little tunes. She paused to poke at bugs on rose petals.

Lottie smiled as she watched her little sister cheerfully enjoying the beauty around her. If only Lottie got to say goodbye to Grandmother, she might be able to enjoy beautiful things too. She remembered something and turned to Orie. "Last week, I saw Mother bring Grandmother some roses from the garden. They were beautiful, and they made her smile really big. We can pick some for Grandmother, too, can't we?"

Orie reached for Lottie's hand and nodded. "We can put them in her room."

With a kick, Tom sent a rock halfway to the orchard. "But Grandmother can't smile anymore." His face looked as hard and cold as that rock. "She can't smell roses or see anything."

"Yes, she can!" Ike crossed both arms. "Father said she is with God now. So if God can see us, as Mother and Father always say, and Grandmother is with God now, then she should be able to see us too. I think she would like it if we picked her some roses." He finished his argument with a quick nod, as if that settled the matter.

Tom looked around at his younger siblings, who were all staring at him for the final verdict. He sighed and shrugged. "All right, then."

Orie helped Sallie avoid sharp thorns while everyone walked around the garden and searched for the prettiest rose they could find. After each found the perfect one, they held their roses ceremoniously in front of them as they filed back inside and up the stairs. Lottie led the way.

When they reached Grandmother's room, Lottie turned the doorknob, cracked the door open, and peeked inside. No one was in there. Fresh white linens covered the bed, and fluttering curtains flanked the open window. Sunlight poured in.

Lottie and Sallie walked in together. Lottie sat on the bed while Sallie dropped her rose on the floor in front of the dresser, giggled, and rushed to the curtains, batting at them as they billowed in a breeze.

Orie set her rose on the wicker chair by the window. "Thank you for all the kind and grandmotherly things you said to me. I forgive you for the mean things you said, which weren't as many."

Ike went to Grandmother's dresser. He arranged his rose atop her Bible, then left the room. Orie took Sallie's hand and followed him out.

Tom wandered to several glass apothecary bottles on Grandmother's nightstand, picked one up, and examined the label. "I didn't know it was that bad. I'm sorry no one could help you and give you better medicine." He returned it and placed his offering among the bottles. "They said you like roses, so I brought this for you."

Lottie stood and spoke quietly while focusing on her rose. "You were strong and did hard things, since even before you were my grandmother. I hope you can rest now." She laid it on the bed. "Goodbye, Grandmother."

Lottie released a deep sigh. She wasn't as confident as Ike was that Grandmother could see them and their roses. She was with God now, and God seemed far away. But it was a relief to finally say goodbye.

Tom laid a hand on her shoulder. "Good idea, Lot. I liked this better than yesterday's funeral."

"Me too." She smiled at the room, now dotted with colorful roses. Another breeze blew in, carrying sounds of her siblings pouring outside through the back door. Lottie and Tom left to rejoin the others. She closed the door behind them.

Now that the funeral was over and all the guests were gone, Anna sat on the parlor sofa and tried to do something normal. She reached into her needle-pointing basket and pulled out her mother's hoop by mistake. The white linen over the hoop looked like the makings of a baby bonnet with tiny summer flowers embroidered around the edges. Fresh tears stung in her puffy eyes. Anna hugged it, but the things that Mother left behind didn't fill her missing presence in Anna's life. Her mother had always been a part of everyday life, so how could she do anything normal without her?

"One day at a time," she said to herself.

For today, Anna cried at the sight of her mother's unfinished embroidery gift. A tug in her heart pulled her to her mother's room. Anna gently put the hoop back and started up the stairs. She labored to climb each step, carrying her grief along with the little life growing inside her. She paused and held her belly. "Had it always been this many steps?"

At the top, she raised a hand to knock on the door. She gasped. Her chest tightened. Her hand flashed to her side and squeezed into a fist. "How stupid of me. There's no need for that now."

She jerked the door open, and a sweet floral aroma washed over her. Roses sprinkled color around the room. It smelled as though the afternoon sun had coaxed the flowers to share more and more of their perfume. This warm, scented air demanded to be enjoyed. Anna sat on the foot of her mother's bed, taking slow, deep breaths. Her eyes closed. They opened when she heard footsteps and Edward sat down beside her.

"She liked roses, didn't she?" he said.

Anna nodded. "She really did."

"I'll miss her."

Anna managed a small, teasing smile. "You will?"

"Of course, I will." Edward offered her a handkerchief from his waistcoat pocket. "Your mother may not have supported all of my ideas for the business or how we raise the children, but she taught me a great deal about how to run this place. I owe a lot to her."

Anna slipped her hand through the crook of Edward's arm and rested her head on his shoulder. "It does me good to hear you say it. We knew this was coming, and we prepared for it, but I still don't know what we'll do without her."

"Lots of things now," Edward said.

Anna yanked her hand away from him and sat up. She thought her emotions were spent after three days of crying, but anger flooded her heart. "Now that my mother is dead, you're free to do as you wish. Is that it?"

He leaned back and sputtered. "Not at all. I will miss her, sincerely, but I can't deny that some things will finally get a chance to change without her protests."

Anna's mouth tightened. "She was my mother, Edward, and I won't have anything unkind said about her, especially now."

He apologized, got up, and headed to the door.

Anna softened. Edward was right. "I understand what you're saying. Things will change."

Edward stopped and turned, facing her. "Things *must* change."

"The girls won't need to hide their stacks of books from her anymore." Anna sighed. "And who knows what my brother will do? He seems to enjoy the church and the apothecary, but no one will stop him from being a missionary now."

Edward sat down with her again. He lifted his brows, making his chestnut eyes look even larger. "You think James will finally go to China?"

Anna sighed and shrugged. "Who knows what people might accomplish if they get the opportunity?"

CHAPTER FIVE

October 1849

A cool gust of wind whirled golden leaves around Lottie's hem. She closed her eyes and breathed in deep. The sun warmed her cheeks. Sweet, crisp air filled her lungs. It smelled like fall. The laughter of Orie, Ike, and the Barclay cousins, Robert and John, sounded hazy and distant as they played ring toss behind her. She opened her eyes and brushed away wind-tossed hair, turning to watch her cousin Sarah on the picnic blanket near the garden.

Sarah was three years older than Lottie and always had her dark hair in a braid. She held the hands of Lottie's one-year-old sister and pulled her up onto chubby feet that were covered in tiny socks. Mother, Aunt Julia, and Sallie sat on the blanket, clapping and cheering her on. "Yay, Mollie!"

Uncle James smiled, leaning back on the iron garden table next to the blanket. Fannie and Peggy were still clearing the dishes from the family's picnic supper.

Mollie's white dress fluttered at her ankles. Sarah let go and joined in on the cheering. "Go, Mollie, go!"

Lottie held her breath. Today could be the day her youngest sister took her first steps on her own! Mollie smiled brightly, looking ready for anything. She lifted her little foot just as another gust kicked up. She wobbled, then crashed onto her bottom. Mollie frowned only for a moment before clapping with everyone else on the blanket. Lottie giggled. Her smile waned as her glance drifted toward the gravestones nearby.

Losing Grandmother was hard. Then two months after that, when the baby was born but never breathed, it seemed Mother might never be happy again. The following year, little Mollie brought much-needed joy to the family. But Lottie still missed Grandmother, and she wondered what her other sister would have been like. She might have been starting to talk if she were here now.

"Lot! It's your turn," Robert called.

Lottie's mind jolted back to the family picnic and the beautiful October day.

Robert cupped his hand to his mouth and called again, waving a tossing ring with the other hand. "Do you want me to go for you?"

Lottie whipped around at her cousin's voice. "No way! Then I'd lose for sure." She marched back to the game and picked up a ring.

After a few successful tosses, Lottie's and everyone else's eyes lifted to Fannie as she came out of the kitchen holding something round and golden brown. Peggy trailed behind her holding another. Lottie dropped her next ring and bolted toward the picnic blanket, where she sat down with her family.

Fannie cut the pies, and Peggy served plates of heaping slices. When Lottie received hers, she jammed her fork in and apple pieces that were covered in warm cinnamon sugar burst out the sides. The crust flaked onto her dress as she lifted a bite. Lottie closed her eyes and let the buttery crust melt in her mouth.

"It's delicious," she said as Peggy served a plate to Sallie.

"Thank you, Miss." Peggy moved closer to Lottie and smiled. "We stuffed as many apples as we could fit in there."

"It's a masterpiece." Lottie spoke around a mouthful.

Mother lifted her nose, her chin pointing at Lottie. "Lottie, ladies eat with their mouths closed."

Lottie leaned to Peggy and mumbled. "Good thing I'm not a lady."

Peggy giggled and handed Lottie an extra napkin.

Lottie cradled her plate in her lap and looked around at all her smiling family digging into their pie. Affection rose in her chest. The golden sun shone around them, keeping them warm for maybe another hour or so. Chilly days were on their way. But Viewmont was only on the edge of change, not yet in its throes. Lottie lifted her mouth into a smile then her fork for another bite.

Uncle James had moved from the table and to the blanket next to Aunt Julia. He looked at Mother and Father. "Thank you for having all of us for the week."

Aunt Julia leaned back on one hand. "October is the most beautiful time to visit Viewmont."

Father signaled to Fannie, and she brought him a bowl of whipped cream. "You're welcome anytime. With Tom away at the university, we certainly enjoy the extra company. But I expect the business keeps you from many extended visits."

Uncle James coughed. His fork screeched across his plate, then fell onto the blanket.

Peggy hurried to him with a fresh utensil and a glass of water.

Father's eyebrows arched. "Something wrong there, James?"

Uncle James glanced at Aunt Julia, as if looking for permission. She sat up and nodded slightly. He set his plate down and spoke loud enough for everyone to hear. "There's something about the business I need to tell you. This is as good a time as any to announce that Julia and I have decided to sell the Scottsville house and close the apothecary."

Father's eyes bulged. He blinked and shook his head. "Has someone approached you with an offer?"

"No buyer yet, but I've got someone in mind," Uncle James said. "We only recently decided."

"That isn't the big announcement." Aunt Julia winced.

"Yes, there's more." Uncle James took Aunt Julia's hand and straightened his back.

Mother gently set her plate down beside her, straightened her back, and lifted her chin. She looked calm, but Lottie knew that was Mother's ready-for-anything posture.

"An opportunity came up that we can't ignore—one of eternal significance." Uncle James's voice rose so that he was nearly shouting. "You know that I've been preaching at the Disciples Church for some time now. Well, they want to send me as a missionary to the Jews in Jerusalem."

The Barclay children sat beaming at their parents. Lottie and the Moon children gasped with wide smiles but didn't say a word. It seemed like happy news, but tension filled the air. Mother and Father looked at each other with restrained smiles.

Aunt Julia leaned forward, toward Mother. "We're only in the early stages of preparing to go. We won't be leaving for some time—perhaps a year. We still need to secure our funding. But we wanted to let you know as soon as we were sure about it ourselves."

"But Jerusalem isn't in China," Lottie said. Every head turned to her. At nearly nine years old, she was new to geography studies, but she felt confident that China didn't have a city called Jerusalem. That was a Bible city.

"It's in the Near East." Sarah answered with her hands folded politely in her lap.

"That's right." Uncle James raised a finger in the air. "It's where Jesus himself walked, and thousands of God's earthly people, the Jews, need to hear that their Messiah has come."

"But why aren't you going to China?" Lottie asked. It didn't make sense that Uncle James would go to Jerusalem after talking about China for so many years.

Uncle James closed his eyes and nodded. "It's true I was set on going to China. It is perhaps the largest mission field in the world. But the Jewish nation must come to faith in Jesus. It has been prophesied. It will happen, and it may happen soon. The signs of the times are ever increasing. The Jews have a special role to fulfill in the Lord's empire of Truth."

Mother and Father both wore grimaces and exchanged worried glances.

Uncle James spread his arms out. "Besides, God's Word says whoever blesses the Jews will themselves be blessed. There are many reasons to go, and the door is wide open."

Was the door to China closed? For years, Uncle James said crowds of people there didn't know anything about Jesus or the Bible, and they needed someone to go tell them. Lottie shrugged. Maybe God would prepare someone else for China.

Father took a cup and saucer from Fannie, who was now offering the family tea. "I know you've lived with this conviction about missions for a long while, James."

"We're going this time." Uncle James spoke seriously. "We have the support of our church. Once we sell the Scottsville property and the slaves, of course, we should have enough funds to comfortably sustain our new life overseas. We now hope to gain the support of our family." He cast a pleading gaze at Mother.

Everyone went quiet again. Mother locked eyes with Uncle James with a strange look on her face, as though she couldn't decide between smiling or crying. After a full moment, Father clapped a hand on Uncle James's shoulder and broke the silence. "You have our support. Frankly, I'm inspired by your faith."

"We'll miss having you nearby, but it's good news to hear you're finally following this call on your life," Mother said with a pained smile.

Uncle James let out a sigh of relief. "Your blessing means more than you'll know." He loosened his grip on Aunt Julia's hand. "Once we get to Jerusalem, we'll faithfully send you letters. And since we'll be here for a whole week, we can discuss details more and try to answer as many questions as we can."

Good thing, because questions swirled in Lottie's head. What was Jerusalem like? Why were Jews more important than the Chinese? Lottie would miss the Barclays, but she was filled with excitement for Uncle James to finally live the adventure he always wanted.

Mother encouraged everyone to finish the pies before the sun went down.

Orie asked Uncle James, "Are you still going to do medicine? Do they need doctors and apothecaries in Jerusalem?"

"That's the plan, my girl." Uncle James picked up his plate again. "We're taking some medical equipment along with our Bibles. Hopefully, the Lord will use both."

After the family watched the sunset together and Edward and James retired to the study, Anna went into the back storage room to fetch games for the children to play in the front parlor. She pulled out her handkerchief just in time to catch the tears that couldn't hide themselves any longer. She covered her face with the white lace-trimmed cloth and breathed deeply. In and out. It was too wet to breathe through. She had soaked it already. She tore it from her face with a soft growl and clutched it at her side.

"Anna?"

She flinched, whirling around.

"It's only me." Julia gave her a fresh handkerchief and a sheepish smile. "Here. I think that one's done all it can for now."

Anna took the offer and attempted to dry her eyes. "I didn't want to upset the children."

"I don't know what James would have done if you and Edward hadn't given your blessing." Julia held her hand over her chest, her eyes soft and glowing.

Anna nodded. How could she not give her blessing? She'd recognized the look on James's face at the picnic when he asked. It was the same look he used to give their mother.

"His convictions have only deepened over the years," Julia said. "When your mother passed, the timing didn't seem right. But now ..."

Anna recognized the look on Julia's face too. It was a glimmer of hope—most likely, hope that their family would finally live as though they actually believed what they said they believed, that the message of Jesus was for everyone and must be shared with all peoples. Hope perhaps that her husband would finally get the blessing he craved to follow God's call on their lives. "I understand. You and James want to be faithful. Now is the time."

Julia wrung her hands. "I'm sorry we didn't tell you and Edward first, in private. I hope it's not a shock."

Anna finished making full use of the second handkerchief. She shook her head. "No, we knew it was coming at some point. It's just—" She held out an open palm, searching for words. "Edward is busier than ever before with growing the business. Tom is away, and I miss him, and it's nearing time for Orie to go to school. Finding the right place for her has been so difficult—not as simple as it was for Tom."

"So much is changing around you." Julia sat on a small settee along the wall and gestured to the space beside her. "Here."

Anna sat down and sagged into the settee. "It's been almost two years ..." Her chest heaved. Her voice quaked. "Since we lost her. But I think about the baby every day, and I miss my mother." Another wave of hot tears overwhelmed her. She didn't try to stop them.

Julia reached an arm around Anna's shoulders.

Anna fidgeted with the soaked handkerchief. She whispered, "I don't want to make the same mistake that she made, forbidding you to go because I miss the ones I've lost, and I'll miss you."

Julia squeezed Anna encouragingly. "That's brave, Anna. Your mother had bravery, too, but you've allowed it to grow stronger in your life than she did in hers."

Anna smiled. "Thank you." Her speeding heart calmed. She turned to face Julia. "I see that James is committed in his calling. All these years, he never truly let it go. Do you feel God's call to foreign missions too?"

Julia laughed. "I think you're the first person to ask me that. Yes, I'm convinced that God is drawing me to missions too. I was concerned at first, taking the boys and Sarah away to live such a different life. But God gave us peace about it all."

"Isn't our family just full of brave people?" Anna breathed easier now, and her body relaxed. "Maybe Tom could visit you in Jerusalem once he finishes his medical training. He could be useful to James."

Julia said it was a wonderful idea and asked if Orie might also be interested. "Orie is pursuing medical education, too, after all, isn't she?"

"Yes, of course—Orie too." Why hadn't Anna thought of that? Witnessing the depths of suffering on the mission field and the transformative power of Jesus could be great for Orie. "Maybe seeing your ministry in Jerusalem will finally inspire faith in their hearts. My Bible bedtime stories sure won't do it. They just don't listen anymore. It's as if they think they don't need Jesus. I fear they've even grown hostile to him."

Julia grasped Anna's hands and looked straight into her eyes. "Keep praying for them, Anna. If either or both of them stay with us in Jerusalem, we will give witness to God's goodness and love to them every chance we get."

Before they went to the front parlor, where a load of children were up to who knows what, Anna and Julia prayed together, laying each of their children before the Lord by name and praising him for calling the Barclays to join his work in Jerusalem.

Lottie downed one of her domino tiles with a slam. "Five more points for me."

Orie sighed as Sarah talked about Israel. She'd started while they were outside and kept it up even during their games in the parlor.

"The voyage itself should be interesting enough, but I hope it isn't too long." Sarah pushed one of her tiles around the table with one finger. "I simply can't wait to wander around foreign mountains and caves and of course meet fascinating people."

"It's your turn." Lottie sat back, waiting for Sarah to go. She couldn't help but frown at her cousin. Father never even took Lottie with him to Louisiana. Now, Uncle James was going to take Sarah on an adventure in a foreign land.

Mother and Father entered the room with Aunt Julia and Uncle James. Mother's eyes were red-rimmed and swollen. Father rubbed her back until she sat down on the settee, then joined Uncle James as he unfolded a large map onto a much-too-small end table. Father held two of the corners up.

"Ike, take over for me?" Lottie got up to see that map. She'd rather listen to Uncle James talk about Israel than to Sarah who was about to live Lottie's grandest dream.

Ike obliged, standing up from his spot in front of the fireplace. Lottie walked over to Father's side and stood over the map covering the table.

"I'll be traveling regularly to evangelize Jews and meet with other missionaries. They mostly live near there." Uncle James pointed to a black dot on the map. "But this will be the new Barclay residence. Right next to that line. It's a river. Or maybe ..." He leaned closer, squinting. "It could be a road. Roads there can be just as windy as the rivers, I'm told."

"What are the houses like?" Lottie asked.

"Stone everywhere! There's stone houses, stone roads, walls—it's incredible. You'll have to come and see it for yourself." He leaned back as if to get a good look at Lottie. "Now that I think about it, you might have the makings of a missionary's wife."

Mother pulled Lottie onto the settee and hugged her close. Lottie's heart warmed as well as her cheeks. She wasn't sure about the wife part, but she liked that Uncle James thought she could have an exciting life as a missionary just like in Mother's stories. If Sarah could do it, surely, Lottie could too.

Everyone looked over as a cheer followed by groans rose from the domino table. It sounded as though Ike won the game.

Father traced a long, squiggly line on the map with his finger. "How far will you be from the Jordan River?"

Uncle James and Father continued poring over the map with Mother. Orie crossed the room and sat with Aunt Julia on the other sofa. Lottie wriggled away from Mother and joined them.

Orie scooted close to Aunt Julia. "Such thrilling days are ahead of you."

Aunt Julia patted Orie's hand. "I believe thrilling days are ahead of you, too, aren't they?"

Orie looked down at her hands, fiddling with a domino tile. "Mother and Father haven't decided where I will attend school. I think they've agreed against the finishing school in Richmond, thankfully. But they haven't told me about any other school. Do *you* know?" Orie's wide eyes jolted up as if searching Aunt Julia's face for any hint of an answer.

"The Lord knows his plans for you, Orie. He will make a way. Please don't worry yourself."

Orie's face fell. "So they haven't told *you* either. I want to be excited for school, but I don't even know what to imagine. My education is just a burden to them. They want me to stay close to home and marry a wealthy Baptist businessman like Father."

Lottie's chin dropped in outrage. It was as if Orie had completely forgotten that Lottie spoke up for her after the library incident with Grandmother.

"You know that's not true," Lottie said. "They made Tom teach you his medical lessons before he left."

Aunt Julia nodded. "Your parents are happy you want to pursue more serious studies. It's just not as easy to find the right school that also wants those things for you—a school that trains girls properly."

Orie folded her arms in a huff. "Tom and Ike only need to go as far as Charlottesville for a good education. But I want to travel farther, anyways." She straightened her back. "I want to see something new and different like Sarah."

Aunt Julia smiled as though she had a secret. "If, after your schooling, you find that you want to see more new and different things, you could stay with us in Jerusalem. Sarah would adore your company. And who knows? Your uncle's medical mission could flourish there. He may need help in a few years."

"Orie can be a doctor in Jerusalem?" Why did Uncle James only say Lottie could go as a wife?

Orie's eyes grew as big as carriage wheels.

"You'll need to keep studying as you are now, no matter where your parents send you to school." Aunt Julia held up a finger. "And until then, keep reading those anatomy and biology books, and ask Tom about what he's learning in school when he's home. Eventually, perhaps you could eat olives every day and walk the ancient roads that Jesus and the disciples walked."

Orie looked dreamily in the distance. "Dr. Orianna Moon, practicing medicine abroad. I love it!" She clasped her hands together, and her domino tile dropped to the floor and bounced under the sofa.

Lottie rolled her eyes. Their stockpile was already missing tiles. She stooped beside the sofa and reached her arm under, feeling around.

When Uncle James talked about Lottie going to be a missionary, she felt excited and special. But when Aunt Julia said Orie might go to Israel, Lottie didn't like the idea at all. She had always wanted Orie to have adventures, but she never really thought about Orie going away without her.

Lottie found something hard and flat under the sofa, but it wasn't small. It felt like a book. She pulled it out and wiped dust off the cover. She smiled and held it up for Aunt Julia and Orie to see. "It's Mother's old missionary book about the Judsons."

Aunt Julia reached for it and thumbed through its pages.

Orie smiled. "I remember that one."

"What do you remember about it?" Aunt Julia cocked her head.

"The adventures and faraway places—Burma, I think."

Lottie's heart raced. Memories of Mother reading the story flashed in her mind. "I remember that Ann Judson got sick and died when she went to be a missionary."

Orie grimaced and leaned back. "That was a long time ago." Her gaze flickered to Aunt Julia. "Uncle James is taking lots of medicine on their trip, so that won't happen to them."

Lottie turned to Aunt Julia. Tears stung her eyes. "Will he have the right medicine if you get sick?"

"Girls, everything will be fine." Aunt Julia laid a hand on Lottie. "He's bringing plenty of medicine, and he knows how to make more. Most people there suffer from curable illnesses, so if I do get sick, your Uncle James will likely have the right medicine ready for me."

Orie's face was still twisted in concern. "But you could get sick with a foreign kind of disease, right? One that Uncle James doesn't know how to cure."

Aunt Julia took a deep breath. She looked desperate for words. "Yes, we do face that risk. We'll face all sorts of risks, and we'll miss out on some things like special visits with you Moons." She tapped Lottie's nose. "But this is what we've always wanted. We waited for years to be missionaries. Now that we finally get to go, do you know what I learned?"

"What?" Lottie and Orie asked in unison, both leaning closer to Aunt Julia.

Aunt Julia closed her eyes. "Following God is the greatest adventure there is."

Orie's face reflected the same confusion that swamped Lottie.

Aunt Julia opened her eyes. Her face shone. "Becoming missionaries was our dream. Now that it's here, I finally feel ready to let it go, if God would ask us to. Because what he wants for us is more exciting and wonderful than anything I could ask him for, whether on the mission field or not. And chasing his heart is more thrilling than going to Israel or China."

What could she say to that? She'd never heard anyone talk about God that way before. He was the one she blamed for being forced to go to church and pray and not doing anything fun on the Sabbath. The one who kept her from adventure, not one who was an adventure in himself.

The Barclay boys called over to Orie and Lottie. "Start a new round with us! This game is blocked."

Aunt Julia smiled and nodded at the girls. They each pecked her cheek, then hurried to rejoin the other children.

Lottie sat down next to her brother. She hadn't found that lost tile under the sofa, but the group seemed content to play with what they had. The boys pushed the dominos to the center of the table, laughing at the idea of Sarah riding a camel around Jerusalem. Sarah smiled awkwardly as if she hoped it was all a joke. Lottie would have gladly taken her place, camels or no camels.

This time next year, Orie would leave for school somewhere. Ike would go away to the University of Virginia like Tom had done. Lottie would be left nearly alone with nothing but Bible stories and a dwindling stock of domino tiles. It seemed that everyone was bound for adventure except for her.

That night, Lottie fell asleep thinking of everyone she had lost or would soon lose. She tossed and turned while a nightmare swirled in her head.

Everyone she ever loved was sailing away on a ship, laughing and happily waving goodbye. She reached out for her big sister with silent screams, but Lottie was left behind, alone, and in the dark. She jolted awake. Hair stuck to her sweaty forehead as she panted and looked around the room. Orie was still there, sleeping in her bed. It was only a dream.

Lottie laid there for a minute. It was too early to get up, but how could she possibly go back to sleep?

She got out of bed, tied her gray wrapper over her nightdress, and ventured downstairs. The parlor and library and dining room were quiet and still. She followed voices to the detached kitchen. Lottie slowly opened the door. A cheery fire glowed in the wide iron cooker. Pots and pans hung on pegs along the wall. Lottie took a deep breath and smelled warm butter and yeast drifting from the oven. Mmm, biscuits.

Fannie and Peggy were busy chatting and sorting out eggs and apples, getting the family's breakfast ready until Lottie said a quiet, "Good morning," and made them jump.

Fannie gasped and clutched a wooden spoon to her chest. "What are you doing down here, Miss Lottie?"

Lottie clutched her wrapper close. "I ... woke up too early." No need to admit that a scary dream had upset her like a child.

Fannie smiled. "Bad dream?"

Lottie flushed then nodded.

Fannie dragged a stool beside the oven. "Sit here, Miss. You need some oatmeal—something heavy to ground you after a bad dream."

"Mama makes the best oatmeal." Peggy carefully added fresh, whole eggs to a pot of boiling water.

Lottie was only a year younger than Peggy, but didn't know how to boil eggs or cook anything. She climbed onto the stool and watched as Fannie stirred a pot of oats and milk. The mixture slowly rose and fell as though it was breathing. Fannie added in some brown sugar, then moved it away from the heat.

"How do you know when it's done?" Lottie asked.

"Oh, it's been going for a while. You just know when it looks right—not tough, but not mushy. Just like that." She spooned some into a bowl for Lottie.

After sprinkling a dusting of cinnamon on top, Fannie handed her the oatmeal and a spoon.

"I love cinnamon." Lottie took a bite.

Fannie winked at Lottie. "I'm gonna make gravy for the biscuits next."

Lottie perked up. "Can I help?"

Fannie hesitated then glanced at the door with a wrinkled brow. "I suppose ... but only 'til Masta' and Mistr'ss Moon wake up."

Lottie nodded. "I'll get back inside before then." Peggy had left the kitchen, and Lottie finished the warm bowl of oatmeal on her lap, then hopped off the stool and joined Fannie at the plain wooden table in the middle of the room. "What can I do?"

As Fannie folded buttermilk into a large bowl of flour, she looked at Lottie then nodded at a salt crock on the table. "You can pinch some of that into the bowl, Miss."

Lottie got the salt and added it to the biscuit mix. She leaned closer and squinted her eyes. There was something on Fannie's hands—two streaks of lighter skin across the top of her dark hands. Why hadn't Lottie ever noticed them before? "Did you burn your hands on the cooker?"

Fannie's face went ashen. She pulled her hands back from the bowl and wiped them on her apron. "No, Miss, I'm careful 'round the oven."

Lottie pointed to Fannie's hands, still hidden in her apron. "How did you get those marks?"

Fannie slightly turned her face away but kept her eyes fixed on Lottie. "I got those back when Masta' and Mistr'ss Harris was in charge."

Lottie tilted her head. That was a long time ago. When Captain Harris was alive, Fannie must have been a young girl. Maybe she had been less careful in the kitchen back then.

Peggy came back with a mound of meat. "When you're done with the biscuits, you can help me fry up the bacon. That can get wild," Peggy said with a laugh.

Lottie helped Fannie and Peggy cook until it was time for everyone upstairs to be awake. Maybe staying at home wouldn't be as boring and lonely as she'd thought.

CHAPTER SIX

1850

The following year, Lottie didn't have scary dreams anymore. But she still liked to sneak into the kitchen and help with what was cooking. Not today, though. Today was a perfect July day, and Lottie planned to spend it outside with Ike, Sallie, Jimmy, and Cary Ann, their sweet-natured neighbor.

Lottie plopped down by the front door and laced up her boots.

Mother came out of Father's study and walked by Lottie. "Going outside?"

Lottie nodded, and her ribbon loosened and fell in her face. "Yes ma'am. Jimmy and Cary Ann came over."

Mother smiled and went into the library, where Orie was reading. "Don't forget to fix your ribbon."

Ike and Sallie whizzed downstairs and halted in front of Lottie.

"Where's Orie?" Sallie looked left then right, swinging her barley curls around her head.

Lottie shrugged and straightened her ribbon. "I couldn't persuade her away from her books today."

"I saw Jimmy from my window." Ike waved for Sallie to follow him. "C'mon. Looks like he's got a new hoop."

The two ran outside and left the door open.

Lottie tugged her laces tight, got up, and grabbed the doorknob. She looked over her shoulder at the library. Was that Orie putting books back on the shelf? Her heart swelled like a batch of Fannie's biscuits rising in the oven. Maybe Orie had heard them and would decide to come along, after all. Orie burst through the library doorway and hurried down the hall into Father's study. Lottie's heart sank as though a vital ingredient was missing from the dough.

Mother came out into the hallway and waved at Lottie. "Have fun, dear." She went into the study after Orie.

All morning, Lottie and the others rolled hoops and played quoits and tag. When the summer sun reached its peak of relentless heat, they raced to the woods beyond the orchard, where a little stream ran through on its way to join the mighty James River.

Of course, to get there, they had to pass the cemetery. Father's parents were buried there, and Lottie had the same name as his mother. As Lottie ran by with the others, she willed herself to keep her eyes up. Most people called Lottie by her nickname, but she still didn't like seeing her own full name on a headstone. Once she reached her namesake's grave, she couldn't help but glance at it.

Charlotte Digges Moon
November 18, 1773 - January 14, 1839
Beloved wife, mother, grandmother

The stone stood in place to remind the world that Grandmother Moon lived between those dates and left behind her family and friends. What else had her grandmother left behind that the engraver hadn't included? The first Charlotte Diggs Moon didn't have books written about her like Ann Judson did. What might Lottie leave behind one day, and would anyone write books about *her*?

Cary Ann paused and shouted back at Lottie. "We're going to be last if we don't hurry up."

Lottie shook the gravestone out of her head and ran to catch up with Cary Ann, leaving little Sallie in last place.

The group settled to rest at their favorite spot under the trees where clear water babbled over smooth stones. Lottie sat on the log of a fallen birch, untied her boots, and kicked them away along with any remaining thoughts about gravestones. She peeled off her socks and sank her feet into a spot where the stream ran deep. The cool water gently washed over her tired feet. Lottie closed her eyes, and her head fell back. "Why is it when my feet are free, I feel free? One dip and my whole self is cooled off."

Jimmy found a pointy stick and began drawing in the dirt. "I'm glad you're so at peace." He waved his hand in front of his nose. "All the rest of us suffer when your stinky feet are free."

Ike laughed, and Lottie threw a sock at Jimmy. He caught it with the pointy stick and waved it around like a white flag of surrender. Sallie giggled, but Cary Ann's brow knit.

"Won't you get in trouble if those get a hole?" she asked. "If I brought mine home like that, my mother would make me darn the whole family's socks."

"I have a few pairs you could fix up, Lottie." Sallie cast her an overly sweet smile.

Absolutely not. Lottie popped up to rescue her sock, then stopped mid-reach. "I haven't gotten into much trouble lately. I really should every so often. Trouble is in my constitution, after all."

Ike raised a skeptical eyebrow.

"If I behave properly too much, Mother might worry I'm ill," Lottie explained. "So I should allow myself some trouble today." She returned to swishing her feet in the water.

Anna sat in a chair in Edward's study, rubbing away a headache from her temples.

Orie clasped her hands and shook white knuckles at Edward. "Please, Father, I promise to do well and make you proud." She turned to Anna. "Let me go to school at Troy this fall, please."

Anna's throat constricted. She never had to go through all of this with Tom. "I know it's difficult, but we must consider the options. New York is far away and very different from Virginia, for better or worse."

Orie stepped closer to her. "It will be for my better—I know it will. It's a serious school, as you said, where they will teach me the same as if I were a boy."

The choices were down to Augusta Female Seminary, which was close to Viewmont but run by Presbyterians, and Troy Female Seminary in New York. Troy held one of the highest scholastic reputations for girls' schools in the country, but it was so far away and notorious for graduating radical abolitionists and feminists like Elizabeth Cady Stanton.

For months, Anna and Edward had mailed inquiries and asked around about these schools. Between themselves, Anna and Edward had already decided on Troy, but they wanted to discuss their reservations with Orie before committing to send her there. Anna also kept the finishing school in Richmond on the table just to give Orie some perspective on the privilege it would be for her to attend a genuine, academically challenging school.

Edward sat at his desk with steepled hands at his stomach. "Please sit, Orie.

Do you believe you're mature enough to be surrounded by liberal Northerners?"

Orie kept her eyes on Edward, nodding frantically, as she felt behind her for the chair and lowered herself down. "Yes, Father, I am."

"You may encounter ideas that aren't customary here in Virginia," Edward said. "The town of Troy seems reliably conservative, but the school welcomes girls from abolitionist and feminist families."

Orie scooted to the edge of her seat. "Yes, Father, I've read all about those things already. You don't need to worry."

Anna sighed. Nothing Orie had said so far eased her worries. Orie may have read about abolition and feminism in newspapers and pamphlets, but those were all from sources they trusted. Orie had never been surrounded or confronted by people who passionately believed differently.

The political differences were one thing. Anna was more concerned about sending her daughter among the wolves of New York's wild religious environment, especially since Orie didn't seem to realize she was only a sheep. Anna shivered, remembering scandalous newspaper stories about spiritualist seances happening throughout the state. Orie was religiously noncommittal at best. Would she be easily drawn away from her Baptist upbringing?

"You'll also find lots of other religions there..." Anna tried to control her voice, which only made it ring higher. "Quakerism and Mormonism. Some spiritualist people even try to communicate with the dead."

Orie huffed and widened her eyes as if she were trying not to roll them. "If I was going to join any sort of religion, I'd be a Disciple like Aunt Julia and Uncle James."

This was not particularly reassuring, but at least Orie didn't seem excited to explore the den of beliefs up North.

At the end of their interview, Edward stood up from behind his desk and walked over to a wall of bookcases. He selected something off a shelf, turned to Orie, and handed her a brand new set of notebooks. "You must faithfully attend chapel. We won't be sending you back for a second semester if you don't have full marks on your chapel attendance."

Orie sprung from the chair and clutched Edward's waist in a hug. She spoke softly. "Thank you."

Anna slowly exhaled and got up to hug Orie. Sending Tom off to school was as simple as following the well-worn road to Charlottesville. She didn't know the way to Troy, but she was willing to grab a spade and clear the way for her daughter.

Back at the stream in the woods, Lottie and the group relaxed and splashed in the water. One by one, their heads turned to listen as a faint yell grew louder from up toward the house.

It was Orie, waving her arms and shouting something over and over. "I'm going to New York!" She was breathless when she reached them. "I'm going to school in New York."

Ike cupped his ear. "I'm sorry, where is it you're headed?"

Orie sneered at Ike. Her chest heaved as she explained with her nose in the air. "I was just discussing it with Mother and Father. We've agreed that I will attend Troy Female Seminary in New York this fall."

Orie sat down on the log next to Lottie. She caught her breath and told the group all about it. By her account, it sounded as if she were an equal member with Mother and Father on The Committee to Decide Orie's Schooling. Lottie pursed her lips. The discussion had likely not gone as smoothly and calmly as Orie said.

Lottie gaped at Orie when she told them the story. "Mother and Father are really sending you up North?" Finding a suitable girls' school must have been hard if they had to explore beyond the Mason-Dixon Line.

"They know I can handle it." Orie propped her fists on her hips and shrugged one shoulder. "Besides, Troy is the best."

Jimmy ran his hand over his head, making his damp hair stick up. "Wow, you're one bricky girl."

"I used to envy you two and Tom." Orie gestured to Ike and James. "As long as you studied, even a little bit, you would go to the University of Virginia and learn whatever you wanted. I studied as much as I could, but I never knew where I'd end up. Now I wonder. Maybe if I didn't envy you and read so much, I'd be going to Richmond in the fall instead for embroidery and French classes."

Jimmy took a sweeping bow. "We're most honored to be of service in furthering your education."

Orie waved him off. "I didn't come find you only to brag. Mother says it's time to come inside."

Jimmy and Cary Ann walked together back to their homes. Sallie hurried ahead to the house, and Ike moseyed at his own pace.

Lottie slid her boots back on and followed Orie, then doubled back for her socks. She snatched them off the log and spun away too quickly, slipping and landing in the water's muddy edge on her hands and knees. She got up and looked down at her dress. Her heart dropped into her stomach. Cary Ann and Ike were right. If Mother saw her, she would surely be in trouble. Lottie wiped her hands on her dress. It was filthy, anyways. She ran to catch up with Orie.

Orie turned at Lottie's presence, gasped, and laughed. "How did you do that so fast?"

"It doesn't matter." Lottie rubbed dirt off her cheek. "When will you leave for New York? How long will you stay there?"

Orie fanned herself with an open palm. "Early September, I expect. Maybe even sooner since I'll be new there and need time to settle in. Father said if all goes well, I can stay for both semesters, maybe more."

Lottie's muscles tightened. She whipped her head toward Orie, who didn't seem anything but pleased at the idea of spending months or even years away from Lottie. The longer Tom was away at university, the fewer letters they got from him. He used to come home for the holidays, but once he started courting Miss Helen Vaugh Wilson, Lottie didn't get to see as much of her eldest brother. What if Orie liked living up there in Troy and decided to stay even after she finished school? She could fall in love with some New York boy and forget about her own sister as Tom had done.

"You'll write to me, won't you?" Lottie started to limp. Her wet ankle was chafing.

"Of course, I will. I'll have loads of adventures to tell you about, won't I?"

"You won't fall in love like Tom and stop writing to me?"

Orie laughed. "It's a *girls'* school. What handsome gentlemen will I meet in classrooms full of girls?"

"Tom went to the boys' school, and somehow he met Helen. Now he doesn't write to us anymore."

"He still writes sometimes," Orie snapped, as if she wished it were true but knew otherwise. "But don't worry. I won't be silly and fall in love. I'm not getting married, anyway."

That didn't shock Lottie. In fact, hearing Orie say it comforted her. Marriage wasn't discouraged at Viewmont. It just wasn't idealized or discussed as the only option for the Moon girls. Lottie's other uncle, Jimmy's father, knew a lot about the law. He actually asked Jimmy's sisters to promise that they would never marry. He said when a woman signed a marriage certificate, she signed all her rights away. Lottie heard that each of the girls agreed. Father hadn't gone that far, but now Lottie wished he had. Then Orie would surely come back home.

Lottie shyly glanced up at her sister. "We still have the rest of the summer together, right?"

Orie paused, and Lottie did too. Orie tucked in a stray curl on Lottie's head. "The whole rest of the summer." She resumed her pace, and Lottie followed. "But I will be busy. Nicholas is going to tutor me before I go."

"Tom's tutor for medical school?"

Orie lifted her face into a breeze. "Mother says he'll teach me some general things to prepare for Troy. But I'll eventually go to medical school after that, so we'll cover science too. There's a school in Boston that teaches female doctors. The one in Pennsylvania where Uncle James went is starting to teach women now. That's where Tom is going, so I'll probably go there too."

Lottie's jaw dropped. Orie had a plan for even more schooling far away from home? At this rate, she would go to New York, Pennsylvania, and then straight to Jerusalem. Lottie's chest tightened, and her stomach felt hollow. Was this the last summer she would have with her sister?

Orie threw her arms wide. "Opportunity is opening up for women! Who knows? You might come up to Troy right after me."

Hmm, that was a new thought. Lottie liked the sound of it. It would be nicer if Orie didn't have to go so far away for school. But maybe she was blazing a trail for Lottie to join her one day.

"It's good Father hired Nicholas again. I'll need all the preparation I can get. As a woman pioneering in the medical field, I have to know the material perfectly if they're going to take me seriously."

"Will Nicholas take you seriously and teach you the same stuff as Tom?" Lottie asked.

Orie's mouth tightened. She looked uncertain for the first time since her grand announcement. "I don't know exactly." She lifted her nose. "But he accepted the job, and Father is paying him to take me seriously."

The girls had nearly reached the house. Sallie and Ike were already inside. Orie and Lottie came in through the back door, hoping to sneak Lottie upstairs before Mother could see her looking more disheveled than usual. They shuffled towards the stairs, then halted at Mother's voice from behind them.

"I see it's providential that I called you inside early today," she said in a teasing way. "You'll need the extra time to wash up before supper."

As Lottie turned around to face her, Mother perched her hands on her hips. Her gaze surveyed Lottie's dress and focused on the filthy socks in her hands. There was a noticeable hole where Jimmy had speared one of them. Lottie bit her lip. Maybe she should listen to Cary Ann more.

"You can take those things to the servants for cleaning. But see to it that you mend the socks yourself." Mother dropped her hands and smiled as though she was trying not to. "I suppose young ladies who are full of life can't be expected to come home perfectly clean every day."

Lottie beamed at Mother and exhaled in relief. Scurrying upstairs with Orie, Lottie cast an I-told-you-so glance at Ike, lurking near the banister.

"You didn't get in trouble?" Ike whispered.

Lottie and Orie giggled as he crossed his arms. Lottie caught Orie's hand and didn't let go until they reached their room.

"I sure will miss you," Orie said.

Confidence lightened Lottie's heart. Orie would leave Viewmont one day, but she wouldn't forget her little sister.

Orie started her lessons with Nicholas the week after she learned she'd be going to New York. On the morning of their first lesson, she wore her most serious and studious-looking dress with an expression to match. She held one of her new notebooks as Father and Mother walked into the library with her.

Nicholas stood from his seat at the table. He looked different than before. His face seemed more chiseled now, and he had grown into his broad shoulders. His short, dark hair curled at his ears.

Rather than be introduced as a child, Orie let Nicholas take one of her hands like a lady. "You may not remember me from when I was a child and you tutored my brother. I'm nearly sixteen now."

He dipped his head in a small bow. "Of course. I remember you from our first lesson, Miss Moon."

Her thoughts froze. "Our first lesson?"

"It was cut short," he explained with a smile. "You ran outside when your angry grandmother scolded you for listening at the door." His face suddenly fell and flushed. "Forgive me, ma'am." He turned to Mother, his employer. "I heard the sad news that your mother passed on. Please accept my condolences."

"Thank you." Mother nodded tightly. "You two should get started. I'll send in some tea."

Father clapped Nicholas's shoulder with a reassuring smile. "Your bag looks fairly stuffed there."

"Yes, sir." Nicholas sounded breathless, but the color started to fade from his face. "I brought my best material."

"You're welcome to any of the books here if they're helpful." Father swept his arm toward the bookcases.

Mother and Father left, and Mother kept the door open.

Orie stood, waiting for Nicholas to say something. His demeanor calmed, and he gestured for her to take a seat. "Your father tells me that you want to attend medical school."

"That's right." Orie narrowed her eyes and slowly sat down. "Is that a problem?"

"Not at all." Nicholas smiled kindly. "He said he would like you to be familiar with the basic terms. But of course, you may recognize many of those already." He unpacked his satchel. "I believe studying the history of some general medical theories as well as learning a few memorization strategies would also prove beneficial to you."

Orie watched him carefully. "You're not embarrassed to teach a woman?"

"I'm not." He began sorting books into piles.

"You don't think I should rather be perfecting my embroidery skills? Or learning to bake a pie?" She inched closer with each question.

"I don't."

Orie leaned back, pressing her lips together to restrain a smile. Maybe Nicholas would treat her more like a student than a girl.

"Unless we're talking about a blueberry pie," he said, with a gleam in his eye. "Then I would enjoy sampling your hard work very much."

Orie fought back a smile. "It would have been strawberry, I'm afraid."

"Pity. I suppose that leaves us with studying the material I've prepared." He handed her a freshly sharpened pencil.

Orie collapsed in her chair, her head back as far as anatomy allowed. "I already told you what the man said. Why do you insist on asking me again?"

Nicholas spun away from the window to face her. "You quoted William Harvey perfectly, but what was he *really* saying?"

Orie heaved a sigh. She appreciated that Nicholas didn't adapt any of his lessons to suit the delicacies of a young woman. Of what she remembered from her eavesdropping days, he taught her the same material he'd taught Tom. The lessons were fascinating and challenging, but not as harmonious as their first lesson together in the library. And today was especially frustrating.

She leaned over the table, pointing a pencil in Nicholas's general direction, not exactly at him. "He was *really* saying that blood circulates from the heart, throughout the whole body, then back to the heart again."

Nicholas offered a weary smile. "Very good, Miss Moon. I only push you because I know you're capable of learning the depths of these complex things. You're a gifted woman."

Orie sat up straight and lowered her pencil. His words melted her heart and disarmed her.

Nicholas crossed to Orie. "Imagine...." He waved his hand in front of him over some invisible scene. "Dr. Harvey presented the theory you just quoted to Europeans who, for over a thousand years, had a very different idea of how the heart works. Harvey was a great doctor and scientist because, while he studied and learned from doctors of the past, he did not hesitate to question their theories."

"But the people didn't accept his theories."

"Not at first." Nicholas picked up her pencil. "But through the empirical evidence that he collected, we now have a better understanding of the human body."

Orie propped her chin up and gazed at Nicholas. "He was brave to stand up to everyone like that, alone with the truth."

"Well, Harvey wasn't the first scientist to challenge the popular theory of the time. Sometimes the truth needs to be communicated to people many times before it's finally accepted."

It didn't take much prodding to get Nicholas preaching on the virtues of science.

"Science is based on experiments and the theories that follow. It must seek the truth. It must always be ready to be wrong, not cling to what everyone else thinks is certain." Nicholas started to pace between the table and the window with her pencil in the air. "A great scientist must be brave enough to build on or challenge the work of others and humble enough to let other scientists do the same to his own work—or hers," he added, looking over his shoulder at Orie.

Orie had read books for years, absorbing their information. But Nicholas's lessons were not only about information. He tested her understanding of how concepts related to each other, and he asked her opinion on medical theories. She loved it and worked hard to keep up with the pace he set for her.

When the time came to end the day's lesson, neither was in a hurry. Orie stood and smoothed her sky-blue dress. She caught one of Nicholas's smiling glances toward her as he gathered his books, one at a time.

Orie straightened her notebooks, then the chairs. "Nick, are you this passionate about your other subjects?"

He smiled whenever she called him "Nick."

"Science is my favorite subject to teach. But music is my greatest passion." Nicholas drummed the book in his hand and looked away. "I get to perform sometimes during mass."

Orie blinked rapidly. She stopped straightening the chairs. "You attend a Catholic church?"

He swallowed hard. "I do."

Hearing Nicholas say "I do" sent a flutter of wedding doves through Orie's chest. Heat rose in her cheeks.

"Is that a problem?" he asked.

"Not for me." She lifted her chin.

He cleared his throat and gave her a small smile. "I'll be back next week to review your progress with the reading."

Orie found another stray chair to straighten up. "I wish it were next week already."

His satchel now perfectly packed, Nicholas stood watching her.

"I enjoy our time together," she said.

Nicholas threw the satchel over his shoulder, checked the doorway with a quick glance, and walked closer. He spoke quietly. "I enjoy your company as well. You're a smart young lady, and you're lovely, if I may say so."

"You may say so!" The words erupted out of Orie's mouth a little louder than she intended. But no one inside the room minded, and no one outside of it noticed. Then, Nicholas closed the space between them with a soft kiss. He tousled the white ribbon in her hair and said goodbye.

After Nicholas left, Orie floated around the house. Everything reminded her of him. The chestnut coat rack in the hallway shared the exact color of his hair. Sunlight bouncing through a glass lampshade in the parlor twinkled just like his hazel eyes.

As she breezed by the open doorway of Father's study, he called her in. Orie nearly bumped into the door frame as she answered him.

"Did Nicholas leave already?" Father lowered his account book. "I'm sorry I missed him."

"I miss him too." Orie's eyes bulged. She coughed. "I mean—yes, we just finished our lesson for the day."

"How are the lessons going, dear? Is Nicholas a good teacher?"

"He's wonderful," Orie said blissfully. "—at teaching." She shook her head to focus on Father and ignore the handkerchief on his desk that was trimmed with the same navy blue as Nicholas's waistcoat today.

"That's nice," Father said, obviously not noticing anything odd. "What have you learned?"

"Oh, um, lots of things." Orie searched the room for an answer. She had just been in a lesson with Nicholas. But his kiss flooded her mind and drowned any scholastic thought. "Circulation!" She finally remembered. "We discussed a great deal about blood circulation today." She softened. "And the heart."

"Sounds as if you're right on track with where Tom was at this stage in Nicholas's tutoring. I'm glad he's giving you decent lessons."

"You like him, Father?"

"Yes, I'll consider hiring him back for Ike to give him an edge before school. And Lottie too. She'll be going before too long."

Orie was nodding her head in agreement up until Father mentioned Lottie.

"Actually, Father, I'm not sure she would be a suitable student for him. He's an excellent teacher, but I think our lessons are so successful because we understand each other. We're good together. Don't you think so, Father?"

He quirked up one eyebrow. "He wouldn't be a good tutor if he could only teach one kind of student. He did a top-notch job preparing Tom for university. I was concerned at first if he could manage tutoring someone with your unique temperament, but it seems that everything is going well."

Her jaw dropped in offense at whatever Father meant by her "unique temperament."

"I think he will be 'good together' with Ike and Lottie, too," Father concluded, returning his attention to his account book.

Orie turned to leave in a much less dreamy state than the one she entered with. Lottie was just a kid, but Orie didn't like the idea of Nicholas tutoring other girls. Did he kiss other girls after lessons? She fretted down the hall, then one glance at the chestnut coat rack had her floating again. He said himself that she was uniquely gifted and lovely. What they had was special.

CHAPTER SEVEN

August 1850

Anna glanced up from reading the latest issue of the *Religious Herald*. She smiled at Orie, sitting on the other sofa in the parlor, twirling a white ribbon around her finger. Orie lounged back and tapped her dangling foot to the tune she was humming to herself. She seemed to be in a remarkably good mood. She must be excited to go to school. No need to question it and risk misunderstanding Orie and riling her into defensiveness.

The idea of Orie going to school so far away in a northern state still set Anna's nerves on edge, but it was nice to see her oldest daughter so happy. If it wasn't the promise of school that lifted Orie's mood, then it must be that the Barclays were on their way over today. Their visits always perked up the household. As much as Anna anticipated them, though, each one confused her more.

Ever since James and Julia announced their missionary plans last fall, Anna had wondered when they would set sail for Israel. It must be soon now. Julia had said the preparations wouldn't take longer than a year. They didn't seem as though they had changed their minds. But here they were—ten months later and still in Virginia.

Since time wasn't telling, Anna resolved to ask James and Julia plain and outright when they were going to serve in Jerusalem. Surely, they wouldn't once again abandon the calling that God put on their lives. Even if they had, she just needed to know if they had decided to stay or still planned to go. Then she could stop preparing her emotions and her table for every visit as if it was their last meal together.

By the time the Barclays arrived in the early afternoon, Orie had left the parlor and joined the children outside. Anna asked Peggy to ensure the garden table was set and ready, then she and Edward stepped out to welcome their guests.

The Barclays poured out of their wagon and scattered toward their counterparts. The children ran off to join their cousins in the yard. Edward greeted James, then the men turned toward the house.

Anna fired off an exasperated sigh. "Running from the women? We have tea in the garden for you."

James turned and waved a packet of papers. "Not today, my sister. A deal is in progress for the estate. Much to be decided."

Anna caught her breath. A deal was in progress? Maybe this was their last meal together after all.

"I'll ask Fannie to send some tea into the study." Edward smiled, and the men withdrew inside.

Julia wrapped an arm around Anna. "We're better off without them. They would only monopolize the conversation with talk of contracts all afternoon."

The two women retreated to the garden. They relaxed on ornate iron chairs, watching the sun dip lower into the sky, taking the heat of the day with it. The scent of summer flowers surrounded them, and the warmth of their afternoon tea filled them as they swapped stories about the days between their visits.

"So I told the boy to climb down from that tree immediately," Julia said, in the middle of a story while Anna nibbled shortbread. "He was so high up there, I was sure he'd faint from the altitude." She smiled and shook her head. "Stunts like that make me anxious about taking them halfway across the world. Who knows what shenanigans they'll get into."

Anna's attention piqued. "If you are still planning to sail to Israel, when will you leave?" She spoke as calmly as if she were asking whether Julia would like more sugar in her tea.

Julia daintily lifted her cup for a sip. It didn't quite cover her playful smirk. "October the ninth."

Anna jolted. "October the ninth?" She steadied her shaken plate of teatime treats. She hadn't expected such a definitive answer.

Julia set down her tea and looked longingly towards the mountains. "Right as Virginia starts her season of splendor, we'll be battling sea sickness with nothing to look at but waves for weeks." She shrugged. "But the house should be sold by then, and there's really nothing else to wait for."

Anna studied her sister-in-law's face. Did Julia seem sad about going? "You were so excited before."

"I was excited," Julia said, then added quickly, "and I still am. We'll finally be missionaries. It's wonderful—a dream fulfilled." She sighed. "It will just be very different. I know it will be challenging, but I don't know exactly what those challenges will be." Julia straightened and smiled. "At a certain point, there's nothing more I can do to prepare other than to just do it. God is providing. I take comfort in that."

Once Anna recovered from the surprise, her heart swelled. Julia and James had faced such disappointment in trying to make a silk business at Monticello. Then they went through that season of uncertainty while living at Viewmont until Mother convinced them to settle in Scottsville and open an apothecary. Through it all, James clearly held onto his passion for missions. Now he and Julia were finally being sent to the mission field—on October ninth. Only a season away.

It was a wonderful thing to celebrate, but Anna understood the conflict that Julia expressed. Unknown challenges lay ahead of them. And they would share family milestones only through letters. James and Julia would miss Christmas that year, maybe for many years to come. They wouldn't get to watch Orie thrive at school. If Tom married Helen soon, the Barclays would likely miss the wedding. But people in Jerusalem needed to know Jesus now. James and Julia shouldn't delay, waiting for some imaginary perfect moment.

Julia looked at the rolling hills and distant mountains as though she was about to cry. She dabbed at her eye, then turned to Anna. "I practiced a little speech in my head on the way over here. I was determined to tell you more gently this time. James and I planned to talk with you and Edward about it together, privately before supper."

"Thank you for telling me. I wanted to know."

Right there in the garden, Anna laid a hand on Julia's and prayed for the Barclays' voyage across the Atlantic, for their adjustment to a culture completely foreign to the only one they've ever known, and for the lost souls they would encounter all along the way to trust in Jesus as their Messiah.

The lowering sun ushered the women inside. Anna paused at the back door and rang the bell mounted on the house. It was an effective way to call the children in, but she tried to avoid using it. Lottie especially never seemed to like being summoned by that bell. Anna smiled at a memory of Lottie years ago stomping inside with a grumpy face.

"We're not cows," she had said.

Anna and Julia walked inside and stepped into the doorway of Edward's study. He waved them in and pulled out two chairs in front of his desk. They took the seats.

"We just came for a moment." Anna smoothed her skirt. "Supper will start soon. The children are on their way in."

"We're almost to a resolution here." Edward returned to stand with James.

James leaned over Edward's desk, studying a pile of what looked like legal documents. "The contract deadline must be September thirtieth at the very latest." He tapped at the papers. "That should clear us for October ninth."

"What's so important about the ninth?" Edward asked.

James's eyes widened as he slowly looked up toward Edward, then to Julia.

"I couldn't wait either." Julia giggled and covered her mouth. "Go ahead and tell him."

James shared the news.

Edward clapped James on the back, beaming. "We'll see to it that nothing prevents you from getting on that ship in October."

"Nothing will prevent it this time, I know it." James shook his head and laid a hand on the contract. "God is providing in every area. The house was the last concern, and we can sell the slaves at any time."

Edward winced and dropped his hand. "You're not taking them to Richmond, are you?"

Anna wasn't an abolitionist by any means, but she was ready to talk James out of selling his servants to the highest bidder in Richmond. It sounded as if Edward was preparing to talk him out of it too.

"No, no." James waved Edward off. "Mr. Staples is taking the bulk of the slaves along with the house. It's right here in the contract." He flipped to the correct page. "The others will stay local in Scottsville with one family or another. No need to visit the capitol and get buried in more paperwork, right?" He elbowed Edward in a joking sort of way. "Mr. Staples gave me a very generous price. Now, the medical work I do in Jerusalem will be strictly for ministry, not for hire."

At supper, James and Julia shared their departure plans with the children. Lottie popped out of her seat, leading the table in a round of applause and cheers. James's eyes brimmed with tears. He laughed joyfully at such a reception of their news.

Orie grinned from ear to ear. "Congratulations."

Ike nodded in approval. "Well done."

As the cheering quieted, Anna rose from her chair and lifted her glass. "Tonight is a celebration. We give thanks to God for making a way for these new missionaries that we're blessed to have in our family."

Everyone lifted their glasses in response. Anna sat and gazed around the table as everyone happily dug into their supper. Tonight wasn't their final family meal together, but her heart stung, knowing it was one of the last.

At Orie's next lesson, she didn't waste any time before informing Nicholas about her aunt and uncle's missionary plans. He didn't say much in response. He just listened politely. In fact, throughout their whole lesson, that's how he interacted with Orie—politely. All he talked about was science and medicine.

When he finally allowed a moment of eye contact, Orie batted her eyelashes. "I'm leaving soon, too—in September."

His gaze darted back to his book. "Yes, I know. Your father told me how long you would need my services."

"Did you know I'm sixteen now, as of next week?"

Was that a smile trying to fight its way through his serious demeanor? "I believe it was you who told me that. Happy birthday—as of next week."

Nicholas looked over his lesson plans, and Orie read an essay. She stared at the same page for much longer than it took to read it. She glanced at him, but he didn't acknowledge her. When he did speak to her, it was as if some daily allotment of words was suddenly imposed upon him and he was dangerously nearing the limit.

He finally spoke without looking away from his papers. "I'm available for assistance if you have any questions, Miss Moon."

"I'm perfectly capable of reading," she snapped.

His head jolted up at her tone.

"Why are you acting so cold? Are you tired of me already?"

He put his papers down and looked at her as though she was a silly, misbehaving child. "Orie, don't."

"You said you enjoyed my company. You said I was lovely." She glanced toward the open door, then leaned closer and whispered. "You *kissed* me. Won't you miss me when I leave for miles away and months at a time? Don't you want me to write to you?"

"I shouldn't have said those things." He shook his head.

Orie's heart dropped into her stomach. His words were a betraying blade that came out of nowhere.

"Not because they're untrue," he added quickly. His shoulders slumped as he dropped the cold, uninterested facade. "I shouldn't have said them because I shouldn't have thought them. I'm a tutor, Orie. A poor man. You see these clothes?" He pulled at his dark, three-piece suit and fine emerald puffed tie.

"Yes." What was his point? He looked every bit the scholarly gentleman.

"This is a uniform, not my typical attire. Any money I hope to make—any success I hope to have depends on my reputation. If word got out about us, people would say I seduce my students. Then who would hire me to teach their daughters? We can't carry on like this."

"I could stay here," Orie said softly. "I could marry you."

He shut his eyes for a moment and sighed. "You can't stay here." He leaned an elbow onto the table and clutched his hair. "This place can't give you what you want. You want more—I see it. Please try to understand, this is for your good too."

She sat there, watching her hands in her lap grow blurry as tears pooled in her eyes.

Nicholas reached across the table as if to comfort her but stopped and pulled back his arm. "You have opportunities that even young men would envy, and I think you could do really well as a doctor. But not here." He sat up straight. "So many people will try and stop you. I won't be one of them."

Orie's mouth hardened. Her arms and shoulders—her whole body tensed. She shoved tears away with her sleeve, but the lace cuffs were no help. How could he do this to her?

"I'm sorry I flirted with you." Nicholas shook his head again, facing the floor. "I'm sorry I kiss—"

"Don't!" She cut him off, throwing two palms up in self defense against such a barrage of pain. "You can't take it back. Don't ruin the memory of it."

"Go to school and forget about me," he pleaded. "Become the first woman doctor from the South. Shock the world with your brilliance, not with a scandal."

"If you believed in me, you would stay with me." Her chest heaved for breath. Her voice grew shrill. Everything they had together was slipping away. "You can at least wait for me to finish medical school. I'll come back, and we can marry."

"You won't come back, not for long." He sounded exasperated at this point.

She sprang from her seat. "You're impossible!" She turned her back to him as fresh tears fell. All her lacy sleeves accomplished was to scratch at her eyes and smear the falling tears across her reddening face.

"Exactly. Impossible." Nicholas made the statement calmly. Yet a frustration seemed to bubble beneath the surface. "Your parents don't want you to marry a poor tutor. Even if they did allow it, they would recant as soon as they discovered I'm Catholic."

Orie reached a hand out. "You know I don't care about religion, Nick. I'll convert to whatever you want." She knew she was begging, but she couldn't let him slip by without trying.

He shook his head and left her reaching for him. "No. I need them to trust me and recommend me. More wealthy families are seeking tutors for their daughters."

Orie crossed her arms tight over her racing heart. "So you want to meet other wealthy young ladies? Maybe flirt with them and sneak a kiss or two?"

Nicholas raised his strained voice. "What I want is a good reputation so I can have a steady career and make a living." His words hung in the air, forcing Orie to face the financial differences between her life and his.

Orie softened. "Of course you do." A long moment passed silently between them. She attempted a smile. "I thought I was the one who was supposed to worry about what people think."

Nicholas's hazel eyes bore into Orie. "What people say and think about me is vital to my success. But your success will depend on not caring a lick what people think about you. You have the money and talent, and soon you will have the opportunity to truly succeed."

Everything Nicholas said sounded reasonable. But if parting this way was right, why did it feel so difficult and awful? Orie wanted to strike out into the world and become a female doctor, just as Nicholas said. But she wanted him by her side while she did it.

Nicholas grabbed his satchel. "I'll send a note to your father that you're ready for Troy and no longer need my services." He bowed his head and turned to leave. He paused in the doorway and glanced over his shoulder. "Goodbye, Orie."

Orie stood alone in the library, her heart racing and her mind blank. Nicholas was gone. She dropped into a chair at the table and let her head fall into her folded arms.

After a few moments, Father walked in and propped a fist against his side. "I missed Nicholas again?"

Orie sniffled.

Father crossed the room and stooped down to put his arm around her. "What's wrong, darling?"

Nicholas had tried to erase their whole relationship, and then he left forever. If she was the only one who acknowledged it, would she remember that it really happened? Orie lifted up her blotchy, tearful face. "He isn't coming back."

Father frowned and his brow twisted. No doubt because Orie hadn't reacted this way at all when other tutors had left. A sudden clarity calmed the panicked confusion in his eyes. "You loved him, didn't you?"

"I did," she sobbed, collapsing back into her arms on the table. "But he didn't want me."

"Orie," Father said sternly. She sat up, and his eyes burrowed into hers. "Did he behave improperly to you?"

Orie shook her head. "He did kiss me, though."

"Gracious!" Father popped up straight. "In this house? During your lessons?"

She told him the whole story. His scowling face grew red, and his mouth tightened, especially during the part where Nicholas kissed her. But he relaxed somewhat when she told him Nicholas left to make sure that she would go to school and become a doctor without being distracted by him.

Blinking back fresh tears, Orie begged Father to not tell Mother. And to give Nicholas a good reference. Sharing her story with one other person was enough to mark that it was real. Father's brow tightened, and he rubbed his forehead, but he didn't deny her requests.

A week before Orie would travel to Troy, she lay on her bed wrapping and unwrapping the special white ribbon around her hand—the one she was wearing when Nicholas had kissed her. It had been three weeks since Nicholas walked away from Viewmont and out of Orie's life. Now she saw more clearly how right he was. If Nicholas had agreed to marry her, she wouldn't be free to learn all she needed to become a female doctor. How could she have let a few weeks of flirtation completely distract her from her goals? It mustn't happen again.

Orie sat up and cast the ribbon to the floor by her bed. She had things to accomplish in life. From now on, she wouldn't suffer a man who dared to step in her way or beckon her off the path to medical school. Education was the only thing that truly offered freedom. The more education she could get, the more possibilities would open for her. Orie straightened her back and set her focus on Troy.

CHAPTER EIGHT

1850

Lottie opened her eyes and rolled over. Peggy had left a bowl of fresh water and a towel on the dressing table and opened the curtains. Sunlight started to peek through the window. Lottie's eyes flickered to Orie's bed. It was empty, as it had been each morning since she left for Troy. Why did Lottie look at it each morning, as if Orie would suddenly appear snoring under the covers?

Lottie sighed. It was late October, and she hadn't received an individual letter from her sister. Orie surely had stories to tell, being away at an exciting school in New York for the first time. Mother had told Lottie not to complain because Orie was busy and going through a big change in her life, so the whole family should be patient and gracious toward her while she adjusted. But Mother only knew that because Orie had written to *her* twice already. Tucked inside Orie's letters to Mother and Father was usually a smaller note for Lottie and her siblings with sweet words about how she missed them all and wished them well. But as Orie's closest sister and confidante for all these years, Lottie deserved more than that.

She threw her blankets back. Shivering, she got up and grabbed a striped wool dress that hung over the dressing table chair. She pulled it on, then went downstairs and gathered around the table for breakfast with everyone.

At the head of the table, Father sat behind a wall of black-and-white newsprint. Ike leaned forward to read the front page in Father's hands. Across from Ike, Sallie and Mollie bickered about something until Mother insisted they keep their mouths closed for a full minute.

Lottie sat down between Mother and Ike and made a quick visual search around Mother's plate. Just silverware and napkins. No letters. She bent over so her head almost rested on her plate, straining to see under Father's newspaper. "Did the post come yet?"

"Sit up, sweetheart. It'll be here soon." Mother placed an apple on Lottie's plate. "Have some fruit."

Lottie pushed it away. She wasn't hungry. She just wanted to know if Orie had forgotten her yet another day. Lottie slumped in her chair. The smell of hot sausages and buttery biscuits suddenly made her stomach growl. If she had to wait for the post anyway, she might as well enjoy a bite. She grabbed a biscuit and savored its warmth in her hands before munching into it.

"A new political party is forming out of New York," Father said as he stared at the paper, addressing anyone who would listen.

Lottie glanced at Father as she reached for the sausages and another biscuit. His news updates always sounded important and interesting, but she didn't usually understand what they meant. Now, where was the jam?

"They call themselves the Know-Nothings. Odd." Father lowered his newspaper but kept reading highlights from an article. "They say the party is gaining considerable influence. It seems these Know-Nothings don't want Irish and German immigrants voting and bringing in Catholicism."

Mother pursed her lips and shook her head. "I don't want the pope's religion in this country either."

"Well, they say if this new party grows and pulls some voters away from the Whig party, that could split the Whig vote and pave the way for more pro-slavery Democrats in Congress. Excellent."

"Who says all that?" Mother frowned.

"The *Richmond Enquirer*." Father carefully folded the Democratic newspaper. "I say, the Whigs won't last much longer. They can't keep their voters happy. Their anti-slavery voters are angry the president isn't tougher on slavery. Their anti-immigration folks are angry, too, and now they have this Know-Nothing party to vote for." Father added more eggs to his plate. "I, for one, appreciate President Filmore's attitude of compromise on slavery, even if he is a Whig—not like that other Whig, Taylor."

Father spoke of President Taylor as though he was angry enough to spit, right there in the dining room.

Mother lifted a reproachful eyebrow.

"May he rest in peace," Father added solemnly. President Taylor had died of food poisoning earlier that summer. "Anyway, Taylor would have led us right into civil war. Outlawing slavery in the western territories and refusing to support the Fugitive Slave Law? Nonsense."

"What's that law?" Ike set his shoulders back and sat up even straighter than he had been already.

"It's a fine example of compromise between the abolitionist states and the slave states. I have a pamphlet in my study I can show you later—'Conscience and the Constitution,' written by Moses Stuart, a *Northern* Baptist." Father leaned back in his chair and pride flickered across his eyes. "Essentially, the South gets help from the Northern states with returning the runaways. That's what a union of states should be doing—working together. Everyone wins."

Fannie and Peggy walked in. Lottie froze while spreading a dollop of strawberry jam across her biscuit. She watched as they refreshed Mother's and Father's coffee, set the morning's letters in front of Father, and left the room without a word and without notice from anyone else.

Father reached toward the pile of letters. Lottie's heart pounded. Surely, Orie would have written to her by now. He grabbed the sugar bowl next to the pile of mail. Lottie sighed.

He dropped a lump of sugar into his cup and stirred the coffee. "Yes, with Filmore's compromise, the new territories get to decide on slavery for themselves."

"I just hope, for Orianna's sake, Troy is keeping all of these divisive politics out of the classroom," Mother said. "There seems to be so much heated passion for political things up there."

Was no one paying attention to what was important? "The post!" Lottie pointed to the bundle that Fannie had brought in.

Father didn't even look her way. "Oh, I'm sure the girls have other things to occupy their attention." Finally, he set the paper aside and sifted through the letters. He piled some next to his plate and set others aside for Mother. Then he paused, smiling. "Lottie, this one is for you. It's from your sister." He handed it to her.

"Orie!" Lottie sprang from her chair, nearly toppling the jam jar. She hugged Father, took the letter, then hurried to the library, leaving little Sallie to cross her arms, kick her chair, and whine, asking why she didn't get a letter with her name on it too.

Lottie ran toward the library but halted by the stairway when she heard Peggy and Fannie in the hallway.

"What did Master say about outlawin' slavery in the West?" Peggy whispered. "I bent down to pick up a napkin and couldn't hear what he—"

"Hush, girl," Fannie snapped.

Peggy lowered her head and did as she was told.

Fannie shot a look at the dining room door. It was closed. "Don't be askin' things like that anywhere they could hear you."

"Why you so scared, Mama? Mistr'ss Moon don't beat us."

Fannie's eyes were fixed on the door as she touched the old burn scars on her hand. "White people can change fast if they get mad 'nough." She blinked, shook her head, and turned to Peggy. "Masta' didn't say anything new, anyways. It's just the same talk. Each of the territories out West are gonna decide if they want slavery or not. We don't know which ones yet."

Peggy lifted her chin. "Well, when we know which ones are free, that's where I'm goin' one day."

Fannie smiled sadly at her daughter. "And definitely don't be sayin' things like *that* in the main house."

Lottie held her breath until they went back into the kitchen. Her heart pounded in her ears. Last year, Fannie had told Lottie she got the burn scars back when the Captain and Grandmother were in charge of Viewmont. Did she mean she got those burns *from* them? Lottie shuddered. If Peggy ran away to a western territory, would Mother and Father get mad enough to use that Fugitive Slave Law to bring her back?

The hallway was empty now, but Lottie tiptoed to the library. She settled into the green armchair with Orie's letter and took a deep breath. She glanced at the empty chair beside her and smiled. Finally, her sister remembered her.

October 15, 1850

My Dear Lot,

After a month here in Troy, I'm convinced that New York and Virginia are more like different countries than two states of the same union. The conversation and vocabulary around me, while in English, sounds completely foreign at times. It's thrilling. Have you heard the word "transcendentalists"? Isn't it one of the longest words you've ever seen? They're a religious group that promotes spending time in nature for spiritual refreshment instead of inside stuffy church buildings. You would like them if they ever started a group down in Virginia. You would never have to sit on a hard church pew again! However, they aren't as popular here as they were because of their radical beliefs about abolition, which people here talk about very often. I heard of them only because one of their famous members, a woman, Margaret

Fuller, died earlier this year on a ship that sank just off the coast of New York. Can you imagine a death more tragic than dying at sea? You'd never finish your final journey to wherever you were trying to go.

Besides the transcendentalists, there are many different groups here that we don't have in Virginia. The spiritualists are very popular among the other girls at school, even though most of the girls' families and the seminary itself are Christian. I can imagine why the girls are drawn to the movement. The spiritualists not only allow women to speak in public in front of men, but they are allowed to be leaders! And spiritualists actually prove their religious claims in their seances. But alas, this is only what I hear. I have never been invited to a seance and am bound by my word to Father to faithfully attend chapel. The sermons in chapel sound just like the ones at home. Nothing interesting to report about that.

Besides the colorful religious landscape around me in New York, the school is a beautiful place. I didn't expect to be so impressed by the scenery here. The autumn air smells crisp. One deep breath of it fills me with energy. The trees around campus glow as they turn to stunning shades of red and gold. They complement the brick building nicely. By the time you get this letter, their branches should still be holding onto some of their colorful leaves. Imagine me walking or lying beneath a tree, staring up to watch the light play on the leaves. That is likely what I will be doing.

The natural scenery has been a much-needed balm to my spirit because I'm not sure if the girls here like me at all. Most of the students and teachers are Northerners. I knew that before coming here, and I even celebrated it. But they don't seem as excited by my Southern-ness. At first, one group of girls socialized with me during meals and invited me *to join them for walks around campus or to class. They asked question after question about life on a Southern planta-tion. When I told them about Viewmont, they asked how many slaves we kept there.*

Lottie flipped the page over. The story went on as Orie briefly recounted the scene that unfolded one day while she walked to class with a group of three girls.

Two of Orie's schoolmates, Sara and Mary, hovered on either side of her while the third, Clara, kept a leisurely pace ahead of them. Their heels tapped slowly on the stone pathway between stately buildings. The season's first fallen leaves danced at their feet. Mary had asked how many slaves were at Orie's family plantation.

Orie searched for an answer. Father must have told her once how many servants they had. "Maybe fifty?"

The girls' eyes grew wide.

"But I myself am interested in abolition," Orie added quickly. She subtly wiped clammy hands on her dress. "Father lets me read plenty about it."

Mary's red curls bounced as she spun around, her dainty, uplifted nose pointing straight at Orie. "Have you read Frederick Douglass's narrative? It's a thorough book about real life as a slave. He gives fantastic speeches with the newspaper man, Mr. William Lloyd Garrison, about abolition, and women's rights too."

"I—I haven't come across it yet. I've mostly read articles and pamphlets." What was the name of an anti-slavery pamphlet that she had read? Her mind went blank. She couldn't remember the title or author of a single one.

Orie clutched at her skirt. Of all the things she'd memorized to prepare for Troy, nothing prepared her for this moment. How could she convince these girls that she was different from what her accent portrayed her to be? She wasn't like other Southern girls.

Sara tilted her head. A blonde braid wrapped around it like a ribbon. "Then perhaps you enjoy *The Liberator*? My family subscribes. You can find top-notch abolitionist articles there."

Orie rubbed her arm and looked down. "I haven't heard of that one. I don't think they send it as far as Albemarle County." With Mary and Sara on each side of her, she couldn't hide her warming face. It must be red by now.

"Hm." Sara's disapproving murmur hollowed out Orie's stomach.

She popped her head up. "The Richmond newspaper runs opinion articles against slavery." There. She'd grabbed the girls' attention again. "But those are usually anonymous. I don't know the authors."

Clara stopped, and the other girls immediately halted. Clara turned and looked at Orie with striking blue eyes. "Orianna, it's perfectly well to be 'interested in abolition,' as you said, but you should know that as long as your food is cooked by slaves and your dresses are washed by slaves, you cannot *be* an abolitionist. It takes real courage to truly live as one against slavery."

Right there on the walkway, I gave them a word or two. How is one supposed to be anything if they are not first interested in discovering what it is? And what did Clara, Sara, or Mary know of anything other than their little lives in their little towns that were only a day's journey away from school? At least I had the courage to travel far away and experience new things.

But, oh, Lot, I may have lashed out more harshly than I should have. I haven't walked with them since. It was two weeks ago.

The teachers have radical beliefs, too, but they're not so rude about it. Many of the teachers are women! It felt like providence when one of them mentioned Mr. Douglass's book the next day. After class, I asked her if I could borrow it, and she said that I may, but only if I returned it with a written response and a list of questions about the reading that we will discuss together. She said in a warning sort of way, "It can change you if you let it." Thanks to my summer tutor, I'm thoroughly trained in writing intelligent responses to new ideas.

That's all I can write for now. The book is sitting on my small desk, inviting me to learn. I sincerely miss your company. Please write to me about life at home.

Your sister,
Orie

Lottie slapped Orie's letter down on her lap and fixed her gaze out the window. Loyalty to her sister rose in her heart, crowding out any bitterness from before about not receiving more letters. How could those girls at Troy dislike her big sister? If only those Northerners knew how Mother taught them to be kind and speak respectfully to the servants. If only Mother and Father had prepared Orie better for life up North and gave her more Northern-style books to read.

Lottie recognized the author's name in the letter at once—Frederick Douglass. He was the man who wrote one of the special books that Father kept in his study. Apparently, Orie never knew it existed until that embarrassing day walking to class. Lottie didn't know of *The Liberator*, but she was determined to read one if she ever had the opportunity. But how would that ever happen? Other than the *Richmond Enquirer* and Mother's women's magazines, the only periodical she'd noticed lying around Viewmont was the *Religious Herald*, a Baptist newspaper from Richmond. At least she knew what *The Liberator* was now.

Lottie folded the letter and tucked it into her pocket. She curled up in her chair and gazed out the window into the front yard, daydreaming about what it might be like to follow Orie to Troy Female Seminary one day. Would she have the same teachers? Or get to live in the same room that her sister had and use the same small desk? If Lottie did get to study in New York, she would be more prepared and wouldn't experience horrid scenes like the one in Orie's letter.

Lottie got up and started down the hallway to ask Mother and Father if Orie told the same story in their letters. She stopped, one foot skidding on the rug. She touched her pocket. What if Orie had only told Lottie that story in confidence? If Orie thought Lottie would blab to everyone in the house, she might not tell her about exciting things that she didn't want Mother and Father to know. No. She would maintain the confidence between her sister and herself.

She turned back to the library, looking for a blank page and a sharp pen, or even a quill. Lottie wrote, relaying stories about home, as Orie had asked. She also told Orie about her commitment to complete privacy in their correspondence.

Not long after Orie's letter came, a packet from the Barclays arrived. Mother handed Lottie a small stack of opened envelopes. Lottie took them and bolted outside near the garden to relish stories of the ocean and distant lands.

It was a chilly November morning. As a gust made its way over the mountains, Lottie closed her eyes and lifted her face up to welcome it as if it were an ocean breeze like the ones her seafaring family must have felt.

She opened one letter after another. The Barclays didn't write about many perilous adventures as they sailed across the Atlantic—not like Lottie read in novels. But they did describe a wild storm and their brief stop in Spain at the Port of Malaga.

Uncle James wrote that word spread quickly around the ship that he was a minister. So he started a Christian service on Sundays and offered counseling for the crew and passengers.

This wonderful ministry was completely unanticipated. It further confirms that God is with us and has prepared good works for us to do. More passengers and crew members typically attend our little church after a storm. The one we experienced recently doubled our group's numbers for two services. The wind thrashed and tore at our vessel so relentlessly that many aboard thought it would surely sink us. Left and right, I heard men promise to live righteously if only God would spare them. But the storm eventually calmed and faded from their memories, and they returned to their distracting vices. Many forgot the tearful promises they made to the Creator. Like in the Lord's parable, gospel seeds continue to fall on rocky soil. Still, we sow on.

Cousin Sarah's letter recounted their day in the Port of Malaga, where they spent the day wandering the busy, bright Spanish markets. She wrote about how the family sat outside at a cafe that smelled like vanilla, coffee, and a blend of mysterious spices. They sipped coffee with milk. She called it *café con leche*. And they listened to the symphony of languages spoken by foreigners from seemingly everywhere. Sarah commented at the end of her letter...

...but I suppose we are foreigners now, too, contributing to the symphony.

The final note on the bottom of the pile was written by Aunt Julia.

It feels surreal that we should write our Jerusalem residence as the return address on this package.

Lottie imagined Aunt Julia's beaming smile behind those words. She pored over the letters again and again.

Between receiving letters from faraway places, Lottie went about her daily life. It was different now. First, she'd missed Tom when he left. Now, Orie and the Barclays weren't around. However, Lottie wasn't always lonely. Jimmy and Cary Ann often came over to play. There was also much work for Lottie to do. She was almost ten years old, so Mother was giving her more challenging needleworking projects—gloves, not mittens.

On top of her own studies, she tutored Sallie and Mollie. Lottie listened to the girls as they practiced reading their primers aloud. She read lines of their own writing and corrected their grammar. She also taught them a few French vocabulary words from her language lessons, easy words such as *lampe, fleur, belle*, and *robe*, or *dress*. Lottie's heart swelled when Sallie and Mollie pranced around the house as though it were Versaille, pointing out every lamp and flower, and complimenting everyone's "belles robes."

Even though Sallie and Mollie weren't obedient students, tutoring them was the fun part of being stuck at home while Orie and the Barclays were out adventuring in the world. Needlework was another story. Mother forced Lottie to practice it much too often.

Another fun part was taking breaks outside on sunny afternoons. Lottie would take a novel or book of poetry along, and revel in the pleasure of filling her mind with beautiful words while nature surrounded her with beautiful things.

On one of those sunny days, Lottie sat on a blanket outside. She looked up while turning a page and sighed over Virginia's hills rolling on forever. A November breeze swirled down from the Blue Ridge Mountains, rustling the season's remaining leaves. Lottie closed her eyes, leaned back onto her elbows, and inhaled the unmistakable fresh scent of pine. Moments like these at home eased her eagerness for a faraway adventure. Her eyes popped open at faint voices yelling in the distance.

It must be difficult for Orie to try and explain everyday life at Viewmont to her schoolmates in New York. They probably didn't have plantations up there.

Another breeze tousled a tree, sending a shower of leaves Lottie's way. One floated onto her lap. She sat up and twirled it by the stem. She smiled. Each fallen leaf reminded her that winter was on its way. That meant Christmas was coming to Viewmont, and when it did, so would Orie.

CHAPTER NINE

1850-1851

Lottie leaned closer to the parlor window and squinted through the falling snowflakes. Each breath fogged the window as she watched and waited for Father to return from the train station with Orie. A lively fire crackled on the hearth, warming the whole room. If Lottie hadn't been so excited, she might have lulled off to sleep right there in her cozy chair.

"They could arrive any minute now," Mother said.

Lottie looked over her shoulder at Mother and smiled.

"Isn't that what you said half an hour ago?" Tom smirked as he moved a knight across the chess board. He sat with Jacob, his classmate from the University of Virginia.

Jacob leaned over the board, squinted, and scratched his curly red hair.

As soon as Orie and Father arrived, the whole family would be home for the holidays.

"The minute hasn't come yet." Mother narrowed her eyes over her needlework at Tom.

Tom's ears turned as red as Jacob's hair. He went back to playing chess. Mother returned to her latest project, freshening up some of Mollie's old infant dresses for the new baby, coming in the spring.

Lottie squirmed back around in her chair and continued her vigil. She inhaled the scent of evergreen. Boughs of it were everywhere—draped over the mantel and looped into wreaths that hung in the windows. The family had even decorated an evergreen tree this year. The whole house was full of Christmas cheer. There was so much to show Orie.

Finally, in the distance, a black spot that was a carriage came into view. Lottie's heart leapt, and she hopped up and hurried over to the bottom of the staircase in the hallway so that she would be the first to greet Orie and Father.

Perched on the bottom step, Lottie leaned back and out of the way as fourteen-year-old Ike dashed past her into the parlor. He had been doing that all month—dashing in and out of rooms. Anything to avoid getting caught by his mother or sisters under the mistletoe hanging in doorways.

Lottie giggled at her brother, then perked up at the sound of horses just outside. Her grin stretched ear to ear when her older sister walked through the front door after their longest time apart ever.

Her wool cloak damp, Orie embraced Lottie. "My little Lot!"

"I'm ten now, actually," Lottie said, smiling up at Orie. "Not so very little."

Father stepped inside and dusted snow off his jacket. "Strong weather out there. Just walking from the carriage to the doorway almost turned me into a snowman."

Fannie took Father's and Orie's wet wraps. She smiled sweetly at Orie. "Welcome home, Miss Moon."

Orie grinned from ear to ear at all the holiday decorations. "It's good to be home."

Fannie nodded and left them to join the rest of the family in the parlor.

After a hearty reunion, Lottie took Orie to the table where the evergreen tree stood. Its branches held small gifts and paper ornaments cut like snowflakes.

Orie handled some of the popcorn-and-cranberry garland that was wrapped around the tree. "What's this?"

"A couple weeks ago, Mother found a photo of Queen Victoria in one of her magazines. She and her family were decorating a tree, so Mother told George to cut down one of our trees too. We decorated it ourselves." Lottie basked in the glow of tiny candles fixed onto the tree limbs. She leaned closer and took a deep breath of citrus from the dried orange slices. She pointed at a paper snowflake. "I made this one. It's not as good as the one in the picture, but it's still a capital tree, you think?"

Orie smiled at Lottie. "It's beautiful."

"I hope we do it again next Christmas."

Lottie released a blissful sigh. Everything was perfect, just like the photo in Mother's magazine. It was snowing on Christmas Eve, and Tom and Orie were home.

One evening between Christmas and New Year's Day, Lottie buried her nose in her new book of Ralph Waldo Emerson's poetry—Orie's Christmas gift to her. Lottie needed more light. She reached over to the round table between her and Orie and raised the wick in the oil lamp. They sat in their library armchairs side by side just as they used to.

The younger girls played with their Christmas gifts on the rug. The boys stayed across the room by the fireplace.

Tom stoked the fire. "They say enrollment tripled over the past few years. We've even outpaced Harvard and Yale. So there are plenty of different groups you can join, Ike. Sporting groups, musical groups, and discussion groups about any topic—it's all there."

Ike sat on the edge of his chair and stroked his chin as if a beard were there. "I want to study the law. Joining a group of other like-minded fellows could help me pass the bar exam."

Jacob stood and stepped closer to the fire. "I'd believe it if they said enrollment had quadrupled. I heard that the board planned just this year to buy a load of bricks and construct new buildings with lecture halls. Then all o' us fellows might finally have space to breathe during class." He and Tom laughed.

Orie's voice rang across the room. "If it's higher enrollment they're after, the board might be surprised at the number of capable women who could boost their numbers."

The boys looked over at Orie. Tom answered her. "I don't think the University of Virginia is worrying over attracting students."

"The way it's looking," Jacob said, "the boys who might have otherwise gone north for school are instead coming to Virginia. Many of our classmates are from different states. Their families don't want them learning any of that anti-South abolition that the Northern schools are spewin'."

Orie set her book down. "Much of what I've learned from my experience in the North is that abolitionists aren't anti-South, *per se*. Rather, they're anti-bondage. Slavery is an affront to the very notion of freedom, which, of course, we Southerners hold so dear." She laid her hand over her heart. "We benefit in many ways from enslaving people, but as Mr. William Lloyd Garrison says, 'Enslave the liberty of but one human being and the liberties of the world are put in peril.'"

Tom and Jacob looked at each other knowingly, as if Orie had just "spewed" the reason why Southern families didn't want to send their sons away to universities in the North anymore.

"Is Mr. Garrison one of your teachers?" He sounded familiar, but Lottie couldn't recall what Orie had said about him.

"In a way," Orie said with a satisfied smile. She turned to Lottie but spoke loud enough for anyone across the room to hear. "He's a journalist who publishes a newspaper in favor of equal rights for women and slaves."

Lottie was just about to ask to hear more when Tom set the poker back in its stand and selected a cup of tea that Fannie had left on the big table for them earlier.

Jacob tapped the fireplace tool stand, then rubbed the back of his neck. "I don't mean to argue, Miss Moon, but I don't see how my freedom is at stake because my family owns our servants."

Mother walked in with a hand on her growing belly and ushered Sallie and Mollie to the door for bedtime.

"Well, you see …" Orie paused, and her eyes widened as if she realized she didn't have an answer for Jacob. "Even besides all that, the personal stories of escaped slaves would stir up the conscience of anyone with strong moral character. Frederick Douglass's stories, for example—"

Mother interrupted before leaving the room. "There must be other interesting things to talk about, right, Orie? Why not give the heated topics some time to cool off?"

Orie ducked her chin and returned her attention to her book, and the boys went back to discussing life at the university.

But later that evening, Lottie sat cross-legged on the edge of her bed, listening to Orie go on about how transformative it was to read *The Narrative of the Life of Frederick Douglass, an American Slave.*

"I've read it cover to cover about three times so far." Orie brushed her hair at the dressing table mirror.

"Well, it's not a very long book."

Orie spun toward Lottie and tilted her head. "How do you know what it looks like? I left it at Troy."

"Father brought a copy home years ago. He took it straight into his study." Lottie tapped a finger to her chin, summoning the memory. "It was brown with gold letters on the front. I haven't seen it since."

Orie gaped, then regrouped in a matter of seconds. She set her brush down and walked over to Lottie's bed. "True, the book is concise."

"Why didn't Mother want you talking about it downstairs?"

Mother had never told them to let topics cool off before. Ever since Grandmother passed away, Mother usually let Tom and Orie and all of them debate about the things they were reading and thinking. Mother and Father would even join in.

Orie rolled her eyes and patted the post on Lottie's bed. "She wants me to behave like a lady in front of wealthy, eligible bachelors like Jacob. She hasn't accepted the fact that I'm never getting married." She clasped her hands around the post and swung freely from side to side. She stopped inches from

Lottie's face. "You know how Mother and Father always taught us to listen to Fannie and behave kindly to the servants?"

Lottie didn't flinch. "Yes."

"Well, there are families who are awfully cruel to their servants," Orie said in a spooky voice.

Lottie nodded solemnly. "After church one day, Martha Harrison told me their servants get whippings all the time. That's why Mother stopped hiring ours out to Mr. Harrison."

"It gets even worse than that." Orie's eyebrows reached toward the ceiling.

She paced the length of the braided rug, retelling Frederick Douglass's story. Lottie's mouth fell open. She forgot to blink as her eyes followed Orie. This was miles away from Mother's bedtime stories.

Frederick Douglass's book had been under the same roof as Lottie for years. And Lottie only learned the story that night because Orie had gone to Troy, where she was free to learn anything she wanted. One semester away from home seemed to have filled Orie with a new boldness and freedom. Could Lottie ever become that bold? That free? She clearly wasn't going to at home, where books were hidden away from her. She must go away to school … and soon.

January came early to collect Orie and Tom and return them to school. On the last Saturday of the month, the boys planned to take a carriage back to Charlottesville later in the morning, but Orie had a longer journey ahead of her. She woke up before sunrise.

Orie pulled the covers up to her chin against the chilly winter morning. She fumed at the thought of riding to the train station with Father. She couldn't forget what Lottie had told her a few nights ago—that Father had Frederick Douglass's narrative locked in his study for years.

Why didn't he ever mention it to her? He knew she was going to school in the North, where lots of people had read that book and would assume that she at least knew what it was. She and Father could have discussed it together. Then she wouldn't have been so humiliated that day with her friends.

Orie wrestled her arms outside and on top of her covers. Her heart raced, and fresh warmth spread through her.

Father only let her read abolitionist editorials in his trusted *Richmond Enquirer*. And he probably only gave her the pamphlets that he read first and approved of.

Orie kicked her feet, fluffing the blanket. She tried to shake away the thought, but if she didn't ask him about the book, it would always sit between them. She wasn't someone who could hide her feelings. And Father would have no idea why she was cold to him. He wasn't the kind of father who got angry at questions, but she had never confronted him before about something like this. Maybe she would ask just one question and see how he reacted.

Orie sat up, stretching and yawning. Her yawn turned into a yelp when she noticed Lottie also sitting up in her bed on the other side of the room, staring at her.

Orie clutched her pounding chest. Worries about her carriage ride with Father scattered from her mind like a cluster of marbles struck by a shooter. "I didn't know you'd be up this early."

"I had to say goodbye," Lottie said quietly.

Orie's heart filled with warmth. Lottie had looked so happy to see her when she came home for Christmas. She looked just as sad now.

"It's not goodbye," Orie said. "I'll be back in a few months."

"Promise you'll write more?"

Orie rolled out of bed with her blanket and shuffled across the room. She squeezed Lottie in a hug. "I'll write more."

When it was time to go, George loaded up the carriage with Orie's bag. She and Father climbed in. Father reached for the heavy blanket on the bench and shared it with her. George signaled to the horse and drove them away from the house. Halfway down the carriage drive, Orie glanced back at Viewmont. The sun had risen enough to illuminate the home she was leaving behind. Her throat tightened, and a tear threatened to fall down her cheek. It would have been better to leave in the dark.

Father patted Orie's hand. She didn't smile back at him or rest her head on his shoulder as he might have expected her to do.

Orie peeked at Father from under the new hat she got for Christmas. As soon as he caught her eye and smiled, she shifted her gaze. Finally, she got up the nerve to ask. "Father, what did you think of Frederick Douglass's book?"

Father's head jerked back. A confused frown replaced his teasing smile. His mouth opened, then shut without answering her question.

Her pulse quickening, Orie dared to pose another question, despite her resolve to test his reaction before plunging ahead. "I know you have it. Why did you hide it from me?"

"I didn't hide it from you."

Orie's face went hot. She glared at her blanket-covered lap and fidgeted with the purse attached to her belt. Was he really denying it? "I've held almost every book in the library, and I've never seen it there."

"I didn't think it was appropriate for you children."

Tears welled in her eyes. "I'm not a child." Her voice cracked.

She glanced up at Father's sad face through her blurry eyes. "Did you read it? Do you believe it?"

Father roughly ran a hand through his hair. "Of course, I believe it. It's the man's personal account."

"Why aren't you an abolitionist, then?" Once Orie got going with questions, it was easier to let them flow, like a water pump after it had been cranked a few times.

"Orie, you know we don't treat the servants the way Frederick Douglass was treated."

She tossed her hands in her lap. "But so many slaves are treated the way he wrote about."

Orie didn't get specific since Father had already read the horrible stories about slave families who were broken apart in every way. Children were sold away from their parents. Husbands and wives were separated, too, or their marriage was not honored by their owner.

"I know. Those masters need to repent." Father gazed out his side of the carriage. "I imagine you hear all sorts of talk about abolition at school. You apparently read about it too. And that's good." He nodded with a furrowed brow, as if trying to convince himself. "It's wise to learn the different sides of things." He turned to her with a pained look. "I thought you understood the Southern perspective."

Orie shrugged. "I've heard it, but it doesn't make much sense."

"Well, you should also keep the Southern perspective in mind when Northerners tell you what they think."

Orie met his eyes. She steeled herself. "Explain it to me. I want to know."

Father took a deep breath. "Some people believe slavery is immoral, but they see it as a necessity. The way of life that you're accustomed to, which provides your clothes and schooling and food ... all of it would completely fall apart if abolitionists had their way."

Orie touched the silk ribbon tied around her new bonnet.

"Others see slavery as a moral institution—'a positive good,' as John Calhoun says. He's a senator. Used to be the vice president of the whole country too. He says Negros have it better here than in Africa or even up in the Northern economy. Those workers aren't guaranteed meals or clothing, and they could lose their jobs at any minute. He says many workers up North regularly go without basic essentials."

"What do you say?" Orie asked quietly.

Father faced forward and lifted his chin. "Our servants want for nothing. I think that says it all. We follow the Bible when Paul wrote to 'give unto your servants that which is just and equal.'" He turned to her, raising a finger in the air. "As a matter of fact, this Christmas, we gave them an extra gift on top of all the meat and candies and clothes we usually give."

Orie nodded but doubt crept up from her gut. Father was claiming the Bible was on his side, but so had the Christians she met up North. She squirmed in her seat. "Northern Baptists say that slavery goes against the whole point of the Bible and what Jesus taught in the Gospels."

"Jesus never spoke against slavery," Father's voice tensed.

Orie leaned closer to him. "What about the Golden Rule?"

"Exactly." He flattened his back against the bench. "That's how we treat the servants—with kindness, as we'd want to be treated. We don't harm them."

The carriage halted, jerking Orie and Father forward, nearly off the bench.

George shouted from the driver's seat. "Sorry, sir. Hit a big rut in the road."

"We're all right, George," Father yelled back.

Father didn't get out to help them break free. George always drove the carriage, except on Sundays. He knew how to maneuver the horse from the driver's seat to get a wheel out. The carriage rocked as he did so, then it went on as normal. Orie straightened her hat and smoothed her dress.

"God has always allowed slavery, Orie. Abraham had slaves. Job had slaves. As long as masters give them what they need and don't harm them, as the Bible instructs, then slaves will have a good life. Paul and Peter in the New Testament wrote that slaves are to obey their masters, even harsh ones."

That reminded Orie about something Sara shared with her. "One of my friends at school is a Baptist. Her family gets *The Liberator*, and she showed me one that was all about the new Fugitive Slave Law and how awful it is. She says it's not right to force Northern people to help capture runaway servants."

Father's face tightened. He spoke firmly. "You tell your friend that law is a decent compromise, and it may well have saved this country from civil war. Northerner or Southerner, we all live under the laws that protect everyone's rights to their property. Everyone must respect the rights of others, or we won't have a country together."

The air felt thick. Neither spoke. But Orie had one more question on her mind. It swelled in her heart and spilled out. "What about a group of Baptist preachers that gathered for a conference in Rhode Island? They wrote in *The Liberator* that there's a verse in Deuteronomy that says when a runaway slave escapes a cruel master and asks for help, you aren't supposed to hand them back to their master. The newspaper published the Baptists' resolutions about how it's more important to obey God's law rather than man's."

He clenched then released his hand in his lap. "Those preachers are mistaken."

Orie's eyes widened. Father didn't usually say that Baptist preachers were mistaken.

Father turned and locked eyes with her and laid a gentle hand over hers. "Even if you don't understand everything right now, know that Southerners can be just as moral as Northerners. And Southern Baptists love God and his word just as much as Northern Baptists do."

A train whistled as the carriage pulled up to the station. The carriage stopped, and they stepped down. With a hug and a kiss, Father settled Orie aboard the train, wished her a safe journey and a successful semester, and returned to the carriage with George.

Father waved as the train chugged along. Once it got moving, it felt incredibly fast, yet the world moved slowly beyond Orie's window. Much like her life —changing faster now than the Southern world in which she grew up. She didn't know what to think anymore.

What everyone at school said about the Bible and abolition sounded right. But in the carriage, Father sounded right too. And he seemed to have more verses to pluck out from the Bible than Northern Baptists did. Orie closed her eyes and shook her head. She didn't really care about the Bible arguments anyway. William Lloyd Garrison always appealed to common sense and left the Bible out of it. That was the way to go about it.

Still, a thought haunted Orie and twisted her stomach in knots. If Mr. Garrison had his way, would Orie really lose her nice clothes and schooling and food like Father had said? Wasn't there a way for the slaves to be free without their emancipation making her life fall apart?

Once Orie made it back to her dormitory at Troy, all anyone could talk about was the big news at school—a spiritualist medium walked among them. A student who claimed she could communicate with spirits. And here Orie had thought abolition would challenge her beyond her comfort.

CHAPTER TEN

1851

Orie sat in her nightgown at the foot of Sara's bed on top of a blue Dutch quilt. "No one knows who she is?" Orie curled her knees up to her chest and smiled. After Christmas break, the girls had started inviting her to walk to class and eat with them again.

"I know who she is," Mary sang as she tied a wrap around her red curls.

Clara sat atop her own bed and leaned forward, squinting her frosty blue eyes.

"You only think you know." Sara unraveled her blonde braid with her fingers. "She isn't going to reveal herself. It would be too risky. She might get kicked out of school!"

"Shush!" everyone said.

Sure enough, a knock came at the door, and the hall mistress didn't ask permission to enter. "Everyone should be in their own beds with the lights out in twenty minutes."

The girls groaned in unison. "Yes ma'am."

When the woman closed the door and left, Mary shot an accusing glare at Sara. "The mystery medium isn't shouting about it like you. I suspected her, so I told her all about how interesting and brave I thought it must be to be a medium and understand divination. Then she confided in me." Mary peeked at the door, then whispered, "It's Margaret Cunningham."

"Maggie Cunningham?" Sara questioned more quietly this time.

While the girls whisper-shouted at each other, Orie considered what little she'd heard and observed about Maggie Cunningham. She certainly seemed strange enough to be in contact with spirits. Her hairstyle and clothes were plain and dark, which was normal for a girl from a humble Quaker family like hers. But there was something steely about her. The way she carried herself around the school. The way she sat so calmly during chapel while all the other girls trembled in their pews, watching the preacher shout about eternal damnation.

Orie chimed in. "I would listen to her ideas about spirits and otherworldly things. It all sounds entertaining."

"You don't say?" Clara drew back a bit. "I imagined you would be the most skeptical of us all, Miss Southern Baptist."

"I think I've proven myself as a woman who thinks for herself, have I not?" Orie answered smugly.

The whole idea of talking with the dead seemed ridiculous and unscientific. But what harm could it do? It would show Orie's new friends once and for all that she was a modern, independent woman. And there was something interesting about Maggie. Her confidence wasn't as easy to dismiss as divination.

"Indeed you have," Clara answered, smiling. "Mary, why don't you ask Maggie if she would like to practice her divination skills and act as our medium?"

Mary nodded so fast that even her curls seemed excited. "I'll ask her to do it next week when there's a full moon. Everything mysterious and meaningful happens on a full moon."

The date was set for a séance with Maggie the following week. Only the four girls were to attend, and they all were supposed to vow that they would never reveal Maggie's identity as a medium before she publicly identified as one herself.

When the day finally came, the girls exchanged solemn nods with each other around the school, as if they had planned some sort of revolution. That night, the moon was full just as Mary said it would be. At midnight, hours after they were supposed to be in bed, Orie and her friends quietly slipped out of their rooms. Dressed in their nightgowns and with their hair tied in rags, they tiptoed down the hall to a small storage room where Maggie had arranged for them to meet. They found Maggie wearing her usual black.

"Won't your roommate suspect you if she saw you going out fully dressed at this time of night?" Sara asked while Maggie was getting the storage room key out of her dress pocket.

"She knows I sometimes venture out in the night, especially on full moons." Maggie smirked. "Good choice on the date. I've learned that the spirits are more responsive on full moons."

Mary stood a little straighter and looked around, bouncing her eyebrows as if to say, *I told you so.*

Maggie unlocked the door. The girls bustled into the room from the exposed hallway, but Orie lingered as Maggie held the door open.

"Other girls who perform séances are like celebrities." Orie cocked her head. "The newspapers love them. If your gift is real, why are you afraid for people to find out about it?"

"I don't care to be a celebrity." Maggie looked away as if even the mention of celebrity wasn't worth her attention. Her eyes cut back to Orie. "Even if I did, you must not have read about smaller cities that condemn those girls and chase them out of town. I only recently discovered this gift. I want to be able to understand it and control it before the public finds out—before reporters start firing questions at me."

"You can't control it?" Orie panicked. What was she getting into?

"I can enough for now." Maggie shrugged and walked in.

This was a mistake. Orie's glance swept down the dark, empty hallway. She could hurry back to her room and forget about impressing her friends. Instead, she followed Maggie into the chilly storage room with her chin held high, her wide eyes probably giving her away. The scene in front of her looked just like the pictures in the newspapers, except for all the brooms and wash rags. The only sources of light and heat were several flickering candles on the shelves along the back wall. They cast strange-looking shadows as the girls shuffled silently around the room to choose a seat. It was barely large enough for the round table and five chairs. They sat down and reached for each other's hands, possibly for comfort or maybe because that's what people did in the newspaper pictures.

Maggie was the last to take a seat. She laid her hands on the table, palms up as if ready to receive a gift. It was all mesmerizing.

What would Mother say if she could see her eldest daughter now? No, Orie wouldn't tell Mother about this. But Lottie always had an ear for interesting stories. Maybe Orie would write to her about tonight if Orie survived unscathed.

"Let's get started." Shadows flickered on Maggie's face. "I need a volunteer —someone with a recent encounter with death."

"Like a ghost?" Sara asked, worry in her voice. "I thought you were going to provide those."

"I mean someone close to a person who recently died," Maggie explained patiently.

The girls exchanged darting glances. No one volunteered information.

"My grandmother died three years ago," Orie finally offered. "She lived in our house."

"Perfect." A mischievous smile curled on Maggie's face. "That's who we'll seek out tonight."

"I—I'm sorry, but I don't want to talk with my dead grandmother right now." Orie's pulse raced.

Maggie folded her hands in her lap and looked around the table. "Well, I'm curious then. Why did you all summon me here?"

"We wanted to see." Mary leaned forward with her eyes wide.

"See what? See if I'm lying?" A hint of defensiveness edged Maggie's voice. She narrowed her eyes.

"No." Clara dropped the hands she was holding and clasped them in her lap. "We wanted to see something real—something new."

"Oh, Orie, can't we please call on your grandmother, just to see if she's here?" Mary turned to Orie and looked up at her with pleading eyes.

This storage room séance was the last place on earth, or in heaven, that Grandmother Harris would be found. But Orie had agreed to participate in this.

"Don't you want to learn about other worlds, as a woman who thinks for herself?" Clara challenged.

"All right, fine. Try to seek her if you want to." Orie relented yet crossed her arms in protest.

"What's her name?" Maggie asked, smiling again.

"Sarah Harris."

The girls held each other's hands again, and Maggie closed her eyes and tilted her face upward. She called out dramatically, "Is anyone there?"

Several seconds passed. Orie peeked around while her hands became increasingly sweaty, despite the draftiness of the room. The other girls' eyes were all closed.

Maggie asked again in a stronger voice, "Are you there, Sarah Harris? Please make yourself known to us."

At a faint tapping sound, Orie's eyes popped open wide, and she clutched Mary and Clara's hands. The other girls gasped. She and Sara exchanged glances across the table. Could this really be happening?

Maggie explained, "They usually prefer to communicate by tapping." She addressed Grandmother's supposed spirit. "With one tap meaning 'yes' and two meaning 'no,' please answer us. Are you happy to be among us?"

There was another long pause before two loud, quick taps.

Well, that seemed right. Grandmother Harris would be absolutely irate about being among this group right now. She might even grab a broom to sweep them out and off to bed.

"We apologize for disturbing your rest." Maggie shifted her gaze toward the candles. "Is there an instruction you wish to give us?"

One tap.

"I imagine she has quite a few instructions for us," Orie muttered under her breath.

"What is it? What do you want to say?" Maggie asked breathlessly.

Mary and Clara fidgeted in their chairs. Sara wiped her palms on her dressing gown. Then the table began to jerk fiercely. Everyone screamed. Orie dropped the hands of the two girls at her side and looked to Maggie. Maggie sneered. Her eyes were full of excitement.

"Do you want us to stay?" Maggie shouted above all the noise.

The table went still, and the girls' screaming reduced to whimpering. Then they heard two strong taps. Their jaws dropped as a few of the candles along the back wall went out, one at a time. That was enough. The girls jumped up and extinguished the rest of the candles themselves and hurried out.

Sara left first, vowing never to return to that haunted room. Mary and Clara whispered to Maggie how thrilling the séance was and how gifted she must be. Orie was the last to leave. As she turned to close the door, she frowned. Was that a light shining and moving through small spaces along the back wall? Weren't those the spots where the candles seemed to go out on their own? But it was too late in the night to investigate any of that.

The following day, Orie struggled to wake up in time for class. Why did they have to choose a school night for a midnight séance? Clara said next time they should do it on a weekend, even if the moon wasn't quite full. Mary nodded while yawning, but Sara and Orie changed the conversation. Orie didn't plan on having anything to do with another séance. But she was glad she'd attended one. It was quite a story, one that she could never tell her parents. Mother would faint on the spot. Especially if she found out that Orie was the one who provided her own grandmother's spirit as the focus of the séance.

That weekend, Orie pulled out some writing paper to relive and relay the thrilling tale to her best confidante at home, Lottie. She wrote all about the room and the tapping and the mysterious candles. It all might have been real. Maggie was a rather convincing medium. But Orie wasn't sure. She wrote that it didn't make a difference to her either way because the experience was decidedly unpleasant. At the end, she included a serious postscript advising Lottie to immediately destroy the letter after reading it and never breathe a word about it to Mother or Father—or Sallie, who could never keep a secret.

Lottie sat in bed as the wind roared outside in the night and a candle flickered beside her. With one hand, she clutched the gray wool shawl around her shoulders. With the other, she held Orie's letter as close to the light as she could without burning it. She read it again and again.

It was by far the best letter Orie had sent her. How could she destroy it? She tucked it inside the book on her nightstand and blew out the light.

CHAPTER ELEVEN

1851

On a cool, mid-March morning, Anna called for Lottie to come upstairs and help with the new baby girl, Robinett. *Thwack*! Downstairs, something fell ... or was tossed. Immediately, footsteps rushed upstairs. Anna laughed to herself. Lottie never missed an opportunity to play with a baby.

Anna left Lottie bouncing little Robinett in the nursery. She headed to the kitchen to tell the cooks about a change they needed to make for the family's supper that night. On the way, she paused at a mess in the parlor doorway. A book and papers were sprawled across the floor. Lottie must have been reading before she dropped everything and darted up the stairs. Fannie was nowhere in sight. Anna didn't want the other children slipping, so she picked up the book and gathered the papers. Orie's handwriting on a letter drew the corners of Anna's mouth up. Her brief smile faded as odd words leapt off the page—séance, spirits, Grandmother Harris's spirit! Horror flooded her mind. Through tunnel vision, Anna could read enough of the letter to understand. She clutched the doorframe to steady herself.

Anna pulled herself up and threw her shoulders back. She marched straight into Edward's study to show him written proof that their daughter was involved in occultist sin. She thrust the letter in front of his bewildered face and waited for him to suggest the obvious—it was time for Orie to come home.

Edward sat back in his chair and slowly read the letter. His lack of immediate outrage was disappointing, but at least he frowned while reading it.

"Did Lottie have questions about this?" Edward peered over the letter with his eyebrows arched. "Is that why she showed it to you?"

"She did not show it to me. She kept it hidden for weeks. See the date? Weeks!" Anna raged, pacing the length of his desk. "I found it on the floor just now. What are we going to do about this, Edward? The girl is partaking in séances."

"It looks as though she attended one séance," Edward said while still examining the letter. "And see here." He pointed to a line in the letter. "She didn't enjoy it. I don't see a reason to worry about her, Anna."

Anna froze and stared at her husband. "What *would* be a reason to worry? What if next month, we discover a poster of our daughter levitating a table, advertising her next séance on stage? Would that be a sufficient reason to worry? Scripture forbids this behavior, Edward. I want her to come home."

"But what would that really accomplish?" Edward held his hands open. "You know Orie. She's not drawn to the religion of this spiritualism. She's drawn to the culture around it—the power and influence it offers to women. That's all. And she wrote that she wasn't interested in participating again. From the sound of it, she suspects it was a hoax, and I agree. Friends of this Maggie person were probably in the neighboring room and blew out the candles through those holes in the wall."

Anna softened enough to consider that for a moment. "Holes in the wall?"

"That's what Orie thinks." Edward shrugged.

Anna's shoulders relaxed a fraction. Maybe her daughter wasn't at risk of becoming a medium as much as she'd thought.

Edward stroked his clean-shaven chin and narrowed his eyes. "I'm more concerned with the way Lottie seems to be treasuring this letter. Lottie is more rebellious when it comes to faith. And you know how she follows Orianna's lead. Lottie is who we should keep an eye on."

They decided to allow Orie to finish her semester at Troy. But she had not followed the spirit of their agreement to faithfully attend chapel, so she would not be sent for a third semester.

Edward pulled fresh paper and a pen out of his drawer.

Faithful chapel attendance, he wrote in their joint letter, *does not allow for occasional attendance to spiritualist séances.*

Edward also wrote that Orie should more thoughtfully consider the influence an older sister has on her younger sister.

"I have something to write," Anna said, reaching for the pen.

We can't force you to trust and obey God. But as a consequence of your séance experimentation, we will now dedicate extra time each week praying for you.

Edward's brow furrowed. "How much extra time?"

Anna dipped the pen into the inkwell and finished the letter.

You're nearly grown now, and either you'll come to your senses and follow the Lord or not. But if not, it won't be for our lack of praying.

When Orie received a thick envelope from Viewmont in the mail, she didn't open it right away. She saved it for a quiet moment so that she could savor a cozy time reading about home.

Later that day, she sat down to read her letter on an ornate iron bench under a hundred-year-old tree with sunshine beaming through its branches that were still bare from winter. Orie gently unfolded the paper and started reading. Her heart and jaw dropped. Somehow, her parents knew what she had done. Orie's stomach twisted in knots, and she chewed her thumb as she read Father and Mother's letter.

Lottie usually enjoyed staying up at night to reread Orie's exciting letter by candlelight. But tonight she sat in quiet contrition, looking at the same letter in her father's hands.

Father and Mother sat on the edge of Lottie's bed, talking for half an hour about the pure and supreme power of God and his *Holy* Spirit. They spoke very slowly and kept asking, "Do you understand?"

Lottie didn't have any questions—not for them. She had a few for Orie, though. She wanted to know more about spiritualism and Maggie Cunningham. And did Orie think all that wild tapping was really Grandmother's spirit?

Mother and Father wouldn't leave Lottie's room until she promised that if she ever had an opportunity, she would not attend a séance or anything of the sort. She agreed.

Once Mother and Father said goodnight and left the room, Lottie dove under her blankets and cried into her pillow. They didn't mention anything about Lottie going to school, but the way Orie handled new opportunities usually determined how much of an opportunity Lottie would get. Lottie still couldn't wander into the woods past the big, mossy rock after Orie went in too far one day and got lost. Though it had only been for half a day.

Orie got to go far away and experience so much freedom at Troy. Now Lottie would never get to go to Troy or maybe to any school in the North.

Maybe Mother and Father would find a good Southern school for her. Like all those Southern boys who weren't going up North anymore for school. But where? Maybe her parents would give up sending her away to school altogether.

Lottie tried to breathe deeply and not panic. She tried not to blame Orie. Lottie was the one who carelessly treated the letter like a bookmark and let Mother find it. But Orie was the one who went to the séance and put the evidence in writing. She must have known that Lottie wouldn't destroy such a letter, at least not right away. Lottie flopped her head to the other side of the pillow. She punched the tear-drenched part.

She used to think Orie was blazing a trail for her at Troy. Now it felt as though Orie had chopped down a tree to block the trail behind her and set the forest on fire for good measure.

Chapter Twelve

October 1852

As Anna walked into the library, Orie and Lottie greeted her from the velvet chairs without moving their eyes away from their open books. The covers looked like ones that Orie brought back from school. Good. Edward had spent a fortune on those. Orie had been reading them, as well as some of Tom's old books, while she was furthering her studies at home until she applied for medical school. Anna smiled to herself as she searched a small desk in the corner for paper. It was good that Orie was sharing them with Lottie, especially since Lottie wouldn't need copies of her own for Troy. Stress stung Anna's heart. Since the best girls' school in the country wasn't an option for Lottie anymore, where would they send her?

Before Orie's séance debacle, Anna didn't wonder much about where Lottie would attend school. She trusted that whatever worked for Orie would work for Lottie too. But now, Troy was completely out of the question for any of her daughters. As far as she was concerned, the bridge from Viewmont to Troy Female Seminary was burned.

A decision needed to be made, soon. Lottie was turning twelve in December, only two months away. Where Lottie had once been content, she now seemed restless. She had consumed many of the books in the library, and now she was working on the new stack that Orie had brought back from her year at Troy. Eventually, Lottie would outgrow Viewmont's library. She would need more space to grow intellectually, socially, and—if Anna and Edward chose the right school—spiritually as well.

"What about that school near Roanoke, the one Charles Cocke runs?" Edward mentioned one evening after the children went to bed.

Anna sat on the chair next to Edward on the sofa. She stopped stitching and glanced at him over her embroidery. "Valley Union Seminary?"

"The very same." Edward smiled at her, holding an issue of the *Religious Herald*.

Anna shook her head. "I don't think that's very prudent, Edward. I wouldn't sleep a night that she's away. I may have stretched myself and seemed more progressive in sending Orianna up North, but at least Troy is an all girls' school. Valley Union is coeducational. I'll not have our daughter alone at school with boys. It's just not prudent." Anna resumed stitching with vigor.

"It *was* coeducational," Edward said, piquing Anna's attention again. "I heard a while back that Cocke was planning to turn it into an all girls' school. It looks as though the rumors were true. He's finally done it." He smacked the newspaper.

Anna stared at the paper in wonder as she left her work in her chair and moved over to the sofa. "Valley Union Seminary is an all girls' school?"

"Exclusively for girls, starting this school year. With a man like Charles Cocke at the head, I think it will be a serious-minded school where we can send our Lottie."

"I did like him that time we met." Anna still struggled to believe this new information. Valley Union wasn't much farther than the boys' university. And Charles Cocke was an upstanding Virginia Baptist. It felt like a miracle.

Edward handed her the newspaper. "It's right here in the *Herald*. Read for yourself. You know Cocke has been pushing for serious, quality education for women. Now he's got Virginia Baptists behind him. I think he even—"

A coughing fit burst out and interrupted him.

Anna's chest tightened with worry. "It's sounding worse, Edward."

"It's only a cough. It's just that time of year." He yanked a handkerchief out of his waistcoat pocket to catch another cough. As he pulled the material away, he quickly tucked it back into his pocket as if Anna didn't also notice the new red blotch.

While Father and Mother talked, Lottie sat quietly on the third step from the bottom of the staircase, just out of sight from anyone in the parlor. She had left her room to find some water, but when she heard that they were discussing her schooling, she slowed and quieted her pace down the stairs, careful to step over that one creaky spot. While they talked, she sat with her eyes closed, listening as hard as she could. Her heart pounded when they talked about the new school near Roanoke. Her eyes popped open at a fit of sudden, violent coughing. Was that awful sound coming from Father?

After the coughing stopped, she was about to stand up and ask them for a drink when Mother mentioned the finishing school in Richmond. Lottie froze, her mouth falling open. How could they consider sending her to a finishing school when a real school had opened so close to home?

Lottie held her breath and risked scooting closer to the conversation.

"I'm not entirely convinced that we should disregard sending her to Richmond." Anna left the *Herald* on the sofa, walked back over to the chair and picked up her embroidery hoop. She stood, fidgeting with it. "They would train her properly. They would teach her Christian manners, and she would get opportunities to practice her French."

"That might be all they teach her," Edward replied a little too quickly.

"What do you mean by that?" Anna clutched her hoop and propped her fists onto her hips. Her heart pounded.

"That place is only masquerading as a school." Edward leaned toward the side table and grabbed his cup of tea. "They'll waste our daughter's potential and fill her head with useless frivolities." He took a sip.

"Useless frivolities?" Anna shrilled. "You do remember that I attended school there, Edward."

"Yes, of course, I didn't mean ... I apologize." Edward looked down to his teacup with a furrowed brow then tilted his head up, squarely at her. "But you want more for her. I know you do. An education like that will either crush her spirit or push her into rebellion. It's not a good fit for Lottie. Besides, she could develop her French at Valley Union. Probably Latin too."

Tears welled in Anna's downcast eyes. "I don't want to crush her spirit. I just want her to be safe. And to honor God and thrive in society."

Edward closed the space between them with a hug. She relaxed into his embrace. His head jolted up and toward the doorway as though he suddenly heard something.

Relaxing, Edward returned to their hug. "Valley Union will train Lottie just as well as the finishing school. Cocke is a strong Baptist. I've heard that the curriculum matches what the boys study in Charlottesville. That kind of focus on academics is what Lottie needs. She will be too busy studying to get into trouble."

Anna smiled through her doubt.

"Well, at least not too much trouble," Edward added. "Lots of decent, local families will send their daughters too. Other Baptist girls will positively influence her—I know it."

Anna was silent for a long moment. "I do want more for her. If you think Valley Union is our best option, I'll pray on it."

"You have plenty of time." Edward patted her back and stepped away. "She won't be leaving home for at least another year. Maybe we're getting ahead of ourselves."

Ever since Lottie overheard Father and Mother discussing the new Valley Union Seminary, she felt light and hopeful. Mother hadn't exactly agreed to the new school, but she had sounded mostly convinced by Father.

By mid-November, school was the last thing on Lottie's mind. Father was coughing most of the time that he wasn't sleeping. For a solid week, the doctor came to visit every other day. Then he came less often. Everything felt unsteady and uncertain. Even Lottie's arms and legs wobbled like jelly half the time. Mother had been bringing Father hot meals in their bedroom and walking with him around the garden in the warmer afternoons. It hadn't snowed yet, and the afternoons still bore the golden light of autumn.

One such bright day, Lottie joined Mother upstairs to take Father on a walk. He said he didn't have the strength.

"The doctor said fresh air is good for your lungs," Mother argued.

"I need you to send for someone." He struggled to raise himself against his pillows.

"Dr. Williams?"

Lottie's head swirled when Father asked Mother to send not for the family's doctor, but for the lawyer.

"There are a few things," he struggled to say between heavy breaths, "that I want to settle if the worst should happen."

Tears pooled in Mother's eyes. She grabbed Lottie's hand, and they left the room. Mother did as Father asked. The next day, the lawyer came and went.

That night, Father called all of the children to come upstairs. Ike and Tom, who was enrolled in Pennsylvania's medical school now, were both home early from university. The boys and Orie seemed somber, yet steady. Lottie took direction from her older siblings and responded like them, even though she'd much rather cry as her younger sisters did.

They gathered around Father, and Mother led them in prayer. Even Tom and Orie bowed their heads and clasped their hands. No one rolled their eyes or snickered. Lottie quietly closed her eyes and listened to Mother ask God, in all his goodness and power, to heal Father. Lottie didn't mind Mother's prayer as she usually did. It actually soothed her heart, like stirring honey into a cup of strong tea, sweetening its bitterness. Maybe God would hear Mother and do as she asked.

Father explained that the children had nothing to be afraid of. Mother was entirely capable of running Viewmont successfully, and each of them would have an inheritance to pay for their education and necessities. As he went on, even Orie and Lottie joined their younger sisters with tears and soft, desperate whimpers. Tom slowly shook his head, while Ike stared at the foot of Father's bed.

Father was sweating, yet he pulled his wool blanket higher up over his chest. "I am ready to die. The only uneasiness I feel is for the hearts of my two grown children." He looked at Tom and Orie. "I feel torment when I think of you both so hostile to the gospel of Jesus," he said, not as if berating them for their lack of faith, but lamenting it.

"Please, Father, don't worry about that right now." Tom kneeled down beside the bed. "You need rest. You can survive this. You must stay alive to see me marry. To see Orie become a female doctor."

Mother told the younger girls to bid Father goodnight. They pouted because they were only allowed limited time with Father. No one knew much about his illness or if it was contagious. The doctor didn't offer a clear answer. He said it might be somewhat contagious, but it might also be simply hereditary. Mother ushered them away for a bedtime story, but Lottie and her older siblings stayed a while.

Ike and Orie left Father to rest. Lottie was about to follow her sister out, but then turned to hug Father again. She whispered, "I want to go to Valley Union and focus on academics, as you said. I'll make you proud."

Father smiled. "I thought I heard someone on the stairs that night." He kissed Lottie's head—like warm, soothing honey again. She sat on the bed, and he took her hand with what he must mean as a firm grip. His gaze burrowed into her eyes. "You make me proud right now, Lottie. Just as you are."

Mother came back into the room with a stack of folded cloths. Behind her, Peggy carried a large bowl of water. She set it down on Father's dresser, glanced at him with a worried brow, then quietly left.

Tom sat on a chair beside the bed, rummaging through his black medical bag. He read the labels on small brown apothecary bottles, returning most of them to his bag. Once he found the one he was looking for, he poured its thick brown contents into a large spoon and gave it to Father. Other than Mother, Tom spent the most time nursing Father, which made sense because he was nearly a doctor now. Tom dipped one of the fresh cloths into the water bowl and cooled Father's forehead as he drifted to sleep.

Lottie stood up. Mother sat in a chair at the food of the bed, knitting faster than Lottie had ever seen her knit before. Lottie and Tom exchanged slightly concerned looks.

"He will make it through this fever, and when he does, he will need a warm scarf for the winter," Mother said in answer to their questioning glances.

Lottie left the room and collapsed onto her dressing table chair, exhausted. Peggy brought her nightdress and helped her tie up her hair for bed. She looked more worried than Lottie felt.

"Masta' Moon's gonna make it through, isn't he, Miss Lottie?"

"I think so. Tom and Mother and Dr. Williams are all taking care of him."

Peggy nodded. "We in the cabins all pray for him."

Lottie nodded. Of course they would pray for him. If Father died, none of the slaves would have an inheritance to help them. When one of the neighbors had died, his widow sold most of their slaves and moved away. But that wouldn't happen at Viewmont. Father said they had nothing to worry about. Maybe God would help them since everyone was praying for him.

The following morning, the whole household celebrated because Father's fever had broken. By Christmas, he was walking around the house and laughing again as though he'd experienced a miracle. He looked much healthier, too— not so thin and pale, thanks to Fannie's Christmas cookies and pies.

At the breakfast table on Christmas morning, Father announced over cinnamon rolls that he felt eager to jump back into work. "It's time to finally build that new carriage drive. It will connect the house to the main road." Mother's eyebrows raised. Before she could say anything, Father went on. "I've accepted an invitation to meet with the business partners in Tennessee and Louisiana right after the New Year."

"That's enough business talk, Edward." As Mother smiled and tilted her head, a couple ringlets framing her face fell across her cheek. "Let's enjoy Christmas."

Lottie dug into her warm cinnamon roll. A simple, happy Christmas was just the ticket after an eventful year with Orie leaving school and Father getting sick. Now that her family was back to normal, Lottie could welcome whatever exciting things 1853 would hold without worry.

Chapter Thirteen

January 1853

Anna sat on the edge of her and Edward's bed next to an open trunk. Fannie had already packed it for his business trip, but he moved around the room, adding items anyway. He set a green paisley cravat inside. Anna picked it up and narrowed her eyes at it as she caressed the fine silk. "A bit flashy for a business trip, isn't it?"

Edward looked over his shoulder at the cravat. "It conveys prosperity. They mustn't think I'm at death's door and planning to fade away from expanding the family's business."

She tossed it back into the trunk and fidgeted with her fingernails in her lap. Her worried gaze followed him around the room. She wasn't subtle about how much she disagreed with him about traveling. His regular trip to New Orleans was one thing. On this trip, Edward planned to meet with men in Memphis too.

"Are you sure your brother can't go to Memphis?"

"You know Isaac is too ill to travel right now."

Anna raised her brow and lowered her chin. "The same could be said of you." Frustration boiled in her chest. Why was he ignoring the fact that he was barely healthy enough for this trip? He was making her state the obvious and behave as a nagging, negative wife. "All of this travel will only stress your constitution, which is still frail, by the way, no matter how jovial you act."

"I'll mostly be sitting down in comfortable rooms and listening to reports about our crop sales in the area. Nothing too strenuous, darling." He winked at her. "Really, I should apologize for taking such a leisurely trip, leaving you at home as the carriage drive project begins."

Anna stood in a huff, walked to the top of the bed, and looked around. She grabbed a pillow and fluffed it. She knew she couldn't convince him to stay home. She accepted his change of subject. "I still think we'll be cutting down too many trees to make room for it. Why must the carriage drive be so wide?"

"We must create space for the future, my dear."

Anna sighed as she threw the pillow back to the bed. To Edward, the future was a bright opportunity waiting to be seized. The Virginia Central Railroad expansion had just finished. Now, cargo and passenger trains ran from Richmond, straight through Charlottesville, into the western counties, and back again. Virginians were more connected now than ever before. Edward seemed convinced this railroad would mean big things for Viewmont. He had said those new tracks could guide trains loaded with their crops to more towns across the state.

"Business is sure to grow, and so must access to and from the plantation. With a wider carriage drive, one wagon can come in while another is going."

"I don't know why this trip can't wait until the spring." Anna crossed her arms. "It's absolutely freezing out there. Tom says your heart might be weakened now, and I'm not sure—"

"Not to worry. That's why I'm bringing this magnificent scarf." Edward held up a heap of wool the size of a large cat. "The only way I'll die on this trip is if I fall asleep wearing this and it suffocates me."

Anna reluctantly smiled at the reminder of her frantic knitting project while he'd battled his fever nearly two months ago. "It's possible Tom's advice is overly cautious. Still, I think January is much too soon and much too cold for you to travel."

Edward closed and locked his trunk. He gripped the edge of the luggage, staring down at it. "Anna, I know that I almost died. I was completely prepared to face it." He turned and looked up at her with big, brown eyes full of hope. "I've been granted another chance at life. I'm eager to make the most of it and get back to work."

Anna softened and released her arms to her side. "I understand."

Silence passed between them as they agreed to disagree.

Anna crossed over to Edward as he rose. "I want to do whatever I can to support you." She walked into his open arms.

"You've done so much while I was ill, managing the servants and making sure the harvest was stored properly." He made Anna smile and blush a little. "Not to mention, making this wonderful scarf." He patted the bundle again.

She laughed. "Enjoy it, because that's the last scarf you'll receive from my knitting needles, after all this teasing."

Edward released her from their hug and breathed deeply. "Should I wait to start on the new carriage drive? I don't want to put too much on you while I'm away."

"I've thought about it. I recently hired out some of the servants to neighboring farms. Just for small jobs. But I believe there are enough men left to handle the trees that we need removed."

"Sounds like a good start." Edward smiled. He patted the closed trunk. "This one is officially packed. The smaller trunk of coins and bank notes is ready downstairs." Edward headed for the door. He turned to Anna and pointed to a corner table. "Kindly grab those tickets? On top of the pile."

Anna did so. Right under them was his updated will. She picked it up. "I'll lock this in your desk downstairs. We don't need it now."

They smiled at each other.

One week after Edward had left, a man came to Viewmont bearing terrible news. Edward's riverboat, the *James Robb*, had caught fire not long after it left the harbor. The man said survivors had witnessed Edward clutching a small trunk as he jumped overboard to swim for shore with all the other passengers. On the bank of the river, Edward was counted among the dead. The small trunk, which Anna remembered had been packed full of money, was lost.

Anna and the girls cried nearly all day. They had prepared for Edward's death, but not now—not after he stopped coughing and got better. As soon as Anna could muster the strength to hold a pen, she wrote two short letters.

Anna sealed them and headed to find George. Hopefully, she could locate him without needing to search the fields or the cabins. She grabbed the handle on the back door. It was already cracked open. At the sound of George's voice outside, she nearly rushed to meet him. He stood with his back to the house, holding Fannie. She was crying.

George gently rubbed Fannie's back. "We just oughta prepare ourselves, is all I'm sayin'. Mistr'ss Moon might not want to carry on the business as big as Masta' ran it. In that case, she might not need all us workers anymo'."

Anna's heart stung. She hated that the loss of her husband was the topic of the day across Viewmont. But it wasn't only her personal tragedy. Of course, the servants would be affected. Of course, they would be discussing it.

Fannie buried her face into her husband's chest, sobbing. "What if we get sold somewhere worse? What if we get sent to different plantations?"

The only answer George offered her was to pray. He and Fannie held each other close and pleaded with God right there by the kitchen. They prayed for protection and for strength. Because whatever was going to happen to them, they had to face it bravely. What else could they do?

Anna was a widow with her own grief, but she felt the weight of their prayer. The fate of their homes and families was up to her.

George's gaze followed Fannie as she walked back to the kitchen, smoothing tears off her face.

Anna stepped outside. "George? Can I get your help with something?"

George whipped around, eyes wide. Scared. "Anything you need, ma'am."

Anna held out the letters. "Would you see to it that these are sent to Thomas and Isaac as soon as possible? They'll need to know."

George took the bundle. "Yes, ma'am, I'll get these out right away."

"Thank you, George. Times like these remind me how integral to Viewmont you are. Fannie and Peggy too." They should know she couldn't imagine Viewmont without them.

The loss of her husband was enough to mourn for the rest of her life. The loss of all that he did for her, their family, and for Viewmont—that was its own grief to face and came with its own decisions to make, but not tonight.

At her reassurance, George smiled, relief washing the worry out of his eyes. He nodded, tucked the letters into the pockets of his thin, brown coat, and hurried toward the stables.

The family didn't eat much at supper. After Anna finally got the girls to sleep, she collapsed on top of her bed, lying awake for hours. She closed her eyes only for moments at a time, ready for a perpetual night. She rolled over toward the window and saw darkness.

"Good," she whispered, "I never want to see the sun again."

It didn't seem right for a sunrise to usher in another day when Anna's world had just ended. But, of course, the sun rose right on time, as it had always done ever since God filled it with light.

Anna, the slaves, and the children all got up that morning. They did the things that usually needed to be done on such days. Anna and the girls pulled on their darkest dresses. Fannie and Peggy started preparing extra food for the guests who would come to mourn with the family.

The day they buried Father, Lottie sat in the parlor with her siblings, all wearing dark clothes just as they would tomorrow and for a long time after that. Orie sat away from everyone else in the corner—not alone, but also not a part of the group. She was eighteen now, practically grown up, but the look on her face was of a girl who was completely lost. Sallie and Mollie were nine and five years old. All day, the two ran around the house one minute, then clung to Mother or Orie the next, as if afraid they, too, might suddenly disappear as Father had.

Lottie, newly twelve, still couldn't believe the news. But everyone was crying and wearing black, and people were visiting as they had when Grandmother died, so it must be true.

Father died. Father is dead.

It sounded strange in her head and too blasphemous to say out loud. Her strongest advocate, her consistent guide—her father would never come home. He was the one who steered Mother away from sending Lottie to finishing school. He was the one who made a way for Orie to learn medicine when Grandmother bullied her away from the library. Who would fight for them now?

Robinett was barely two years old and didn't seem to understand what she'd lost. Still, it broke Lottie's heart when Robinett asked for "Da-Da." Later that spring, Mother renamed the baby Edmonia, after Father. Calling her by a different name after all this time would be strange. Not like a nickname. But no one argued.

One day after the renaming, Lottie sat atop her bed and cocked her head to the side to get a better look at her baby sister toddling across the braided rug. The baby made her way to some wooden blocks that all the other Moon children had once played with.

"Edmonia," Lottie said slowly, as though she was learning a new word in a different language, listening to the sounds it made. "It suits you. You even look a little like him—for a baby."

Lottie joined Edmonia on the rug and scooped her into a hug. A powerful concern suddenly filled her. Edmonia had Father's nose, so at least she could see part of him whenever she looked in a mirror. But who would tell her about the things Father said and did? How would she learn the names of the flowers and the trees on the way to church? How would she know that Father loved her and worked hard so that she could have a full life? Surely, Mother would tell her. But just in case, Lottie whispered to little Edmonia a promise to tell her all about him.

CHAPTER FOURTEEN

July 1853

Anna sat at her vanity table, watching herself in the mirror gently fastening the last black button on her collar. She kept her hair and clothes simpler these days and didn't need much help from Fannie once her corset was tied up. She picked up an ornamental silver hair comb and thumbed over the engraved and swirling vines and leaves, savoring the texture. It had been a gift from Edward after Tom was born. She tucked it behind the braid wrapped around her bun. Ready.

A good bit of time stood between then and supper, but Anna got dressed, anyway. Mostly because she craved time alone to sit quietly, far away from questions about how she wanted to move forward with the business. Ike and Tom were both home for a visit. They wanted to know what was to become of Viewmont. Anna understood it was important to them, especially to Ike. He would likely be the one to run the plantation after her since Tom was now practicing medicine. The boys' questions piled on top of the usual ones that peppered Anna about what was for supper that week and who was right in the daily argument, Mollie or Sallie. She hardly had answers anymore for the usual questions, much less those regarding the business. So she didn't deal with it at all.

The slaves continued with the annual schedule of sowing and reaping. Everything went on as normal—except for the growing stack of letters on Edward's desk. What quandaries and dilemmas awaited her in those envelopes? As soon as she remembered them, she shoved them out of her mind.

Edward had died barely six months ago. Now, Anna was a forty-four-year-old widow with a plantation to run and seven living children to raise. Her eyes stung. She would have no more children.

As a land-owning widow, she had choices. But with choices came decisions. And those decisions weighed so heavy on her shoulders that, without the corset, she'd surely struggle to sit up without slouching. At her vanity table, the only decision she faced was whether to wear a silver comb in her hair or another one of Edward's jewelry gifts from throughout the years.

Anna got up and crossed to the window, watching the clouds move slowly across the summer sky. Hope attempted to flicker in her chest. Clouds usually made for vibrant sunsets. The sky was beginning to pinken already. She could stay in her room and enjoy it till supper. Edward would say she should step out into it to lift her spirits. She sighed. *Why not?*

Anna went downstairs and smiled as Tom and Helen also headed toward the back door. Her older son had brought Helen Vaugh Wilson with him on the visit—always a delightful girl. They were a few paces ahead of her. Anna stepped outside after them. She shut the door, and Tom nearly jumped as he whipped around. He shot her an oddly panicked look. Was he so afraid she might join them? Why?

Anna stayed by the house, puttering in the opposite direction. "Am I allowed a little fresh air before supper too?"

Tom's tense shoulders relaxed. "Of course, Mother." He looked relieved but still a little put out.

Helen playfully grabbed Tom's arm. "Why are you being so silly?" Her blonde ringlets bounced as the couple strolled across the grounds, up toward the orchard.

They looked so fine together. Anna's heart ached. Her oldest son would surely be married soon. Helen seemed like an excellent choice—beautiful, educated, and from a Baptist family. She even got along with the girls, especially Lottie, and she adored little Edmonia.

Anna breathed in the moment. The evening air was sweet and warm. Crickets started to chirp. Anna watched the sky fade from pink to orange. Then the clouds became like red flames over the nearby flowers and distant mountains. Each sunset was beautiful, of course, but God certainly outdid himself tonight. She didn't try to reconcile that knowledge with the belief that God was also the one who could have, yet did not, prevented Edward from boarding that doomed riverboat.

The empty place beside Anna was full of what might have been. Edward might have stood beside her and reached for her hand or pulled her close for a hug. It was completely different from when Grandmother died. When she died, it didn't feel as though Anna had lost a limb. The sky grew blurry as tears welled in her eyes. This stunning evening would have been so romantic for a couple.

She gasped. Could Tom have been acting so strangely because of nerves? Anna quickly wiped her eyes and peered at the orchard just in time.

Helen was clutching her shawl tightly around her shoulders. Tom dropped to a knee and lifted up something small, maybe a ring! Helen raised a gloved hand over her mouth, and her shoulders heaved a little, as though she was crying or laughing or both.

Fresh tears fell down Anna's cheeks. She clutched her stomach. Her little Tom. He was always such a sweet boy. He would be a fine husband.

At supper, the family cheered the news and ate a special meal of Helen's favorite foods, which Tom had planned with Fannie ahead of time. The couple shared the story of Tom's proposal. Helen's breathless *yes* was the most beautiful sound Tom had ever heard. That's what he told everyone, immediately sending a blush across Helen's face.

"I didn't know Mother would watch the whole thing." Tom laughed. "I almost lost my nerve when you came outside with us."

"I had no idea," Anna said apologetically. "It's such a beautiful night. I'm glad you went through with your plan."

"As am I." Helen rested her newly jeweled hand on Tom's arm.

He took her hand and kissed it. His sisters giggled around the table. He stood up. "I'd like to take this opportunity to toast my intended. And my mother."

Anna's heart caught in her throat.

Tom raised his glass toward Anna. "To Mother—you and Father, may he rest in peace, lived and worked side by side, always together, showing us all what a wonderful thing marriage can be." He turned his glass toward his new fiancée. "To Helen—wherever you go, you inject the world with joy and laughter. I've learned this year that life is unpredictable and can be cut much too short. Whatever time I have left, I want to live it by your side."

Helen and Anna dabbed at their eyes with napkins as everyone else raised their glasses in a toast.

"When's the big day?" Lottie unfolded her napkin with a flourish and laid it across her lap.

"Sometime in December." Tom's face glowed.

Anna fumbled her fork as her eyes widened. "This December?" She tried not to choke on her corn. She'd be hosting a wedding at Viewmont in only a few months?

"If it's possible," Helen said with the dreamy smile of a new bride.

Anna managed a tight smile in return. She nodded, counting the tasks to be done.

When Edward was alive, he and Anna had dreamed and whispered about a lavish society wedding for their son on the hills of Viewmont. If Tom and Helen's ceremony was held near the orchard in the early fall, the scent of ripe apples might permeate the air. Or if they wed closer to the main house in the spring, all the blooming flowers would practically do the decorating for them. But since their wedding was to take place in December, it would no doubt be indoors and require a lot of decorating. The house would need extra cleaning, and the furniture would need precise rearranging. At least the expanded carriage drive should be finished in time to welcome all the wedding guests.

"I'm glad you're getting married." Lottie dug into her sweet potatoes. "You make Tom much happier than he was by himself. You can marry on my birthday if you want—it's on the twelfth."

Helen laughed and beamed at Lottie. "What a generous offer. Thank you. I think we should let your mother choose the exact day, as we hope it will be in her home."

Tom looked at Anna with pleading eyes. She could say no and suggest Helen's family home. She could ask them to wait until after her year-long mourning period.

Lottie was right. Tom seemed like a happier man since he started courting Helen. Even now, even after the loss of Edward, hope and joy radiated from Tom's face. It was clear he adored Helen. Why should they wait any longer to marry? Tom and Helen's wedding could breathe fresh life and love into Viewmont again.

Anna set her shoulders back and lifted her chin. "We are a house in mourning."

Tom's face fell.

"But there's a time to mourn and a time to dance," Anna continued with a sneaking smile. "I think soon, it might be time to dance."

Tom looked at her in pained confusion.

"Ecclesiastes," Helen said excitedly.

Anna smiled and confirmed with a nod. "Ecclesiastes." The girl knew her Bible. Hopefully, she would influence Tom to pick his up once in a while.

Agreeing to host the wedding at Viewmont lifted Anna's days with a new purpose. It was as if planning the wedding shook her awake. She even decided to chip away at the stack of envelopes on Edward's desk.

She sat down one morning in the padded leather desk chair and lit the lamp. She reached for the envelope on top of the pile, then for the letter opener. Like wielding a sword in battle. She ripped open the first letter. It was something to do with taxes. She set it down and opened the next one. Taxes again. She frowned. Were all of them about bills?

The third letter was from the family's lawyer who had updated Edward's will when he was ill. Anna picked it up and noticed the next few letters were also from the lawyer. Her heart tightened. While she had been wallowing in grief, the lawyer was trying to reach her. After Edward died, the lawyer had said something was wrong with the newest will—a date or signature or something. The firm had needed time to corroborate the facts, so there had been no customary reading of the will after the funeral. Anna opened the envelope and pulled the letter closer. Her heart pounded faster as she read each line. She got to the end and shoved it to the edge of the desk. That couldn't be right. Was it?

Anna hadn't read Edward's will before, when he was ill and she thought he was dying. She wrenched open the drawer in Edward's desk and dug out the copy that she had stored in there, back when she thought she wouldn't need it for a long time. She skimmed it once, then she read it again more slowly, and a third time to make sure. Her gut hollowed as she consumed the words. She held her hand over her mouth and whispered, "Edward, what have you done?"

As the widow of a Virginia landowner, Anna was lawfully entitled to a third of the estate. But in her husband's will, she wouldn't own any of it or have any true authority over her home or their business. She would just be the steward, and Ike would inherit it one day after she passed.

Anna shut the document back into the desk drawer, then stormed out of the room, through the hallway, and out the back door. She didn't shiver in the chilly morning as she marched through fog and over dewy grass toward Edward's grave. She had some things to say.

She sat down on her heels in front of her husband's headstone, ignoring the bench behind her. Mud already half covered her skirt. Wet hair stuck across her forehead. She clutched fists full of damp grass for support as she spoke to Edward's name, engraved on the stone.

"We ran Viewmont together. You always discussed things with me and asked for my opinion, acting as if you valued it. I had the experience and the tools—everything I needed to be the next owner—a successful owner. But you denied me that right." Anna released the grass and pounded the ground. "Why?"

She hung her head. She knew what she needed to do next. When Captain Harris died and her mother became a widow for the second time, he'd also left her as the steward of Viewmont rather than its owner. When her mother petitioned the Captain's will in court and won, she explained to Anna exactly what she had done every step of the way—just in case. Now

Anna found herself facing the same situation that her mother faced back then.

Anna turned to her mother's gravestone. She pulled herself up and closed the three feet between the two stones.

When her mother had won her case all those years ago, Anna had said she was proud of her for being so brave and strong. She hadn't said that she wished Mother would have been that brave and strong earlier in life. When her mother's first husband, Anna's father, had died, Mother was much younger and less confident in her abilities, but she was just as adamant about protecting her independence. She had not petitioned the court for her rights as a landowning widow and run her deceased husband's estate. She certainly did not remarry as soon as she could have. Remarrying would have secured a home for all four of her children, but she would have been a subordinate wife again, not a wealthy, independent widow. Instead, she sent her three older children away to live on the plantations of one aunt or another. James had only been two years old at the time. Mother had kept Anna with her because she'd only been an infant.

"I was furious with you when I realized why James and the others didn't live with us until you finally married Captain and we moved to Viewmont." Tears mixed with sweat and mist on her cheeks. "James was eleven. I was nine and had never lived with my siblings before. You let us all, everything, slip away just so you could keep your precious freedom."

For a few minutes, Anna cried loudly. She wiped her face, smudging the tears around.

Then she steadied her breathing. Strength returned to her. "I'm not furious anymore, though. You were a younger widow then than I am now. And your mother never made you learn to add and use figures, as you made me, even though I hated it." A laugh escaped like a breath from deep within her. "You learned from your mistakes and fought for your full rights the second time you were widowed. I understand better now. You didn't want to send them away. You just crumbled under the weight that was suddenly dropped on your shoulders. That same weight is now on my shoulders. Oh, Mother, I wish you were here." A fresh wave of tears overcame her.

Psalm twenty-three was engraved on the stone. She remembered who was there with her in the shadow of the valley of death. He was her portion. He was all that she had and all that she needed.

She would fight for the full amount that the law entitled her to.

Anna stood up. "The Lord will save me. I won't doubt him. I won't crumble. My daughters will stay with me. Viewmont will be our home, and the business will thrive."

By the time Anna walked back to the house, the mist had cleared and the fog had vanished in the sunlight. She returned to the study, sat down in her husband's chair, and drafted a letter to the family's lawyer, informing him of her decision. Anna would refuse what her husband bequeathed to her and file papers to contest his will, just as her mother had done. Hopefully, she would win just as her mother had won.

Not only did Anna grieve the loss of her husband and her old life with him, but now she also would have to wrestle for the inheritance he should have left her. The year ahead would be fraught with struggle. But it would end with Tom and Helen's wedding. By then, she could hope for a fresh start for their family.

Lottie wandered through the house before Tom and Helen's ceremony was supposed to start. Fannie and Peggy had decorated Viewmont beautifully for a Christmas wedding. As Lottie walked downstairs, she tapped the brilliant white ribbon entwined with evergreen boughs that wrapped around the banister. Last Christmas, Father had walked down these same steps without holding the rail for support, beaming with joy and health. More greenery swept over the parlor doorway, like Father's open arms ready for a hug. Lottie's throat tightened. She swallowed hard and shook her head.

In the parlor, she scooted past the evergreen tree atop a table in the back of the room. Warm, refreshing citrus notes filled her senses as she breathed in the scents of the stringed cranberries and dried orange slices. Last year, the tree's branches had held so many presents that after the family picked them off and opened them, the tree looked as if it stood a bit taller, relieved of its merry burdens.

All season, Lottie couldn't seem to enjoy the beautiful decorations and sweet traditions without remembering the Christmas before—Father's last Christmas. It had been such a happy and hopeful time because he had gotten well. But the memories of laughter, delicious food, and presents also swirled with sadness. Father had died too soon after Christmas for the two memories not to mix. Lottie's chin quivered, but she didn't cry.

She meandered through the newly arranged rows of chairs to the front of the parlor, where delicate lace and white roses surrounded the wedding altar. She sat down and fixed her eyes on the altar. If she tried her hardest to be happy today and collect as many joyful memories as possible from Tom's wedding, maybe Christmas wouldn't sting her heart so much.

Lottie's family came downstairs, and the wedding guests began to arrive and fill the parlor. Mother still wore her black crepe dress, but she left her mourning cap and veil upstairs even though lots of people were around. She'd said Orie, Lottie, and the younger girls didn't have to wear black at the wedding since they had almost finished the year of mourning. They got to wear their navy blue, forest green, and plum dresses. Wearing a color again was refreshing. But it felt strange not wearing any black all of a sudden. So Lottie had wrapped a small ribbon of black velvet around her wrist.

Lottie's mother and sisters joined her up front close to the altar. Ike eventually sat at the far end of the row with one of their neighbors, Margaret, who went by Meg. The two had started courting earlier that fall. Meg clutched her reticule and beamed, glancing around the beautiful room.

Orie leaned to Lottie and whispered loudly, "Look, it's snowing! That means they will have a happy life."

Lottie craned her neck to see snow falling outside. It was beautiful. She studied the scene, embedding it into her mind.

"Plus, it's a Monday, an omen for good health," Orie said.

Lottie frowned at her. "What's an omen?"

Sallie jabbed her elbow into Orie's side. "Shh! Here she comes."

Lottie turned in her seat with the rest of the guests to watch the bride entering the room as a string quartet began to play. Helen wore white, just like Queen Victoria had worn. As the bride made her way toward Tom, whose face shone, Lottie touched her bracelet.

She tried to catch some of the happiness radiating from Tom's face, but a darker thought clouded her mind. Her breath turned quick and shallow. Heat spread from her chest to her head, and her hands felt clammy. This wedding was only the first family milestone that Father would miss. He wouldn't see Tom and Helen walk back up the aisle as husband and wife. He wouldn't watch Orie or Lottie walk across any graduation stage, and he barely got to see little Eddie walk at all. Lottie's eyes watered. Since crying was normal at weddings anyway, she let the tears fall.

Crying eased the building tension, like when they released the gate on a swelling lock in Scottsville's canal. Once the preacher started talking, it was easier to focus on the ceremony. He led Tom and Helen in vows to God to love and honor each other faithfully for life, no matter what.

Lottie stiffened and crossed her arms. She stopped crying and settled into bitterness. Making promises to God? He was surely an unreliable being, if he existed at all. If God saved Father in November last year, why did he let him die two months later? What sort of God was that?

After the ceremony, Lottie followed the crowd and the happy couple into the library, which had been transformed into a reception hall. She softened at the smell of a delicious wedding breakfast. She didn't count the preacher's words as one of the day's happy memories, but that meal certainly made the list.

CHAPTER FIFTEEN

June 1854

Anna opened her sleepy eyes to a window full of morning light. The bright sun and blue sky might have promised a warm spring day if not for the few patches of snow left over from winter's latest howl. She lingered on her side of the bed, clutching the blanket to her chin. She wasn't crying herself to sleep anymore or waking up in a panic, searching the room for Edward. That must be progress. But was she healing?

Last year, while Anna completed the carriage drive, prepared for Tom and Helen's wedding, and sorted out Edward's will in court, the buzz of it all had carried her through her grief. There were always things to do and needs outside her own pain to focus on. Now, as her days settled into the slower rhythm of normal life, Anna didn't know what to do next. Even if she had known, she didn't have the energy to do it. There was no big project to accomplish, no battle to fight. Only each day.

More sunlight poured into the room. It was a Sunday, but Anna didn't move. She dreaded gathering the girls for church. They had been getting harder to manage. Only a woman with an innerspring of endless energy could keep up with mothering them well, not Anna. She didn't engage with each conflict that screamed out to her. It was impossible to discipline them every time she found Sallie and Mollie fighting, or Lottie sighing loudly during family prayers, or Orie snapping at someone, especially if they were playing keep-away with the mail. Orie had finished studying all of Tom's old textbooks and applied to the women's medical college in Pennsylvania after his and Helen's wedding. The response should arrive any day now.

Anna rose. Even if she didn't have the energy to teach and discipline her daughters, she could at least lead by example. She shuffled to her wardrobe and opened the doors to a row of black dresses. Fannie must have tucked in that plum dress and a blue one, as if that would coax Anna out of her mourning. It had been over a year since Edward's death, so the girls didn't wear their mourning clothes anymore. Her hand started to reach for the plum, then it found a black sleeve. Today, it felt like a lie to wear anything other than black.

Anna pulled on the dark dress and lumbered downstairs into an empty dining room. Her eyes shut, and her head fell back in defeat. The children were nowhere to be found and likely nowhere near ready to go. She went into the kitchen and grabbed some bread and fruit for the journey, then headed back through the house, praying as she went. *Lord, I need you.*

She peeked out a window on her way back upstairs. A group of slaves waited outside by the wagons, ready to drive to Scottsville.

Anna opened Sallie and Mollie's door, then crossed her arms at what she found. They were sitting on the floor with Eddie playing with their dolls. "Girls, why aren't you ready yet?"

Sallie and Mollie shouted together as if it were rehearsed. "We don't want to go to church!"

Anna stared at them. The girls often whined and moaned about going to church. And she didn't always make them go, especially after Edward died. She turned and walked toward the older girls' room. Maybe Lottie and Orie could rally the others.

She went in and saw them sitting perfectly upright on their beds, holding opened books that they clearly weren't reading. It appeared that they were in on the protest. "What's this?"

Orie held her chin high. "We prefer to stay home and rest today, Mother. We'll watch over Sallie, Mollie, and Eddie."

Anna looked at Lottie, waiting for her to say her line. Nothing came. As Lottie sat on the edge of her bed, her gaze flickered to her older sister. Then she stood and addressed Anna. "I don't like going to church, Mother. The air smells weird in there, and the songs are boring, and Pastor Fox talks too long."

Anna's heart stung. After years of visiting church together as a family, this was how her daughter thought of it. The hurt awakened Anna, but not enough to argue. "Fine. But I'm taking Edmonia."

Anna went back to the other room, picked up her youngest child, and walked outside.

Eddie played with the ribbon hanging from Anna's hat. "Mama, where are we going?"

Tears welled in Anna's eyes, threatening to overcome her. Her voice quivered. "To sing to God and listen to the Bible."

Eddie looked straight into her watery eyes. "I like to sing."

Anna hid her face as she kissed Eddie's cheek. She still smelled sweet and warm like a baby. "I like to sing, too, darling."

Anna hurried through the door and out to the covered carriage. She didn't dare cry in front of the slaves, who were waiting in their wagon. She helped Eddie onto the padded bench, then stepped up herself. George caught Anna before she could close the door.

"Pardon, ma'am, but this letter came yesterday evenin'." George handed her an envelope. "It got dropped on the way inside."

She took the envelope. "Thanks." Another word would have surely broken the levy that was barely holding back her tears.

Anna wept half of the journey to Scottsville Baptist Church while Eddie sat on her lap, gazing at the world outside, singing little songs. After Anna spent herself crying, she breathed as deeply as her corset would allow. She leaned Eddie back to look into her eyes. Eddie laughed and dove into Anna's bosom. She smiled and teared up again. Out of all the children, Eddie looked the most like Edward. Anna kissed her daughter's soft hair and gave her a gentle squeeze before Eddie wiggled to her own seat and went back to her songs.

It wasn't easy showing up to church, first without her husband and now without most of her children. Years ago, maybe fourteen by now, when Edward and Anna had helped finance the church building, she would grab his hand as they walked up the hill to Scottsville Baptist. It felt like a joint effort and something that they were proud of together. When the children were smaller, she went and prayed for her kids to be impacted by the preaching and the worship. Now, going to church only made her miss Edward and her children more and those times when they would all sit together and fill a pew toward the front.

When the wagons arrived, Anna helped Eddie walk up the hill to the brick building. Pastor Fox stood at the tall double doors and beamed at Eddie. "Good morning, young lady."

Eddie scooted closer to Anna and clutched her dress.

Pastor Fox smiled at Anna. "She's growing by leaps and bounds."

Anna stroked Eddie's hair. "Half an inch taller every time I turn around, it seems."

"It's good to see you both today." He looked at her with a strong, focused kindness that made Anna's throat tighten and her eyes sting. Were they red-rimmed? How could one body produce this many tears?

She nodded silently and followed his arm that swept toward the sanctuary. Anna stood upright as she walked in, but her heart limped over the threshold.

The slaves quietly trailed behind them and made their way up to the balcony with the other Black members. Anna glanced up and behind her. These days, the balcony looked fuller than the sanctuary floor.

Anna and Eddie settled at the end of their pew, sharing it with another family. The wood creaked as they sat down.

The woman next to Anna turned and greeted her. "It's nice to sit with you. I'm glad you're here."

Anna smiled. "It's good to be in God's house."

Back when Anna and Edward hosted Baptist services at Viewmont, they'd dreamed about one day worshiping in a proper church building with a crowd of other believers. After Edward donated the funds and the church was finally built, many Sundays at Scottsville Baptist weren't exactly as they'd anticipated. Sometimes Pastor Fox preached too long, as Lottie had said, but that was only because he spoke slowly, leaving room for the congregation to think. Anna didn't notice a bad smell like Lottie had complained of, but she didn't like *every* song they sang. For every disappointing Sunday, there were seven far more wonderful than all she had imagined.

At Pastor Fox's instruction, the congregation stood and opened their hymnals to "Come Thou Fount of Every Blessing." They raised their voices loud as they sang the hundred-year-old song together once again. Some voices grew louder at "streams of mercy never ceasing call for songs of loudest praise!" Others nearly shouted "prone to wander; Lord I feel it; prone to leave the God I love!" Then the whole room prayed aloud together, "Here's my heart, Lord; take and seal it. Seal it for thy courts above."

As she held Eddie and sang, Anna looked around. These people weren't perfect, and their lives weren't perfect either. That's why they gathered here. Some faces were lifted high while others bowed low. Peoples' eyes were either wide open or slammed shut—whichever helped them better see the Holy One present in their midst. Tears fell freely down cheeks that were lifted in smiles. Life could be hard, but this crowd knew where their help came from. Anna wasn't the only one looking around. Sprinkled around the sanctuary, children gaped up at the adults. They were learning what it looked like to worship in spirit and in truth. Anna's chest tightened. She patted Eddie's back and turned to face the front.

There was nothing special or spiritual about the building on Harrison Street. The bricks came from plain old Virginia red clay. Mr. Moore on the fifth row made the steeple. And as beautiful as the pulpit was, there was no power in that pine. But the book that Pastor Fox held as he preached from it— there was power in those words. The people all around Anna who believed in the Word of God carried around the Spirit of God with them. In that way, she was completely filled and completely surrounded by God.

No teatime visit could replace this holy communion with God and his saints. No book of poetry could match the peace of listening about how God was their strength, their trustworthy safe place, and always in control. Church was a regular realignment of thought and heart to God.

Pastor Fox finished preaching. The congregation finished singing, praying, and fellowshipping. Anna, Eddie, and the slaves loaded into the wagons again and headed home. Anna left more full than when she arrived. The community, the worship, and the Word had revived her. Although she had woken up parched, she'd received all and more than she needed at the well of living water.

Anna didn't have a wedding to plan or a court case to fight anymore, now that she had successfully contested Edward's will. But she had four children at home who did not seem to want anything to do with God. They needed her. Even if they didn't realize it, they needed Anna to pray for them, to engage with them, and lead them. On her own, it was too much. But with God, it was possible.

While Mother, Eddie, and the slaves were away, Lottie sprang into action. The plan to stage a coup and skip church had been Orie's idea, but Lottie took it one step further.

Lottie and Orie had wandered into Sallie and Mollie's room and congratulated them on a job well done. Lottie sat down between her two younger sisters and laid a hand behind their shoulders. "Why don't we show Mother how nice Sundays could be without going to church?" She looked up at Orie. "Then we won't have to convince her every time we want to stay home."

Orie held her chin and squinted her eyes. "How would we do that?"

Lottie spoke slowly, emphasizing every syllable. "With a hot, delicious meal."

Sallie's face twisted in confusion. "But it's Sunday. The servants don't cook on Sundays."

"No one is supposed to cook on Sundays." Mollie shook her head with her eyes wide.

"Exactly!" Lottie popped up to her full height. Sallie's and Mollie's captivated gazes followed her. "After church, we always sit down to a cold meal that was made the day before. Cold ham with cold bread, applesauce, and cold vegetables."

Orie held her hands up. "We get it. A hot meal would be nice."

Mollie smiled, looking into the distance. "I like applesauce."

"We can keep the applesauce. But imagine a Sunday dinner of warm roasted chicken with the skin still crunchy, butter melting down a pile of mashed potatoes, and cobs of hot corn. And then a fruit cobbler fresh from the oven."

Was that a glimmer at the corner of Sallie's mouth, as if it was actually watering? Lottie paused, letting the idea simmer. "It will be a surprise for Mother. The servants won't even know about it."

Orie smirked and tapped her finger tips together. "Let's do it."

Lottie and her sisters giggled as they hurried down the stairs and out the door to the kitchen. They halted and their faces fell. An iron padlock wrapped around the door.

Orie's jaw dropped as she stared at the locked door. She crossed her arms in a huff. "It's as if she doesn't trust us."

Lottie examined the lock, then wandered around, surveying the building. "Well, we are trying to break one of her top commandments—no work on Sundays."

Mollie's face twisted in deep concern. "Is the applesauce trapped in there too?"

Lottie spotted an open window. She rallied Orie and Sallie to hoist her up. Once Lottie reached the window, she easily climbed through and lowered herself inside. She unlocked the door, and everyone filled the room and looked to her.

"This was your big idea." Orie grinned. "What should we do now?"

Lottie had never prepared a whole Sunday dinner before. But she had helped Fannie and Peggy make food for years, and she knew where all the ingredients were. Lottie assigned the group tasks of peeling, chopping, and baking.

"Mother will be home in a few hours." Lottie hoisted a wooden spoon in the air. "Let's get to work."

Everyone scrambled to their tasks. It took all the time they had to put the ingredients together in a way that tasted good. With only a sliver of time to spare, they finished the meal and set the table, running plates and bowls of food from the kitchen to the dining room.

Lottie inspected the place settings while Orie and Sallie cleaned themselves up after they had dropped the flour sack and became engulfed in a small explosion of white powder.

Mollie ran into the dining room. "The wagons are coming up the drive!" She giggled as if it were the most thrilling thing to possibly happen.

The girls rushed into the dining room and lined up together in front of the table. They were ready just in time.

The main door burst open, and Mother's voice filled the house. "Girls!" Her footsteps indicated she was checking all the front rooms. The shouting grew louder as she bustled into the dining room with Fannie right behind her, holding Eddie. "Girls! There's smoke rising from the kitchen chimney!" Mother searched the room with wild eyes, as if flames might be devouring the walls.

Sallie stood calmly next to Lottie with her chin tucked to her chest and her hands folded sweetly in front of her. "Hello, Mother."

Mother fixed her gaze on them and bobbed her head as she did when she was counting them.

"We made Sunday dinner for you," Mollie said.

Lottie gave her sisters a signal nod. The four of them parted down the middle and stepped aside to reveal savory-smelling dishes neatly presented along the center of the table. The silverware twinkled in the candlelight beside empty plates ready for filling.

Eddie clapped and bounced in delight.

"We did it all ourselves—for you." Lottie's chest swelled.

Mother turned to Fannie, whose face had clouded in a look of confused fear.

Orie stepped forward. "The servants didn't know anything about it. It was just the four of us."

Lottie had expected the stunt to surprise Mother, but she hadn't expected the silence or the tension swelling in the room.

"Doesn't the food look good? I scooped the applesauce. It's right by your chair." Mollie pointed behind her to an unusually large and ornate bowl of applesauce sitting on the table. Lottie had tried to convince her to use a smaller crock, but she'd insisted on the fancy dish.

Mother broke into laughter. She stepped over the threshold and took Mollie's face in her hands. "It looks delicious, darling."

Mollie smiled as Mother kissed her face.

Eddie started to kick, so Fannie let her down. Immediately, Eddie scurried to the large, ornate bowl, reached up on her tiptoes, and stuck her finger in for a taste.

Mother pulled Eddie away and sat her in a chair as she spoke to Fannie. "The house isn't burning down, after all. You can continue on to the cabins with the others."

The meal was surprisingly delicious. Mother ate two helpings of everything and complimented the cooking.

Mollie leaned across her plate for another roll. "It was Lottie's idea! She taught us how to cook."

Lottie's face flushed. "Shh!" She didn't want all the blame if this went wrong. They had agreed to bear it as a group. But Mother didn't seem angry. She only lifted an eyebrow and offered an impressed smile. Ah, the scheme seemed to have worked. All Mother needed was a hot Sunday dinner.

Releasing a sigh, Lottie bit into her chicken and tapped her heels against her chair. Much better than cold ham.

Later that night, Mother perched on the foot of Lottie's bed. Lottie sat up against her headboard. Here it came, more praise of her baking.

But Mother wasn't as jovial as she had been at dinner. She gave Lottie a look. Lottie knew that look, even if she hadn't seen it in a while. It was a look of disappointment that tried to be friendly. And it usually came before a long talk about acceptable morals and behavior.

Mother turned to Orie. "Would you please excuse us for a little while?"

Lottie's heart pounded. Her wide eyes pleaded with Orie to stay.

Orie's face twisted. She slowly got out of bed then paused and glanced back at Lottie.

"There's a new box of peanut brittle in the study desk," Mother said. "You're welcome to a piece or two."

Orie perked up. She shrugged and left Lottie alone with Mother looking at her like *that*.

CHAPTER SIXTEEN

1854

Lottie looked at the back of her closed bedroom door, down at the braided rug, then at her hands clutching a quilt spread over her—anything to avoid eye contact with Mother, still sitting at the foot of her bed.

Mother tilted her head down to Lottie's level and caught her eye. "What inspired your little adventure today?"

Her tone wasn't angry. Maybe there was still a chance to convince her. Lottie released the quilt and held out her hands on her lap. "You always say that Sundays are for God and resting, not for working. That's why we can't have hot meals—because the servants have to work to make them." She raised her head. "But I think it's more restful to eat a nice hot meal instead of cold food. If you let us stay home from church more often, we could make more Sunday dinners. You said it tasted good, right?"

"Yes, Lottie, I enjoyed our special meal together. I know a hot dinner is usually nicer than a cold one. It's not about that. God made the Sabbath for us to rest. The servants need that, and so do we. Without resting, we can't heal." Mother's gaze shifted to a blank spot on the wall as though she had just remembered something. A funny look clouded her face.

Lottie crossed her arms. Clearly, Mother didn't understand.

Mother's focus returned to Lottie. She leaned forward and patted Lottie's leg. "Trust me. Developing a habit of Sabbath when you're young will help you later when life gets more complicated and challenging. You won't always have this spunky energy."

"Yes, I will!" She was going to have an exciting life that wouldn't be bothered with observing Sabbaths.

Mother chuckled. "Even so, resting is important. This year ... was very hard." She took a deep breath. "I haven't been very attentive to you or your sisters, and I'm sorry." Lottie lowered her arms as Mother continued. "But if I didn't have a Sabbath, if I didn't pray and sing to God with the church, I would keep being a bad mother."

Lottie sat up and scooted closer to the foot of her bed. "I don't think you're a bad mother." She leaned into Mother's open arms. "After last year, we might need a month of Sabbaths to rest and heal."

Mother nodded against Lottie's cheek. "You're full of grand ideas today." She twirled some of Lottie's hair around her finger. "The meal was truly delicious. Did you really plan it all yourself?"

Lottie broke their hug and smiled up at Mother. "I did! I thought about it for a long time. When Orie said we should all stay home, it was the perfect opportunity. Only, I forgot about the kitchen being locked, so I had to climb in through the window and—"

"Through the window?" Mother gaped at Lottie.

Lottie bobbed her head, then continued without stopping for another breath. "And I looked around to see what food we had. There was a chicken already plucked and prepared. Then I told Orie and the girls what we could do with it all. They liked the idea."

"You sure know how to rally a group." Mother slowly shook her head. "I would have chosen a different aim, but you showed real leadership today, Lottie. I believe you'll do great things one day."

Lottie frowned and rubbed the back of her neck. *One day.* She'd begun to despise it when grownups said that. Uncle James said she might travel the world as a missionary one day. Mother said she might go to school one day, whenever that was.

Mother's brow furrowed. "What's wrong?"

"I just ..." Lottie jerked her arm down. Her hands fiddled in her lap. "When will I get to do big things? I'm already thirteen." This conversation wasn't part of Lottie's plan for the day. It all came rushing out. "I want to go to school at Valley Union like Father said. When is it going to happen?"

Mother drew back. "How did ...?" She didn't finish asking how Lottie knew about the school. She looked straight into Lottie's eyes, which were beginning to water. "Would you like to go to school in the fall?"

"This fall?" Lottie's heart swelled. Her stomach fluttered. Her wildest dream was coming true.

"Valley Union is a respectable Baptist school for girls, and the lessons are modeled after the University of Virginia's."

Lottie fell back in amazement, plopping onto her bed or maybe dropping onto a cloud. Good thing she had been sitting down for this.

Mother laughed, then spoke with a hint of sternness. "I'll remind you that Orie didn't go away to school until she was older. But Valley Union is designed for girls your age, and it's much closer to home."

Lottie tested how the words sounded out loud. "I'm going to school in the fall."

Mother smiled at her. "I'm excited for you, darling. But Lottie, I need you to understand something."

Lottie sat up to listen, still floating on the wonderful news.

"Your father provided for your education and expenses. But one day, if you choose not to marry and you want to live as independently as I imagine you might, it would be wise to have a way to provide for yourself. This school is a very special opportunity. You're smart and quick. You could be a teacher one day." Those two words suddenly didn't bother Lottie anymore. Mother leaned forward. Her earnest eyes burrowed into Lottie's. "You have more opportunities than most people, but you still need to work hard at them. Do you understand?"

Lottie nodded, trying to fight back a smile. "Yes, ma'am." No amount of serious talk could faze her happiness right now. She closed her eyes for a moment and saw Father's face. He had wanted a good school for Lottie, and he had made a way for her to go. Affection filled her heart for him. She could finally walk in his plan for her.

"We'll take it semester by semester." Mother leaned back, seemingly satisfied. "Depending on your progress, you can stay through the two-year program. Remember, we didn't let Orie return to Troy after that séance nonsense. Please don't put me in that position again."

"Yes, ma'am." Lottie couldn't stop smiling. She was going to school, not *one day*, but this fall. Her adventures were about to begin.

Anna was smiling, too, when she left the room. Her daughter would go to a school nearby and study the same curriculum as the boys. That wasn't even possible when she was Lottie's age.

She ventured downstairs to find Orie. She checked the library first.

Orie, in her blue dressing gown, sat curled up in her favorite chair in the corner by the window, gazing out at the clear night sky. She straightened when Anna made her way to one of the bookcases.

Anna ran her fingertips over leather spines, some smooth and others cracked. "Was the peanut brittle any good?" Her fingers found the one about the missionary experiences of Ann and Adonirum Judson. She rubbed the title in gold letters and sighed. Orie would never sit for a missionary bedtime story these days. Anna felt Orie's eyes on her.

"I liked the crunch," Orie said from across the room. "It didn't stick to my teeth like usual."

Anna nodded at the shelves. "Good, I'll try to get Mrs. Barnes' recipe. She gave me the box at church today."

Orie huffed at the mention of church and crossed her arms. "Is it my turn for a scolding?"

Anna glanced over her shoulder at her eldest daughter. "Oh, I suspect we're both too tired for that, and you're too old for a good scolding, anyway. Besides, what could I say?"

"You could say that I'm wicked for wanting to skip church, and it was dangerous to let the girls sneak into the kitchen." Orie waited for Anna to respond, receiving nothing more than a quizzical eyebrow. "But I kept watch on the fire and made sure that Sallie and Mollie didn't get too close to the stove. I even gave Sallie a dull knife to cut potatoes. Mollie only scooped the applesauce and set the table."

"It seems you already know what you did wrong."

Orie slouched, then stood up and hugged her arms as she started toward the door with her face cast down. She stopped and looked up when Anna spoke.

"But you missed one thing." Anna turned away from the books to squarely face Orie. She brought her hands flat together, as in prayer, pointing at Orie. "You forgot that those girls have looked up to you their whole lives, especially Lottie. She watches what you do and listens to what you say."

Color flooded Orie's face. She started pulling on her ear.

Anna crossed the room and opened her hands. She gently held Orie's arms and spoke tenderly. "It's time you start taking your influence over them more seriously. Being the eldest sister is not as light of a responsibility as your behavior today suggested."

Orie lowered her gaze again. "I'm sorry."

"You haven't asked me about the mail today."

Orie slowly shook her head. Her mouth wobbled. "It doesn't come on Sundays."

Anna held out an unopened envelope addressed to *Miss Orianna Moon*. "George gave it to me this morning."

Orie's face brightened. She gently took it in both hands. "How can the weight of my future feel so light?"

Anna crossed to the desk and dug in a drawer. "The women's college doesn't determine your future, Orie."

"But they do." Orie walked ghost-like to the desk, holding the letter as if it were something sacred. "If they don't accept me, where else can I learn medicine?"

Anna handed her a letter opener. Orie gently ripped open the envelope, dropped the heavy opener, and unfolded a single sheet of paper. She swallowed hard before she began to read it out loud.

"'On behalf of the dean of the Women's Medical College of Pennsylvania, I am pleased to inform you of your admission ...'" Orie clutched the paper to her chest. She locked her teary eyes with Anna's. "Oh, Mother, I'm going to medical school! I'm going to be a doctor!"

Anna laid one hand over her stomach and covered her smile with the other. Pride radiated from her heart. She enveloped Orie in a hug of laughter and tears, relishing the joy of that moment and the promises it held for the future.

"Praise the Lord," Anna whispered.

Orie wiped her eyes with her dressing gown sleeve. "I wish Father were here. It feels like his accomplishment too."

Anna smoothed Orie's hair away from her tear-streaked face. "Once your father got word that the school was accepting women, he knew you would go there one day and become an amazing doctor. We both knew all along."

A clock chimed from the bookshelf several times.

"It's getting late." Anna tilted her head toward the hall. "You should get to bed. I believe Lottie has good news to share as well."

Orie held the letter to her chest with both arms and walked out of the room as though she was leading a wedding processional.

Anna sat in Orie's chair to rest a moment before going up to her room. But as soon as her aching body nestled into the soft cushions, she groaned. If she stayed here, she would surely fall asleep in the library. It had been a long day, exhausting and energizing at the same time. She'd had quality conversations with Lottie and Orie, and before that, she'd also engaged Sallie and Mollie in a talking-to about how it was more important to obey their mother than their older sisters. A satisfying day, in the end.

The girls still needed her. Isaac was nearly finished with his schooling, and Tom was married now and would soon start a family along with his medical practice. Sending her children out into the world without her husband had not been part of Anna's plan. But while her walk through life with Edward was over, she wasn't alone. The good God who held her together and gave her the strength to keep going would stay by her side.

As Anna walked to her room, she paused at Orie and Lottie's door, which muffled only some of the giggling and whispering. She continued down the hallway, a smile on her face.

The next day, Anna walked into the kitchen. A savory aroma stopped her in her tracks. She took a deep breath. "Is that for supper tonight?"

Fannie stood drying a bowl beside a large bucket of dishes in soapy water. "Yes, ma'am. Chicken and vegetable pie."

"It smells heavenly."

Fannie smiled bashfully.

"I came in to tell you that Peggy will accompany Lottie to school in Roanoke in the fall."

Fannie's drying rag slowed.

"I understand there are quarters nearby where the servants live."

Fannie set the bowl and cloth on a small table beside her. She gripped the top with one hand and gently held the other over her stomach, which was rising and falling with deep breaths.

Anna moved a step toward her with open hands. She had never seen Fannie so clearly distressed. "Peggy will come home with Lottie at Christmas and summertime. I know you will miss her as I'll miss my Lottie, but this will be an exciting opportunity for both of them. Peggy will see new places and meet new people."

"Yes, ma'am." Fannie released her grip on the table and dabbed at her brow with the back of her hand. "May I ask, ma'am, when is Miss Lottie fixin' to leave?"

"We'll take the train mid-September."

Fannie's eyes widened. Her breath quickened again. "The public train? Not the family's carriage?"

"Yes, I'll take the girls myself." Anna took another step closer and touched Fannie's arm. "I will keep Peggy in first class with us. She won't be alone in the back."

Fannie exhaled. Relief washed over her face. "Yes, ma'am. Thank you, ma'am ... for telling me."

"Of course." Anna patted Fannie's arm. "Mothers should know these things so we can prepare ourselves as well as our children."

"Yes, ma'am." Fannie nodded to the floor.

"Glad we're settled." Anna turned to let Fannie get back to work. Her stomach rumbled with that enticing scent of chicken pie. Biscuits would be nice with supper if there was enough buttermilk left. With her hand on the door, she looked over her shoulder to suggest it but quickly closed her mouth. Fannie had turned her back. Her shoulders heaved and her head bent into her hands.

Anna's mind raced. She was being generous and considerate by informing Fannie ahead of time. What more could she have said to comfort the woman? She'd seemed fine just a moment ago. Anna quietly crossed the threshold and closed the door.

When mid-September came, Anna waited beside the carriage that would take her and the girls to the train station. She glanced toward the sun shining down on them between fluffy white clouds. It was a beautiful day, still warm. A chill in the breeze hinted at the changes to come.

Lottie had already hopped in the carriage, ready to go. George loaded the luggage onto the back then joined Fannie in saying their goodbyes to Peggy over by the horse.

Fannie's eyes shone as she fussed with Peggy's travel pass. She tucked it into a pocket on the inside of Peggy's coat. "It's right here if anyone stops you and wants to see your pass." She buttoned the material closed and nearly smacked her own eye to catch a fallen tear. "If you get lost, at least your travel pass won't."

"I won't get lost, Mama."

"Right, you won't." George knelt in front of Peggy and looked into her eyes. He lowered his voice, but it still carried to Anna. "You'll stick close to Mistress Moon. Keep quiet, and keep your eyes low. Don't do nothing to draw attention."

As Peggy nodded solemnly and her parents embraced her, Anna turned away, her stomach tightening. Fannie clearly was awash in anxiety about her daughter. Anna was perfectly capable of safely transporting Peggy to Valley Union. Why didn't they trust her?

When George stood up, he asked his daughter, "What do you remember if you get scared?"

Peggy closed her eyes and recited, "God is with me. I don't have to fear."

After one more hug, Fannie released her daughter. George helped Peggy up onto the front bench. He came around to the side of the carriage, and after Anna climbed in, closed the door. Then he joined Peggy and grabbed the horse's reins. At a click of his tongue and a crack of the leather, they were off.

Lottie nearly bounced in her seat, staring at the drive ahead of them. "Do you think we'll see the Colemans on the train?"

The carriage curved around the carriage drive. Anna gazed out the side window at everyone waving. "Mrs. Coleman said they were leaving tomorrow to have more time with Cary Ann." Orie and the other girls went inside, but Fannie stayed in front of the house. Anna watched Fannie grow smaller and smaller until George turned the carriage onto the main road. Guilt stung Anna's heart. She chewed her lip. Maybe it wasn't necessary to take Peggy away from her family. But it was normal for prosperous families to send a slave with their children to school, especially younger children. Lottie was only thirteen. Wouldn't she need help being so far from home? Anna wrapped her arm around Lottie's shoulder and kissed the top of her head. She had been impatient with Fannie once or twice in the past, but by preparing her for this day, not to mention providing for them all, Anna had risen to the Apostle Paul's call in Colossians to treat slaves with justice and fairness. What more could she have done?

CHAPTER SEVENTEEN

1854

Going away to school at Valley Union Seminary was supposed to be Lottie's big chance for freedom and endless adventure. No more enduring Mother's Bible lessons or spending hours on needlework. Lottie didn't have to practice needlework anymore, but her days at school were plenty full of everything else that she was required to do.

She rose early each morning for breakfast, then chapel. From eight in the morning until four in the afternoon, she was studying or in classes, except for a dinner break at noon. After evening devotions, supper, and more study time, she enjoyed two unscheduled hours a day. It wasn't much, but two hours was enough for a girl like Lottie to make a little adventure with her friends—Cary Ann Coleman and her cousin, Mary Moon.

One day, Lottie left the study room early and snuck outside. She lifted her face into a gust of autumn air. It smelled like fresh possibilities. Her heels tapped quickly on the brick walkway leading to her favorite bench. She sat down and dug into her bag. She'd spend the precious few minutes between afternoon studying and evening devotions reading. Novels were forbidden at Valley Union, so Lottie cracked open her French grammar textbook, placed her latest story inside, and picked up where she left off.

When classes and study time ended, Cary Ann walked up. "Still fighting off the native cannibals, I see." She nodded to Lottie's book.

Lottie clutched both books to her chest in a panic. "How did you know?"

Cary Ann pointed and laughed. "The French book is upside down." She shook her head in mock disappointment. "You're getting sloppy. Plus, I noticed *Robinson Crusoe* was gone from your stack this morning." She sat down beside Lottie on the bench. "This must be the third time you've read that one since school started."

Lottie shrugged. "It's short. I'm glad I brought *some* novels with me. There's not much to choose from in the library here. It's all math and science and music theory. Something must be done to fill those shelves."

"Don't make the teachers think they don't give us enough reading as it is." Cary Ann lifted her finger. "Raise a fuss, and you might be sitting out here truly reading textbooks."

Lottie smiled and nodded, tapping the side of her forehead. "Always thinking ahead." She closed both books. "You know, of all the thrilling moments in this book, I think the most tension is at the beginning. Just imagine, Crusoe almost stayed home and studied the law to please his family. The whole story of traveling and cannibals and mutineers never would have happened."

"I'd study law any day if it meant avoiding cannibals." Cary Ann shivered. "But it *is* fun to read about other people's wild choices. That book is filled with decisions I'd never consider."

"Well, *I'd* consider them."

"If you're that eager for adventure and willing to travel where cannibals run around, maybe you should marry a missionary."

"No, missionaries want to marry nice Christian women, not wild devils like me!" Lottie shook her half-pinned-up hair for effect.

Worry spread across Cary Ann's face. "You don't mean that."

Lottie gathered her things and linked arms with Cary Ann as they stood up and walked to the chapel together. "No need to worry about me, dear friend." Lottie patted Cary Ann's arm. "Mr. Cocke's devotion this evening will probably chase all the devilish decisions out of me."

Cary Ann raised an eyebrow. They both knew that wasn't true. If Mother hadn't converted Lottie into an obedient Baptist girl by now, Mr. Cocke sure wouldn't be able to.

Now she knew better than dreaming of becoming a missionary. When she became a teacher, she would be able to earn a living and travel and read books as much as she wanted.

Once they got to the chapel, Lottie led Cary Ann to the middle-most row, and they sat in the middle of the pew. It proved to be the safest place to sit during devotions—equidistant from Mrs. Green's piercing gaze as she surveyed the students from the back of the room and Mr. Cocke's spittle from the pulpit.

While Mr. Cocke preached, Lottie watched the day slip into evening through the chapel windows. She sighed when autumn's warm sunset receded and twilight took over. The days were rapidly getting shorter, and she was wasting precious time in devotions.

When Mr. Cocke was deeply moved by his own preaching, which often seemed the case, he ended by praying with his right hand high in the air as though he was reaching up to God in heaven. The other hand would grip his Bible as if Mr. Cocke wanted to be sure it would come with him if God ever reached down and snatched him up like Elijah.

Mr. Cocke's voice grew louder as he prayed. "Holy Father in heaven, I plead on behalf of these girls. Lead them in the way everlasting, through the narrow gate. And should they drink from other wells in rebellion, Lord, may their hearts be utterly restless until they taste your sweet and satisfying waters."

Lottie hadn't heard anyone pray like that before. Back home, Pastor Fox signaled it was time for prayer by politely folding both hands in front of him and bowing his head. And he always prayed with such long pauses, which Mother had once called "space for him to hear from God." Lottie rolled her eyes at Mother's voice in her head. *Prayer isn't just talking to God, Lottie. We must listen too.*

Weeks ago, when school and devotions first started, Lottie had asked Mrs. Green, the lady principal, why Mr. Cocke prayed in such a unique posture.

Mrs. Green had squinted at Lottie. Somehow, she had spoken through pursed lips. "It is not ladylike to peek during prayers, Miss Moon."

Lottie started to squirm in her seat as Mr. Cocke went on praying.

"And we thank you, our Lord, for the blessings and the trials of the day behind us. Grant each girl here the grace to obey you wholeheartedly. Amen."

Mr. Cocke opened his eyes. His countenance fell back down to earth at the lack of open and tearful repentance in his audience. That concluded the last devotion of the day.

Mrs. Green rose from her seat behind the students. "Girls, you may proceed to supper now—quietly. Meditate on Mr. Cocke's message, and we will gather again for morning prayers as usual."

After Mrs. Green, Lottie was the first to stand. She needed to eat supper quickly and get her studying done early in her room. On a different evening, she might have played a game with her friends or written a letter to Orie. Tonight, she had a promise to keep.

After supper and studying, Lottie hurried back to the dining hall and met Ann Scott, a slave at Valley Union Seminary. The students and staff were all in their rooms by now, so they had the whole room to themselves. They sat at a table farthest from the doors and windows.

Ann set a candle between them and lit it. The flame flickered, casting a light that danced across her face. Once it steadied, it burned bright for being only one candle. Ann sat quietly while Lottie rustled around in her bag for a pen and paper.

The other students had told Lottie that Mr. Cocke had hired Ann, her husband, Claiborne, and their daughter, Bettie, from their owner to work at the school. As the story went, when their owner's daughter got married last year, he gave her Bettie as a wedding present. Then she took Bettie and moved to Missouri with her new husband. The whole school knew that Ann and Claiborne were devastated to lose their daughter. But Mr. Cocke couldn't help them because Valley Union had only hired the slaves. He didn't have authority to keep Bettie against her owner's wishes.

That all happened before Lottie started at Valley Union. Ever since Bettie was taken away, students took turns secretly helping Ann write letters to her daughter and read her the ones that Bettie sent back. Lottie had promised to help her write one this evening.

Lottie uncorked her ink and dipped her pen in. "Ready. What would you like to tell Bettie?"

The candlelight revealed Ann's soft, loving smile. "I'd like to say 'Hi, Honey' to start."

Lottie put pen to paper, then paused. "Not 'Dear Bettie' or something like that?"

Ann laughed in her deep voice. "Then she wouldn't believe the letter from me. If we gonna do this, Miss Lottie, all the words gonna be from me."

Lottie smiled back with a nod and started transcribing all that Ann wanted to tell her daughter since her last letter. Claiborne had recovered from his cough, but Bettie was welcome to keep praying for him as long as she liked. Their baby son had finally learned to say "Bettie," so he was ready to meet his big sister whenever they got the chance, which Ann prayed would come one day soon.

Lottie slightly hunched over her papers, listening as the woman went on talking sweetly to her daughter through Lottie's scratching pen. Ann looked forward to October apples. What was Bettie looking forward to in the fall?

Lottie nodded, imagining a crisp bite of a fresh apple. "Nothing like October apples in Virginia."

Ann talked smooth and slow, so Lottie didn't have to scribble too quickly. Ann asked how Bettie was getting on and if she was still going to that nice church she had written about.

A sudden bang sounded, as though someone was trying to open the door. Lottie jumped. Her pen accidentally added a long tail to the period at the end of the sentence. She and Ann jerked their heads toward the door. Lottie held her breath, waiting for something to happen. But nothing did.

"Must be the wind," Ann said.

What they were doing wasn't exactly within the school rules. Although Lottie had never heard of anyone being caught and punished for helping Ann, Mr. Cocke always seemed serious when he instructed the students not to fraternize with the slaves.

Lottie took a breath and flipped the page over. She looked up, ready to start again. "What else?"

"Write down Psalm 17:8."

Lottie hesitated. "I don't know that one."

Ann closed her eyes and quoted the verse. "'Keep me as the apple of your eye. Hide me under the shadow of your wings.'"

Lottie copied it. "How did you learn that? I thought you couldn't read."

"Same as I learn all my verses. I listen to 'em, and I pray 'em. I heard a preacher pray that one a long while back, and it stuck with me. I prayed it over me and Claiborne. I prayed it over Bettie back when she was a baby and woke up crying like she was scared. And now I pray it over my baby boy. Bettie will know it when she reads it. Mr. Cocke taught her to read 'n' write. She taught me a little before—when she was here."

Lottie put her pen down and slouched while she held her hands in her lap. "My mother taught me Bible verses, but I don't remember many of them too well."

"They stick good when you close your eyes and imagine 'em. Just picture it—God cuddlin' you close, coverin' you with his wings like a mama bird."

Lottie closed her eyes and tried it. "'Hide me under the shadow of your wings.'"

"You got it." Ann smiled. "Bettie used to swap out the words a bit. After all the laundry was done for the day, we'd be headed back to the cabin through those woods over by the hill. And she'd lift her little face up at the moonlit leaves and say, 'Hide me under the shadow of your branches.'" Ann laughed. "But you couldn't laugh then because that sweet baby meant it with all her heart."

"Who did she want to be hidden from?"

Ann turned her face away and looked at Lottie from the side of her eye. "Why don't we finish the letter so you can get to bed, Miss Lottie? It's gettin' near ten o'clock."

Lottie leaned forward. "Who was looking for you?"

Ann faced Lottie square on. "It's like this. No one really sees us enslaved folks, but everyone knows when we're around, especially if they want something. In the woods, under those branches, no one could see me or Bettie or tell us to do anything. We was covered. I don't know if God meant for trees and branches to be the same as wings and feathers. But he covered us with 'em just as good."

They were hiding from more work? Lottie had expected something of a chase story. She didn't know what to say. She held out the letter and her pen. "Do you want to sign your name?"

"I would, in fact." Ann took the pen and signed, *Mama*.

"I'll send it out tomorrow." Lottie folded the letter and packed it into her bag.

Ann got up. "Thank you, Miss Lottie. You did me a kindness." She nodded like a small bow and left toward the cabins beyond the woods.

Lottie glanced up at the clock. 9:55. A touch of panic stung her chest. Cary Ann had promised to cover for Lottie if any of the staff noticed she wasn't in their room by ten o'clock. Still, Lottie hurried back to her room as quietly and quickly as she could and burst through their door.

Cary Ann jolted in her desk chair and dropped her textbook. "I thought surely you were going to be late, but you're right on time." Her gaze followed Lottie as she set aside her bag and started unpinning her hair. "I had a whole story ready about you getting sick and needing to go out to the outhouse right away."

Lottie laughed. "Good idea. Disgust the teachers so they won't ask more questions."

Cary Ann picked up her textbook, the one for natural science class. Lottie fell back dramatically onto her bed, bemoaning the subject. "Science is entirely impossible. I'm going to fail Mr. Muller's exam tomorrow, I'm sure of it." An idea popped into her head, and she sat up speaking as if it were a revelation. "If I fail it abysmally enough, then he might completely excuse me from science studies."

Carry Ann was getting ready for bed, fluffing her pillows. "Oh, Lottie, I'm sure it won't be that bad."

"I am confident I will manage through life without being able to quote Newton and his laws." Lottie grabbed her gown from the drawer and quirked up one side of her mouth. "When I see a newly fallen apple, I take it and bite it, not stare at it and let it rot, wondering why and how it fell."

"What would you do, anyway, if you were excused from science?"

"I'd have more time to read and explore the campus and actually study my French book."

Cary Ann turned, gaping at Lottie with an incredulous smile. "But you don't need extra time to study French. Remember your scores last week? Some of the best students here don't have your knack for languages."

"Well, you're right about that." Lottie buttoned up her night dress. "Most girls here can't translate a French menu."

"Not exactly my point, Lottie. I hope you don't get excused from science. It's a wonderful way to study God's creativity," Cary Ann said dreamily. "He created this world—biology, physics, and all. The more I learn the science of a flower, the more I marvel at it and give thanks for it."

It took all of Lottie's strength to refrain from rolling her eyes. Last time the eye-rolling urge overtook her, Cary Ann sulked and ignored her for hours. Even though Cary Ann often disregarded the rule about silence and sleep after ten, she was much more obedient and pious than Lottie. She probably even enjoyed the mandatory sermons, songs, and prayers held at two of the sleepiest times of the day. Who thought that was a good plan?

Still, Valley Union was more than long days and mandatory chapel times. The studies were hard and the rules were strict, but this was the place she belonged. This was where Father had imagined her at school. Where else in all Virginia could a girl learn Latin, French, writing, math, and especially natural science? Although, Lottie wouldn't mind forfeiting the privilege of being taught that particular subject.

She glanced at her nightstand with a frown. There was usually a clean towel there.

"Peggy came and went while you were gone." Cary Ann pointed to Lottie's dresser. "She took some clothes for washing and left the towel and a water basin for you over there."

"Good, I want to at least look clean as I fail the exam tomorrow." Lottie crossed the room, dipped the towel into the water, and scrubbed her face.

"You won't fail." Cary Ann tucked into her bed and blew out her candle. "You've studied. You just need a good night's sleep. It'll be fine."

Lottie sat on her bed and blew her candle out too. "Only if I dream the answers."

CHAPTER EIGHTEEN

1854

Lottie needed some cheering up after Mr. Muller's science exam. She followed Cary Ann to the paved circle in front of the main school building.

Cary Ann gently patted Lottie's slumped shoulders as they walked. "I'm sure you'll get a passing grade. It's based on participation, and you certainly participated." Her lips twitched as if she was trying to restrain a smile. "What did you hope for in there?"

Lottie slowly shook her head and widened her eyes. "I don't know, but that wasn't it." The fresh memory of the exam's paralyzing difficulty splashed embarrassment through her chest. Lottie unbuttoned her coat and let October's chill cool her down.

A week before, Mr. Muller had told Lottie's class to be ready to discuss chapters four through eight in their natural science textbook for the exam. He had told them it would be like a class conversation. He would introduce different topics from the textbook, then randomly call on students to discuss them. If that student wasn't confident in the topic, she could choose another topic from that section of the textbook, as long as no one else had already talked about it.

When it came time for the exam, most girls addressed their topic well, then rambled nervously about anything they could remember until the teacher stopped them.

As class neared its end, Lottie hadn't been called yet. She had lots of practice in academic conversation with her tutors, but not in a conversation about science in front of the whole class. With only a few more minutes before the bell, Lottie had held her breath. But then, Mr. Muller finally called on her together with the other last two girls, requesting they tell the class about Isaac Newton's three laws of motion. Lottie's heart had dropped into her stomach.

Why hadn't she bothered to study those more? Her mind went back to holding her French textbook only to hide *Robinson Crusoe*, a novel she had already read so many times. She'd gotten so angry at herself, she could have stomped on her own foot. Her panic must have shown clearly on her face as Lottie signaled to the other girls to start the discussion. That had given her more time to think, but she still couldn't remember Newton's third law. And all of the similar topics that she did know about had already been covered.

Cary Ann kicked a pebble several feet ahead of them on the circle. "It was smart of you to discuss the history and implications of Newton's laws, rather than try to explain the laws themselves. But what was all of that about the Scientific Revolution and how science replaced church, and—what was it you said about the scientific method?"

Lottie heaved a sigh and quoted herself dryly. "'It gave the masses a way to discover the truth about themselves and the world instead of blindly accepting a faith handed down to them by their parents and grandparents.'"

Cary Ann flinched. "Ouch. Yes, that was it. You might get a personal visit from Mr. Cocke after that one."

"Or from Mary." Lottie nodded toward her cousin, who was quickly approaching them.

Mary waved. "Lottie! Cary Ann!"

They stopped to let her join them.

Mary bounced up to the girls. "I wanted to be sure you were all right, Lottie. That was rough in there. But I think you did a fine job with your answer."

"Thanks, Mary." Lottie lifted a small smile.

"It's ridiculous of them, anyway, to make us perform like that and learn every detail about science like the boys have to learn." Mary huffed. "It's not as if any of us are going to be doctors or chemists."

Lottie straightened and tilted her chin up. "Actually, my sister is studying to be a doctor right now. She's expected to know every bit of science as the male students. Women can learn to be anything these days."

Mary's face brightened, probably at something else to gossip about. "Of course, that's right. How is Orianna doing at school?"

"Very well." Lottie lifted her chin a little higher. "She said a few women have dropped out already, but she's sticking it out to the end."

"Capital!" Mary cheered. "If she becomes a female doctor, she won't need to marry. That's why I'm here. Father says he doesn't want any of us girls to marry and give up our rights. I'm supposed to become excellent in something so I can have an occupation."

"I want an occupation too." Lottie folded her arms over her chest.

"I'm sure there's one out there for you. You're a sharp, clever girl. But, of course, if you found a man to marry you, then you needn't worry at all about not being capable of learning science."

Lottie turned to Cary Ann and let her eyes roll freely this time.

Cary Ann quickly stepped between the two girls. "Mr. Cocke himself says young ladies require the same mental training as young men."

"Yes, yes, of course." Mary waved her off. "I believe women should be educated, too, obviously. I'm just saying there's no need to worry about performing at the boys' level in things like natural science, especially since your father never forbade you to marry."

Anger flashed through Lottie's chest and flamed across her cheeks. Mary had some nerve to mention Father. With great effort, Lottie held her tongue while Mary's continued to flap.

"Glad to see you're feeling better now, Lottie. You looked ghostly white walking out of class. Anyway, I must run and check on Rebecca Carlisle." Mary let out a giggle. "She's been walking around all week with a giant scab on her forehead. She must feel awful. Bye!"

Mary flitted away as quickly as she had come.

Lottie's tense shoulders collapsed and rounded on Cary Ann. "Can you believe her?"

With her eyebrows as high as they could reach, Cary shook her head. "That was tactless, what she said about your father. But, you know that's how Mary is. She doesn't mean any harm."

"Just because she doesn't mean harm doesn't mean she's not guilty of it," Lottie snapped. She wanted to spit on the ground, but that was probably against the rules. Her spinning mind couldn't remember the long list at the moment.

Cary Ann threw her arms in the air. "And what nonsense about science!"

"'Not capable,'" Lottie scoffed. "I must remember to tell Orie that one." Mary sometimes said ridiculous things, but she was still Lottie's cousin and friend.

The bell rang to officially start dinner, so Cary Ann and Lottie headed back inside. Lottie did remember to tell her sister in the next letter she wrote, and Orie responded quickly. At first, when Peggy brought the mail one morning, Lottie thought she got two letters on the same day. But Cary Ann snatched the other envelope.

"What are you doing?" Lottie asked. "That one is from my cousin Jimmy."

"I know. It's for me." Cary Ann's scarlet face looked away. "We write to each other sometimes."

Lottie silently questioned her through squinting eyes, but she let it go—for now. They sat across the room from each other on their beds and opened their letters. After a while, Lottie laughed and read aloud a portion of what Orie wrote.

"'Foolish people don't want us to think we're capable of anything beyond matrimony and motherhood. They don't want women to vote or work because then we'll realize we don't need men to do so for us. I'm surprised at Mary. She has obviously believed the lies fed to her. Be sure that you don't. Stay strong, little sister.'"

Cary Ann obliged Lottie with a smile, then returned to her own letter.

"I suppose you don't want to read out any of *your* correspondence?" Lottie attempted to add a teasing note to her question. "Is it full of love poems and heartfelt promises?"

Cary Ann dropped her hands in her lap and wearily cocked her head. "Lottie —"

Lottie lifted her hands in surrender. "No, no. You enjoy it. I'll read over here, quietly to myself."

Further down in her letter to Lottie, Orie wrote that Tom planned to practice medicine out West.

Once I get my medical degree, I'll go to wild and dangerous places, too, where they'll need my skills and not mind that I'm a woman.

Lottie looked up at the back of James's letter that was now fully blocking Cary Ann's face. "It's actually good you're forgetting about me now. That'll make it easier for when you leave me to marry him."

"I thought you were reading quietly to yourself," Cary Ann said from behind her letter.

As Lottie read the last line of Orie's letter, her face must've turned as ghostly white as when she'd left Mr. Muller's classroom.

You are capable of learning anything, Lot. People will tell you otherwise. They will say it's not appropriate or necessary to learn or do or say certain things. You must be diligent to learn everything placed in front of you, or you risk proving them right. Not only for your own sake, but also for the sake of all the girls coming up behind you.

Lottie slowly lowered the page onto her lap as Orie's words sank in. She hadn't thought about it like that. She wasn't only failing a science class. She was failing womankind.

Lottie was distracted through the rest of the day. Orie's letter tossed and turned in her head. She didn't answer the teachers' questions in her classes. She didn't engage her friends at meal times or break times. She quietly let the day happen to her, then went to bed early.

Later that night, after classes, evening devotions, and supper, Cary Ann stirred in her bed and sat up. She whispered in the dark. "Lottie?"

"I'm sleeping," Lottie answered after a long pause.

"You're sniffling—and loudly." Cary Ann wrapped a blanket around herself, then slid out of bed.

Lottie's weary eyes were adjusted to the dark and focused with no trouble on Cary Ann as she hobbled over and rolled onto Lottie's bed. "What is it, Lot?"

Lottie lifted her face from crying into her pillow and opened her mouth, but she couldn't say it. It took her a minute to get the words out between gasping sobs. "I'm not—working hard enough. I'm not d–doing well enough."

Cary Ann looked confused. Or maybe she still couldn't see in the dark yet. "But you *do* work hard. You're doing great here."

Lottie shook her head as she rolled onto her back. Cary Ann didn't understand. "Father was so proud of Orie for being special, knowing science and medicine." She roughly wiped her face and struggled to breathe evenly. "I can't even understand three basic laws, or even one of them. I have to get better, or I'll be incapable, just as Mary said—not as smart as boys are."

Cary Ann seemed more alert now. Her eyebrows furrowed as though she was angry, but Lottie knew she was just working her hardest to understand. "You know your father was proud of you too. And I don't think he wanted you to go to school and be just like Orie. I think he wanted you to go to school and become even more like you."

Lottie sniffled and spoke in a small voice that belonged to a much younger her. "Okay."

"I listened to your little speech in class. You understood so well how Newton's laws affected people and history."

"But I couldn't say what the laws were," Lottie whined.

Cary Ann sat up in a huff. "Lottie, it's okay. You can't know everything.

them."

Lottie reached for Orie's letter on her nightstand and showed Cary Ann the last paragraph that had sent Lottie into a worried fog all day. Cary Ann held it close to her face. After a moment, she tossed it toward the foot of Lottie's bed.

"I love Orie, but that's nuts. You don't have to learn *everything* just to prove you can. What if they offered a class about ... I don't know, underwater basket weaving?" Cary Ann waved her arms in the air. "Would Orie insist you master that one as well?" She leaned forward, smiling.

Lottie laughed. "No, she wouldn't."

"Are you sure?" Cary Ann teased. "It might earn more respect for our gender and inspire generations of women behind us."

They giggled at the idea of parading soaking wet baskets in front of Jimmy and Isaac back home.

Lottie breathed deep and relaxed. She should have told her friend much earlier in the day. "Maybe I'll ask Mr. Cocke about dropping science for next semester." A memory sprang across Lottie's mind. She sat up, facing Cary Ann. "I forgot to tell you! I heard about why he's always away on Sunday afternoons."

"Mr. Cocke? He preaches every Sunday night. I'm sure he prepares in the afternoons," Cary Ann said dismissively.

Lottie slowly shook her head, relishing her secret. "He takes his horse and rides over to Big Lick, five miles there and five miles back every Sunday afternoon."

"But why?" Cary Ann leaned toward Lottie and squinted.

"To teach a Sunday school class for servants!" Lottie's words burst out of her like water from a hot spring. "He teaches them the Bible and how to read and everything."

Cary Ann's jaw dropped, and her eyes bulged. "But that's against the law! Where did you hear that?"

"Peggy told me." She rushed on, savoring Cary Ann's surprise. "And when I helped Ann write that letter, she said her daughter learned to read from Mr. Cocke."

"Why does he try to teach them?"

Lottie shrugged. "Maybe it's the same as with us. Mr. Cocke just wants everyone to get the chance to learn—girls and servants too."

Cary Ann leaned back and grimaced. "Mother says they're not as capable of learning as we are."

"Mr. Cocke is a professional teacher and a really busy one." With shrugged shoulders, Lottie held both hands out at her sides, as if asking an obvious rhetorical question. "Why would he waste that much time every week if they weren't able to learn anything?"

"Even if they can read, I'm not sure they should. It's illegal." Cary Ann stressed each syllable of that last word. "I don't want to fight about it." She yawned, reminding Lottie how tired she was too. "You're not sad anymore, so we can sleep now."

Cary Ann gathered her blanket around herself again and rolled off Lottie's bed, back to her own.

Lottie flipped her pillow over to its non-teary side and settled in for sleep. "Laws, laws, laws. First Newton's, now Virginia's. Rules are more troublesome than they're worth."

Later that week, Lottie explained to Mr. Cocke in his office why she wanted to stop taking science classes. She stood as confidently tall as her four-feet-and-some inches would let her and said that she had accomplished what she could in the subject. She wanted to focus on learning other things. Mr. Cocke smiled kindly from behind his crowded desk and encouraged her to keep at it for now. He would confer with Mr. Muller about a final decision.

Lottie's stomach twisted in knots all day.

Immediately after devotions that afternoon, Mr. Cocke called her back from the crowd of girls rushing to the dining hall. Her heart jumped when he told her the wonderful news. She would be excused from further science studies after she completed that semester. She was free!

She joined her friends in the dining room, sitting next to Cary Ann and across from Mary, and another classmate, Julie Toy. Now that Lottie's anxious stomach had relaxed, she realized how hungry she was. The meal that evening did not disappoint. The slaves served them ham with rolls, corn, turnip greens, and stuffed eggs. A basket of red apples sat on each table. As they enjoyed the hot meal, slaves came around again with trays of ginger snaps.

Julie took a couple cookies, then grabbed an extra handful before the man moved the tray to the other girls.

Mary lifted an eyebrow at Julie. "I don't think we're meant to have that many cookies."

Julie looked haughtily at Mary. "It's like Mr. Cocke said this morning. 'God is faithful to just forgive us our sins.'" She popped a ginger snap into her mouth.

Lottie reached for an apple and held it to her nose. It smelled sweet. "It's 'He's faithful *and* just to forgive us our sins.' And you have to confess them first." She took a bite. Her friends froze and turned their heads toward Lottie.

She wasn't the kind of girl who usually quoted Bible verses at people for taking extra desserts.

A smile spread across Cary Ann's face. "Lottie, did you actually pay attention in devotions?"

Three astonished faces gaped at Lottie. She had shocked herself as much as she had clearly shocked them. Lottie stammered. "O—of course not." She shifted in her seat and mustered what sounded like casual confidence. "You know my mother. No one can escape her house without being forced to memorize a few verses. Besides, everyone knows that one."

They didn't question her further. Thankfully, Mary changed the subject. "Now that you're excused from science classes, you can practice French more —lean into your strengths."

"I've been thinking about that," Lottie said.

"Your strengths?" Cary Ann laughed. "How humble you are." She devoured a few of her own ginger snaps.

Lottie wanted to do something new with the extra time she would soon have, something challenging and interesting. It wouldn't break any school rules, but it might bend one. She leaned over the table and looked each of her friends square in the eyes in turn as she whispered, "I want to start a literary society, and I want you all to join."

Lottie proposed that as a real literary society, the group would gather regularly to discuss books and articles, probably on Wednesday afternoons during reading time. The meetings would be completely independent of teachers, unless the group decided to invite one to give a special lesson and join in the discussion. And as a literary society, it would be important to have a society library. So all the members should contribute books to share too. As long as they were considered scholarly literature—not novels— the group shouldn't expect any trouble.

It didn't take long to convince Cary Ann and the girls. It took the rest of the fall semester, however, to settle on a name.

Lottie came to supper one day with an idea. "We could be called the Philomathean Literary Society. It's Greek for 'lover of learning,'" she said while exploding her arms out to expand on her words. "Oops." She'd accidentally knocked a biscuit covered in raspberry jam right out of Julie's hand and onto her lap.

Julie shoved Lottie's arms away from her face.

Mary waved a napkin across the table at Julie. "Here, before it stains!"

Julie glared at Lottie as she snatched the napkin.

Lottie lowered her arms, sat back, and waited for her friends to be impressed with such a capital name. "Well? What do you think?"

Julie dabbed at the bright red spot on her dress. "Philo—what? How do you even spell that?"

"Don't worry about it. It's a literary society, not a writer's society." Lottie looked at Cary Ann for support. Julie was probably too angry to agree with Lottie on anything at the moment.

Cary Ann was nibbling on a piece of cheese. She set it down on her plate. "I also thought of a name to consider. The Euzelian Society. It's Greek, too, but it's about the zeal for good."

Lottie tilted her head.

Cary Ann pushed the basket of biscuits to Julie, who took one and ate it plain this time. "Because we'll read and discuss good things that make us grow, not just anything for no reason."

"Euzelian." Lottie listened to the sound of it. "Even better."

Cary Ann nodded, looking pleased with herself. Truthfully, Lottie preferred Philomathean. But, remembering a teary evening when Cary Ann had comforted Lottie and told her she didn't have to worry about learning every single subject in the world, Lottie didn't argue.

"Well, I'm not sure that one is any easier to spell, but I'm in," Julie said.

"So am I!" Mary leaned over the table and looked around the group excitedly. "What is our color?"

"Our color?" Lottie clapped a hand to her forehead. Organizing a literary society for only herself would have been much faster and easier. But deep down, she didn't want to start one alone. She wanted her friends to be involved, which apparently meant they needed to decide on a color.

Once the name and the color—green—was settled, they started meeting in the spring semester. By then, Lottie had convinced five other girls to join. All spring semester, most of those nine girls showed up to Euzelian meetings every second and fourth Wednesday before evening devotions in Mr. Blair's classroom. He was the rhetoric teacher and had allowed the girls to gather there, as long as they left the classroom exactly as they found it.

They continued meeting until the last couple weeks of school. Instead, Lottie spent every waking moment studying for the end-of-year exams. She made it through that last stretch in the school year and went home to Viewmont for the summer.

Lottie spent warm, bright summer days with her siblings and Cousin Jimmy, traipsing around the garden and through the woods then enjoying tea and books in the library. And there was a new baby to play with! Tom and Helen brought their new baby, little Tom, for a long stay at Viewmont this summer before they embarked on an adventure out West, where Tom planned to offer his medical talents. Despite the warm memories of that visit, by the time Lottie got back to school, her blood ran cold at any thought of Tom. When they came to mind, she would blink a lot and shove the stinging thoughts away.

When the Euzelian Society resumed meetings in the fall semester of the next school year, the group had nearly doubled. One new member in particular had been talking nonstop about joining ever since Lottie had described it at home during the summer break. Sallie had joined Lottie as a student at Valley Union and was warmly welcomed as a fellow Euzelian.

Similar to her first year at school, Lottie carried a new painful burden into her last two semesters. Grateful for a full schedule and plenty of distraction, Lottie determined to keep moving forward.

CHAPTER NINETEEN

1855

On the fourth Wednesday of October, Lottie wandered outside in the crisp afternoon, making her way to the main building. She meandered through a gust of wind that lifted fallen leaves and tossed them around her fluttering skirts and flyaway hairs like red and gold confetti, celebrating cooler days and the new school year. Lottie took a wide step to the left and stomped on a satisfyingly crunchy leaf. Resisting the urge to stomp on more of them, she picked up her pace to Mr. Blair's classroom. Cary Ann was sure to be there already because it was her turn to lead the group.

The Euzelian meetings meant more to Lottie than she had thought they would. She loved the extra reading and free discussion with her friends. It was exhilarating to learn so much without worrying about giving a proper, correct answer to a teacher staring at you down his glasses. The society was almost like talking with Orie back at home in Viewmont's library. A lump caught in Lottie's throat at the thought.

When she arrived, the girls arranged their seats in a circle so that it didn't feel like class. Lottie smiled as she sat next to Sallie.

Cary Ann stood and called the meeting to order. But before getting to the afternoon's discussion, she reminded the group about the decision from their last session that all Euzelian Literary Society members would wear a green ribbon during meetings—the same green as Hollins Institute, the school's new name.

Sallie leaned toward Lottie and whispered, "Why is the name different now? Mother still calls it Valley Union."

"Older students still call it that too." Lottie winked and whispered back. "The Hollins family donated money over the summer that apparently saved the school from closing."

Cary Ann coughed, clearly calling for Lottie's attention. She said that small gestures like wearing a green ribbon would show the teachers that their literary society was a peaceful part of the school, not a rogue group.

"Given the controversy of some topics we discuss and the rowdiness of some valued members here," Cary Ann said, looking pointedly at Lottie, "every little gesture helps our group build a respectable reputation."

Lottie responded by slowly tapping a green ribbon pinned to her dress. The other members joined in by holding out their green bracelets, hair ribbons, and pins. The two new girls who had asked to join this week leaned in and looked around at the options for displaying their own badges of loyalty to the group. During this unplanned fashion display, Lottie daydreamed about walking into some future meeting completely covered in green ribbon. It would be an expensive prank but worth it.

"Lovely, everyone." Cary Ann swept her hand toward the two newcomers. "I'm pleased to welcome our new members." They turned pink and smiled bashfully while everyone clapped. "Also, Mr. Blair agreed to join us at the next meeting and give a reading from Mr. Thoreau's *Walden, A Life in the Woods.*"

Many of the girls around the circle giggled at the mention of the school's most handsome teacher.

"Let's settle down," Cary Ann said with her hands on her hips.

"Hey!" Lottie immediately grabbed the group's attention. "Let's act as though we're a literary society and not a bunch of silly debutantes, shall we?" She nodded to Cary Ann encouragingly.

The circle hushed.

"Thank you, Lottie. As I was saying, after the reading, Mr. Blair will lead us in a discussion about existentialism and Thoreau's search for personal independence. That's all for announcements. Let's give a big thanks to Lottie for penning our latest article, which will be the topic of our discussion this afternoon." Cary Ann gave Lottie the floor amid a round of applause.

"Hear, hear!" shouted one girl.

Another pouted. "I didn't get to read it yet."

Cary Ann settled in an empty chair. "She's going to read it aloud, so we'll all hear it."

Lottie stood in the middle of the circle with her shoulders back and chin up. She raised her paper high enough to read it without covering her mouth. "The question. Do women have the same intellectual curiosity as men?" After every few lines, Lottie rotated to face all sides of the circle. The girls silently watched her, some in slack-jawed awe, others with pensive brows. Once she finished reading, she sat down and let Cary Ann moderate the discussion.

Julie stood first to give her thoughts, and the girls debated back and forth. They more or less agreed with each other, but they pushed each other further to clarify their logic and evidence.

At the end of the discussion, Lottie asked to address the group before it was time to leave. "One last item needs attention before we adjourn. These lively and deep discussions, which we all enjoy, are fueled by the resources we share, are they not?"

"Here she goes again," a girl murmured.

Lottie stood and raised her fist with fervor. "We must contribute to the group library. If we hoard our literary resources, thinking that we'll grow on our own, ahead of the others in this group, we're wrong." She paced around the circle with open, pleading hands. "When we share resources, we grow more, together."

The bell started to ring and cut short Lottie's speech. The Hollins bell rang exactly on the hour every hour, but somehow, it always seemed to ring too early for morning prayers and evening devotions, and far too late for meal times.

"Thank you, Lottie." Cary Ann glanced at her with a slight frown as she rose. "Everyone, bring in more books. Mrs. Greene will scold us all if we're late for devotions, so let's close this meeting."

The girls hurried out, but Cary Ann and Lottie lingered to make sure the chairs were back in their exact right place. They worked quickly and carefully.

Lottie grabbed two chairs from the edge of the room and set them where they were supposed to be. "Next time, we should tell the girls to move their own chairs."

"I agree." Biting her lip, Cary Ann flitted a look her direction. "You know, just because they aren't bringing in many books to share doesn't mean they're hoarding them."

"I know," Lottie said quietly. She hadn't meant to get that loud about it.

"Why is it so important for our society to have a library?"

Libraries and books had always been important in Lottie's home, especially to Father. Her heart suddenly ached for Christmas a couple years ago in the library with her siblings all together. It was the last Christmas that felt normal—before Orie went away to school, before Father died, and before Tom—. Lottie swallowed a lump in her throat. She shrugged. "We're a literary group. It seemed like a good idea."

Cary Ann must have noticed Lottie's eyes beginning to water. She crossed the room to Lottie. "You just seem a bit, I don't know, different lately. If you want to talk about what happened over the summer, I can listen."

Lottie roughly dropped the last chair in its right place, making Cary Ann shudder and take a step back. "What do you want to hear? Tom died hundreds of miles away on a boat, and I couldn't do anything to save him. That's all there is to it."

Cary Ann moved closer again. "You couldn't have saved your brother even if you were right next to him. There's no cure for cholera."

The muscles in Lottie's hands tensed. "I could have told him to leave the sick people behind and keep going west with his family."

"You know he wouldn't have listened to that. He went west to help people, and that's why he stayed on the boat."

"A lot of good it did! Now that he's gone, he can't help anyone, baby Tom lost his father, and I lost my brother." Lottie's pain-filled shouts sat heavy in the air. She hugged her arms tightly and turned away from her friend. Cary Ann still had her father. She didn't understand.

Cary Ann laid a hand on Lottie's shoulder. "Have you prayed about these things?"

Lottie threw her head back and spoke toward the ceiling. "Do not talk to me about God right now." She took a deep breath and looked down. "If I prayed, all I would do is scream, and he still wouldn't listen, anyway."

"Talking with God might really help."

"Why? Things don't turn out well even for people who pray and try to do what God says."

"That's not true, Lot."

Lottie rounded on Cary Ann. "We prayed for Father, and God healed him only to let him die two months later for no reason. Now my brother is dead because he got too close trying to help people with some contagious disease."

Cary Ann glanced nervously at the clock on Mr. Blair's desk. "We're going to be late. We should get to the chapel."

"You go. I'm not going. God does as he wills and so do I."

Cary Ann's eyes were shining now. "Lottie, that's incredibly rebellious to say, even for you."

Lottie surveyed the room where the Euzelian Literary Society had just gathered. The girls had free and open discussions of complex and controversial questions. They were growing and seeking knowledge together, without a man preaching Bible verses at them, telling them what to do. Lottie looked at Cary Ann with fire in her eyes. "This is my chapel." She grabbed her bundle of books, including a Nathaniel Hawthorn novel, and marched outside.

Lottie plopped under a tree, fuming. She opened *The House of the Seven Gables* and tried to read. Everyone at home had told her to go to God with her troubles—Mother, Pastor Fox, and now Cary Ann. But if God was real, then he was the one who brought all the troubles into her life. How could she trust him or even talk to him?

"Hello, Miss Moon."

Lottie jolted. She hadn't noticed Mr. Cocke walking over to her. "What are you doing here?" Shame instantly stung in her chest. That wasn't the Hollins way of speaking to teachers, especially the head of the school.

"I could ask the same of you," Mr. Cocke said with a smile.

Lottie stared at him, bewildered. Devotions couldn't be finished already. She looked down at her book. How long had she been trying to read that page?

"Pastor Gwaltney from Enon Baptist is preaching this evening," he explained. "I thought it would be a treat to hear someone different for a change."

"I've heard him on Sundays." Lottie glanced at Enon, the church across the road from Hollins. "I think I would prefer to stay out here with Hawthorne." She patted her book.

Mr. Cocke laughed. "I don't blame you. Mr. Gwaltney's a kind man, but he can be a dry speaker." As he lowered himself down onto the grass across from Lottie, she shifted.

Was she in trouble?

"I'm not going to make you go to the chapel," he said. "Actually, I'm glad I saw you out here."

"You are?"

"I haven't had a chance yet to give you my condolences." Mr. Cocke gave her a very sincere look of great concern. "It's a tragic thing what happened to your brother. I was sorry to hear of it."

Lottie froze. How did Mr. Cocke know about Tom? "Yes. Tragic."

"Miss Moon, I see that you're a brave and strong young lady, but if ever you feel the need to sit and talk, I can sit and listen. Or Mrs. Greene, if you like. She's not as harsh and prickly as she lets on."

Lottie's gaze fell to her lap as tears pooled in her eyes. "Thank you." A tear dropped onto the page, splashing her frustration and sadness across Hawthorne's words.

Mr. Cocke picked up a dry leaf, fiddling with it without crunching it. "I'm sure you've heard lots of condolences that come with advice. I hope at least some of them have been helpful to you."

Lottie relaxed her shoulders and sighed, still gazing toward her lap. "They tell me to pray and trust that God is still good even though people die." She shut the book, tossed it to the side, and locked eyes with Mr. Cocke. "But it's all so awful that I'm not sure God cares. How can he if he lets all of this happen?"

Had she shocked him? But he had nodded as Lottie spoke. He didn't seem offended. He was just staring up at the empty sky, fiddling with that dead leaf.

Mr. Cocke lowered his gaze to her and spoke slowly. "When sad things happen in my life, it comforts me to remember that God is sad about them too. You're right to remember that God lets things into our lives. The world isn't as it was meant to be. Evil is always going after people, trying to destroy them—even kill them. God has the power to keep that evil away or allow it to touch our lives when it serves his good purposes."

Lottie bristled. Her heart was beating fast. She wanted to stand up, tower over Mr. Cocke, and shut down such nonsense. "What good purpose is God trying to accomplish?"

Mr. Cocke leaned forward with a holy fire in his eyes. "Repentance—restored relationship with his beloved creation." He swept his arm around them, then poked a finger on the ground. His voice rose with passion, not simply volume. "That's what God wants. He wants people to know him. To make that possible, he allowed his own Son to be crucified—a very sad thing, was it not?" He didn't wait for Lottie to answer. "God can use every sad thing to draw people close so that they can know him and enjoy his strength, his goodness, and joy, even in the sad things." He paused and lowered his voice, each word still resounding with zeal. "I advise you to trust that God cares—more than you know."

Lottie sat silent, stunned. Her heart was still beating fast, but not in fury.

The fire in Mr. Cocke's eyes had reduced to the friendly twinkle he usually wore around the school. "There I go, adding more advice to the pile." He smiled. "Forgive me. You didn't come out here for a sermon."

CHAPTER TWENTY

1856

Lottie and the girls gathered in the study hall at their usual table. Unlike classrooms with individual desks, the study hall room held a collection of tables for quiet group study. Mrs. Green presided from her desk at the front.

Mary came in last and hastily set her textbooks on the table with a folded newspaper page on top. "Did you all hear the latest news from Kansas?" Before anyone could answer, she informed them, "Even though President Pierce himself said the pro-slavery government is legitimate, jayhawkers still won't back down about the election being a sham. It's getting violent, they say."

Julie grimaced. "I've heard that too. They're calling it 'Bleeding Kansas.'"

Lottie leaned over the table. "How did you get a Kansas newspaper?" She turned the paper around to read the headline.

Cary Ann took out her other book. "Why do you all read about such awful things?"

"My brother lives in Kansas now, so I like to stay informed," Mary said. "He's a newspaperman and sends us interesting copies."

"Study hall..." Lottie and the other three girls jolted at Mrs. Green's sudden appearance. "...is not for leisure reading."

"Yes, ma'am," they said in disharmony, breathless from the scare.

Lottie and Julie took textbooks from their bags as Mary packed away her newspaper.

Julie opened her book and spoke quietly, looking as if she were discussing the content on the page. "April Fool's Day is coming up. Anyone got any good ideas? My roommate is due for a prank."

"Isn't Elizabeth your roommate?" Mary shook her head in what looked like pity. "Shouldn't we leave her alone? She is having such a rough time with her family, after all. I heard her brother returned home after years in California, married to an Indian woman! I heard her parents are beside themselves, as you can imagine."

As Mary gossiped, Lottie savored a daydream of her April Fool's Day plan. It was the perfect prank that would surely allow not only her, but the whole school to skip morning devotions and maybe even the first class of the day.

Cary Ann grimaced at Mary and changed the subject. "I forgot about April Fool's. Last year it was on a Sunday. I remember it felt sinful to do any pranks on a holy day."

"Well this year it's on a Tuesday." Julie shrugged. "There's nothing holy about Tuesdays."

"I love April Fool's Day," Lottie said dreamily. "It's a perfect day for devils such as myself to revel in a little mischief."

Cary Ann looked exasperated at Lottie. "Please don't call yourself a devil."

Lottie held her hands out innocently. "But it's my name. That's what the D stands for— Charlotte Devil Moon."

Cary Ann and Julie gasped. Mary smirked and raised an eyebrow at Lottie.

"Shhh!" Mrs. Green frowned at them from the front of the room.

Lottie didn't say a word about her prank. Mary would end up telling the whole school anyway, and Cary Ann might try to stop her. Lottie needed the help of only one person, and she knew exactly whom to ask. She just hoped for a chance to talk with her before the big day.

On the Thursday before April first, Lottie sat hunched in her bedroom chair, tapping the sill by the open window as she watched for the washerwomen. When she spotted them walking up to Hollins in their Sunday best, as usual, to deliver the girls' clothes, Lottie's shoulders snapped back, straight and alert. They looked so poised, carrying the large laundry baskets atop their heads. Smaller than many of the washerwomen, Peggy still balanced her basket perfectly.

When she knocked on Lottie's door and walked in, Lottie hopped out of her desk chair and stumbled over a stack of books.

Wide-eyed, Peggy dropped her laundry basket, darted to Lottie, and helped her up. "You alright miss?"

"Of course." Lottie smoothed her hair and brushed her skirts. "Do you know where Ann might be?"

Peggy leaned back and eyed Lottie with a concerned frown. "Down the hall, I expect. She washes clothes for a few girls."

Lottie hurried out the door and down the hall. Her inner conscience, which often sounded like Cary Ann's voice, repeated the school's rule —*Students are not to fraternize with the servants.* She shoved it aside and continued searching for Ann. She found her in an empty room unloading a laundry basket. Perfect.

Lottie stepped in and closed the door behind her. "How did that letter turn out, Ann?" She spoke as casually as she could manage. But she didn't have another plan if Ann wouldn't help her. Asking Peggy would be too risky.

Ann turned from hanging dresses in a wardrobe. "Hello, there, Miss Lottie. Just posted it the other day, so I 'spect it'll reach Bettie real soon. I'm much obliged to you. If there's anything I can do in return, lemme know."

Lottie's heart leapt. As Ann picked up her basket and started to move on to the next room, Lottie nearly shouted. "Since you mentioned it... It's almost spring, but it still feels like the dead of winter at night, doesn't it?" She exaggerated a shiver. "Are there any extra blankets or bedsheets to spare?"

"Of course, Miss Lottie," Ann said cheerfully. "I'll leave some on your bed before the evening."

Lottie had secured the extra sheets! Everything was in order. It would have been much easier to ask Peggy for the extra linens, but Lottie didn't want to involve her. If the prank was traced back to Lottie, the teachers would surely assume that Peggy had helped her get the sheets. It was a harmless prank, really. Still, if the teachers got angry, they wouldn't think to ask Ann, and now Peggy would be innocent if she got interrogated.

The evening of March thirty-first started off like any other. Lottie sat at her dressing table in her nightgown as Peggy tied and set Lottie's hair.

"After the graduation in a couple months, we head back to Viewmont—this time for good." Lottie smiled at Peggy in the small mirror on her table. "Are you excited?"

Peggy beamed back at her. "Very much, miss. It's been a long while away from Mama and Papa and Viewmont. I expect you're excited to see your mama too."

"I am." Lottie often thought about home. It was impossible not to with Peggy and Cousin Mary around Hollins—and now Sallie. Her heart was starting to ache for a glimpse of Mother's face.

Peggy finished her duties for the day, wrapped her shawl around her, and headed toward the door. She paused and held it open, turning back to Lottie with a bashful smile. "I think my mama and papa gonna be proud of me. They never been this far off the plantation. I was scared at first, but I think I do good work here. Mrs. Cocke even told me so."

"Of course, you do good work," Lottie affirmed. "Your parents will be proud and happy to see you."

Lottie hopped into bed and slid under her extra mound of sheets and blankets. Fondness rose in her heart as she watched Peggy leave. Lottie was ready with her plan. She waited for midnight. Everyone would be sleeping deeply by then.

When it was time, she sneaked into the night, where the shining sliver crescent in the sky looked more like a restrained smile than a moon. If God was really up there, he must be smiling at her.

Lottie gathered up a bundle of bedsheets, then quickly shuffled toward the kitchen behind the west building—where the bell tower was. Lottie's past experience climbing through the kitchen window at home to make Sunday dinner proved helpful in reaching the bell on the kitchen roof. Once she shimmied through the window, she hopped down into the kitchen, made her way up the belfry, and wrapped half of the fabric around the bell's clapper and stuffed the rest into the bell.

She couldn't stop the bell ringer's faithful work, but those sheets should stifle the clanging sound. When the ringing bell was supposed to awaken the whole school at daybreak, all the noise would be muffled and meaningless. The slaves who worked in the kitchen were older. It would surely take them some time getting the bedsheet off the clapper. Then Lottie and everyone else could sleep peacefully into the April morning—hopefully, all the way through morning prayers.

She tugged on the knots to make sure the bell wouldn't simply shake off the bedsheets when it started ringing. They seemed thick enough to work and secure enough to stay put. Now all Lottie had to do was get back into bed without waking Cary Ann and try to sleep with excitement buzzing through her.

CHAPTER TWENTY-ONE

1856

At daybreak, Hollins Institute was silent—until the biological bells of some of the girls and slaves began to wake them.

A giddy frenzy gripped the school that day. In Lottie's first class, whispers and giggles created an undercurrent as students shared their experiences and theories of what had happened and who was responsible. The flustered teacher shushed the class so often that he seemed to struggle to focus on the lesson himself.

When Lottie received a summons to Mrs. Green's office, she tried not to smile the whole way there. She'd expected her reputation alone to land her on Mrs. Green's list of suspects. And she would confess if a teacher directly asked her about the bell. Whatever punishment she received would be worth it.

When Lottie reached the office, she found Mary sitting outside Mrs. Green's door. Lottie stopped in her tracks. "What are you doing here?"

"I have a meeting." Mary lifted her nose a little.

Lottie settled into a chair next to her. "Caught eavesdropping on teachers again?"

Mary didn't deign to answer the accusation. "What are *you* doing here?"

Lottie restrained a smile and bounced her gaze innocently around the hallway.

Mrs. Green called in Lottie first. "I have some questions for you about this morning, Miss Moon."

As Lottie followed her inside, she glanced back at Mary, who couldn't have looked more stunned. She mouthed silent words at Lottie. "It was you?"

Lottie winked, then shut the door behind her.

She confirmed Mrs. Green's suspicions that she was responsible for the bell tower prank. But when Mrs. Green asked where she got the linens for the bell, Lottie said she simply pulled them from her own bed. Mrs. Green raised a brow and asked if Lottie was cold, sleeping the rest of the night without bed linens. When Lottie said no, thankfully, she didn't push the question further. The plan had worked perfectly, except for Lottie getting caught. But at least Peggy and Ann weren't suspected.

Lottie went to her next class, then joined her friends in the dining room to celebrate the successful April Fool's prank. The gazes and whispers of girls all around the hall followed her. Mary must have already spread the word that Lottie was behind the morning's chaos.

"What did Mrs. Green say?" she asked as Lottie sat down next to her. "The door was shut, so I couldn't hear."

Julie groaned. "Will she force you into some awful cleaning task for punishment?"

"Will you have to study in solitude? Are you expelled?" As Mary leaned closer with each question, Lottie backed away.

Tears swam in Cary Ann's eyes. "Oh, Lottie, please say you won't be sent home."

Truly? They were *this* concerned? Lottie held her arm out as if trying to calm a flock of nervous hens. "Mrs. Green was steaming angry, but she said because the bell wasn't damaged, I wouldn't be dismissed."

Lottie's friends let out a sigh of relief and leaned forward for the rest of her story.

"Mr. Cocke was in there too. I'll lose a point in deportment and be given extra assignments to better occupy my mind. He said although my behavior wasn't destructive, it was 'highly undignified and void of any self-restraint.'" Lottie laughed.

"Well, it *was*." Cary Ann crossed her arms.

Mary shook her head. "Now all the teachers will think you're a troublesome girl. And most girls will write home about your prank."

"I sure will." Julie chuckled. "My brothers are going to love it!"

Lottie held her hands out. "Perhaps all of Virginia will think less of me. But wasn't it wonderful skipping over devotions and sleeping beautifully into the morning?"

A smile crept over Cary Ann's face.

Lottie took that as encouragement. "Hasn't today been fun? Seeing the teachers run frantic?"

"Watching the French teacher race around the halls with rags still in her hair was definitely a high point of the year." Mary giggled. "Students might tell that story years after you graduate."

"You could be a legend!" Julie threw her arms in the air.

As the group laughed, Lottie locked eyes with Ann across the dining room, carrying a tray toward the kitchen. Her expression hardened, then she hurried away. Did she think Lottie had betrayed her?

Mary turned to Lottie as if she had just remembered something. "I haven't told you what happened after you left."

"After I left Mrs. Green's?"

Mary nodded fast with a big smile. "They left the door cracked."

Mary said that Peggy was brought in for reprimanding too. Mrs. Green, Mr. Cocke, and Mr. Cocke's wife, who was in charge of the female slaves, were all in the meeting. Mary had peeked through the sliver of open doorway at Peggy standing in the middle of the room, hanging her head, shivering with fear. Tears fell down Peggy's face as Mrs. Cocke berated her for abetting such a disruptive, shameful activity.

Lottie's heart sank. Her hands turned cold. "But they can't prove that. Didn't Peggy speak for herself? Didn't she say she had nothing to do with it?"

"I didn't hear Peggy say a word." Mary answered Lottie's frantic query with wide, innocent eyes. "Besides, Mrs. Cocke didn't really need to prove anything, did she? She's in charge of the female servants."

But that wasn't all. While Peggy was in the office, two slaves, Hannah and Ann, came to Mrs. Green's office. Hannah chased after Ann, who was marching straight to the door with a fierce look in her eye. Mary said it was all so thrilling.

Hannah had caught up to Ann and pulled at her elbow. "Are you crazy? I didn't tell you so you'd go barging in there un'nounced."

Ann shrugged her off without taking her eyes off where she was going. "A girl Bettie's age won't take the punishment for somethin' I did." She paused at the office door for a moment, as if gathering up all the courage she had. Then she opened the door and told them what *she* had done, not Peggy.

The bell rang, ending Mary's story and the midday meal. Apparently, someone had finally loosed the linens and freed the bell's clapper. But Lottie couldn't move. Her stomach swirled as she reeled from all that she heard. Peggy was innocent but had endured such an awful meeting in Mrs. Green's office anyway. And Ann knew that Lottie had lied to her.

A strange conviction rose within her. She needed to fix things. But what should she do with the guilt that rose in her throat whenever she saw Ann?

Lottie mustered up enough courage to apologize to Peggy. The next time Peggy came to collect laundry, Lottie sat on her bed, picking at her nails while Peggy silently loaded her basket with Lottie's dirty clothes.

Lottie started to open her mouth a couple times before she finally broke the silence. "I didn't know you'd get in trouble like that."

Peggy paused her work only for a moment. She clenched a skirt as she added it to the basket.

Lottie rubbed her arm. "I thought by asking Ann instead of you, you'd be protected if the teachers asked you any questions."

Peggy lifted her basket, turned to Lottie, and sighed. "We slaves don't get asked questions, Miss Lottie. We just get told what to do."

If only Lottie could melt into her bed like a puddle. She couldn't undo the terrifying experience in Mrs. Green's office that she had brought upon Peggy.

After that, Lottie didn't contrive any more elaborate schemes to get out of going to devotions. She just stopped going.

Toward the end of the semester, Mother found out about Lottie skipping devotions when the school sent her a report. But, miraculously, Mother must have thought Lottie's point deduction in deportment was because she'd skipped so many devotions. Mother sent her a scathing letter, saying she ought to remove her from Hollins immediately and let her miss her own graduation, but in grace, she would let Lottie finish her schooling. Relief washed over her. If Mother had heard about the bell tower prank, that might have been one sin too many for Mother's grace.

One afternoon in May, Lottie and Cary Ann took a break from their studies to walk to the Botetourt spring. Its waters were supposed to benefit one's health. With exams approaching, Lottie would take any extra help she could get.

She jumped ahead a few paces and twirled with her arms in the air. "Aren't these woods refreshing? We're almost to the spring."

Cary Ann pawed at a leafy branch protruding into their path and pursed her lips.

Maybe the walk was longer than they'd remembered and the sun was hotter than expected. Maybe Cary Ann was just nervous about writing her speech for the graduation ceremony. She was the only student selected to write one. For whatever reason, she seemed on edge.

"They should have the graduation outside instead of in that stuffy church," Lottie said. "Wouldn't it feel glorious to receive our diplomas with the wind embracing us and a choir of birds celebrating us?"

Cary Ann grabbed a piece of fallen branch and used it like a walking stick. "They might not even allow you to participate in commencement. You've missed so many chapels already."

"Two dozen, and they haven't kicked me out yet," Lottie bragged.

"What if you miss my speech?" Cary Ann threw the stick back into the woods.

Lottie pushed her hair off her shoulder. "What does it matter?"

As Cary Ann whipped her head toward Lottie, she tripped on a stone. Lottie lunged to catch her friend's elbow. Cary Ann yanked her arm away and glared at Lottie, quoting her words back to her. "What does it matter?"

Lottie's mind scrambled. Clearly, she had offended Cary Ann. Why had she been so careless with her words? "I—I only mean that, well, you're not reading it. Isn't Mr. Blair going to read your speech on stage?"

Cary Ann looked down as she tapped the ground with the toe of her shoe. Lottie had to move closer to hear her small voice. "You know we're not supposed to speak in front of groups of men."

"They'll miss out. You read so well at Euzelian meetings."

A smile twitched on Cary Ann's face.

Lottie ventured to take another step closer. "I'm sorry, Cary Ann. I'll be at the commencement to hear your speech, no matter what."

Cary Ann lifted her chin. "Let's get to the spring first. Aren't the waters supposed to make us relax and perform wonderfully on our exams?"

"That's the plan."

"What's your speech about, anyway?" Lottie asked.

Cary Ann grinned. "All of us." That was all she would give away.

On commencement day, the Hollins girls gathered at Enon Baptist Church across the street. Graduates sat in the front pews while their classmates and families squeezed into rows behind them.

Mr. Cocke beamed with pride at the girls as he welcomed their families and a host of Virginia Baptist leaders to the ceremony. Throughout the event, some graduating students went up on stage and performed music, showing their skills with their flute or violin. Mr. Cocke and some other men addressed the crowd. Toward the end of the ceremony, Mr. Blair got up to deliver Cary Ann's speech. Despite his skill as a rhetoric teacher, he fidgeted and wiped sweat from his brow as he read about women's infinite capacity to learn and grow—how it needn't be stifled or confined to conventional female topics, but rather, when nurtured and challenged, a woman thrives—and not only the woman, but also her children, husband, and community.

Lottie's mouth hung open in a wide smile. She couldn't have been more proud to be Cary Ann's friend. The students, teachers, family, and other Baptist guests rigidly stared forward with polite smiles. They all seemed to finally relax as Cary Ann's speech took a turn, affirming that the best place for a woman to reside with this grand education was in the domain of her home, under the protection and leadership of her husband, rather than in the noisy and boisterous worlds of politics and business.

Lottie's mouth closed and her brow furrowed. Learn all you can, but stay at home? Confusion swirled in her mind. It was the same as when Grandmother was alive and Lottie and Orie lived in the tension of having access to a whole library and being told only to read so much.

When Lottie's name was called, she shook the memory away. She walked up to receive her French diploma and paused at the sight of a hundred girls all wearing identical white dresses with blue sashes, waiting their turn. They had worked hard over two years to earn these diplomas. Who knew what was next? Hopefully more adventures before they were confined to the domain of the home.

Over the sea of white dresses, Lottie's gaze found her family. Mother and most of Lottie's sisters sat toward the back, beaming at their graduate. Her tall brother especially stood out, looking very uncomfortable with a church half-full of smiling girls sneaking peeks at him. Lottie giggled and smiled back at her family, then returned to her seat and watched her friends get their diplomas.

After the ceremony, Lottie searched for Cary Ann, which would have been much easier if they weren't all wearing the same dresses. When they finally found each other, they waved wildly.

Lottie shouted over all the noise. "You would have delivered that speech better than Mr. Blair—or at least not have sweated so much."

They were laughing when Mary walked up to them.

Cary Ann stopped laughing immediately and touched Mary's arm. "I heard about what happened in Kansas. Is your brother safe?"

Mary took a deep breath. "Mother just told me he telegraphed that he's well. Although, his news office isn't well at all. They completely tore it apart."

Lottie winced. Barely a week before graduation, a pro-slavery mob had terrorized Lawrence, the town where Mary's brother lived. It had been in all the papers. They set fire to a hotel, looted businesses, and destroyed the printing presses at anti-slavery newspaper offices. After what happened there, an abolitionist named John Brown had rallied his own mob and murdered a bunch of pro-slavery farmers. That was just a few days ago. It seemed that the bleeding in Kansas wasn't stopping anytime soon.

As Mary told Lottie and Cary Ann more about what her brother had reported, other groups of fathers and brothers clustered together, whispering, probably about the same news.

"Why is your brother an abolitionist, anyway?" Cary Ann asked with a kind curiosity. "I thought your father owns a plantation with lots of servants."

Mary nodded. "He does. And I have plenty of other brothers who'd like to take it over. John said he wanted to go out West and try to make it as a journalist. He's not like these other abolitionists. He just says that as long as slavery exists, the only people who have a chance at success are wealthy landowners like my father. He didn't expect people to get so violent over it all. He said he wouldn't be surprised to see a war soon."

Lottie gasped. "A war in Kansas?"

"In all the states," Mary corrected.

Julie bounced up and wrapped her arms around Lottie and Mary. "Don't you all look cheery? We graduated!"

Lottie, Cary Ann, and Mary smiled awkwardly.

"I didn't want to leave without saying goodbye. My family is over there." She pointed to a group of young men near the door. "We have a special supper planned."

One of Julia's brothers who was facing them was particularly handsome. Lottie wrenched her eyes off him and embraced her friends in a tearful group hug. They all said goodbye and promised to write, then they went home with their families, taking a crisp new diploma with them, along with many happy memories of the past two years.

When Lottie and her family reached Viewmont, the summer sun still glowed faintly in the sky. As soon as the carriage stopped, Peggy got out and ran straight to her mother. Fannie buried her face into Peggy's hair and clutched her tight in a tearful hug. Lottie lingered outside with Mother and Ike around the garden table while Eddie chased Sallie and Mollie down toward the flowers. Orie had another year at medical school in Pennsylvania before she could rejoin the family at home.

Over the years, Viewmont had seen loss and change, yet its beauty and happiness somehow survived. Lottie's heart swelled, and she let out a laugh. How could a war ever break out in beautiful Virginia?

Chapter Twenty-Two

Summer 1856

Fifteen-year-old Lottie didn't have a plan for life after Hollins. For the first time in over two years, she stared ahead at an indefinite portion of time with nothing in particular to do.

"You have a French diploma," Mother said, dipping her quill into the inkwell on her desk. "Teach the girls French." She smiled at Lottie and went back to her correspondence.

Lottie had always taught her younger sisters whatever she was learning, but never a real lesson. Gaining more teaching experience might be useful if she were ever to make a career of it as Mother had once suggested.

She taught the older girls French and Latin and how to write English clearly and persuasively. Eddie was only five years old, so Lottie focused on teaching her to read English. Eddie was a darling student who listened to Lottie and clutched her pencil with all her might as she practiced the alphabet. Her little face screwed up with determination. Lottie told her that Father had looked just like that when he was thinking hard, which brought a smile to Eddie's lips.

Sallie, on the other hand, acted as though she didn't need Lottie because she was going back to Hollins soon for her second year. Mollie followed Sallie's lead. Maybe being a teacher wasn't such a good idea.

On a sunny morning in June, Lottie sat in her chair at the library table crossing her arms. Her sisters had pushed her to exhaustion during their lesson. "Try the sentence again."

"I already know those words." Sallie wrinkled her nose and pushed the Latin book to the middle of the library table.

Mollie sat back and crossed her arms. "Me too."

Lottie groaned and unfolded her arms. "But you're using them incorrectly." She stood, leaning on the table with her head down between her shoulders. She was about ready to give up and leave the room. Spending the day outside would be infinitely better than this.

Thankfully, Ike wandered over from his spot in one of the velvet chairs across the room and surveyed the lesson. He stroked his clean-shaven chin, nodding. "I'm impressed. What you're teaching here is what we learned in my third year at school."

Lottie lifted her head as he spoke. He smiled as he patted her back. Her gaze followed him as he went to work in the study. Since Ike had passed the bar exam last year, he had moved back to Viewmont and had been helping Mother run the estate. He had also continued courting Meg. He was nice to have around.

Lottie turned to Sallie with renewed energy. "See? If you listen to me, you'll get a head start before you go back to Hollins, *and* you'll know more Latin than any of the boys your age."

Sallie pursed her lips, then smiled.

From then on, Lottie's lessons went smoothly. Of course, her class size shrank when Sallie returned to school in the fall with Peggy, but Lottie gained her third student back quick enough. In November, a terrible outbreak of typhoid spread around Hollins. When two students died from the illness, Mother brought Sallie and Peggy back home immediately.

At first, Lottie's extravagant amount of free time was as jarring as it was welcome. Like unlacing a corset, she could breathe and move more freely. Even if Hollins hadn't been infested with typhoid, she found plenty of reasons to not miss university—sleeping in her own bed, for one. She also enjoyed more opportunities to roam and read.

But being at home wasn't the same as before she went away to school. Lottie had changed. She wasn't content anymore to fill her afternoons with lounging in the garden, browsing the library, and sipping tea in the parlor with her family and visitors. She still enjoyed those things, but she craved more now, which was hard to talk with Mother about. There was too much to explain about what the Euzelian Society meant to her, how she relished learning languages with other students, and how she couldn't forget the way

Mr. Cocke prayed and preached so differently from what she had heard growing up at Scottsville Baptist Church.

"You all sat in a classroom and read even outside regular class times?" Mother said after Lottie tried to tell her how she missed the Euzelian meetings. Mother shook her head in amazement. "You must be relieved to rest your mind at home."

Lottie mustered a smile while a longing twisted in her stomach. Her friends at school would understand her right away. She never used to feel as though she had to explain herself before—not at home. Lottie's studies and experiences over the past two years were like new parts of her that her family had to get acquainted with. At least there was plenty of time for that now that she was home indefinitely.

An unexpected announcement from Helen, her brother's widow, further interrupted Lottie's ability to concentrate on lesson plans. Helen was going to remarry and move to Alabama with little Tom. Lottie's head spun at the news. Her only nephew, her strongest connection to her brother, was moving so far away.

Helen had said she wanted her son to spend this Christmas with his Viewmont family before they left. Mother planned a special holiday supper. When it was time to eat, everyone made their way, laughing and talking, from the festive parlor past the evergreen-wrapped staircase and through the hall, decked with wreaths, to the dining room. Candlelight glowed in the room and sparkled against the gold-rimmed plates. All the bouncing curls, beautiful dresses, and bright ribbons added to the decorations.

Ike pulled out a chair for Meg, who had recently become his fiancée. Lottie sat between him and Jimmy, who was home from the University of Virginia and had apparently grown the beginnings of a mustache while he was away. Mother hadn't invited many people to this Christmas supper, but she had invited Jimmy, probably to help Ike not feel completely outnumbered as the only man. Orie, who was home for the holiday, sat across from Lottie and next to Sallie and Mollie, who were already giggling about something together. Helen maneuvered around the room gracefully, despite her fashionably wide hoop skirt. She and Tom settled nearest to Mother at the head.

Fannie and Peggy served a gorgeous Christmas feast complete with creamed potatoes, candied yams, and a golden turkey—the biggest anyone had ever seen.

Once Isaac gave a heartfelt prayer of thanks, nothing stopped the group from digging in.

"I've been so focused on school lately, I feel I've lost touch here," Orie said between bites of green beans. "What have I missed?"

Mother raised her eyebrows as she sipped from her glass. "I'm sure you already know everything important from my letters."

"Yes, but that's it—you write about the big, important things. I want to know all the daily happenings—every tiny detail." Orie grinned around the table as if inviting stories.

Ike cleared his throat. All eyes turned to him. "You may not know, I've decided to become a Baptist. Officially."

Margaret smiled proudly and reached for his hand.

Orie spluttered. "Well, that's no tiny detail."

Sallie shrugged and reached for the gravy. "Your prayer did sound different."

Lottie gaped at Ike, stunned into silence. Ike had never seemed to dislike going to church as much as Orie and Lottie, but Lottie would have never guessed he was actually interested in becoming a Baptist like Mother and Father.

With shining eyes, Mother beamed at her only living son. "How did this happen?" Her voice broke.

Ike explained, still holding Margaret's hand. "A buddy of mine from the university took me to Charlottesville Baptist Church one Sunday. That's where the school chaplain, John Broadus, preaches. I took to his preaching and went back to the church a few times before committing my heart to God. Of course, I looked into other denominations before settling on joining the Baptists. It's all been sinking in while I've been home. I just wrote to Broadus to tell him."

All these years, Ike had sat through the same sermons at Scottsville Baptist Church that Lottie had without walking down to the altar. What about John Broadus made Ike want to finally join the church? Did Mr. Broadus preach like Mr. Cocke?

Mother reached for a napkin and dabbed her eyes. "Oh, son, this is the best Christmas gift you could ever give me."

Ike's face flushed. "That same buddy of mine..." Seeming eager to shift such attention off himself, he changed the subject. "He's marrying one of our neighbors over the Christmas holidays. You remember Mr. Thompson's eldest daughter?"

"I do." Orie snapped her head toward him, bouncing the ringlets that framed her face. "She's sure to have a magnificent event."

"No more so than yours will be." Helen smiled at Margaret and touched the black stone in her broach that was pinned to her fan-front bodice. "Weddings at Viewmont are wonderfully beautiful."

A hush fell over the room in remembrance of the last Viewmont wedding.

Orie shifted in her chair. "All this talk of weddings is the most I've heard in years. When we're in school, it's the furthest thing from our minds. All we talk about is studying, and all we think about is graduating with perfect marks. The teachers say anything less would only be an excuse for a medical practice to not hire us."

"I love talking about weddings," Mollie said dreamily, spinning a pea in her spoon.

Sallie giggled. "Jimmy probably likes talking about weddings, too, but he never gets to at home—not with four sisters all committed to singleness."

Jimmy ducked his head over his plate and blushed.

Mother darted a suspicious glance at Sallie. "What's this about?"

She smirked. "At Hollins, Cary Ann Coleman got lots and lots of letters from Jimmy."

Jimmy cast a hurt, accusatory look at Lottie.

"I promise, I didn't tell!" Lottie pressed a hand over her heart, pleading for Jimmy to believe her. How did Sallie find out about those? Lottie wouldn't put it past her little sister to have snooped around her and Cary Ann's room at school.

Jimmy lifted his head high and defended himself. "She's my close neighbor and a friend."

But Sallie wouldn't quit pestering. "We live closer, and I never got any letters from you."

Mother raised a firm hand as well as a commanding voice. "That's enough. This is a nice family meal—let's enjoy it as though we are a nice family."

Sallie and Mollie snickered.

"You two will enjoy it in silence until we're done," Mother added.

With Sallie and Mollie quiet, the rest of the family finished the meal in peace, then moved back to the parlor for Christmas gifts and games.

Lottie stood with Orie and Margaret by the crackling fire. They chatted and sipped Christmas punch while watching Mother and Helen help Tom open a present across the room. The drink cooled Lottie's warm cheeks and gave off a perfume of cranberry and cinnamon.

Margaret cupped her glass of punch and shifted closer to Lottie and Orie. "Will Jimmy's sisters really never marry?" It wasn't easy to hear her whisper.

Orie shrugged. "They promised their father, and they still haven't married yet."

Margaret nodded solemnly. She glanced down at the fire, as if uncertain if she wanted to ask another question. She looked at Orie. "Will you do that too?"

Lottie sipped her punch and fixated on the group opening presents. She had asked her sister that before and knew Orie didn't ever want to marry.

Orie hesitated. "If I find a good-natured man who loves me and can keep up with me, I might be persuaded to marry."

Lottie whipped her attention back to Orie and Margaret, spilling some red punch onto her dress. What did Orie just say?

"But..." Orie held out a firm finger. "He must genuinely admire my ambition, not just tolerate it or think it amusing. Otherwise, I won't bother with marriage."

"You're not afraid at all of a life of maidenhood, are you?" Margaret said in awe. "I think that's very brave."

"I believe you're the brave one." Orie laughed, handing over her glass when Peggy hurried over with a damp napkin for Lottie. "You must be if you're going to marry into this family and take me on as a sister-in-law."

Lottie stared at her sister while dabbing at—or somewhere near—the stain. Orie probably only said she'd consider marriage because Margaret and Helen were both getting married soon. Maybe Orie needed someone on her side to say what she really thought—that she'd never marry. Lottie chimed in. "I don't plan to marry. Not ever. I can't imagine a man so wonderful that I'd exchange my independence for him. I'm going to have a meaningful life of adventure, and no man will keep me from it."

Margaret smiled and laid a gentle hand on Lottie's shoulder. "You say that now, but you might meet such a man one day."

Lottie narrowed her eyes, heat rising in her chest. She wrenched away. "I do say that now, and I mean it."

"You two are an impressive pair." Margaret snickered. "I'm grateful my children one day will have such strong aunts."

Lottie crossed her arms and looked across the room, to where her younger sisters took turns holding little Tom and showing him Christmas toys. Orie hadn't agreed with Lottie as she'd thought she would have. How could Orie have changed that much? Orie had said herself that she never thought about weddings and marriage while away at school. Not only did Lottie feel she had to explain herself to her family, but now it was as if she didn't know them.

Mother stood and addressed everyone in the room. "I would like to take a moment and give thanks for the blessing of this special evening."

Lottie rolled her eyes to the ceiling and grumbled. "We already prayed and read the Christmas story before supper."

"Yes, dear," Mother said, looking instantly exasperated. "I meant the blessing of this special group of people." She softened and looked around the family as she spoke. "Gathered here are the people who are dearest in the world to me. Although, ever since Edward and Tom passed on, our group is smaller than we'd all wish. But we've been blessed to know and love Helen and little Tom." Mother pulled Helen closer in a one-arm hug. "You'll always be part of this family, and we send our love with you as you start a new life in Alabama."

"Thank you." Helen beamed at her, though she wiped her eye. "We will stay in touch."

Mother raised her glass and turned to Isaac, who had joined his fiancée by the fire. "We look forward to welcoming Margaret next month, although you're already my daughter in my heart. Isaac has brought me not only another daughter but also much peace in managing the business. Then there are my darling girls who, one by one, are going out into the world and meeting success. And dear Jimmy, who has been more of a brother to you all than a cousin. Indeed, 'the Lord gives and the Lord takes away.' Although he has seen fit to take away much, tonight I look around at you all and remember how much he has given. And I want to say, 'blessed be the name of the Lord.'"

Isaac raised his Christmas punch in a toast. "Amen, Mother."

Mother certainly hadn't changed at all. She'd been quoting Bible verses to the family all of Lottie's life. After Mother's blessing speech, Lottie moved away from Orie and Margaret. Thankfully, she found an open space next to Helen on the sofa.

Mother joined Eddie on the rug, playing with little Tom. Lottie's heart swelled as Mother lifted Tom in the air and Eddie made silly faces at him. He giggled and squirmed in delight. Lottie stored up the memories to treasure for the years her nephew would grow up somewhere else. Mother pulled him in for a snuggle.

Tears stung Lottie's eyes, threatening to overcome her, but she set her face and clutched her dress. She turned to Helen and nearly whispered, "We'll always love you and little Tom. I won't forget you when you leave."

Helen reached over and held Lottie's fist full of fabric. "I know. I promise to remind him where he comes from and that there are wonderful people in Virginia who love him very much."

Lottie's tears triumphed and fell down her cheeks. A promise of her own was rising from her heart. She wiped her tears away and looked Helen square in the eyes. "If anything should ever happen to you, I want to care for him. I will get a good job as a teacher so I can support him."

Helen smiled and squeezed Lottie's hand. "Lord willing, Tom won't need to claim it, but I have no doubt that you would take good care of him. I see how you love him."

Lottie relaxed her grip and embraced Helen. She was more committed than ever to working as a teacher when she got older.

Chapter Twenty-Three

1857

Orie missed Ike's wedding in January, but he missed her graduation in February, so she didn't let herself feel too guilty. The newlyweds were still on their bridal tour, visiting family, while Mother and Orie's sisters traveled to Pennsylvania to witness her graduation. The Moon family alone nearly outnumbered the graduates.

One by one, Orie and the other six young women crossed a platform, pausing to shake the dean's hand before taking their diploma to the other side of the stage. It was a simple ceremony, but the fact that two of the seven graduates were the first women from the South to earn a medical degree added a historical importance to the usual graduation pomp.

"You were really the first one," Lottie told Orie on the train back home. "Since that girl from South Carolina walked up after you, you were really the first Southern woman to get a medical degree."

Orie smiled at her sister. Her heart fluttered as she thumbed the roll of smooth parchment with her name inscribed on it. Shouldn't it have felt heavier? Shouldn't the whole car have erupted in cheers once she boarded with it in her hand? That diploma was a dream come true—something she had worked toward for years. But the baggage man had taken her luggage without notice, and she'd waded through the aisles to her seat without even a simple congratulations. Even though no one outside of her school and her family knew what that parchment meant, it made her special. If only she felt as special as it proved she was.

When Orie returned to Viewmont, all the Moon women were once again under one roof. But the house wasn't always occupied solely by women. Her brain froze when she heard that Mother had hired Nicholas again to tutor Sallie, Mollie, and Eddie. How was Orie to deal with that?

Lottie put her hands on her hips as they confronted Mother together right after they learned the news the first week in March. "Is my teaching so insufficient that you had to hire a tutor for them?"

"He's mainly going to teach the girls music, not languages," Mother said. "They still need you, especially since Hollins is still closed."

Lottie pursed her lips but dropped her arms to her sides. "Very well."

Orie had her own reasons for not wanting Nick around, of course, reasons she didn't explain beyond having a general dislike of the man.

Mother tossed her hands up at that protest. "But you loved him when he tutored you."

Orie froze.

"You grew so confident in your studies and did so well at Troy."

Orie breathed again. She had only told Father how she felt about Nick. It wasn't as if she'd wanted to keep a secret from Mother. She just hadn't wanted to talk about it right away. Then time had gone by. Father had obviously kept his word if Mother was inviting Nicholas back into the house.

Viewmont was a large estate. It should be easy for Orie to avoid their tutor —if only she wasn't so fond of the library.

Nicholas was giving a lesson in the library one April morning when Orie walked in. She halted immediately. She could quietly back out of the room, but Nicholas and her sisters were looking at her. Even Lottie sat at the other end of the library table.

Orie's legs had gone too numb to move, anyway. Heat flushed through her body, and she suddenly needed to wipe her hands dry. She clutched at her cotton skirt. "You're still here?" Her voice croaked. "I must have gotten the time wrong."

Nicholas stood and sent her a wide smile. He looked just as handsome as ever. He kept his hair longer and more relaxed than before. A tuft of curls entwined at the top of his head and lightly touched his face. "I hear congratulations are in order. Your sisters tell me you've just completed your medical degree. Well done, Orianna."

How calm he was. Orie absorbed the shock and addressed him as casually as if she had never loved him or kissed him before. "Yes, I'm quite pleased. I suppose I owe much thanks to you, even though I graduated sixth out of seven." No need for him to feel too proud ... for tutoring her *or* for leaving her.

"You've done a historic and brave thing." Nicholas held his hands open. "You did the work. All I did was give you some books and get out of your way."

"You weren't in my way," Orie snapped.

"I wish you were first in your class." Sallie groaned. "The valedictorian's speech was awfully boring—not a thing like Cary Ann's. Now that was a capital speech, wasn't it, Lottie?"

"Yes, one she deserved to give herself." Lottie giggled. "Although I have to admit, it was fun watching Mr. Blair give a women's rights speech."

That piqued Orie's interest. "She spoke on women's rights?"

Lottie nodded. "About women's intellectual curiosity—how it's the same as men's and needs to be nurtured and challenged in order to grow."

"Well done, Cary Ann!" Orie cheered. "If women stay focused, we can learn and accomplish anything."

"Indeed!" Nicholas raised his hands as if to applaud.

Orie shot him a vicious look, and he dropped them. He was not welcome on her side, not even if they agreed.

Lottie leaned forward onto her elbows. "But at the end, Cary Ann said that once a woman learns everything at school, her proper place is at home."

Orie shook her head. "What an odd way to end such a speech. A woman's place is wherever she plants her feet."

Lottie sat back and smiled. "I like that."

Mother came in as Orie spoke. "Well, Sallie, Mollie, and Eddie's place is here, learning their lesson from Nicholas." She raised her eyebrows at Lottie and Orie. "Is there something else you two could be doing?"

"I'm observing Nicholas since I'm going to be a teacher one day." Lottie tapped her pencil on her notepad.

"I need to write some inquiries about jobs. I just came in for the medical dictionary, but it can wait." Orie turned to leave with an air of great importance. She paused at the doorway and looked back over her shoulder, catching Nicholas's eye.

His plan had worked. They didn't marry, and now he was a successful tutor, and she'd made history with her diploma. Was he happy? She gave him a small smile, which he returned before they both turned away.

She didn't regret going to medical school, but it had cost her. Now it was time to leverage her new degree into a job. Surely, that would make it all worthwhile.

Starting a career in medicine was more difficult than Orie had imagined. By the fall, she still hadn't found a job, but she kept sending letters. She even sent one to Uncle James and Aunt Julia, asking if there were any opportunities overseas for educated female doctors.

It had been over half a year since graduation, and she was living almost the same as she had before. The hope of her prestigious new degree was slowly being crowded out by dread that it didn't matter at all. She had the qualifications and the passion, just not the opportunity to actually practice medicine.

One afternoon in early October, she ran outside to screams and found Lottie and Cary Ann gaping at Jimmy, who was writhing on the ground and clutching his shoulder. Apparently, he had fallen on it wrong, walking along the short fence by the garden—probably showing off for Cary Ann. Orie got to put her knowledge to good use and reset it. But that was the extent of her medical practice.

Her sisters, on the other hand, were thriving.

After almost a year at home, Sallie was finally going back to Hollins with Peggy. Mother had received a letter from the head principal himself, all about the school's commitment to health and the adjustments they had made to prevent a disease outbreak from happening again. They'd even advertised in newspapers. One major adjustment was the new, separate accommodations for the slaves, as if they and their homes had been to blame for spreading typhoid on campus. Now, the slaves would live much farther away on an old field beyond the woods.

Lottie had some excitement on the horizon too. Mother had decided to send her to the new Albemarle Female Institute in Charlottesville. Ike said that his pastor, John Broadus, was instrumental in starting it. Apparently, the school went by the University of Virginia curriculum, so Lottie could add to her two-year degree from Hollins and earn a full university education. She would start the next fall and be in the school's second-ever class.

Virginia Baptists were progressing and starting girls' schools, but they weren't ready to have a female doctor just yet. In fact, it seemed that not many people in the States were willing to have a female doctor. Orie might need to go even farther away for that.

CHAPTER TWENTY-FOUR

1858

Lottie laced up her boots and pulled on her coat. Cary Ann had already left their dorm room and said she'd meet Lottie in front of the main building for their new-student orientation.

The rough transition from Hollins to home had smoothed into a pleasant and productive past year at home. Lottie had gained valuable experience as a teacher. Now Eddie could read, and Mollie's writing had greatly improved. Between Lottie's and Nicholas's efforts, Sallie would return to Hollins as prepared as though she hadn't been away from school for almost a year. And Lottie had been given the exciting opportunity to continue her own education at Albemarle Female Institute—with Cary Ann, Mary, and Julie.

Lottie scurried out the door. When she spotted Cary Ann leaning against a stone half wall outside the education building, Lottie waved and made her way over. A young man was marching straight up to her. Had he thought she was waving to him? She picked up her pace and fixed her eyes ahead at Cary Ann, but he didn't seem deterred.

The stranger walked up to both of them and looked at Lottie with a wide grin. "Miss Charlotte Moon?"

Once he got closer, he looked familiar. Where had Lottie seen him before? She had noticed men from the nearby University of Virginia coming to ask the principal if they could call on the older students. He didn't look as young as those boys, but he didn't seem as mature as the institute's teachers either. She scowled at him. "How do you know me?"

The man took a respectful step back. "Please forgive me for being direct. I asked someone to point you out to me." He removed his hat and dipped his head. "I'm Crawford Toy. Pleased to finally meet you. My sister has told me a lot about you."

"Your sister?" Lottie had never experienced a more confusing introduction than this one. She glanced at Cary Ann for help, but she seemed just as bewildered by this man.

"Julie. Julie Toy. She told all of us at home about your time at Hollins."

The fog in Lottie's head instantly cleared. He was Julie's handsome brother that Lottie had noticed at their Hollins graduation. Now that she had a better grasp on the conversation, she relaxed. "Yes, of course. It's good to meet you. This is another friend of Julie's, Cary Ann Coleman."

Crawford nodded to Cary Ann, then leaned closer to Lottie with playfully narrowed eyes. "Did you really climb a belfry and stuff it with blankets just to skip devotions?"

Lottie blushed. "What a wild tale. Have you heard that one, Cary Ann?"

"Yes, but I heard the girl used towels, not blankets," Cary Ann said.

Lottie clasped her hands behind her. "Whoever she was, she must be a free and adventurous spirit."

"And brave," Crawford added. "If ever she were to continue her schooling here, I, as a teacher, might need to keep an eye on her."

Lottie's heart fluttered. She tried to restrain a smile. "Yes, you should."

Cary Ann coughed, breaking the moment between Lottie and Crawford. "What subject do you teach, Mr. Toy?"

"Natural sciences." His eyes were still fixed on Lottie.

Lottie nodded and forced a smile as if someone had very kindly offered her a disgusting treat. "Fascinating subject."

Crawford bowed again and put his hat back on. "It was delightful to meet you, Miss Moon. Miss Coleman. I believe the orientation is starting soon. I'll see you in class."

Lottie's gaze followed him as he walked into the building.

Cary Ann giggled. "Think you'll take up science again?"

Lottie tilted her head. "It might be worth another try." She shrugged. "You never know. A new teacher could make a real difference."

"Yes, I'm sure a teacher like him will make all the difference." Cary Ann nudged Lottie and looped her arm around hers. "C'mon, Julie and Mary are saving us seats."

In the large classroom, Lottie and Cary Ann took the two empty desks behind their friends. They were all just in time for the start of the orientation.

Lottie tapped Julie's shoulder and whispered, "You didn't tell me your brother was a teacher here."

Julie turned around and rolled her eyes. "One of the founders with Mr.

Broadus too. I'm sure he's already found you and told you. He just graduated and is so proud of this job. It's all he talked about at home."

"He did, in fact, and he also said that *you've* been talking plenty at home, too—about me."

Julie scrunched her face. "What?"

Cary Ann shushed Lottie and Julie, who were growing louder the longer they whispered. "People are looking. Shouldn't we wait at least a few days before getting into trouble here?"

They quieted down to listen to Mr. Hart, the principal at Albemarle Female Institute. He spoke about Virginia Baptists' new endeavor to educate young women with the same academic standards as young men, and how it was an opportunity for their generation to grow and formally study things that women before them never had the chance to. He charged them to read, think, and study diligently in their years at the school.

As it turned out, Lottie learned more about Albemarle from the returning students than from the orientation. Everyone said the school's first year was a trial in more than one sense of the word. They didn't have as many dorm rooms, and they had to gather for classes in the basement of Charlottesville Baptist. Now that the school had moved into a renovated building up the road from the church, sixty girls could live on campus, and there were ample classrooms. The school was also close to the general store, which was convenient for when they needed treats.

The older students all seemed thrilled that a dog they had befriended last year had followed them to the new building. The white dog was exceptionally friendly and furry with big dove-gray spots on its ears and back. He roamed the schoolyard, accepting treats and pats on his head. Lottie enjoyed his playful presence. He seemed to think of himself as the girls' guard dog, growling at some of the young men who came to call from UVA, which Lottie approved of.

She might have flirted with Crawford, but she had been caught off guard when she met him. The plans for her life did not involve suitors.

One Sunday afternoon in the middle of October, Lottie walked into her room and found Cary Ann, Julie, and Mary crowded around an unusually large book.

Julie popped up and smiled. "There she is. You can help us. You're capital at languages, and—" She squinted at Lottie and laughed. "Is that hay in your hair?"

"I was reading out by the haystacks." Lottie searched for the straw stuck in her hair. "What are you doing?"

Cary Ann beamed at her. "Mr. Broadus preached a wonderful sermon this morning."

Not this again. Lottie crossed the room and set her book down on her desk. Mr. Broadus preached most Sundays at Charlottesville Baptist Church, on top of founding AFI and being the chaplain at UVA. Everyone thought he was brilliant. Lottie was growing so tired of hearing how amazing his sermons were, she just might develop a twitch at the mention of his name.

"We're looking up disciple in this book." Julie flipped it closed for a moment and read the title on the cover. "'*Liddell and Scott's Lexicon, Greek to English.*'"

Lottie paused and peeked back over her shoulder. They were searching through a Greek dictionary? Maybe she could borrow it when they were done looking up Bible words.

Mary came to sit on Lottie's bed next to her desk. "You should have seen the number of people who went up to the altar after his sermon. Mr. Broadus talked all about the Great Commission in Matthew 28, how Jesus called all of his followers to make disciples and baptize people in all the nations. It was incredible! I noticed several AFI girls go down and give their lives to missions."

"He talked about missions?" Lottie tried not to look too interested, but some long-forgotten ember warmed in her heart. Of course, foreign missions was a popular topic discussed and celebrated in Southern Baptist churches. But it felt personal and special to her, as though she wanted to take the word out of the air and keep it in her dress pocket.

Cary Ann traced the lines of text in the book with her finger as if they held the key to all knowledge. "He mentioned that we don't have a good verb in English for *disciple*, so we're looking up what it means in Greek. Come and see. You would love this."

Lottie didn't move. She sat at her desk and unclipped her purse from her belt. No need to encourage Cary Ann, making her think Lottie was interested in studying the Bible. Foreign missions travel, maybe. But not the Bible.

Julie glanced up at her. "You should come to church with us next week and hear Mr. Broadus for yourself."

Lottie cackled at the invitation. "I was better occupied this morning reading Shakespeare than sitting in church listening to a preacher. I'll happily attend Mr. Broadus's school, but I have no interest in his church."

Cary Ann shook her head. "You can't ignore God your whole life, Lottie."

"He doesn't seem to mind," Lottie mumbled.

Cary Ann looked at Lottie with pure pity on her face.

Lottie glared back at her. "I'm here to learn about more important things.

You heard Mr. Hart at the orientation. We have an opportunity to learn things that other women throughout Virginia—throughout history!—couldn't even dream of. So no, thank you. I will not be wasting time filling my head with Mr. Broadus's sermons or searching Liddell and whoever's lexicon to decipher Bible mysteries."

Lottie's friends gasped, but they didn't have time to respond before she stormed out of the room. Her feelings were too big to stay indoors. She stepped outside and filled her lungs with brisk autumn air. It cooled the heat rising in her cheeks. She had forgotten her coat but wasn't going back in to get it.

She marched away from the dormitory, holding her arms. She passed several trees, looking for the one maple tree with a groove in its trunk that fit her back just right. It was the most beautiful one on campus too. Some of the leaves on its top and edges had already started to turn red.

Lottie had learned in Crawford Toy's science class that the first leaves to change were the ones farthest from the tree's roots. The lack of nourishment made them fade from green to fall's vibrant colors—a beautiful but short-lived demise. Then, even the faintest wind could send them skittering from their branches.

The sound of barking quickly grew louder and closer. Lottie looked all around, and that white dog was right behind her—the one that all of the older girls loved. It didn't seem angry, but it barked and circled around her, not letting her move forward, almost as if it was trying to herd her back to the dorm.

"Not now!" Lottie tried to shoo the dog away. The mad thing wouldn't stop barking at her.

"Miss Moon!"

Lottie looked up. Crawford grabbed a stick from the ground, then waved it around and whistled at the dog. That got the creature's attention. Crawford tossed the stick clear across the yard, sending the dog off on a chase. Lottie steadied her breathing and straightened her skirt as Crawford walked up to her.

"That dog sure was fixed on you," he said with a smile. "You must have some dried meat in your pockets."

"Only bits of hay." She found another straw and pulled it out.

He arched a brow and leaned his head forward, so she told him what she had done that morning and what had happened with her friends when she got back to her room.

"Well, I won't argue against a morning spent reading Shakespeare." He tucked his thumbs behind the suspenders at his chest. "But I applaud your friends for researching. Too often, I think, we misunderstand the true meaning of Scriptures. English sometimes doesn't fully convey the depth of the original Hebrew and Greek words. I often find it helpful to read passages in their original language."

Lottie made a face. "Maybe you would like to join them."

"I'm content right here, talking with you." He offered a relaxed smile.

Lottie's cheeks burned, despite the chill in the air.

He swept his arm out toward a walkway. "Join me for a walk?"

She fluttered her eyelashes and nodded. "Where to?"

Crawford breathed deep and lifted his shoulders. "Anywhere and nowhere."

He held his hands behind his back and kept to her pace as they walked around the campus. It was easy to forget that Crawford was a professor. Since he was a new graduate, talking with him felt more like talking with a friend than a teacher. When he mentioned the Bible, he spoke about it in an academic way that Lottie could tolerate. He didn't pressure her or seem to expect any certain answer from her. They reached a fork in the path, and Lottie smiled and led them to the right—it was longer.

Lottie studied hard all semester and developed a reputation for excellence in languages and writing. She also became known for her determined refusal to humor anything religious. By the time Christmas break came, she felt like collapsing as one did at the end of a race. The students scattered to their family homes across Charlottesville and Virginia to rest and celebrate the holiday.

At Viewmont, Lottie treasured time with Uncle James, Aunt Julia, and her cousins as they visited from Israel. It was good to see them after eight years apart. She was beginning to imagine Uncle James's signature at the bottom of a letter when she thought of him rather than his face.

Uncle James said that after they had received Orie's letter, he made some inquiries about how the people in Israel would welcome a female doctor. The need for doctors was great enough that Uncle James confidently invited Orie to visit, not only as his niece but also as a professional doctor with work to do. Orie had never expressed the slightest interest in being a missionary, but she had been at home and unemployed too long to turn down the offer. Since no one in Virginia or any other state would hire a woman to be a doctor, Orie prepared to join Uncle James and Aunt Julia on their next voyage back to Israel in January.

When it was time for Orie to leave Viewmont, Lottie squeezed Orie good-bye. When would she return? Or would she never? "You can't get enough of faraway adventures, can you?" She released her grip. "First to the North, and now across the ocean."

Orie kissed Lottie's head and drew back. Her eyes were shining. "Once I settle in, I'll write about when you can come join us if you like."

Lottie's eyes widened. She might finally get a chance to follow her sister on an adventure.

Back at school, while Lottie grew in her studies, Julie and Cary Ann grew in their faith. They even started a prayer group on campus. Mary sometimes attended the group, but Lottie never did.

Through the semester, something was shifting in Lottie's relationship with her friends. Cary Ann seemed to tiptoe around Lottie when anything about God came up in conversation. Julie stopped sharing all the things she'd said God was stirring in her heart.

One morning, Cary Ann and Lottie found a spot outside where they could lay a blanket down and study together. Before they opened their books, Cary Ann asked again if Lottie would visit their prayer group that week.

"The weather is getting nicer, and we're going to meet outside, just like this," Cary Ann said. "It might be fun."

Lottie didn't take her eyes off sorting her notebooks from her textbooks. "It would be more efficient to toss a coin into a magic well than sit around telling God my wishes for an hour."

Cary Ann snatched a notebook out of Lottie's hand and slammed it onto the blanket. "Stop saying those things!"

Lottie jolted and stared at Cary Ann. "I thought we could be honest with each other. We're close friends."

"How can we be close when you dismiss and laugh at the person who is most dear to me?" Tears suddenly fell down Cary Ann's face. "I'm committed to being your friend. But I love Jesus, as ridiculous as that seems to you. It's not fair that I listen to you about things, but you won't listen to me talk about him or come even once to my prayer group."

Lottie spoke quietly. "I do listen to you. You just want to change me."

"It's not me who wants to change you, Lottie." Cary Ann's words spoken so quietly fell heavy on Lottie's heart.

"I can't change." She plucked a piece of grass and tore sections off, bit by bit. How could she move forward out of this awful moment with her friend? "Let's just study."

Cary Ann sniffled and nodded. They opened their books.

"Then let's take a walk like friends do," Cary Ann said. "Julie and I planned to walk later today. Will you come?"

Lottie looked up with a pained smile, wanting to say yes to anything Cary Ann suggested. "Yes, I'd like that."

Neither Cary Ann nor Julie mentioned anything about God when they walked by Charlottesville Baptist Church with Lottie. They just kept chatting along the roadside, heading nowhere in particular.

"Has Jimmy talked with your father yet?" Julie's question pitched high with excitement.

Cary Ann turned red. "We haven't even talked with each other yet about getting married. Well, at least not much—not in detail."

The bells from Charlottesville Baptist told them it was four in the afternoon and time to start walking back to campus.

Julie sprinted a few steps ahead and spun around, facing Cary Ann, pointing at the belfry. "The church bells are ringing for you already!"

Cary Ann looked longingly at the church, then shook her head. "Enough about me and Jimmy. I want to hear more about you and John."

Julie sighed at the mention of her beau while Cary Ann and Lottie caught up with her. "We've spent time together for almost three weeks now, and I still like him. He's wonderful, really. Crawford was shocked at first, but he's getting used to the idea of me with his university pal. John is in his final year of school, but they still get together." She brightened and turned to Lottie. "Speaking of Crawford, what about you? Any suitors strike your attention lately?"

"My attention is focusing on becoming an accomplished academic and teacher," Lottie said with her nose in the air.

"Are you sure you wouldn't want to also *marry* an accomplished academic and teacher?" Julie leaned on Lottie's shoulder, bouncing her eyebrows.

Lottie tried not to smile. "I have no idea what you're talking about. I have no plans to marry, and I have no suitors, which perfectly suits me."

"Well, if you change your mind, Hope sure has enough suitors." Julie rolled her eyes. "I'm sure she could spare one or two."

"Or all," Cary Ann added gravely. She turned to Lottie. "Hope is the one who let us borrow her lexicon."

"I've seen her." Lottie stepped ahead of Cary Ann, making room on the sidewalk for a passing couple. "She's very beautiful."

"She's also very talented in Greek," Cary Ann said. "She wants to teach and travel, like you. She doesn't want to marry."

Lottie maneuvered back beside Cary Ann. Her eyebrows came together. "Then why does she see any suitors?"

"In our prayer meeting last week," Cary Ann said, pausing for a second as if to check Lottie's face for any sign of offense, "Hope said her father insists that she makes a good marriage. She's going along with it until she can figure out what to do. It all seems very hard on her, and she asked for prayer."

Lottie only nodded. She made sure not to pounce on Cary Ann for bringing up the prayer meeting. She had never seen her friend explode as she had a few hours ago. Lottie didn't want to drive her friends to that point of frustration ever again. Cary Ann had always forgiven Lottie when she said something out of line. After that morning, a nagging fear sat heavy in the pit of Lottie's stomach. If she didn't change soon, she could lose her friends.

From that day on, she resolved to live more peaceably with them. She held back her laughter when they told her they were praying for her. She didn't heckle them when they talked about Mr. Broadus's latest sermon.

Lottie also showed more and more interest whenever Julie and Cary Ann borrowed Hope's massive lexicon. Lottie hadn't formally studied Greek yet, but she wanted to dive into that book and learn every word. By November 1858, she had earned a degree in Latin from Albemarle Female Institute, but she wasn't going to stop there. If she learned Greek, too, she could better understand ancient works of Hesiod and Homer. Then she could show her friends there were more benefits to studying Greek than just researching Mr. Broadus's New Testament sermons.

CHAPTER TWENTY-FIVE

1858

O ne Sunday evening in December, Lottie studied alone in her room. Cary Ann and a bunch of other students from AFI were all at Charlottesville Baptist Church for the start of the revival. Mr. Broadus was going to preach a service each night that week. Of course, Lottie had no interest in the revival. Even if she had wanted to see what it was all about, exams were coming up before Christmas, and there was so much to study.

After a certain point, though, Lottie needed a break from her textbooks, so she reached into her desk to open Orie's latest letter—all the way from Israel. She'd received it earlier that day and had been saving it for a treat. She put away her textbooks and freshened up her cup of tea. She unfolded the small paper.

October 13, 1858

Dear Lottie,

It may surprise you to read how happy I am here in Jerusalem, as I never set out to be a foreign missionary. But you know it was a hard year for me after my graduation. You watched me write all those job inquiries and study to maintain my knowledge, hoping that someone somewhere would hire me to practice medicine. I did all I could do, but

I still couldn't move forward. I love our home, but I felt hopelessly stuck. Getting on that ship with Uncle James and Aunt Julia seemed like the only open door. So I walked through it, and I'm glad I did! I'm starting to suspect it was God who made it happen.

That line will surely have surprised you too. I'm learning more about the wonder of God's ways. It's amazing here. Last week, Uncle James helped heal a Jewish man with a simple chemical compound, and he decided to follow Jesus right then! After a lifetime of unbelief, his heart was changed. It was incredible. I see now that God truly cares, and he cares for everyone.

I'm getting much use out of my medical education here. People are less particular about whether a man or a woman helps heal them. It's as if they see me as a Western doctor first and a woman second. As long as I uphold their ideal of the first, they'll overlook the second.

Lottie didn't finish the letter before she shoved it back into her desk drawer and slammed it closed, shaking her teacup. More about God! And in a letter from Orie?

Dazed from the letter and exhausted from studying, Lottie got ready for bed. She didn't wait for Cary Ann to get back from the revival service. Right as Lottie was falling asleep, Cary Ann slowly opened the door and walked in.

Lottie yawned. "It must have been a long sermon."

Cary Ann jumped. "Sorry, Lottie. I tried to come in quietly. I saw it was dark in here and thought you'd be sleeping. Since you're awake ... yes, it was a wonderful sermon." Her whisper was full of excitement. "I know you aren't interested in church, but this revival is special. You should come next time and see for yourself. Oh, and they're hosting prayer meetings each morning of the revival week. Julie, Mary, and I are going. You can come with us if you want."

Lottie's foggy head was spinning to keep up with what Cary Ann was saying. "Have you gone crazy? I don't go to church or prayer meetings. Least of all, in the mornings."

Cary Ann didn't say another word. She just got ready for bed and went to sleep.

When Lottie woke up in the morning, she looked over and saw that Cary Ann's bed was empty. Lottie hit her pillow. No matter how sincere her resolution, she couldn't help but hurt her dearest friend. Cary Ann hadn't invited Lottie to church in months. This revival must be something that she really wanted to share with Lottie.

Lottie sat at the desk next to Cary Ann's in their first class that day and leaned over to her. "Did I offend you so much that you didn't want to see me in the morning? I'm sorry. I don't know why I say those things."

Cary Ann turned to look Lottie in the eye. "I wasn't in the room because I woke up early for the prayer meeting. We all prayed for you, Lottie. And I will keep praying for you, no matter what."

However silly a revival seemed to Lottie, she needed to go to the next service. It would be a small gift to such a great friend as Cary Ann.

"And just so you know," Cary Ann said as the teacher stood up to start the class, "you say those things because that's what's in your heart."

Class started before Lottie could defend herself, which was just as well because she didn't have anything worthwhile to say back.

That night, the girls scanned the chapel for enough seats where they could all sit together. Once Mary found four in a row, she nearly ran to grab them. The room was full, not only of AFI students, but also some teachers, UVA students, and other people Lottie had never seen before. Once they settled in their seats, Lottie noticed Crawford Toy a couple of rows ahead. He turned around and offered a genteel smile. She smiled back.

When it was time, Mr. Broadus took the pulpit, opened a Bible, and started reading from the Gospel of Matthew. He read about God's kingdom where those who mourn are comforted and the meek inherit the earth, where the pure in heart see God and his children are peacemakers.

Lottie squirmed in her seat. It all sounded beautiful. She even craved it, but she felt so disconnected to it. She had mourned and not felt comforted. She wasn't meek or a peacemaker, and her heart wasn't pure. Was that why she wasn't blessed in the ways Mr. Broadus preached about?

Mr. Broadus continued reading about how anyone who is angry with someone or lusts over someone is guilty of murder or adultery. And if God's people are hurt or offended, they are not to retaliate.

Now people besides Lottie shifted uncomfortably in their seats. One man on her row bowed over his lap with his hands clasped behind his head, and the prayer time hadn't even started yet.

Mr. Broadus looked up at the crowd. "The way of God isn't easy, is it?"

"Amen," responded several people in the crowd. More silently nodded.

The preacher went on to read about how God cares for his people, clothes them, and feeds them. They have no need to worry with the Lord as their

God. Lottie listened closer when Mr. Broadus said not to worry about your life because God will provide what is needed. He stepped out in front of the pulpit and quoted Matthew 6:33 from memory. "'But seek ye first the kingdom of God and his righteousness, and all these things shall be added unto you.'"

He leaned toward them as he preached. "None of us can do these things on our own." More *amens* erupted from the crowd. "It's not easy to trust in God day in and day out. It's not easy to follow his ways. But when we repent and believe in Jesus Christ, our hearts will be changed. He will be forever with us, and the Spirit of God who then dwells in us will be all and more of the power that we need. God tells us through the Apostle Paul in 2 Corinthians, 'My grace is sufficient for thee. For my strength is made perfect in weakness.' Friends, God is good, and he is for you. As we continue what I sense will be a truly impactful week of revival, I implore you. Trust in the sufficient grace of God. Let it wash over you, fill you, change you completely, and strengthen you."

When Mr. Broadus opened the altar for prayer and repentance, seats emptied all around the sanctuary. Lottie flattened her back against her pew, her heart pounding into the wood. She gripped the edge of her seat and didn't let go until her friends agreed it was time to leave.

Lottie didn't say much on the walk back to the dormitories. It was late, and after two days of early-morning prayer meetings and late-night revival meetings, Cary Ann went straight to bed. Lottie laid her head back onto her pillow and closed her eyes, willing sleep to come. She didn't want to think about what the preacher said or how it made her feel.

Her eyes popped open at the sound of barking. That dog must have wandered over to the campus again. Cary Ann didn't seem to notice it. She was sound asleep from the moment her head hit her pillow. Lottie waited and waited for the dog to go away or at least to be quiet. Whatever it was barking at must have scurried away by now.

Lottie flipped onto her stomach and covered her ears with her pillow. The creature had to be barking straight at the wall of her dorm. The pillow wasn't working. She flipped back over and stared at the ceiling, trapped with only her thoughts about how her heart had pounded when Mr. Broadus read from Matthew, and how her gut had felt hollow, even hungry, when he spoke of grace. Was there maybe something to all of this faith stuff? Something real? Even Orie was writing about God.

Lottie shook her head. She had to be losing her mind from exhaustion.

Tuesday morning, Lottie woke up, so she must have slept. Across the room, Cary Ann was getting ready for the prayer meeting. Lottie found herself stepping out of bed and getting dressed too.

Cary Ann paused and faced Lottie with a puzzled look. "Where are you going this early?"

"To the prayer meeting." Lottie dug through the back of her desk drawer for the Bible that Mother had made her bring.

That was all Cary Ann asked. She must have been shocked. Lottie sure was. But she never knew anything more clearly than that she needed to go to this meeting.

When they showed up, Julie and Mary started waving to Cary Ann, then slowed to cover their gaping mouths when they noticed Lottie beside her. Cary Ann sat down with the group. When whispering girls flocked to her, she shook her head and shrugged her shoulders.

Meanwhile, Lottie kept marching straight up to Mr. Broadus, who was standing off to the side with a couple other men. She said she had some questions for him. He kindly invited her to sit on a nearby bench.

Despite the early hour and her lack of sleep, energy coursed through her body. She tried not to burst her arms out or shout her questions. Why couldn't she make herself be kind and peaceful on her own? Why was her heart more angry and prideful than it was pure? How did God's "sufficient grace," as Mr. Broadus had called it, fix all of that?

He listened to her with a pensive brow until all of her words came out. "You've heard the phrase 'simple, but not easy.'" He smiled. "Salvation is simple, but it sure isn't easy. That's why God did most of the hard work."

Lottie leaned in, her eyes squinted in skepticism. "But what was 'the hard work'? People have told me my whole life to trust God. What am I supposed to trust about him?"

"All those things you said you can't fix on your own—those are sin." Mr. Broadus matched her earnestness. "Sin is what gets in the way of people being with God, and it has a heavy price to pay off. But because God loves us and wants to be with us, Jesus came to pay the price that settles our debt. He came to cleanse us from all that sin. That's why he went to the cross and the grave, and came back to life—so that we can know God and be with him forever. It's all because of love, you see?"

Lottie nodded silently, slowly, at the ground by her shoes. She understood deep down, maybe for the first time.

"And all that's required of us is to choose him by believing and trusting that what he did is enough. Do you think that you, a young lady with clearly a great intellect, could submit to something so simple? Do you want to trust in Jesus, Lottie?"

Lottie met his gaze. How could he look so peaceful when she felt so torn and tortured? Her heart had been at war for a long time. Last night, it had twisted and burned with the fury of a final battle. Now that the billows of smoke were clearing, she could see the victor.

That night, even before Mr. Broadus could finish inviting people to the altar, Lottie stood, made her way down the aisle, and shared her decision with the whole sanctuary. She confessed that Jesus Christ was now and forever the Lord of her life and the Savior of her soul.

Cary Ann, Julie, and Mary clutched each other, watching her with tears in their eyes. Many in the congregation gaped and then cheered.

The next day, Wednesday, December 22, Lottie prepared to be baptized by Mr. Broadus. Her friends asked if she would wait a few days. Then her mother and more of her family could come see it. But Lottie was adamant.

"I need to do this now," she said. "I've waited long enough to come to Jesus. I don't want to wait any longer to make our relationship public."

That afternoon, Lottie waded into the frigid Rivanna River with Mr. Broadus as a crowd of her AFI classmates and members from Charlottesville Baptist Church clutched their wool or fur coats.

He laid a hand behind her back and whispered, "It'll be quick. I'll save the sermon for this evening."

She nodded as her teeth chattered.

Mr. Broadus lifted his voice and asked if Lottie had trusted in Jesus as her Savior. She shouted "yes" then held her breath as he plunged her into the waters. After a crash, everything went silent. In what must have been only a split second, she was as still and breathless as all the loved ones she had ever seen in a coffin. Strong hands lifted her up and she burst through the surface. Lottie gasped for air and laughed as the crowd whooped and shouted. She had been dead for the past eighteen years. Now, she was alive.

When Lottie went home for Christmas and told her family what happened, Mother burst into tears. The tears continued throughout the holiday. At times, when Lottie sat minding her own business, reading her Bible, which looked new but was actually several years old, Mother looked at her with a sweet smile under watery eyes. At one point, Mother got it in her mind that Lottie might be pulling a prank on her. But Mary came by and confirmed the whole thing. Lottie Moon had indeed become a Christian.

"And baptized at the Baptist church?" Mother asked, dabbing a handkerchief to her eyes.

"Yes, Mother, I'm a Baptist now," Lottie said. "There's even a record. I can take you to the church secretary to see it if you'd like."

Mother took Lottie's word for it, which was backed up with a whole new demeanor. Lottie was still herself, but something deep was different about her, as if she had an unshakable peace.

CHAPTER TWENTY-SIX

1859-1860

Everything was different for Lottie, not only because she was following Jesus now and was finally, truly free, but also because so much had changed around her. After two years at Albemarle Female Institute, Cary Ann and Mary had completed "enough" school, as their parents had told them. They did not come back for the fall 1859 semester. But Julie Toy was still a student, so Lottie could still share a dorm room with a familiar friend.

Lottie missed the daily camaraderie with her old friends, but she now enjoyed their letters. She did not miss science class, which she wasn't taking anymore. Dropping the subject wasn't as easy a decision to make as she'd thought it would be. Lottie had actually done well in Crawford Toy's class. She understood the content and performed much better than she had at Hollins. Maybe the teacher really had made the difference. While it was reassuring to know that she could succeed in the subject if she had to, she would never be a scientist if she could help it.

Of course, Julie teased that Lottie only dropped the class because Crawford wasn't teaching it any longer. He had been appointed by the Southern Baptist's Foreign Mission Board as a missionary to Japan. But first, he had to prepare at the new Southern Baptist Seminary in South Carolina. Mr. Broadus left AFI for South Carolina, too, as a founder of the new seminary.

With two dear friends, a favorite teacher, and her pastor and mentor no longer at AFI, Lottie had plenty of spare time to get to know her new friend in Jesus. She focused much of her free time on studying Scripture and attending worship services under the new pastor at Charlottesville Baptist Church.

However, on a mid-October evening, she and Julie were excited to see their old pastor, who was back in Charlottesville for a special service while the seminary was on fall break. The church planned to take up an offering for Southern Baptist missionaries. With Mr. Broadus back in town, it was sure to be a full sanctuary, but Lottie and Julie didn't hurry, as a couple of gentlemen had promised to save them seats.

The sun was setting earlier on these autumn days. Lottie and Julie walked toward it on the way to the church. Julie whistled as she kicked a fallen pinecone down the road. Lottie touched the leather chatelaine purse clipped to her belt which contained the half-cent coins she had saved for the missions offering. That whole month, she and Julie hadn't bought any ice cream from Hazel's, their favorite restaurant in town, so they could give more to support the missionaries. As they got closer to the church, Lottie clutched her Bible and notebook to her chest—the one with a marbled cover that held all of her church notes from the past several months—and nibbled her lip.

Julie slung her arm through the crook of Lottie's. "Are you looking forward to seeing him?"

"Of course, we haven't heard him preach in months."

Julie frowned for a moment, then smirked. "You know who I mean."

Lottie let out a nervous laugh. She knew Julie wasn't asking about Mr. Broadus. But what could she say? "I don't know how I feel about seeing Crawford. We never really got going, not like you and John." She didn't know what he wanted or what she wanted in that relationship, and she had no clarity on what God wanted.

"But he always seemed sweet on you. And he asks me about you. He's asked John about you too."

Julie sounded as though she was trying to encourage Lottie, but it only made her more frustrated. She held onto her books but dropped her arms in exasperation. "Why doesn't he ask *me* about me?"

"Doesn't he write to you?"

Lottie's heart stung, and heat rose in her cheeks. She looked away. "He hasn't."

It was hard enough to catch her own dreamy thoughts about Crawford and remind herself of the obvious truth that he wasn't interested in her. Julie's insistence that Crawford fancied Lottie only made it more difficult.

"Oh." Julie's eyebrows sprang up. Then she frowned at the road ahead of them. "Maybe he doesn't know what to ask you. He's going to Japan for who knows how long. It's not as if he could ask you to marry him and be the mistress of some homestead he's setting up somewhere outside of town."

"He knows that's not me." Lottie shook her head. "That's not what I'm looking for."

"So what are you looking for?"

"I'm—I'm not really sure anymore."

"Well, he's annoying sometimes, but he's kind and exceptionally smart, like you." Julie tugged her arm.

"And handsome." Lottie smirked, then she chuckled. "I'm sorry—I know he's your brother." She took a deep breath to steady herself. "Everything used to be so clear. I wanted a big adventure out of life, and to teach, and I didn't really need a husband for any of that. Now that I know Crawford ... well, maybe he's what God wants for me. I only want what God wants." Lottie never would have uttered those words before that day when she gave her life to Jesus.

Julie beamed. "It's amazing how much you've changed in a year."

"It's dizzying sometimes, but I'm grateful God is working in my life. He's completely redefining everything for me—freedom, happiness—things I thought I understood better than you churchgoers." She nudged Julie.

"What if God was the one who put those dreams for adventure and teaching in your heart? And now that you're a Christian, he will make those things happen, even better than you imagined!" Julie's arms burst out in an explosion of excitement.

Lottie laughed at her wild friend. It was a nice thought. When they arrived at the sanctuary, they found John and Crawford toward the front. Julie took her seat next to John. Crawford moved his Bible from the spot next to him and looked expectantly up at Lottie. Her heart pounded and her mind raced. Were her dreams of being with Crawford from God, or were they distractions from him? She quickly sat next to Julie on the other end of their group. Crawford's face fell. She settled into the pew with her notebook open, ready to record whatever God would show her. Surely he had a plan for her. If only he would tell her what it was.

The pianist signaled for the congregation to stand and start the service in song. Though Lottie had stood up and sat down and stood up again through church services all her life, for the past year, it felt as though she was actually singing to God. Standing as tall as her four feet and some inches would allow, she lifted her voice. "'How firm a foundation, ye saints of the Lord, is laid for your faith in his excellent Word!'"

When Mr. Broadus read and preached from God's Word, its truth pierced Lottie's heart, surely to burn there for days, changing her from the inside, consuming the dross and refining the gold, as it said in the hymn they had just sung. *When through fiery trials, thy pathway shall lie, my grace all sufficient shall be your supply. The flame shall not hurt you; I only design thy dross to consume and thy gold to refine.*

Lottie had certainly known fiery trials along her path, but for the next one, she wouldn't just struggle through it. She would let God refine her in it.

After the service, John and Crawford offered to walk Julie and Lottie back to school. Crawford didn't seem to be hiding the fact that he kept glancing over at Lottie. They all talked and enjoyed each other's company. Once they reached the girls' dorm, they all kept walking past the door and wandered the school grounds. Crawford's face brightened when Lottie maneuvered next to him and asked if, while at seminary, he was getting even more excited about going to Japan.

"It's an amazing opportunity." Adventure sparkled in his eyes. "Japan has been closed to missionaries for so long, until now. And after spending so much time with Mr. Broadus, I'm convinced it's my duty. He says every man who wants to go into ministry and is able should first go minister among the heathen who've never heard the gospel."

"Hear, hear!" John applauded.

They paused in the light of an oil lamp along the path.

"What's this?" Julie smiled wide. "You sound as if you're going with him, John."

John's eyes lingered on hers for an extra moment before he answered. "If God wills it, I will go to the ends of the earth. The missionaries who left for Japan last year were the first to go there in over two hundred years! Can you imagine?"

"If you're going that far from home, you'll need to bring a wife who will take care of you." Julie's comment sent a red wave across John's face.

"It's an exciting time for missions." Crawford turned to Lottie. "What do you think?"

Lottie grinned and tossed her head. "I think you'll all have a wonderful time and do wonderful things."

Crawford smoothed his light brown hair away from his face. "You're not coming with us?"

She shrugged. God had stirred her heart to missions, but his direction was not yet clear. So she made a little joke of it. "I would, but I haven't finished my Greek class yet." Everyone chuckled. "Besides, the board doesn't send unmarried women as missionaries."

Crawford shot a quick glance her way. His mouth remained shut, but it turned up in a small, hopeful smile.

"While God provides for me to be here, I'm going to get as much of an education as I can," Lottie said decidedly.

She had already started learning Greek before she became a Christian, but now, she couldn't wait to learn all she could about the language that the New

Testament had originally been written in. She strove harder than ever in her studies. No one must think she left her brain behind with her old self. In Christ, she was a new creation. And this new self was a young woman who worked heartily as unto the Lord for his glory, not for her own. Everything was different now, and she would give all she had to God—heart and soul, mind and strength.

They returned to the dorm. John and Julie settled on a nearby bench, not yet ready to say goodbye. It was a beautifully clear night. The longer they looked up, the more stars there were to see. But it was too chilly to stand around waiting for Julie. Lottie waved goodnight to everyone and looked toward the door. Suddenly, a hand grasped hers. She turned back in surprise and met Crawford's desperate gaze.

"Lottie, I've never met a girl like you," he said, still holding her hand. "When I'm away, my thoughts are often here with you." He paused as if hoping for a response beyond Lottie staring at her hand in his. "I think we're a suitable match, and—when I'm back at seminary, may I write to you?" It was a simple question, but his eyes were pleading.

A joke crossed Lottie's mind about having too many pen pals as it was—Mother, Orie, and Cary Ann. But she would not repay his earnest plea with a joke. "Yes, I would like that very much."

Relief and joy washed over Crawford's face. He released his tight grip on her hand and lifted it for a kiss. A chill that somehow warmed her shivered up her arm.

She and Julie said goodnight to the boys and went inside. They giggled and shared only some of the special things their gentlemen friends had said to them. Julie had been right about Crawford. After a while, they settled into their beds.

Lottie looked over at her friend. She treasured Julie's friendship even more now that Cary Ann and Mary had finished school. Soon John would marry Julie and probably whisk her away to Japan. But even that didn't persuade Lottie to drop everything and join them on the mission field.

Of course, she wanted to go. Foreign missions had captivated her heart since she was a little girl, and now that she was a Christian, her long-dormant dream began to awaken. But something about Crawford didn't sit well in her heart. She had to do well where she was until God clearly told her to do something or go somewhere else. Crawford couldn't take center stage in her mind or heart.

Tomorrow, she would keep studying. She might even look for Hope and invite her to start a regular study time together. After all, it would be nice to have another friend nearby.

The next evening, when Lottie approached Hope in the dining hall about studying together, she learned that Hope wouldn't be coming back to school after Christmas. A wealthy young man had asked to marry her, and her father insisted that she leave school and take the opportunity. Tears slowly fell down Hope's beautiful face as she told Lottie that she would study with her while she could. But soon she wouldn't be able to study Greek anymore, and she wouldn't become a teacher or likely travel anywhere beyond visiting family and maybe accompanying her husband on business trips. Everything was decided for her. There was nothing to be done about it. Hope would leave Albemarle Female Institute after the semester and get married in the spring.

Lottie went straight to her room and sank into the nearest chair, overwhelmed at the injustice of it all. Lottie's and Julie's textbooks and papers were scattered over every surface. What were all these schooling opportunities for if something like what happened to Hope could happen to any of the AFI students?

Lottie's thoughts drifted to Orie, as they often did when she thought about women and work. Even if Hope did get to finish school and became an expert in Greek, would a school hire her to teach? After all, Orie had gotten all the medical education that was necessary and possible, probably more than some male doctors in America. But people still wouldn't let her do the work she was trained to do. Because a female doctor was considered so awfully immodest and inappropriate, Orie had to leave the country for an opportunity. Of course, it was more acceptable for women to be teachers than doctors, but female teachers were still mostly restricted to music or deportment classes, not Greek. Women's opportunities for work simply weren't keeping up with their growing opportunities for education.

As Lottie anguished, something nagged at the back of her mind. Oh, yes. She was a Christian now. She could pray to God about all of these things! So she did. In prayer, she remembered one of Orie's letters she got after Christmas that had contained the most wonderful news and flashed a smile to the sky outside her window.

Lottie dug it out of her box of letters and re-read that Orie had decided to follow Jesus and get baptized in Jerusalem. If mother had cried all through Christmas about Lottie's salvation at the Baptist church, she must have fainted to learn of Orie getting baptized in the same city Jesus himself did.

Lottie tucked the letter back into her box. If Orie had easily found a medical job right after she finished school, then she probably wouldn't have gone to Israel with Uncle James and Aunt Julia, and she might never have recognized her need for God. It was like a verse Lottie had just memorized. *All things work together for good to them that love God, to them who are the called according to his purpose.*

Lottie had closed her eyes and was meditating on this verse when Julie burst through the door, startling Lottie into laughter.

"Sorry I scared you," Julie said. "I was hoping to find you. Are you praying?"

Lottie was still laughing, clutching her heaving chest. "I was—before my heart jumped out of my chest." She told Julie all about Hope's upsetting situation but how God had comforted Lottie in prayer. "Isn't that amazing? I wish I had been praying years ago."

Julie dropped onto her bed. "That's so sad about Hope."

"An outrage, is what it is." Lottie sighed. "You should have seen her face when she told me she was getting married. So lost. So heartbroken."

Julie shifted and coughed to clear her throat. She hesitated before saying what was on her mind. "Maybe it's not the best time, but I have some news to share with you too."

"Is it happy? I can't take anymore sad news today."

Julie took a deep breath and spoke slowly. "John has asked me to marry him." Wincing, she watched Lottie as if waiting for an explosion.

Lottie looked at the floor, then back at Julie. "And you said yes?"

Julie nodded. "I did."

Lottie got up and silently crossed the room. She sat down by her friend and took her hands. "Then this is very happy news!"

Julie said they planned to marry in the spring, and then in the fall, they'd go with Crawford through the Foreign Mission Board to Japan as missionaries. Julie would leave school sooner than Lottie. "But I've had three years here," Julie said with a shrug. "That's much more of an education than most girls get."

They stayed up late that night talking all about John and Japan.

"The more I consider it, the more I think God might be calling me to missions, too," Lottie admitted.

Julie lit up as though an idea had just occurred to her. "Has Crawford written to you? Oh, Lottie, if you married him, you could come to Japan with all of us. We could be sisters!"

"He's written." Lottie fidgeted with the pleats on her wool dress. "He hasn't asked me anything like that yet, but I enjoy his letters. I just—I don't know what it is. I can't imagine marrying anyone right now, not even him."

"Well, if he hasn't asked you, I won't try and convince you to marry him—yet." Julie winked. "If you're set on staying single, I actually heard rumors that the mission board might send unmarried women."

Lottie's eyes turned to slits. "Why would they do that?"

"Apparently, many foreign women don't listen to men. Or maybe they're not allowed to. I don't remember that part, but the board needs women missionaries, and they're willing to send unmarried ones. Baptist preachers are even starting to say that God can call a woman to do something, even missions, not just help her husband with whatever he's doing."

Lottie raised a skeptical eyebrow. She had read in the Baptist newspapers about pastors beginning to affirm women's callings in work and ministry, but Baptists sending unmarried women as missionaries? That sounded too good to be true.

"Crawford told me," Julie said, as if reading Lottie's doubtful mind. "It's the word buzzing around the seminary. The board might really send single women."

Lottie frowned. "Why wouldn't he mention something that important to me?"

Julie laughed. "I can't say for sure, but I imagine he might prefer it if you didn't know, especially if he's planning to ask you a certain question. But even if he asks you to marry him—if the mission board will send single women, then you won't need to marry if you don't want to." Julie grinned from ear to ear. "The world is changing for women, Lottie."

"Yes." Hope dawned in Lottie's heart. "But will it change fast enough for me?"

Julie and John married in the spring of 1860, and it was beautiful. The bride wore her best Sunday dress and her brightest smile, which grew wider with each step she took down the aisle. Butterflies arrived right on time to dance around nearby patches of blue aster flowers, and white dogwoods in full bloom sprinkled the surrounding woods of tall pines. Matching the flourishing scenery, the wedding couple radiated hope for good things ahead. They were not only starting a new family that day but also embarking on a mission together in only a few months.

A couple weeks into Julie and John's honeymoon, Hope got married too. Her wedding was probably the most beautifully decorated one Lottie had ever seen outside of a magazine. Hope's parents clearly spared no expense. She looked stunning in a brilliant white gown. The bride held her chin up as she made her way to stand beside her groom. She looked strong, yet very delicate, like a mature tree with something rotting inside, ready to crumble at any moment. The young man smiled as he took Hope's hand as though he had won the greatest prize in all his life. Given the sincerity on his face, hopefully he would treasure Lottie's friend every day as much as he seemed to then. It wasn't a sad wedding, but it wasn't nearly as happy an occasion as a wedding should be.

That summer, Orie returned to Viewmont from two years in the Middle

East. She marveled aloud at how much Eddie had grown in her time away.
Sallie and Mollie were growing into young women as quickly as they could,
relishing any chance to enjoy a social gathering. They were especially excited
when Peggy and one of the field hands, Matthew, asked Mother if they could
marry.

Most times, when a slave couple got permission from Father, and then
Mother after he died, they married by their own wedding traditions out where
the cabins were. Lottie had never seen one of their weddings before, but she
had heard the story of back when Father had officiated a ceremony for Fannie
and George right on the family's front porch. Peggy asked Mother if she could
marry on the porch like her parents had.

The family stood as witnesses and a crowd of slaves gathered in the yard to
watch Isaac read a Scripture and pray over the young couple. Matthew,
wearing his best clothes, took a weed broom and laid it down in front of them.
Tiny white and purple flowers sprouted from Peggy's braids that swirled
around her head like a crown. She smiled up at Matthew, grabbed his hand,
and they jumped over the broom as everyone cheered.

Lottie clapped with all her might and smiled at Fannie, standing in
George's embrace. Both beamed at their daughter with shining eyes. Change
swirled all around Lottie as many of her friends became wives.

One mid-July morning, Mother continued her new habit of reading the
newspaper at breakfast, then going into Father's study to check the ledgers.
She and Ike were giving those ledgers plenty of attention lately to ensure that
the estate could keep the promises that Father had made for the younger girls'
education. Ike's and Orie's had already been paid for, but Lottie planned to
study at Albemarle for a fourth year, and the younger girls still had a lot of
schooling ahead of them.

Mother and Ike seemed to have trouble maintaining the merchant business Father had grown in other states. Selling crops and maintaining relation-
ships with buyers in different states took lots of organizing. Mother didn't
have the time on top of running the home, and Ike didn't seem to have the
same interest in it as Father had. At least the plantation's crops were doing
well. They were sure to have a solid tobacco harvest in the fall, and the rest of
the South was still celebrating a record-setting season for cotton. Mother said
the family's finances were stable—for now. But newspapers were full of
rumors about war and Southern states threatening to secede from the Union.
Tensions were running higher than ever before, especially after what happened
last October in 1859.

Lottie had found out later that while Crawford had held her hand that
autumn night in front of her dormitory and asked to write to her, the same
John Brown who had made Kansas bleed during Lottie's graduation from

Hollins was in Virginia, taking over the arsenal at Harpers Ferry, capturing slaveholders, and freeing their slaves. That November, Brown had been caught, tried for murder and treason, and hanged. Ever since that shocking series of events, newspapers seemed convinced that civil war was inevitable. If war between the North and South did come, the success of Viewmont depended on a Southern victory.

As Mother worked in the study, Ike went out to check with the slave overseers. It was a bright summer day, so Orie and Lottie set out for a walk in the woods near the stream they had loved as children. Once they reached the spot, Orie sat down on a smooth log while Lottie freed her feet from their boots and dipped them into the cool water.

Orie looked over at Lottie. "Did you know in China, they bind girls' feet to keep them tiny like a child's?"

Lottie shot her a glance. What a strange thing to say. "How is that even possible?" She tapped her toe here and there, sending ripples across to the other side.

"As the girls' feet grow, parents tie them really tight. The bones shift into awful contortions, apparently. But when they're all wrapped up into tiny silk shoes, everyone says they're beautiful. It helps girls make a good marriage and lift their family's social rank."

Lottie's stomach turned. She scrunched her face in disgust. "That's incredibly savage. How did you learn that?"

"People from all around come through Jerusalem." Orie shrugged matter-of-factly. "Uncle James met a Chinese medicine man there who told him about it."

Lottie stood, lifted her cotton skirts above her ankles, and waded into the shallow stream. "Will you go back?"

Orie's face fell. "Only if God wills it." She shook her head. "The Middle East is a difficult place for women. I saw and learned a lot there, to be sure. But I'm grateful to be here now."

Lottie wasn't bothered that she hadn't had the chance to visit Orie in Israel as they had dreamed about. But she still wanted to hear all about it. She kicked and wiggled her toes then joined Orie on the log. "What else did you learn?"

They spent the afternoon sharing stories about everything—Orie's adventures in the Middle East, Lottie's life at AFI, and Jesus, whom they both knew intimately now. From their letters, they each knew that the other had become a Christian. But only now did they realize they were both baptized in December 1858.

"Amazing! We were baptized at the same time all those miles apart." Orie had plucked some marsh marigolds near the log and sat braiding the yellow flowers together.

"Yes, but you were baptized in *Jerusalem*." Lottie reached behind the log and picked a few to make her own chain.

"It wasn't any more special than yours. And it wasn't nearly as freezing cold as yours was either, I'm sure. A December baptism in Virginia? You couldn't wait, could you?" Orie laughed.

"Not another minute!"

Lottie told Orie about Julie, John, and Crawford's plans to be missionaries in Japan. Orie pressed her, asking why she was going to school for an extra year since she talked about them as though she wanted to jump on their ship and go with them.

"I don't know for certain if God wants me to be a missionary," Lottie said a little defensively. "Anyway, the mission board isn't sending unmarried women right now."

"But they will—they must." Orie set her flowers aside, stood up, and kicked at some dirt. "Things are changing for women. No matter who wins this war that's sure to come, things will be different afterward. And the Foreign Mission Board will have to change or be left behind when single women find some other way to go."

"You sound like Julie." Lottie smiled up at her sister.

"I'm only saying that with something as important as missions, there will always be a reason not to go. Keep your eyes set on the one reason to go."

CHAPTER TWENTY-SEVEN

1860-1861

Classes were starting up again soon at Albemarle Female Institute, but Lottie couldn't bring herself to pack her bags—not yet. Not until she heard back from Principal Hart about what to do. She had been nervous the last few weeks of summer, ever since Mother sat her down and told her plainly that the family's finances were not stable enough to send Lottie back to school for a fourth year. Lottie immediately took up her pen and wrote to Mr. Hart, explaining the situation and asking for advice. The more she wrote, the more the realization sank in that she might not return to AFI to finish her schooling.

One morning near the end of summer, Fannie handed Mother the day's mail at breakfast, and Lottie asked again if anything had arrived for her. As Mother sifted through the stack, she gently reminded Lottie that this was a chance to practice patience and waiting on the Lord. Lottie slumped in her chair, moving her breakfast around with her fork. Then Mother's face brightened as she plucked out an envelope with Lottie's name on it.

Lottie held her breath as she read through Mr. Hart's pleasantries and inquiries about her well-being. She fixed her eyes on the last line.

With a mind like yours, you are welcome to continue your studies here and pay the tuition when you can.

She exhaled with a laugh. Tears filled her eyes. God had made a way for her!

By the time classes resumed, Lottie had said her goodbyes to Julie, John, and Crawford. She wished them well and promised to keep praying for them and saving money to send to the mission board. But at the last minute, poor John came down with both typhoid and the measles. He wasn't healthy enough to walk to the drugstore, much less travel to the Far East. Julie cared for him and consoled his disappointment by reminding him that they planned to meet up with Crawford and the rest of the missionaries in Japan next year.

But the oddest thing happened. Crawford didn't get on the ship either. He wouldn't say why, and no one could figure it out. Maybe he didn't want to go to Japan without his sister and close friend. Maybe he felt God keeping him back. Whatever the reason, he simply returned to Southern Baptist Seminary.

It wasn't the same as when they were roommates, but Lottie kept up with Julie, Mary, and Cary Ann through letters. Cary Ann and Lottie's cousin, Jimmy, still seemed sweet on each other, but there wasn't a hint of any matrimonial announcement in Cary Ann's letters. Reading Mary's letters, on the other hand, felt like reading a tell-all society newspaper. They were filled with mentions about possible engagements and other interesting tidbits about the extended Moon family and their old Hollins classmates.

The latest letter from Julie contained a clipping of a serious newspaper. She didn't write very much. It was all too horrifying to put it into her own words, she said. Julie let the article relay the details to Lottie. The ship that Julie, John, and Crawford were supposed to be on never reached Japan. It sank somewhere in the Pacific Ocean. The authorities couldn't find it and didn't know what went wrong. Whatever they would decide had happened wouldn't change the fact that the other missionaries and everyone else aboard that ship were lost at sea.

Shock hit Lottie like a roaring wave. The loss of life was a tragedy. That was clear. But what was the word for the shock of a near tragedy? Gratitude, confusion, horror—these all swirled around in Lottie's heart. John would survive the measles, but none of them would have survived a sinking ship in the middle of the ocean. Julie, John, and Crawford nearly lost their lives, Lottie nearly lost three dear friends, and the Japanese still needed people to live among them and give witness to the gospel.

Soon after, Crawford came to Charlottesville. He sent a letter ahead of him, asking to see Lottie. They met at Lottie's school and tried to decide where to go.

"You should pick," Lottie said. "You aren't in town for very long." His face looked thinner and dark circles rimmed his eyes.

"Lady's choice." Crawford dipped his head.

"If you insist," she said as if he had been warned. She knew just the place to bring some fullness back onto his cheekbones.

Lottie led him over to Hazel's and paused under the little red-and-white awning as Crawford opened the door for her. The evidence of a kitchen hard at work greeted them right away—the smell of fresh coffee and the warmth of the stove and its buttery creations. Lottie smiled at the familiar scene. They sat down at a small round table by a window that was big enough to watch people bustling through the intersection. Lottie smoothed her yellow dress and shifted in her seat, maneuvering her small, domed skirt under the table. A server brought two menus then left them to decide their order. Lottie didn't look over hers for long. "I'm having the chicken salad sandwich and then coffee and ice cream." Along with Crawford ... ingredients for a perfect day.

Crawford shrugged out of his gray frock coat and gazed at the people outside with a furrowed brow. "I'll have a coffee," he said without looking away from the window.

Lottie cocked her head at him. "Julie and I used to come here for ice cream, but they have good food too. Turtle soup? Ham? Chicken pie?"

He turned to her and sighed. "Just coffee."

Lottie tensed. Why did he insist she choose if he was going to sulk and only order coffee? "You hate it here. Let's go somewhere else." She started to push her chair back.

"No—please, let's stay," he said, reaching across the table. "I want to be somewhere you're happy and at home. I—I haven't been very happy." He looked down and out the window again. "I've been lost since the news about the ship."

Lottie's brown curls bounced as she scooted her chair forward and took his hand. She offered sympathies and affirmed that it was a deeply unsettling thing to have happened. Of course, he would feel unhappy and lost.

"I don't know why it happened." He ran his hand through his hair. "I've studied God and his ways for years, and I can't figure out why. Why didn't I get on that ship? Why did it sink with all those missionaries on board?"

"There's not always a reason," Lottie said in a soothing voice. "Awful things happen, and God is sovereign over them, of course." Now she was somewhat lost, unsure of what to say. "You know more about theology than I do, but I do know that every good thing comes from God. The fact that you're still alive—that's a very good thing. I praise God for it."

Crawford smiled, but the lines around his mouth remained tight. He quoted from the Book of Isaiah. "'I make wellbeing and create calamity. I the Lord do all these things.'"

"'So that people may know that there is none besides me,'" Lottie continued from the same chapter. It wasn't a coincidence that she'd been reading through Isaiah for the past month. "*Everything* God does is to draw people to himself so that he will be glorified."

He narrowed his eyes at her and nodded slowly, as if a question in his head was starting to find an answer.

Lottie convinced him to order some hearty chicken pie, and they enjoyed their meal together. They spent the fall afternoon walking around the town and then the campus.

"Why did you come to Charlottesville?" Lottie asked as they wandered toward her dormitory. "Are you seeing your old friends from UVA later?"

Crawford stopped on the path. Lottie paused and turned toward him. He looked even more serious than he had at Hazel's.

"I came to see you—only you," he said. "I'm going to get on the next ship, but I don't want to go alone. I want a wife to come with me."

Lottie's heart might have completely stopped. He wouldn't. Not now, surely.

"I want *you* to come with me," he added.

Lottie's mind was spinning, trying to make sense of what was happening. "You're asking me to marry you?"

Crawford got down on one knee and took her hand. "Miss Charlotte Moon—Lottie—will you marry me?"

Lottie looked into those familiar, pleading eyes. It would be so easy to say once again as when he had asked to write to her, *Yes, I would like that very much.* A vision of her life flashed before her eyes. She was sailing across the ocean, safely tucked against Crawford's chest. She was teaching Japanese children and strolling arm in arm with Julie. Everything would have been wonderful if not for the obvious truth. "You're still in shock from the news about the ship. You're not thinking clearly."

Crawford jolted back. If he wasn't in shock before, he certainly was now. "My thinking is perfectly clear." He grasped her hand tighter and pulled it to his heart. "This might be why I didn't get on that ship. We should go as missionaries together, as husband and wife."

"I don't know if we should do anything as husband and wife. I don't even know if you love me, Crawford."

"I love you, Lottie!" he shouted.

"Well, that settles it, then, doesn't it?" She didn't mean to sound sarcastic, but that proposal was completely ill-timed. He'd admitted himself how unhappy and lost he felt. Was he expecting her to make him happy and find his way? No. He needed to heal first and decide in a sound mind if God truly wanted him to propose.

They argued until Crawford dusted off his knee and left Lottie at the school, warning her that he would ask her to marry him again so she had better be ready next time.

The school year couldn't have been fuller of distractions for Lottie. Her family's financial stress, the shipwreck, and then a proposal. She didn't think the world could get any crazier—until Christmas came along and she went home for the holidays.

At breakfast one morning, Fannie set the newspaper down as usual, and Mother leisurely picked it up. At her first glance of the front page, she gasped and dropped her apple-buttered toast.

Lottie froze, as did everyone else at the table. "What's wrong, Mother?"

South Carolina had announced itself as the first state to secede from the United States of America.

"A war is coming." Mother lowered the paper and looked at Ike with shining eyes. Her only living son would likely go to battle if a war did come.

Anger between the North and the South seemed to have been simmering ever since Lottie could remember. But After Abraham Lincoln was elected president the month before, the South had gone into a frenzy. No man that Lottie knew of had voted for him. Everyone said the Northerners were making decisions for the whole nation. When Lottie had arrived for Christmas, Mother and Isaac were angry that Mr. Lincoln would be the president once inaugurated in springtime. Orie had assured the family that he would find a solution to the problem of slavery. Ike had rolled his eyes, and Mother had raised her eyebrows, but everyone mostly humored Orie and hoped for the best. This morning, however, Mother looked terrified.

Fannie had left the dining room with the tea. Lottie volunteered to go bring it back. Mother needed some extra fortification this morning. Lottie reached to push open the already cracked door to the kitchen, then froze when Peggy exclaimed.

"She said what?" Peggy nearly dropped her stirring spoon.

"Keep yer voice down," Fannie whisper-shouted.

Lottie put her face as close to the door as she dared while Fannie told Peggy what Mother had just read aloud from the newspaper.

"So it's finally happening," Peggy said with wonder in her eyes.

Fannie propped her hands on her hips. "There was nothin' about Virginia in that news article."

"South Carolina's only the first." Peggy beamed. "Soon, the whole thing will break apart, and when there's a war, me and Matthew are gonna go West to be free together."

"I liked Matthew ever since he was a scrawny boy, runnin' folks' luggage all around. I didn't mind you marryin' him, but do y'all have to go away?" Fannie asked. "We might could stay on here as free folks. The Moons have been good to us."

Peggy's face went sour. "Not good enough to set us free."

Fannie didn't argue with that. She grabbed an empty tray and turned to collect the breakfast dishes.

Lottie staggered back as Fannie opened the door. She lunged to grab the falling tray, but it clanged on the floor.

"Miss Lottie," Fannie exclaimed, patting her face and straightening her head wrap. "Pardon, I didn't see you there."

Both Lottie and Fannie caught their breaths.

"I came for the tea," Lottie said. "You brought it in but didn't leave it on the table."

"Oh." Fannie's gaze darted around the room, then spotted the silver teapot on a table. She set it on another tray. "Here it is. My apologies, miss. I musta lost my head for a moment."

"Indeed." Lottie took it and headed back into the house, steaming along with the tea. Fannie and Peggy spoke as though they were certain a war would come and just as certain, if not hopeful, that the South would lose. Why did they want Viewmont to break apart? This was their home too. Lottie paused at the dining room door and breathed slowly to calm down.

Although the news about South Carolina cast a shadow over the holiday, the Moon family celebrated the birth of their Savior, clinging to the comfort of remembering Emmanuel—God with us. If ever they needed that reminder, it was now. What would become of South Carolina after its secession? How many other states would follow their lead? Would Virginia be among them?

Sure enough, secession announcements filled January's newspapers. Mississippi was the first to follow. Florida announced its secession the day after, and then Alabama. The next to break away from the Union were Georgia, Alabama, and Texas. The country hadn't even celebrated its centennial, and now these states were banding together as a new union called the Confederate States of America. In February, they chose a man named Jefferson Davis as their president. The South was finally standing up to the tyranny of Northern control.

All the while, during Albemarle Female Institute's new semester, students were buzzing with rumors and news about the coming war that the North would surely declare on the South.

Lottie stood with a few other fourth-year students one February morning before class was about to start. There were only a handful of fourth-year girls, so they spent more time together than they had in their first few years at AFI.

Emma, a girl with silky curls tied in expensive ribbon and a naturally booming voice, seemed the most eager for a war. "All of my brothers plan to fight," she said. "Mother and I've been practicing our knitting. All the men are going to need warm socks when they're fighting next winter."

"Next winter?" Lucy gasped, as if the thought might make her faint. "I can't believe it's coming to this. My father's family is in Illinois, and he says he doesn't want to end up on the same battlefield as his brother."

"It's a horrifying thought," Jo agreed. "I have cousins in Missouri."

Emma turned her nose up. "Virginia will join the Confederacy soon enough, and then we'll have a grand Southern nation, completely outside Lincoln's control."

A loud ringing sent the girls scattering to their desks. Lottie blessed the bell for starting class. The war was already so distracting from her studies, and it hadn't even officially started yet. Lottie narrowed her eyes, forcing herself to focus on what the teacher was saying at the front of the classroom. But her heart raced as thoughts flashed across the front of her mind—war, her home, and the horrors of slavery that Frederick Douglass described in his book. If only Southerners could have figured out how to fix the problem of slavery themselves, no one might be considering war at all. Now that the North was trying to take control, everything was at stake—not only Viewmont, but the whole way they did life. The longer Lottie thought about it, the more anxious she became.

That evening, she spent her time studying God's Word and her class text-books. With everything so unsettled, focusing on the task at hand was comforting. That's all she could do right now, anyway, unless she wanted to join a sock-knitting circle for the soon-to-be soldiers. And knitting was almost as boring as needlepointing.

Principal Hart insisted that the school continue with its schedule. There wasn't an official announcement of war yet, but there *was* an official date set for their exams. Lottie continued working hard. Mr. Hart believed in her enough to let her come back to school without paying tuition right away. She wouldn't let him down. She excelled at languages, mastering Latin, Greek, Spanish, French, and Italian. Her heart swelled when Mr. Hart told her he had written to Mr. Broadus about her, saying that one of her recent papers was much superior to anything he had ever read from a student before.

A month after Lincoln was inaugurated in March 1861, the announce-ment of war came in the form of a headline: **WAR BEGUN! First Shots Fired!** Newspapers reported that Confederate soldiers had stormed Fort Sumter in Charleston, South Carolina. The Confederate States were now offi-cially fighting with the United States.

After that, Virginia finally seceded, along with Arkansas, Tennessee, and North Carolina. Sides had been chosen. The war had begun, and Lottie had two weeks of school before graduation. Mr. Hart seemed more determined than ever for the girls to finish the year. He told Lottie and the other fourth-year students that come graduation in May, they would have done enough scholarly work to earn full masters of art degrees. They might even be the first Southern women to do so! This prestigious prize helped focus Lottie's attention on completing the school year with her best work, rather than focusing on the national chaos around her. Lottie and the other fourth-year girls studied together and often exchanged their papers with each other for review.

As the Confederacy was setting up their government seventy miles east in Richmond, Lottie attended a small graduation ceremony to receive her hard-earned diplomas. This graduation was different from her graduation at Hollins or any other she'd been to. Orie's, Ike's, and Tom's ceremonies had been full of hope. The graduates were applauded, admired, and assured of a bright future with wonderful possibilities.

But when Lottie's moment on the stage came, she glanced up at Mr. Hart as he handed her a rolled-up diploma. He struggled to keep his chin from quivering. He seemed overcome with pride for his students. Or he might have been scared and sorry for them. The AFI graduates were now equipped with one of the highest levels of education they could possibly attain. But they were entering a society at war, and no one could assure them of a bright future.

While Lottie moved back to Viewmont with her diploma and scholarly gown, young men across the state traveled to northern Virginia with their guns and gray suits to join General Robert E. Lee's brigade. Ike joined the Confederate Army. So did John, Crawford, Jimmy, Lottie's other cousins, and most of the other young men that she ever knew.

When she got a letter from Crawford, she let it sit for a day or two on her bedside table, afraid it was another marriage proposal before he went to war. But when she finally summoned the nerve to open it, she found only a few lines of information about his company unit and how to write to him.

Whatever was important before the war was now set aside. Because whatever was important before the war now depended on life continuing in the same way after it was finished. Mother knitted socks for the troops just like every other woman who had a man away in the army. She took the family's support for the war a step further. Mother said they had to be completely invested in a Confederate victory.

One day that summer, Lottie helped Mother gather up the coins and every bank note in the house into suitcases. All of the Moon women loaded into the carriage with the suitcases and set out for Charlottesville.

The city was already different than when Lottie had graduated in the spring. Men in gray suits walked wherever they were going with intense purpose. New flags that she assumed must be for the Confederacy had been raised around the city. Mother led the girls straight to the bank, where they

converted all of their money into Confederate dollars—the money in the suitcases and the money the bank was holding for them.

Eddie stood on the tips of her toes to look at the new money Mother
packed back in the suitcases. None of the Moon women could boast about
their height, but there was hope for ten-year-old Eddie, who still had some
growing to do. She pointed to a fifty-dollar Confederate bill. "That's what
Jefferson Davis looks like?"

"Yes." Mother tapped each stack as she counted. "We must pray for
him."

"I think the hundreds are the prettiest." Mollie reached in and touched
one. "Who is that woman?"

"That's Mrs. Pickens. First lady of South Carolina." Mother moved
Mollie's hand out of the way and snapped the case shut.

"They call her the Queen of the Confederacy," Orie jeered.

"She's not a queen," Mother said. "We must pray for her too. Women have
an important role in this war. We're doing our part today by supporting the
Confederacy."

"I plan to do my part to support the boys." Orie raised her chin. "While
we're here, I'd like to visit the hospital and see if there's a place for me to serve
the wounded."

Lottie and her family got dinner in the city, then they all accompanied
Orie on her mission. She didn't get to meet with the men who ran the hospital, but she got the names of some men in charge. She would write them once
they got home.

Back at Viewmont, Orie didn't get a quick response from her letters. But
later that summer, the first battle broke out in northern Virginia—the Battle
of Bull Run, they called it. After that, wounded Confederate soldiers poured
into Charlottesville's hospital, churches, and other places that formed the
city's new hospital network. The man in charge finally responded and let Orie
join as the head of all the female nurses.

Lottie, Sallie, and Mollie volunteered as well, but not nearly as often as
Orie did. Everyone Lottie knew of was involved in the war some way or
another. Cousin Jimmy and his brothers were gaining prestige by surviving
important battles, and her Ohio cousins Ginny and Lottie—sometimes
referred to around Viewmont as "the other Lottie Moon"—served as nurses
for the Confederacy, too, but they seemed to travel quite often to and from
Union territory. If Lottie didn't know any better, she might have guessed they
were spies.

At the Charlottesville hospital, Orie was unstoppable. Until one day, she
collapsed at work. They sent her home to rest at Viewmont, where Lottie took
care of her. One young, single doctor from the hospital, Dr. John Andrews,

was especially worried about Orie. He sent a letter every couple days, asking about her and even coming to visit on his days off.

Orie wasn't the only one who caught men's eyes at the hospital. The hospital chaplain noticed Lottie's hard work and passionate faith. He even had the courage to ask Lottie to marry him, but she declined. Surely, she hadn't been acting in a way that invited another marriage proposal. Maybe it was the war and its atmosphere that anything could happen at a moment's notice.

CHAPTER TWENTY-EIGHT

1863–1864

April 1863 marked two years since the war started. At the beginning of the year, Abraham Lincoln issued his Emancipation Proclamation, promising to free slaves in the Confederate states if the Union side won the war. He even welcomed runaway slaves into the Union Army. A lot of slaves heard about it and hurried across the Mason-Dixon line to join Lincoln. But most slaves at Viewmont and everywhere else stayed where they were and continued working.

As the war dragged on, Lottie tried to occupy herself with productive work. She moved her church membership from Charlottesville Baptist to Pine Grove Baptist and taught Sunday school there. It was closer than Scottsville, and Lottie liked its humble wooden building and the country fields all around. She came alive whenever she opened God's Word with those children. Both the white and black children were quick to learn the songs and catechisms she taught them. She also occasionally volunteered at Orie's hospital in Charlottesville.

Once Orie regained her health, she married Dr. John Andrews at Viewmont, and the two moved to Richmond to work at the army hospital there. The marriage didn't surprise Lottie in the slightest. It was plain that Dr. Andrews was as enamored with and devoted to Orie as she was to her profession. If there ever was a perfect match for Orie, Dr. Andrews was it.

After helping Orie get well then get ready for her wedding, Lottie picked up a familiar role—teaching her younger siblings. Mother wouldn't send Eddie away to school, not with Union troops invading Virginia. They couldn't afford a school like Troy or Hollins right now, anyway. But under Lottie's tutelage, Eddie would be just as educated as any twelve-year-old girl at a fancy school up North.

Whatever dreams Lottie had of going as a missionary with the Foreign Mission Board were set aside indefinitely. Word spread that the board had run out of money. They were funded by Southern Baptists, many of whom were serving in the Confederate Army and facing the real possibility of their own poverty if this war didn't turn out the way they planned. Southern Baptists could barely afford to sustain the missionaries they had already sent. They certainly weren't sending any new ones, much less unmarried women.

God had given Lottie meaningful work to do at home, at Pine Grove, and at Orie's hospital. But none of that was paying work, and it certainly wasn't what Lottie had imagined her life to be after becoming one of the most educated women in the South. After the war, she would strike out on her own and find a job to support herself. Until then, she tried to be content with the work God had given her.

"Does it make you sad?" Eddie pulled her knitted sweater tighter up over her shoulders against a morning chill in late-April.

Lottie turned to face her sister. "What's that?" She had been staring out the library window for longer than she realized, watching the raindrops fall down the glass. They each dropped at different speeds. Some went straight down the window, while others seemed to change course suddenly when they hit some unforeseen spot on the glass.

"You're stuck here with me instead of going off on an adventure some-where." Eddie sulked as if she thought she was the one holding Lottie back. "Orie got to go to Jerusalem after she graduated, but you have to stay home and teach me."

"I *get* to teach you." Lottie winked. "You've always been my favorite student."

That didn't exactly answer Eddie's question, but she smiled, anyway. "Okay, then. You just look sad."

"I'm not sad." Lottie slumped and sighed, knowing she wasn't very convincing. She turned back to the window. "I think I'm supposed to be here for now. I just wish I knew what God was doing." She gathered herself and sat up straight. "You're lucky, you know."

Eddie grimaced and shifted her gaze to the pile of math books on the table that they had been working on for most of the morning. "A lucky person would have lost these books in the river."

Lottie laughed. "I mean, when you're in school, you learn one subject and then another, moving up through the years. It's such a clear path. Until one day, you graduate, and then there's no clear pathway—no next step." She sighed again. "Then nothing makes sense anymore."

Eddie grimaced and lifted the cover of an algebra book as though it was something filthy. "That's what I thought when you opened this one."

Lottie flashed Eddie a smile. "But the more you worked on it, little by little, it started to become clear, and now you can solve any algebra problem in that book—well, in the first half of the book." An idea sparked. "Maybe that's what I need to do—keep working and then all of this will make sense one day."

"Maybe." Eddie hesitated. "But God and life aren't much like math problems."

Lottie was taken aback. "That may be the wisest thing you've ever said." Lottie shrugged since she couldn't argue with that. Eddie hadn't even claimed faith in Jesus yet, and there she was, seeming to understand him fairly well. "I guess trying to figure God out is easier than trusting him sometimes."

Lottie only spent the mornings tutoring Eddie. In the afternoons, she took walks around the plantation, read books in her green velvet chair, and kept up with reading and responding to letters.

Orie wrote about Dr. Andrews, how kind and talented he was. All of Helen's letters assured the family that she and little Tom were safe and well in Alabama. The other Lottie and her sister, Ginny, wrote every so often to check in on the family and confirm their own well-being. Ike did the same. Mother read the newspapers religiously, especially after a battle, muttering prayers that Ike's name wouldn't appear in the casualty lists.

Crawford Toy still wrote to Lottie. When she read that he thinks of her before each battle and prays to see her face again, her gut went hollow. She replied with her own written prayers for him. In his latest letter, he said that he'd started learning German to pass the time in camp. That made Lottie smile. Even during a war, Crawford couldn't help but grow academically.

Lottie's cousin and friend, Mary, sent a shocking letter. Mary must write letters nonstop because she knew from someone currently at Hollins Institute that two of the slaves there, Ann and Claiborne Scott, had taken their young son and escaped!

Lottie settled in her library chair and pulled the letter closer to her face as she carefully read each word about how they supposedly fled to Missouri to be with their daughter, Bettie, who had been taken away from them years ago. Lottie stood up. This was too exciting news to take sitting down. After all those letters that students had helped Ann write to her daughter, their family was finally together.

Lottie began pacing the room. Ann didn't wait for the end of the war to go and live her life as a free woman. Maybe Lottie didn't need to wait for the war to end either. She couldn't go be a missionary, but maybe she could get a paying job as a teacher somewhere.

It didn't take long to find a teaching job, not with an excellent reference like Mr. John Broadus. In October, Lottie would take the train south to Valdosta, Georgia, and live with a family there to tutor their sixteen-year-old daughter named Katherine.

Mother let Lottie go without much of a fight, as if she knew she couldn't stop her. But Eddie sat at the library table, crying as Lottie sorted which books to bring to Georgia. She would take more advanced ones because the girl was older. She left Eddie's school books and made notes about what Eddie should study during the next several months to a year.

"A year?" Eddie sobbed. "You're leaving again for a whole year to teach some other girl?"

"I don't know exactly how long I'll stay in Georgia," Lottie said in a comforting voice. "I just want you to have a study plan and know where you're going. That's all."

Eddie tore up the stairs, crying. Sallie and Mollie, who were teenagers now, grumbled about Lottie leaving, too, but only because they weren't allowed to go anywhere or do anything fun anymore, not since the war started.

That October, Before Lottie boarded the carriage that would take her to a southbound train, she paused and studied the stunning scene around her. Mountains in the distance had turned gold. On a perfect day, the warm autumn sun would bake the apple orchard, and then a light breeze would carry the sweet air through Viewmont's open windows. A more peaceful person would have been content living at home and teaching Eddie until the war was over. But what if the war went on for years? Lottie couldn't wait that long to work and teach people outside of her family. This job in Georgia was a start. It was a real job with a contract and a salary.

The family had offered Lottie a room in their home with a view over their backyard. They agreed that Lottie would have two hours each afternoon to rest and read her Bible. They seemed impressed at her piety when she insisted that she would not work on Sundays.

When Lottie arrived in Valdosta, she was taken aback by the plantation where she would live and work. It was even grander than Viewmont. The house looked strong and beautiful with its tall white columns. Blue shutters flanked each of the many windows, and a wide porch wrapped all the way around the house.

The air of a prosperous Southern family felt familiar, but slight differences reminded Lottie that she wasn't quite home. The family was Presbyterian, not Baptist, and their plantation grew cotton, which was much prettier in the fields than Viewmont's tobacco. Also, preparing to teach Katherine was completely different than teaching Eddie or her other sisters. Lottie didn't know what the girl had already studied or how she best learned new things. In their first lesson together, Katherine joined Lottie at a writing table in the back parlor without a word. She just sat there, scowling in her fine clothes.

The aggression emanating from this teenage girl didn't alarm Lottie. She was certainly used to pouting students. Maybe this job would be similar to teaching Sallie and Mollie.

"Good morning, Katherine," Lottie said.

Katherine roughly crossed her arms. "I was planning to daydream through your lesson today about the ball this Friday, but I've just been informed that it's canceled."

This could be a very short first job if she didn't get along with Katherine and her parents sent Lottie away. Or worse, it could be a very long year if they didn't get along and her parents still kept Lottie on. She needed to find a way to show that she was on this girl's side and that she was someone to be trusted and respected.

"I see." Lottie folded her hands on the table. "On account of something about the war?"

"Like everything else." Katherine tossed her arms up as though she'd had enough of this war nonsense.

"Right. That's a shame."

Katherine started listing all the unpleasant ways the war had affected her life. "I can't go to school with other girls because of the war. My brothers are all away because of the war, which makes this place awfully boring. But at least I had a wedding to look forward to. My sister was supposed to marry David, and they were going to have a splendid wedding with a big cake, but can you guess what happened?"

"Did he enlist?" Lottie humored the girl for now, but how could she steer the conversation toward the day's lesson?

"Of course. The wedding is postponed, and he might not even come back!" Katherine leaned forward and spoke in a spooky voice. "If he dies, she might not ever love again."

"Hmm, yes, that would be very sad."

"It would." Katherine nodded, brushing her silky dark hair behind her shoulders. Her crystal blue eyes were huge and concerned.

"After the war, what will you do?" Lottie asked.

Katherine stared at her, frowning slightly.

"What's something you've always wanted to do?" Lottie asked again, then sat quietly as Katherine cocked her head for a moment.

"I'd like to go to France and eat ice cream at an outdoor café near a river."

A smile spread across Lottie's face. "Well, then, you'll need to know how to use a few French words. What if you want to order lunch with your ice cream and you need some salt? The word for *salt* sounds almost identical to the word for *saddle*, and I imagine that one tastes much better than the other."

Katherine laughed while Lottie took up her pen and started making a list of things that Katherine needed for her adventure in France one day. "You'll probably do well to know some math, too, so you can convert the prices and exchange rates in your head. And let's find some maps. You'll need to know how to get around a new place."

"I've seen maps in here." Katherine smiled and sauntered over to a roll-top desk at the other end of the parlor.

For most of their lessons, it was just Lottie and Katherine. A slave woman came in quietly a few times each morning with sweet iced tea, buns, and then eventually lunch. They didn't usually see Katherine's parents during that time, so they were both startled when one day that first week, the door burst open and Katherine's father suddenly walked into the room. He stood clutching the blue lapel by his puffed-up chest. He seemed to be frowning, even though it was impossible to see his mouth under such a full beard.

"Is she minding you, Miss Moon?" he asked, looking at Katherine instead of Lottie.

"Yes, very well, sir," Lottie said breathlessly, still recovering from the surprise entry. "Your Katherine here is extremely bright."

"It's good that she's applying herself." He turned to Lottie. "You can join us for the Presbyterian service on Sunday if you like, but I suspect you'd prefer the Baptist church. It's farther up the street. If we leave earlier, we could get you there on time. Our driver will drop us off, then take you the rest of the way, if that suits you."

"Yes, please. Thank you. That's very generous."

"Well, then. Continue on." He left the room in just as big a huff as when he came in.

After the interruption, Lottie flipped through a few pages in a French book, attempting to push through the new tension in the room and get back to their lesson. Had Nicholas ever felt this awkward at Viewmont?

Katherine broke the silence. "Father's been different since the war started. His warmth got cold. Not that he was ever very warm."

Lottie set down the book. "It's impossible not to be different from before it started."

Living in another family's house was completely different than living at home or even at school with other girls. She felt it most once she started riding with them to town on Sundays. There was something so familiar yet completely different about it without her own father, mother, and siblings.

Growing up, she'd treasured the wagon ride to Scottsville but loathed the service once they arrived at church. Now, she loved the Baptist church in Valdosta, and even though Katherine's father could be unpleasant, Lottie was thankful to not have to walk there every week, especially during the oppressively humid summer. Over the months, with the help of wise people at church and her own time in prayer and Bible study, she learned to anchor her heart in Jesus. Wherever she lived in the world, she always belonged with him.

Fellowshipping with other Christians and resting in God became essential as the war progressed. Ever since General Sherman of the Union Army took Atlanta that summer, then left it broken and burning in the fall, the whole family was on edge, not just Katherine's father. No one knew where General Sherman's army was headed next. From September of that year of 1864 on, Lottie clung to her Bible like never before. In the early mornings and in the afternoons, she memorized Psalm 23 just from reading it over and over.

On a Tuesday afternoon in late November, Lottie was resting her eyes and praying in her room that overlooked the back cotton fields. She thanked God for his faithful presence over the past year as she grew in the challenges of her first job away from home. It was a peaceful afternoon until Lottie flinched at an awful sound. The crack of a whip and then a scream. Then again. And again.

Her eyes were wide open. Lottie held her breath and slowly crossed to the window. She moved the curtain aside. Katherine's father stood about fifty feet from the house clutching a whip. He had blood splattered on the front of his clothes and a look of anguish on his face, a mix of fury and fear. A shirtless slave shook at the foot of a wooden stake in the ground to which he was tied. Katherine's father lifted the whip again then yelled, tossed it to the ground, and walked away. It was as if he knew that no matter how tight he gripped that leather handle, everything it sought to hold together would soon fall apart. As soon as Lottie lost sight of him walking around the house, a group of four or five men rushed to the whipped man and gently carried him toward the cabins. Two women followed them, holding onto each other, crying.

Lottie later learned what happened from the woman who brought tea each morning. Apparently, Katherine's father had found out that the man was planning to make a run for it, join Sherman's army, and try to start a new life with his forty acres and a mule that Sherman had promised.

Lottie struggled to fall asleep that night. Clutching the bed sheet up to her chin, she stared with wide, burning eyes at the closed door of her room. She couldn't look at the window on the opposite wall. If she could forget it for a moment and force her eyes shut, she might fall asleep. A cool breeze drifted through the open window behind her, sending a shiver down her neck and reviving the memory of that poor man, limp yet shaking in the arms of the other slaves. Lottie whimpered, and her eyes flooded. She blinked tears down the side of her face, dampening her hair and her pillow. Lottie recited Psalm 23 in her head, praying and imagining the slave as a little sheep being led by the Good Shepherd, even through the valley of the shadow of death. She took deep breaths and blinked more regularly now, longer and longer.

That week, it became clear that Sherman and his troops were marching to the coast, to Savannah, not south toward Valdosta. That was a relief, but the events of that summer and fall had planted seeds of doubt that the Confederate Army could win the war.

Lottie couldn't go on as before. For the rest of the week, sitting at the same dining table as Katherine's father made Lottie's stomach turn. That Sunday at church, she waited for him to go to the altar and collapse in confession of his violent sin, but he remained in the pew with his family singing about God's grace. Lottie's stomach turned again. She couldn't stay there.

Lottie decided to return home that week, at the start of December. Katherine's parents didn't pressure her to reconsider. As Lottie packed her books and clothes, the expected satisfaction failed to come. God had given her peace about taking this job, but once she got there, it wasn't exactly peaceful. Katherine's father made the stories in Frederick Douglass' narrative come horribly alive, and General Sherman had brought the war closer than it had ever felt at Viewmont. The war wasn't just on battlefields anymore. Cities and homes were burning.

As Lottie buckled her trunk, something buried deep in her memory resurfaced. Her sister's question after a bedtime story about Burma and her mother's answer. *Sometimes when we follow God, He takes us to places that aren't very nice, and He asks us to do things that aren't very easy.* If that was true, maybe Lottie was right on track with God's plan.

General Sherman's army left Georgia almost the same time Lottie did. Both headed north. After traveling by a mix of carriages, steamers, and what was left of the railroads, Lottie made it home in time to enjoy Christmas with her family.

A couple days before Christmas, Lottie sat on the floor with her sisters, folding pages out of Mother's old magazines and cutting snowflakes. Lottie held hers up to a candle on the small table behind her and watched the light flicker through the shapes.

Orie leaned back against a pillow on the sofa. "Very nice, Lottie." Her hands rested on top of her burgeoning belly as she slowly worked long needles, knitting mittens for her new baby. This was their third baby, and Orie said she was sure it was another boy. She and John hadn't stayed working in Richmond long before buying a home closer to Viewmont.

Eddie's head popped up, a pile of crumpled paper in her lap. Her gaze landed on Lottie's paper snowflake. "How do you get so many tiny triangles?"

"Fold your paper a few more times before you cut." Lottie winked.

Lottie got up and fixed her ornament onto the tree, breathing in the evergreen. As a child, the Savior's birth hadn't really meant anything to her. But ever since Lottie became a Christian, she enjoyed Christmas so much more deeply. She stood back, reflecting on God's patience.

After the people of Israel waited four hundred years in heaven's silence, God sent Jesus at the perfect time. Even though four years of war wasn't as long as four hundred, it took a lot of faith to pray and wait through it. She was praying for the war to end with everyone she knew intact. And she was praying to somehow, someday serve God in foreign missions. Christmas reminded her that God answers the prayers of his people and doesn't make them wait forever ... just until the perfect time.

CHAPTER TWENTY-NINE

1865

By early February, Orie's occasional labor pains had picked up speed. Everyone went to Orie and John's home near Viewmont to help. Lottie's younger sisters cared for little James. Mother and Ike's wife, Meg, stayed with Orie and John as she labored. Lottie couldn't stay still, so she rushed around the house with one of the slaves, running pitchers of clean water and bundles of fresh towels up to the room.

Lottie was hurrying up the stairs with another pitcher of water when she ran into John slowly making his way down.

"Just taking a break," he said, running a hand through his hair.

Lottie stopped and propped the heavy pitcher on her hip. "The other boys were born healthy. This one should be, too, right?" She tried to give John a reassuring look, but the pitcher was digging into her hip.

John nodded with a tight smile. He was a doctor, after all, and had seen how these things could turn unexpectedly.

A door slammed. Lottie and John jolted and turned around as Mother stormed down the stairs in tears.

"What happened?" John asked with wide eyes full of worry.

"I have been asked"—Mother sniffled—"to leave the room."

Lottie and John scooted out of her way as she marched past, keeping her quivering chin up.

John gave Lottie a wry smile. "Everyone's more tense than usual today."

Not surprisingly. Ever since Orie's first baby died of croup before his second birthday, Mother had fussed over the way Orie raised little James, her second. When Mother would complain that Orie let them run wild and play in the dirt too much, Orie reminded her how much time they had spend in the woods as children, and they all turned out fine. Apparently, Mother's worries for Orie's next child had started already.

By the end of the day, Orie gave birth to a healthy baby boy. Mother handed Lottie the little bundle when it was her turn. She held him close and snuggled his chubby cheeks. When she leaned back to get a good look at him, she gasped.

Orie's other sons both had John's blue eyes, but this baby looked up at Lottie with the same deep brown eyes as her oldest nephew, Tom. Those were the Moon brown eyes—Father's brown eyes. Lottie glanced at Mother, who was beaming with joy, perhaps thinking the same thing.

That whole first month with baby William, Lottie didn't think once about armies marching across Virginia or Southern cities burning. It was as if the war was a bad dream. God had graced their family with new life, and that was all that mattered.

In March, however, Lottie and the family were wrenched back into the reality that was raging just beyond their front door. They heard that Northern soldiers were marching through the area, destroying the canals down in Scottsville and moving through the countryside, confiscating food, livestock, and anything that might be helpful to the Confederate cause. Rumors of ransacking drove John and Orie to gather their boys and stay at Viewmont so the whole family could face whatever may come together.

Lottie was in the nursery, watching William nap in the mid-afternoon. When he began cooing and kicking in his bassinet, she crossed the room and scooped him up. It had been a long nap. He must be hungry.

Lottie carried William around the house, searching for Orie. The rooms and hallways were eerily empty. She peeked into the parlor. No one. She went to the library next, which was empty, and then the dining room. She found Peggy sorting and counting an unusually large amount of silverware on the table. Only a wedding party would need that many utensils. Lottie quietly left Peggy to her work, whatever she was doing, and ventured out to the kitchen. She stepped through the doorway and halted.

Half the household was bustling around the kitchen. Meg was dragging sacks of what looked like sugar and flour from the back of the room. Orie was placing some apples into a small basket. Others went into a large wooden crate.

Mother was pointing around the room, giving Fannie directions. "Bundle up the bacon and any other food we can spare for the next several days."

Fannie nodded and started stacking bacon onto a clean white cloth.

"Do you think George can manage all of this?" Mother asked Fannie.

"Yes, ma'am, he's readyin' the wagon now." Fannie folded the cloth over the bacon. With a shaking hand, she reached for a box on a shelf. She pulled out some twine and tied up the bacon.

Mother rubbed her crumpled brow. "Oh, I wish Ike were here to help protect us."

"He's out with the army protecting us." Meg heaved a sack of flour at Mother's feet.

Mother melted and reached for Meg's hand. "Yes, of course he is. I'm sorry, Meg."

No one seemed to notice Lottie had walked in. William wailed in her arms. He must have realized he was hungry.

Orie immediately looked up from sorting her apples. She smiled with pity and wiped her hands on her dress as she crossed the room to her baby. "Here, darling boy." After picking him up, she sat on a chair in the corner and fed him.

Lottie's empty hands twitched. "What's going on?"

"Yankees are raiding the area," Mother said.

Lottie's stomach dropped. *Not again.* "What can I do?"

"Peggy is collecting all the silverware and jewelry into the dining room." Mother stepped around and over sacks of food toward Lottie. She held Lottie's shoulders, looking straight into her eyes. "I want you to take it into the woods and bury it."

"The jewelry too?" Even the pearls that had been on Mother's wrist at weddings, funerals, and holiday suppers? She had always insisted they be kept clean.

"All of it, Lottie. Bury it good, and be sure to cover the loose dirt with any leaves and sticks."

Lottie looked around the kitchen. "Is all of this necessary?"

"You weren't here last year," Orie snapped. "They'll burn what they don't steal."

Lottie turned to face her sister with her fists mounted on her hips. "Did you forget where I was last year? I saw what Sherman did to Atlanta. I just don't understand why they're here now."

"This is war—it doesn't have to make sense. Last year, they burned wilderness and farms in the Shenandoah. You weren't here. You didn't worry about them coming into your home and destroying everything and everyone."

"Enough!" Mother shouted.

William started to cry. Orie rocked him. Lottie lowered a raised finger and closed her mouth, even though she was ready to tell Orie just how wrong she was. Of course, Lottie knew what that fear and worry felt like. General Sherman had marched past the grand home she was staying at in Georgia.

"Go, Lottie," Mother said with enough indisputable force to make a cat jump into a river. "No Yankees are taking my mother's silver—not today."

Lottie nodded and rushed into the dining room. The family's heirlooms sprawled across the dining room table—Mother's pearls, her silver-plated hairbrush, and all the fine things that Lottie had seen while growing up. They were beautiful, all together, glittering in the candlelight like pirates' loot in a novel. Peggy asked what they were supposed to do with it all.

Lottie took a deep breath. "We're going to bury it in the woods."

"In the dirt?" Panic carved lines on Peggy's face. Burying the silver was quite a different task than her usual assignment of polishing it.

"They're convinced the Yankees are coming." Lottie rubbed a headache twisting above her eyebrow.

They were filling their apron pockets with the treasures when John burst into the room, breathing heavily as though he had been running.

"Where's your mother?" John swept the hat from his head. "Carter's Mill is burning."

Lottie froze, holding a large spoon. The Carters had been their neighbors her whole life. She pointed toward the kitchen with her spoon-less hand. John rushed in that direction. Lottie followed him wordlessly, silverware clinking in her pockets. Mother, Orie, and Meg stood there crying, listening to John. Fannie moved quicker, packing up the food and handing bundles to George, who then loaded them into a wagon just outside.

"The Barnes' boy rode through and gave me the news." John's chest was still heaving. "I could see the smoke rising in the distance as he was telling me."

"The poor Carters." Mother shook her head. "Was the family safe outside?"

John opened his arms to Orie, holding his youngest son. "The boy didn't say. He just gave me the news and rode off to warn the next house. Once Viewmont is secure and the soldiers have passed through, I'll check on the Carters."

Orie sobbed into her husband's chest. "What are we going to do?"

"We're going to pray," John said, sounding more confident than he looked.

Lottie stepped further into the kitchen. Peggy, who had apparently trailed her, joined her mother. Fannie, Peggy, and George stopped to bow their heads too. The family huddled together as John asked the Lord to cover them and somehow divert the soldiers away from Viewmont.

After John said *amen*, Mother hugged Lottie. "Run hard, Lottie." She kissed Lottie's cheek, leaving it damp with her tears. "If you see smoke from the house, stay in the woods."

Tears filled Lottie's eyes as she nodded. "We will."

Mother blinked and cocked her head. "'We'?"

"Peggy and I."

Mother's gaze shifted to Peggy. She leaned close to Lottie and whispered, "I want you to go alone. Do not let her take any silver."

Why on earth would she suggest such a thing? Mother had never accused the slaves of stealing before.

"Can I put the silver in the wagon with George and the food?" Lottie whispered back.

Her brow furrowed, Mother cast a sideways glance at George as Fannie handed him the last bundle of food.

"It's *George*, Mother." Lottie spoke low but propped her hand on her waist.

Mother shook her head so slightly that only Lottie noticed ... hopefully.

"You go ahead, George." Mother waved him on. "The other servants should stay in their quarters. Northern soldiers won't burn those."

Without being asked, Peggy pulled the silver from her pockets and handed it to Lottie. Lottie tossed Mother an *I-told-you-so* look. Peggy embraced her father, then quickly left with her mother for the cabins. George set out into the woods with the wagon loaded with food.

Lottie hurried back into the dining room. She shoved as much more silverware as she could into her apron pockets, then wrapped the rest of her family's treasures into the tablecloth and scooped the bundle into her arms. After making her way down the porch steps, she clutched the bundle close and ran with all her might in the other direction from the one George had taken.

The woods were dark even though the sun hadn't gone down yet. She ran farther into the forest than she had gone before. Eventually, she slowed and stopped. Her arms and legs ached, but the energy coursing through her veins kept her focused on what she had to do.

Lottie looked around her for a good spot. She found one between two trees and dropped to the ground. She grabbed a sharp stick and started digging a hole in the ground as deep as she could. Then she dumped all of her family's treasures in. She frantically pushed the dirt back over the hole and covered it with leaves, sticks, and small rocks, just as Mother had said, so that it looked natural like the rest of the wooded area.

Lottie got up and didn't bother brushing the dirt off her hands or her dress. She just ran back home, relieved with each deep breath that she didn't smell smoke. Once she got out of the woods, she could see the sun setting over the fields, painting the clouded sky with vibrant reds and oranges. It looked like war.

They hunkered down together in their home all night, waiting for something they hoped and prayed wouldn't come. And it didn't. One by one, Lottie's siblings and nephews went upstairs to bed or fell asleep in the parlor. Orie left her seat on the settee to feed William upstairs. John and Mother sat across the room from Lottie, wide awake in a chair near the fireplace. She stared at the glowing logs, reciting Psalm 23 as she had done while Sherman was burning Georgia. Lottie got up and silently followed after her sister. She wanted to finally tell Orie what she saw in Georgia.

She climbed the stairs and opened the door of the nursery. Orie rocked in Mother's chair, smiling and swaying with her baby while she fed him. She motioned for Lottie to come in.

Lottie stepped in and sat at the foot of the rocking chair as she had when she was a child, listening to Mother's stories. This time, she had her own story to share. Lottie clutched her knees to her chest and told Orie all about that day in Valdosta, about Katherine's father whipping the bleeding, shaking man, and the other slaves who carried him away. "Reading about it in a book was so different than living in the middle of it."

Orie's eyes brimmed with tears. "I'm so sorry. That poor soul."

"When this war started, I hated the North for assuming such power over us. But now I don't know." Lottie pushed her hair away from her forehead. "No one should be able to do what Katherine's father did to another man without consequences."

Orie pursed her lips and shook her head. "No, they shouldn't."

It was plain to see by now that the Confederacy was going to lose this war. Sherman's army had crushed them. These raids might be the final straw that breaks Richmond's back. Lottie straightened her legs and leaned back on her hands. "When this war is over, and the slaves are free, things will be different."

Orie lifted a pained smile. "Yes, I'm afraid so."

By morning the next day, Lottie relaxed a little, but everyone seemed wary of the peace. Had the soldiers really moved on? Of course, it was what they'd prayed for, but it wasn't what they'd expected.

Fannie came up to the house as she usually did, but Mother told her the slaves should stay in their cabins until she could sort out where the soldiers went and what was happening on the other farms. Mother said George could bring the wagon back from the woods, but he should leave the food packed in the wagon and cover it in case he needed to run it out again. Orie cared for her little ones while Lottie, Mother, and Meg put together a simple breakfast for everyone.

John grabbed an apple, then went over to Carter's Mill to offer any help he could. He came back after noon, bewildered. Carter's Mill was fine. Mr. Carter had told him no soldiers came through and nothing had burned.

"Then why did the Barnes boy give us that warning?" Mother demanded.

John sat down at the dining table with everyone, and Orie handed him a plate of cold ham biscuits.

"I wondered that, too," John said, taking a biscuit. "He probably saw dust clouds, not smoke. Mr. Carter said he was worried about raiders just as we were, so he moved his cattle all at once, out of sight from the road. When I saw the herd today, they all needed a good washing. They probably kicked up a mighty dust cloud."

Mother pursed her lips, as if she was fighting to keep strong words from escaping.

"They were still glad I came by." John shrugged. "Mr. Carter threw out his shoulder herding all those cattle. I set it right and made up a sling for him so it'll heal properly."

"Did they pay you anything for it?" Orie's gaze jolted up at John. She had stopped pulling the ham into pieces that were small enough for James to eat.

John shook his head sadly. "They don't have money to spare any more than we do."

"He's gonna choke on that," Mother snapped at Orie.

Orie furrowed her brow and tore the piece of ham again, in half, then gave it to James.

Lottie felt as angry as Mother apparently was. She'd run as she had never run before. Her legs were sore, and her arms ached from carrying the silver and jewelry. War was hard enough without people spreading rumors and causing unnecessary panic.

Mother heaved a sigh. "Well, Lottie, I suppose you can bring the silver back now. There's still plenty of daylight. Maybe by tomorrow we'll dine with proper silverware again."

Sallie and Mollie asked to go too.

"In the woods to dig in the dirt?" Lottie's eyebrows arched. Her prissy sisters had clearly been cooped up for too long, hiding from apparently imaginary soldiers. The girls might regret it and complain about dirtying their dresses, but Lottie needed the help. She didn't have the strength to carry that load by herself again.

Sallie and Mollie walked with Lottie back into the woods, but Lottie couldn't find the same spot. It all looked so different in the daylight. After what must have been an hour, Lottie clutched her hair as she turned in circles searching for freshly dug earth.

"How far did you run?" Sallie asked nervously.

Lottie fixed her gaze to the ground. The twisted bun at the top of her head was unravelling. "I don't know—farther than usual. I buried it between two trees."

Sallie and Mollie exchanged a knowing glance, then surveyed the endless trees that surrounded them.

When they returned for supper empty-handed, Mother didn't scold Lottie. She silently nodded, then joined the rest of the family in the parlor for the evening.

Lottie thanked God that her family and her home were safe, but the Barnes boy's false alarm added a sting to the loss of her family's silver and jewels. If Peggy had been allowed to help Lottie, would *she* have remembered where the treasure was buried? And if Mother had allowed George to take it in the wagon, he would have rolled the silver up to the house along with the food.

Down the road in Appomattox, General Lee surrendered to General Grant of the Union Army on April 9. The war had finally ended, and so did the Confederate States of America.

The day the news reached Viewmont and was confirmed by neighbors, Lottie tried to comfort Mother, collapsed on the parlor sofa and crying into her hands. A Union victory meant the Southern economy their family depended on had just changed forever. However, couldn't this dramatic change signal an opportunity for something new, maybe even better?

"We'll be okay, Mother." Lottie placed her hand on Mother's shoulder. "The Lord will lead us into what's next. He will provide for us."

Mother straightened and patted Lottie's lap with a weak smile.

"Our men fought bravely, and now the war is over," Lottie said. "That's something to celebrate, isn't it?"

"Now Ike can come home," Meg added, beaming.

"I thank God that Ike made it through, and we all survived." Mother clutched Lottie's and Meg's hands. "It's a miracle. But the fighting isn't over. I fear it's barely begun."

Peggy walked in with a tray of tea. Mother, Lottie, and Meg immediately locked eyes on the young woman who didn't yet know that she was free.

At all the attention, Peggy's brow furrowed. "Pardon, ma'am, is now a bad time?"

The next night, Peggy helped Lottie get ready for bed. Peggy wasn't enslaved anymore, but Lottie had asked for help, and Peggy obliged. Lottie sat at the vanity table, and Peggy stood behind her, tying up Lottie's hair as they had done for years.

Some of the emancipated slaves had left Viewmont as soon as they heard the news. Some, like Fannie and George, took the offer to stay on as employed workers. Others, including Peggy and her husband, stayed on without committing, as if they weren't sure what to do next.

Lottie handed Peggy more rags as she told Lottie some of the freed slaves had gone looking for a factory job up North or a new opportunity out West. Some left to join their families around the country.

Lottie glanced at Peggy in the mirror, chewing her lip. She had never talked with Peggy about where she would go if she were free. But now that Peggy was free, she wouldn't get in trouble talking to Lottie about these things.

"Do you and Matthew know what you're going to do? Now that the war is over?"

Peggy met Lottie's eyes in the mirror while her hands continued twisting Lottie's hair into rags. She didn't answer right away, as if she wondered about getting into trouble too. This new world was an adjustment for everyone.

"We've talked about getting work at Hollins," Peggy said.

Lottie raised her eyebrows.

A soft smile bloomed on Peggy's face. "I liked it there when we were girls —most days, anyway."

Lottie's cheeks burned. Her April Fool's prank rang in her memory.

Peggy shrugged. "Matthew thinks we're more likely to have steady work there, more than—"

Peggy cut herself short. Her hands froze, and her face went scarlet. She looked down as if reprimanding herself for getting too comfortable in the conversation.

"More than at this struggling plantation, you mean," Lottie said kindly. "I plan to find work elsewhere too. Leaving is wise."

Peggy relaxed and went back to work. "I disagree."

Lottie jolted. "You want to stay here?"

"I told Matthew we need to leave Virginia altogether." Peggy sighed and shook her head. "The school will pay us, but they'll still treat us the same as when we were slaves. That's all folks know."

Lottie's eyes widened. She nodded slowly.

"I want us to start new out West so our children have a fresh start."

Lottie gasped. Her jaw dropped. "Are you expecting?"

Peggy laughed and blushed again. "I just told Matthew this week." She closed her eyes for a moment and laid a hand on her belly. "All our babies are gonna be born free."

"Will your parents go with you—out West?" Lottie tried to calm down and sound unconcerned. Losing a strong young man like Matthew would be a blow. But Mother might be more likely to lease the land to sharecroppers, anyway, than be able to pay a freedman's wage. And since the Moon girls would be going away to school or finding a job soon, they could get on just fine. But Fannie and George seemed essential to life at Viewmont. Mother would be lost if they left.

"They say they're too old to start something new like that," Peggy said, relieving Lottie's concerns. "Mama wants to stay at Viewmont. Once Matthew and me get settled, and especially when we have more babies, she'll ask Mistress Moon for permission so she and Papa can visit."

Lottie cocked her eyebrow at Peggy in the mirror and almost laughed at Peggy's modesty. "Well, I don't think they need to ask permission anymore, do they?"

Peggy smiled at her as though she knew that—she was just testing the waters. "I suppose not anymore, Miss."

Celebrating the end of the war didn't last long. In the weeks that followed, President Lincoln had been assassinated. The newly reunited states were already breaking apart.

Lottie paused as she walked by the study and her Mother's crying drifted into the hallway. She paused and peeked around the cracked door. Ike stood next to her, patting a reassuring hand on Mother's heaving shoulders as she slumped over the desk.

Good, she's not alone this time.

Lottie didn't need to ask what was wrong. She already knew. The Moons had fifteen-hundred acres of farmland, no slaves to work it, and no money to hire laborers. All the Confederate dollars Mother had exchanged their cash for were worthless now. And the neighbors who owed her from hiring Viewmont's slaves had no way to pay her back—not with their Confederate money. Any valuables that the family could have sold were still buried in the woods somewhere. Lottie had gone back again to check, and George had looked too. Nothing had turned up.

Selling some jewelry and silver spoons wouldn't restore the Moon family fortune, but still, guilt rose up in Lottie's throat when she remembered them. Of course, she cared and prayed about the future of Viewmont. But those were Mother and Ike's decisions to make. Lottie and her sisters had their own futures to worry about.

There was enough money from Father's will to send Eddie and Mollie to Richmond Female Institute but not enough for them to come home for Christmas. Sallie had finished her schooling and was qualified for a job now, if she could find one. John had enough work in the area, but no one could pay him, at least not as much as he needed to keep up a profitable practice. John and Orie had started talking about settling in Alabama. John said he heard of paying work there.

Lottie's missionary dreams felt more distant than ever before. She had read in a Baptist newspaper that the Foreign Mission Board only had a dollar and seventy-eight cents in its bank account. Life wasn't like it was before the war in any way. Before, teaching was a fun idea and an adventure. It never felt necessary—not with her family's fortune to rely on. But now, she needed a job, so she began writing inquiries. She couldn't stay at Viewmont, not when the estate didn't have enough means to support her.

Chapter Thirty

1869

Lottie looked up from her writing desk in her room at Danville Female Academy. Out the window, students were lazing under trees, enjoying the sunny, October afternoon and walking arm in arm, maybe sharing their secrets and dreams with each other. It made Lottie smile.

Teaching the girls in Danville, Kentucky, was like experiencing some of the best parts of her own childhood all over again. When Lottie had been in school, she'd never enjoyed deportment classes, and here she was instructing her students on manners and behavior. Even with such a dull teaching assignment, Lottie was grateful. As young and lively as the students often made her feel, working to support herself and sending money home to help Mother reminded Lottie that she was one of the adults now.

Life in the former border state of Kentucky was different from living in the heart of the old Confederacy. While Southern states were slowly reconstructing after the Civil War, Kentucky came out in much better shape. People here still had enough money to send their daughters to fine schools and support a staff of qualified teachers. John Broadus had given her a glowing reference that cleared the road for her.

Once she got here, however, Lottie's connection to the Confederacy certainly hadn't made her popular among the other teachers or the people in her church. They didn't make much of an effort to welcome her or invite her to tea. It was as though they thought they already knew everything they needed to know about her—Lottie was a slaveholder's daughter from a Virginia plantation. On campus and on the street, people sneered at her as though she was responsible for starting the war and taking away so many of Kentucky's sons, fathers, and brothers. Over time, however, Lottie's vivacity, sharp mind, and servant-hearted devotion to God had won most people over.

After her first year at Danville Female Academy, a group of Presbyterians took the school over from the Baptists and renamed it Caldwell Institute. The Presbyterians increased the teachers' pay, and Lottie had been promoted to teach more interesting subjects like languages. She'd even influenced the school board to hire her sister, Mollie, as a teacher. God was providing so perfectly for her here.

Lottie had assured the school board that Mollie had thrived at Richmond Female Institute. Her essay was even read at graduation, just like Cary Ann Coleman's was back at Hollins—or, Cary Ann Coleman *Moon*, which became her name when she and Jimmy married shortly after the war. Cary Ann seemed so happy, from her letters. Apparently, Jimmy was a model husband and could do no wrong, which, as Lottie knew from growing up with the boy, was completely untrue.

The good thing about having her sister work in the same place was that Lottie only had to write half as many letters home. When it was Mollie's turn to write to Mother, Lottie could simply add a line and a signature at the end. Today it was Lottie's turn.

Group by group, the students outside her window began to pack up their things and get ready for supper. Lottie returned her focus to her desk and continued writing about her promotion from teaching deportment to languages, which she wrote:

> ...is not only much more interesting and rewarding to teach, but it also means that I can send more money home, as you've asked.
>
> I'm grateful God gave me favor with the people here and with John Broadus, whose reference has proven invaluable once again! I truly enjoy teaching at Danville Female Academy, now Caldwell Institute. Mollie is doing very well too. It's a joy to see my former student now teaching girls who some-times give her the same struggles that she used to give me. The new Presbyterian school doesn't seem to mind us Baptist teachers, even Mollie, who as you know calls herself a Catholic now.

At Danville Baptist Church, I've been teaching the girls the Twenty-third Psalm. The Lord reveals more of its beauty to me whenever I teach it.

How is Uncle James? There's a man at the church, Dr. Burton, who often makes me think of him. He was a medical missionary to China. It's a joy to spend time with him, listening to his stories and seeing his passion for the spread of the gospel. Mr. Cabaniss, another retired missionary to China, is here working among Kentucky Baptists to promote missions. It appears as though I am surrounded!

Lottie signed the letter but didn't seal it. Soon, she would hand it off to Mollie.

She reached into her desk and touched another letter she had received from Crawford shortly after the war. She couldn't throw it out ... not yet. She carefully opened it again and let her eyes rest on those words—*Marry me.* It was quite a thorough, well-thought-out proposal, almost like a business proposition.

The board still isn't sending missionaries right now, but we can be married for a while and then go to Japan when there are funds.

You once said you didn't know if I loved you. I don't express love as flamboyantly as others, but I do love you. Thoughts of you sustained me during the war. Memories of simple days in Charlottesville, listening to your voice, treasuring each breeze that carried the scent of your hair to me. I'm convinced that if we marry, you and I will make a good match.

But when he finally asked, Lottie felt deep in her heart that it wasn't right. Shortly after she got that letter, she accepted the offer to teach in Danville instead. Crawford didn't respond to her reply letter. Julie told her later that he had gone to Germany to study theology. Whatever the reason for that decision, at least he would get to practice his German.

Later that week, Mollie stopped by Lottie's classroom to add a few lines to their joint letter before sending it in the next post.

"I wish you would write all the letters, and I could just sign them," Mollie said. "Yours are always more interesting and well written than mine."

"Yours are perfectly fine." Lottie cleared off her desk for the end of the week. "Besides, if we started doing that, Mother might worry you've run off and gotten married or something."

Mollie sighed and looked dreamily into the distance, as if that wasn't such a bad idea.

Lottie propped a fist onto her hip and tilted her head. "I wasn't serious, Mollie."

Mollie snapped back into the moment. "Hm? Oh, yes, of course. It's just that ... Dr. Shepherd is such a wonderful man, isn't he?"

Confusion swirled in Lottie's head, then it suddenly dawned on her. "The doctor who helped that student who fell last month?"

Mollie patted her braided chignon bun at the nape of her neck. "He's so talented and kind. I see him at mass, too, very regularly."

Lottie tried not to frown at the thought of Mollie at mass. Both Mollie and Sallie had been more influenced by Nicholas's Catholic faith than Lottie had realized when she was observing their tutor's lessons years ago.

Mollie studied her nails. "I'll try not to run away, but it would be so nice to marry him one day."

Lottie smiled, unconvinced and unconcerned. She'd learned to not worry about Mollie's latest crush. Both Mollie and Sallie had always been romantics.

Mother's response to their letter came quickly.

Thank you for sending the money. It went straight to paying off debts. It's been difficult owing money to family, especially when I'm owed money myself by some neighbors. But I won't detail all of that again.

Sallie seems to be intentionally leaving her rosary beads around the house, which she knows upsets me. You should see the way she handles them and mumbles her "prayers." It's nearly pagan. Every time I see them on a table some- where, regret rises in me for hiring Nicholas. Do you remember him? She recently told me that he was a Roman Catholic, too, as if that would comfort me and show how such wonderful people are Catholics. I appreciate your advice for tolerance, but it's difficult in my own house. Still, I will treasure her presence while she's here. She recently got a job teaching in Bristol, Virginia. I'm thankful she won't be too far away from home.

I miss you, Mollie, and Orie. But that's the price a mother pays for having such accomplished women like you as daughters. You make me proud, Lottie. Your father would be, too, if he were here. Even your grandmother. Although, she'd be completely horrified at all the Catholicism in the family now.

Eddie has earned her diploma and is still deciding what to do. She is just as anxious as you were at that stage in life. I'm anxious for her, only because she's my last chick to leave the nest. I know she's a charming, smart girl and will thrive in whatever she does.

As you know, your Uncle James has been teaching at the college in western Virginia. He and Julia have set their minds to retire to Alabama and live with your cousin there. I don't know yet when they will leave. Ike and Meg send their love.

Lottie's eyebrows came together as she set down the letter. She immediately pulled out a fresh sheet of paper and filled it with encouragement for her youngest sister. An educated woman with Eddie's sensible mind and passionate heart would surely find a mountain of desirable opportunities soon enough.

Thankfully, Mother hadn't detailed her worries about the estate again. They'd ended up selling portions of the land to some cousins whose finances were still in decent shape because they didn't depend solely on farming for income. Mother also let local farmers use some of Viewmont's land in exchange for the first pick at the crops. To make ends meet, and only as a last resort, Mother had borrowed money from extended family.

It troubled Lottie to witness her home and inheritance dwindle, but Mother seemed completely broken by it. Lottie and her siblings reassured Mother they understood she was making the best decisions she could in such dire circumstances. But it wasn't lost on Lottie the shame Mother must feel for being the generation that lost the family fortune her ancestors had built up ever since they sailed from Scotland and stepped foot in America.

After one semester working at the Danville school, Mollie left in a huff and returned to Virginia to teach. Apparently, Dr. Shepherd wasn't responsive enough to her flirtations, and she told Lottie that she needed to become an independent woman, away from "that obstinate man." Lottie tried to convince Mollie that Dr. Shepherd was probably being calculated with the relationship, not wanting to seem hasty or improper. If Mollie stayed and continued getting to know him, he might ask to marry her. But she was insistent on making her own way, which, judging from Mother's letters after Mollie had returned home, proved more difficult than she'd thought.

With all the chaos going on at home, Lottie wasn't exactly surprised by Eddie's latest letter in March 1870.

Mother's not doing well. I wanted to tell you because I'm sure she didn't mention it.

Indeed, Mother hadn't mentioned her ill health at all. But it was obvious from her letters that she was consumed with stress about the future of Viewmont and, at times, her daughters. And as far as Lottie knew, Mother and Orie still weren't talking—not after their latest argument about the methods by which Orie was raising her children.

A lump rose in Lottie's throat. She would go see Mother and comfort her, but the end of the school year was still a few months away. As soon as the semester ended, Lottie would leave for Virginia.

Lottie missed having a family member nearby, but there was much to do in Danville that kept her occupied. In addition to keeping up with her family back home and teaching her students, she had become a leader at the Baptist church, even a deaconess, but without the title. She didn't crave the posterity of a title, but she had written a two-part series of articles, advocating for Baptists to give women official religious orders as other Christian denominations did. If the Baptist church assigned deaconesses, more women would work in God's harvest fields.

Lottie had no idea the *Religious Herald* would print her articles on the front page. In the first one, she wrote about a Catholic priest in Strasburg, Germany, who had set up a deaconess house, where over three hundred women have now served the poor and needy for pledges of five years at a time.

Baptist newspapers didn't usually print articles shining a favorable light on Catholics, so Lottie signed her article on the Strasburg Deaconesses as "M" from Kentucky. In part two, the *Religious Herald* editors endorsed her article:

> *We commend the article below to the careful attention of our readers, especially of our city bishops. We have long been convinced that our churches have failed to employ usefully their female members. They occupied a sphere of activity and usefulness in the apostolic churches, it seems to us, which has not been assigned to them in modern churches. Let us think of the matter.*

The editors' support emboldened her to sign this one as "L. M." from Danville, Kentucky. In the article, she moved away from foreign Catholics and focused on what the Episcopalians in Philadelphia were doing about creating opportunities for women in the church to serve in nursing ministries, sewing circles, Bible classes, and Sunday schools! They were organizing their women like the Catholics had done, blessing the people of Philadelphia with a host of eager, capable servants.

Lottie had volunteered herself at the Baptist church in Danville, but she had to be bold and find her place there. So many Baptist women were not serving because there seemed to be no place for them, leaving scores of hurting people in their cities without help and hope. After sending her articles out into the world, Lottie went back to the plow, teaching a girls' Sunday school class and helping her pastor with research and correspondence.

Spending time at the church was always exciting, especially when Dr. Burton was around. The way he talked about the Chinese people and their need for the gospel could make anyone leave everything and run straight to San Francisco to catch the next ship for China. The thought tempted Lottie, as missions always did. The more she learned about the need for foreign missionaries, the more she considered asking Helen to release her from that promise to care for Tom. No. The Bible said to not break one's vows. Lottie couldn't go as a missionary, but she could pray for them and give money to the cause, and she did.

Another letter from Eddie in May shocked Lottie into action.

> *Come home as soon as you can. Mother might not make it through the summer.*

Eddie wasn't one to exaggerate. Lottie reached under her bed and pulled out her traveling bags right away. "The Lord is my shepherd. I have all that I need," she whispered to herself as she latched her bags closed.

Lottie had arrived one month before Mother passed on June 21. Sallie and Mollie had come into town even earlier, but Orie couldn't come right away. She wouldn't be able to receive the news and arrive in time for the burial on Friday. It was already Wednesday. Soon, they'd lay Mother to rest beside Grandmother, Father, and her other babies, whom she'd joined in heaven.

Lottie wrote to John so that he could break the news to Orie that Mother had passed peacefully.

June 21, 1870

Dear Brother John,

The worst, no, the best has come. Mother went home to God today about two o'clock. We bury her Saturday. She spoke of Sister often—said 'my affection for Orianna is unchanged.' She said, 'all of my children are dear & sweet to me.'

She died peacefully & happily. For about three days, there was no pain. The last moments were, of course, sad, but I think I can never fear death after seeing her triumph over it. I wish dear Sister could have seen her. We told her we would all meet her in the many mansions. How happy she is now with the husband & children gone before! She said to me on yesterday, 'Lottie, my darling, don't cry for me. I want not a tear at my grave to be shed.' Then added, 'You must rejoice with me.' I will write more fully soon. My precious sisters & brother bear it with Christian resignation. I do so sympathize with dear Sister. Tell her this with my love —Mother said, 'Peace, live at peace among yourselves.' She meant her children.

I am too exhausted to write more.

Yours,

Lottie.

Two weeks after her mother's funeral, Lottie slouched in her chair, fanning herself as the late summer sun poured in through the large library windows. The painted flowers on the folded paper fluttered as her wrist flicked back and forth. Each tiny gust of manufactured wind tossed strands of hair back from her sticky face.

Mother's death had come quickly, although it wasn't as untimely as Father's or Tom's or the babies'. It didn't knock Lottie down with shock, but the grief had its own weight. She was nearly thirty years old, without a parent to guide her or children to distract her. God didn't give her a reason, but he gave her peace about rejecting Crawford's last marriage proposal.

Eddie walked in and silently locked eyes with Lottie. They had to get out of the house, even if it was a scorching July day. They strolled down through the gardens and admired the roses in bloom. They ventured past the shady apple orchards and dipped into the woods.

Eddie walked down to the water lightly swinging a rose bloom by her side, and then laying it on top of the gentle current. It had been several years since Lottie had tutored her. During Eddie's time at the Richmond Female Institute, she had become an eloquent and confident young woman. She came back up to the shaded area of the woods, slid an arm around Lottie, and rested her head on Lottie's shoulder.

"When did my baby sister become so grown?" Lottie pecked the top of Eddie's head with a kiss.

After Eddie went to school in Richmond and Lottie went to work in Kentucky, they'd kept up over letters as much as they could, but there was a lot that didn't make it into the mailbox. There by the river, Eddie told Lottie that she wanted to become a missionary.

Lottie gasped and lurched back to get a better look at her. "Where did this come from?"

Eddie laughed, straightening after she fell off Lottie's shoulder. "From you. And Uncle James's influence and Mother's too." Her face clouded.

"Did she know?"

"Yes, I made sure to tell her every good thing I could think of."

Lottie smiled. "I'm sure that filled her with joy, just as it fills my heart with joy."

Eddie's eyes sparkled as she beamed at Lottie.

Lottie patted her sister's arm. "That's a beautiful dream for one day."

Eddie's eyes cut to the ground. She bit her lip then glanced up at Lottie in a restrained smile. "No, actually, I want to be a missionary very soon."

Lottie shook her head. "From what I know, it's very difficult to do that right now." Without intending to, she slipped into her teaching voice. "Missionaries have to raise much of their own support, and the Baptist Foreign Mission Board still doesn't send single women."

Eddie's face fell.

"I'm sorry, Eddie. I don't mean to put you off such a worthwhile dream. I just don't see how you can go as a missionary right now. Unless ..." Panic flashed in Lottie's heart. "You don't have more news to share, do you? You don't have a beau?"

Eddie exhaled with a sharp laugh. "No, God is calling me to go to China as single as I am, and I think it will be very soon."

Lottie tried to think how to encourage her. "Mother left you some money, and you have a top-notch education. Think about the exciting ways God could put that to good use."

"You don't think I can do it," Eddie said with a bite in her voice and fire in her eyes. "I'll always be your baby sister. You can't even imagine me doing something as wild as sailing across the world to minister to Chinese women!"

Lottie lurched back again. "No, of course, you can do it, and you should do it. It's just not possible right now. I thought that I wanted to be a missionary to China, too, but I probably won't because of—" Her nephew's name filled her mind, finishing that sentence in her head. For some reason, she didn't want to say it out loud. "There's just so much need right here. You could try teaching. And then you'd have an income. You could support foreign missions as I'm doing."

"Is that what you really think?"

"It's sensible." Lottie shrugged. She had accepted the reality that being a missionary was impossible right now. Eddie would accept it, too, once she let it sink in.

Eddie nodded curtly, but her eyes smoldered.

It took a while before they spoke again and walked back up to the house.

Lottie stayed at Viewmont for the rest of the summer. An awful occasion had brought her home, but she relished time with Eddie, Ike, Meg, Sallie, and Mollie. Getting to know her siblings more as adults was an odd but satisfying experience.

Shortly before the school year started up again, Sallie returned to Bristol. Mollie was still sending out inquiries about another teaching position, but she said she was considering returning to Kentucky. The doctor had written to her over the summer, which seemed to have softened her resolve to stay away from him forever. Eddie stayed at home for now but vowed to find God's path for her soon enough.

Lottie left Viewmont in good hands with Margaret and Isaac, who became the estate's executor after Mother died.

Lottie returned to Danville, Kentucky, in the fall to teach for another school year. She arrived more tired and weary than when she left in the spring. That weariness drew Lottie to relax in a common area of the teachers' dorm. She was startled when a bright, blonde woman suddenly walked up to her—a new teacher whose energetic smile seemed like a permanent fixture on her face.

She thrust her hand toward Lottie. "Anna Safford's the name. Pleased to meet you."

CHAPTER THIRTY-ONE

1871

Anna Safford was the daughter of a Presbyterian minister who traveled and preached throughout the South. She and Lottie became fast friends, not only because they were both passionate about missions and women's education, but also because they were the only Southerners on staff.

One day in the teacher's lounge, Anna was pouring herself a hot drink at the tea service when Lottie, sitting nearby, yawned loudly.

"Out late on the town again?" Anna teased.

"You know me—wild as a western stallion." Lottie tried to cover another yawn.

Anna stirred honey into her cup. "You went straight to church right after yesterday's last class, didn't you? How long did you stay?"

"The pastor needed research help again, and Dr. Burton was speaking that evening about ministering among the Chinese, so I had to stay and listen. In the time between, I got to prepare my lesson for the girls on Sunday. It was all very exhilarating. I just didn't expect it to go so late." Lottie yawned for a third time.

Anna handed her a hot cup of tea. "Looks as though you'll need this to make it through the rest of the day."

"Thanks, friend." Lottie paused for a moment over the steam and took a sip.

"Has Dr. Burton convinced you to be a missionary yet?" Anna tilted her head. "That's why he's here, right? Recruiting Baptist missionaries?"

"I'm sure that's part of why he's here," Lottie said between sips. "Mostly, he's raising support for the missionaries still in China. I joined in supporting them. I'm thankful to work here, where I'm needed, and still get to support missions."

"I feel that way, too, but sometimes, I wonder if I'm needed here as much as I think I am. Have you ever wondered if you'd be of more use on the mission field?"

"This is where God has me." Lottie shrugged as though she hadn't often wondered the same question when she was still and her heart was quiet. "Anyways, no one would send me without a husband."

"What about that man at the seminary?" Anna's eyebrows bounced. "You said he just wrote to you."

"He did—to tell me he's found a wife." Lottie didn't try to keep the irony out of her voice.

Anna winced. "Sorry."

"It's fine." Lottie waved a hand at Anna. "I had my chance with Crawford. The idea of marrying him never sat well with me. What about you? You seem to like the idea of going abroad."

Anna flashed a confident smile. "I'll go one day. I wouldn't mind going with a husband, but I'm growing more comfortable with the idea of keeping my singleness, which wouldn't be a problem except that the Presbyterians are just as hesitant to send unmarried women as the Baptists are."

"At least they're not as broke as the Baptists. If it weren't for people like Dr. Burton and Mr. Cabaniss raising support for missionaries, I shudder to think what would happen to them." Lottie enjoyed the last sip of tea and set her cup down. "That's enough talk of men and missions. Let's get back to work before we give them a reason to finally fire the Southerners."

The students in Anna's and Lottie's classes were best behaved and the most prepared when test time came. The girls loved them and flooded them with tokens to show it. Whatever fruit or flora was in season could always be found on Anna's and Lottie's classroom desks. The hard work of teaching and Anna's spark had rekindled the fire in Lottie's spirit—the fire that had nearly been doused by the war, her family's loss of fortune, and now the loss of her mother. With Anna around, Lottie had a guiding, grounding friend again, as she had with Cary Ann and Julie.

In February 1871, Lottie received word from a distant cousin who was starting a new school for girls in Georgia. It would be in Cartersville, only a short way from Atlanta. He wrote that Georgia was still rebuilding from when General Sherman came through years before. The local families were devastated, he wrote, and the girls were in desperate need of education. The world had changed, and the girls needed to be prepared to enter it boldly, able to earn their own way in life. Men weren't as plentiful as they were before the war, so there were fewer husbands to go around. Her cousin said he'd heard how talented Lottie was as a teacher and invited her as well as Miss Safford, whom he'd also heard so much about, to come run the place as associate principals. Cartersville could use two teachers like them.

"Let's do it!" Anna threw both arms in the air.

Lottie laughed. "But I've barely finished reading you my cousin's letter." She had been reading while Anna paced Lottie's room, wearing a very serious expression.

"What an amazing opportunity! And the timing is so perfect, it must be the Lord's planning."

Lottie wasn't as certain as Anna was. "It could be, but how do we know our work here is finished? God paved the way for me to be here. I can't ignore that."

Anna sighed. Her serious expression returned. "There's no future for us here, Lottie. The parents simply don't want women of the old Confederacy teaching their daughters. One of these days, they'll find a reason to dismiss us."

Lottie couldn't deny that. And the offer did sound like a smart, professional opportunity as well as an amazing adventure. Lottie had never dreamed it—to start a new school from scratch as associate principals in a town full of girls who desperately needed them. There were other teachers for the students in Danville, but not all teachers would want to go to a war-devastated town in the South. If she didn't go teach the girls in Cartersville, who would?

When Lottie and Anna handed in their notice at Caldwell Institute at the end of the spring semester, they were met with polite pleas to stay followed quickly by gracious well wishes. Lottie's students and pastor expressed the most distress. But after the initial surprise, her pastor quickly transitioned to congratulating her and thanking her for her faithful service. Her students, however, tried to persuade her to stay with extra gifts and sweet notes up until her last day. Once everything was settled with their Danville community, Lottie and Anna gleefully took the train to Cartersville as soon as they could.

Right when they arrived in early June, they began planning and preparing for the school to start that fall. Lottie and Anna had been busy meeting with parents of potential students and setting up lesson plans. By September, the new girls' school in Georgia was open. That first year was a complete whirlwind.

Lottie and Anna determined to start the institution with a reputation of discipline and scholarship. They made themselves indispensable by investing in the success of every student who enrolled. They worked to become an inspiration too. When the girls looked at two hard-working Southern women who were successful, even without husbands, they were looking at possibilities for their own futures. The townspeople welcomed them wholly as well, thanking them that though they were talented and educated enough to teach anywhere, they chose Cartersville, Georgia.

Lottie and Anna lived in the same boardinghouse and worked at the same school, but they peacefully went their separate ways on Sunday mornings. Cartersville Baptist Church welcomed Lottie, and the local Presbyterian church welcomed Anna.

By spring of the following year, 1872, the school had dozens of students. It was a lot of work, but as the school grew, so did Lottie's confidence that this was where she was supposed to be. God's blessing seemed all around her.

In the few quiet moments Lottie had alone in her room, she caught her thoughts wandering across the ocean to little girls stumbling around on painfully bound feet and so many Chinese stumbling around in the dark, bound in sin, as Dr. Burton had described. Back in Kentucky, conversations about foreign missions and China had surrounded her. She had felt so much more a part of it all, and she missed that. Still, she wasn't considering anything drastic. The girls in Cartersville needed her. And Tom might need her one day too. Lottie intended to keep her promise to Helen, who had become a widow again, sadly.

And yet, each thought of all the people in China who didn't know God softened Lottie to the possibility of revisiting her old dream. She had dismissed it for so long, but maybe God was trying to tell her something. Oh why did she discourage Eddie from being a missionary that day by the river? She must write to Eddie and apologize, to encourage her sister to follow the Lord, and he would make a way somehow. Before Lottie had a chance, she got a letter from Eddie, saying that she had become a missionary with the Foreign Mission Board!

"And you're sure she's not married?" Anna said when Lottie asked for her help in processing the letter.

"I keep wondering that too. She's the most beautiful of us all, but no—no husband. I can't believe it. I do, of course, but still, I just can't believe it. Eddie is going to China as a missionary," Lottie said in awe.

Lottie told Anna how Eddie wrote that over the past couple years, she had been collecting accounts of other unmarried missionary women, proving why she should be able to go with the Foreign Mission Board. She found that a Baptist woman from a nearby county in Virginia had gone overseas with the Northern Baptists' mission board even though she was from Virginia because she knew the Southern Baptists wouldn't let her go. And Eddie had heard of a few single women who'd accompanied a family on the mission field. It appeared that there was no shortage of women who were capable and willing to go. And when they found avenues to do it, they didn't go alone. They always lived with other missionaries on the field and worked together.

Once Eddie had her accounts in order, she contacted the Foreign Mission Board's new corresponding secretary, Mr. Henry Tupper, for a meeting to share these stories. She also showed him a letter from Mrs. Crawford in Teng-chow, China, inviting Eddie to live at her and her husband's home. Mr. Tupper seemed very interested in that and read it for himself. Eddie then pulled out a reference from the principal of Richmond Female Institute, and she even proposed paying her own salary with her inheritance until proper support could be raised. Even if Mr. Tupper had been hesitant to send single women, her case was convincing. But as it happened, he was eager to start sending more Baptist women, married or not. Eddie made herself look like the perfect candidate for this new initiative.

Mr. Tupper held a special meeting with the board on April ninth, and that day, they appointed her, Edmonia Moon, as a genuine Southern Baptist missionary. Eddie's handwriting was difficult to read when it got to that part of the letter—as if her pen couldn't keep up with what she was trying to say. Apparently, Mr. Tupper knew of a group of Baptist women in Richmond who were organizing a society to support missions. They would support Eddie along with a few other Virginia churches. God must have been preparing it all!

Anna's open-mouthed smile grew bigger the more Lottie talked. "That's incredible," she finally said. "It will change everything for Baptists. More single women will go—just you wait."

Lottie folded the letter, and her arched eyebrows drew together. "I'm starting to think that waiting has been my problem."

Lottie left Anna to run the school while she traveled up to Virginia to help Eddie prepare for her journey to China. When she got to Viewmont, she wasn't the only one who seemed surprised by Eddie's decision. While Isaac, Margaret, and Sallie all helped Eddie fold linens and pack, they looked at their youngest sister in mystified curiosity, as if for all these years, they didn't really know her. Uncle James and Aunt Julia sent a letter of prayer and congratula-tions from Alabama, which arrived just in time before Eddie left. They were beside themselves with joy and proud to have "another missionary in the family."

By May 1872, Eddie was on a steamer ship, and by June, she was in China, writing to Lottie about it.

China is wonderful, Lottie. The weather is pleasant. The community with the other missionaries is delightful, and there's an abundance of good work to do. You would love it here. That day by the river after Mother passed and you tried to convince me to stay in America, you didn't ask if God had called me to go. I think you know that's the only question that really matters. And I think you didn't ask me because you haven't asked yourself that question. Of course, there are a million reasons not to go, but if there's something keeping you home, I pray that you will set it aside. I'm not asking you to let it go. Only, set it aside for a moment and honestly ask the Lord if he is calling you to go. Remember the psalm, if you hear God's voice don't harden your heart.

If Lottie asked herself the question, was she ready to live the consequences of God's answer?

CHAPTER THIRTY-TWO

1873

The plan was for Anna to join Lottie the last week in January at the Baptist church. Every once in a while, they visited each other's church out of as much curiosity as kindness. Lottie's pastor, Dr. Headden, had just returned from a pastors' conference, which meant he was sure to be fired up about something. So Lottie had suggested today might be an interesting day for Anna to visit the Baptists of Cartersville.

No doubt, Anna would be a little bit late, as usual, so Lottie meandered to her writing desk and carefully cleared off a pile of students' papers. She gasped. There was that terrible tintype photograph again—the one Anna had pressured her to have made in Atlanta a few months ago. It made her look as a student, and she hated that giant bow the photographer had suggested she pin at her collar. Lottie kept the photo hidden in her drawer, but after Anna visited Lottie's room, it would somehow be set out in random places, waiting to spook her.

Lottie shoved it back in the drawer where it belonged and sat down to sort through her mail. Hopefully, there would be another letter from Mrs. Crawford in China. It had been a while since her last one.

Eddie had introduced them by mail at first, and now, Lottie and Mrs. Crawford wrote to each other regularly. Lottie read and re-read her letters about life and ministry among the women in China. Mrs. Crawford had told her that women missionaries were particularly needed because whenever Mr. Crawford went into a new village to preach the gospel and minister to the people, the Chinese men would meet with him, but not before quickly ushering the women out of sight of the foreign white man. Lottie explained how it was wonderful for her and Anna to have so much authority and influence in running the school in Georgia. How did the women missionaries rank as decision-makers in a group with male missionaries? Mrs. Crawford had assured Lottie that ministry among the women in Tungchow was very much led by the women missionaries. Not long after Lottie started praying for and corresponding with Mrs. Crawford, God filled Lottie with a passion to start contributing to Mr. and Mrs. Crawford's financial support. So she did.

Sorting through her small stack, Lottie brightened at a letter covered in stamps, many with Chinese writing on them. She carefully tore it open to start reading right away before Anna came in. Lottie's gaze darted from the left of the page to right, then back again. Her heart pounded in her ears, and heat rose from her chest as she read a particular line several times. She slammed the letter down onto the desk. "How could she?!" Lottie popped up out of her desk chair.

Anna had just walked in, ready for church. "I'm not *that* late, am I?"

"It's not you." Lottie smoothed her dress and calmed down. "It's from Eddie. Apparently, my wise, all-knowing sister has decided I'm to be a missionary."

Anna's brow furrowed. "Well, that's not so bad, is it?"

Lottie shoved the offending paper toward Anna. "Eddie actually had Martha Crawford write about me to the corresponding secretary of the Foreign Mission Board."

Anna leaned forward and squinted at the letter. "Oh dear," she said, raising a gloved hand to her mouth.

The letter wasn't from Mrs. Crawford, after all. It came from Lottie's youngest sister. Apparently, in one of Lottie's letters, her excitement and support for Eddie's work among the Chinese had been misinterpreted.

Lottie collapsed into a plush chair by the window and looked up at her friend, searching for answers. "Eddie says I should join them, and Mrs. Crawford has actually written Mr. Tupper. It's completely horrifying." She glanced at the letter again. "I'm still employed here. Wasn't anyone going to ask me?"

"Well ..."

"Yes?" Lottie arched an eyebrow at her friend.

"Hasn't *God* been asking you for years?"

"It's still not right." Lottie crossed her arms and turned her face toward the window.

The work in China that Eddie described had indeed captured Lottie's heart. Eddie was teaching alongside one of the other missionaries who had opened a school for girls. At first, they didn't have many students. The local people exercised a deep distrust of white people, and they didn't bother much with educating their daughters, anyway. However, in Eddie's latest letters, she'd reported a growing number of girls who were hungry to learn, even from foreign teachers. Lottie couldn't help but write in response about how amazing that opportunity was and how proud she felt of Eddie for doing such noble work, serving and loving those girls in the name of their Lord Jesus. No wonder Eddie interpreted Lottie's enthusiastic response as interest in joining her.

Of course, she wanted to. She wanted to teach and minister to the Chinese girls with feet that were bound and ears that had never before heard the precious name of Jesus. But her students in Cartersville and little Tom filled her mind. Didn't they all need her to stay in America? Truth rose in her thoughts and demanded to be recognized. Tom wasn't so little anymore. He was nearly old enough to care for his younger siblings if needed.

Lottie turned back to Anna. "They need us here." Was she trying to convince Anna or herself? "What would the school do if one of the associate principals left?"

"They'd probably go out and hire another one," Anna said matter-of-factly.

Lottie's jaw dropped. She didn't hide her offense.

"This is a successful school now. It'll be easier to fill teaching positions than when we first started. Think about the girls in China who really need teachers." Anna started to count Lottie's qualifications on her hand. "How many other women are gifted in languages like you are, passionate about the gospel, *and* have connections in China and teaching experience and—"

"Okay, okay. I get it." Lottie threw her hands up in surrender, which was just as well because Anna was running out of fingers.

"God has been directing your steps all your life. He has prepared you so thoroughly, but besides all that, it's his calling that qualifies you. Is he leading you to China?"

Lottie closed her eyes for a moment and set aside the thing that was holding her back, imagining that she had never made that promise to Helen. Her heart started to race ahead of her. She shook her head and willed herself to slow down. "But even if I decided to go and if the board would send me, who would support me? All the Virginia churches who know me are supporting Eddie."

Anna laughed. "There sure are lots of reasons not to go, aren't there?"

Lottie shrugged and forced a smile.

"The church here sure seems to like you an awful lot."

Affection for Cartersville Baptist Church rose in Lottie's heart. Teaching the girls in her Sunday school class. Baking cookies for the charity bake sale. Accompanying her pastor on some of his faithful visits to the sick and the homebound church members. Listening to him with rapt attention as he pounded the pulpit, calling the people to advance the good news of Jesus in the world around them. She loved them all, and she had a hunch that they loved her too.

"But would they give their own money for me to go?" Lottie had served the church since she'd arrived in the city, but she had never asked them for money.

"From what I've seen in my last few visits, that church adores you." Anna checked the timepiece on her belt. "Now let's get moving so when you ask them to pay for your missionary expenses one day, they'll think of you as a responsible woman who shows up to church on time."

Lottie set the letter onto her desk, grabbed her Bible and chatelaine purse, and followed Anna out the door. They arrived at Cartersville Baptist and sat down in Lottie's usual pew just as Dr. Headden was walking up to the pulpit. He asked the congregation to turn to John 4. Lottie knew that story before she opened her Bible.

Dr. Headden read about Jesus at the well, waiting for his disciples to bring food. He talked with the Samaritan woman who was hiding, trying to avoid scorn from her neighbors. She was living each day in desperate need of Jesus without knowing him. When the Samaritan woman believed Jesus's claim to be the long-awaited Messiah, he was so satisfied that he didn't feel hungry anymore.

Lottie leaned forward in her seat. She thought of the Chinese women, hidden away from the good news of new life in Jesus. She thought of Mrs. Crawford, Eddie, and the other missionaries working so hard day after day in a foreign land, completely satisfied in doing the good work that God had prepared for them to do.

Tears filled Lottie's eyes, blurring the pages of her Bible. She fumbled in her purse for a handkerchief. Her life was firmly planted in Georgia with a dream job and a loving church. But as she sat in that pew, she felt her heart sailing away to China.

"'Lift up your eyes,'" the pastor read. Lottie did. "'Look on the fields; for they are white already to harvest.'"

When the sermon ended and the offering was taken and the last hymn was sung, Lottie wordlessly left the pew and walked out the door.

"Lottie!" Anna called after her. "Are you okay?"

Lottie paused to turn and wave that all was well, but her head was spinning. Was she really considering becoming a missionary? It was something she'd always wanted but had never seemed possible. And now, her whole world was screaming at her to go. She needed to decide today. If she left the question unanswered and cried like this whenever someone mentioned missions, she'd need a new set of handkerchiefs every month!

Lottie went straight to her bedroom, shut the door, and prayed all afternoon. She read her Bible and paced her room. She prayed for her students, Cartersville Baptist Church, Eddie, Mr. and Mrs. Crawford, the Chinese, and for clarity about her place in all of it. She emerged from her room in time for supper. Nervous glances followed her as she joined Anna, the couple who owned the boardinghouse, and one or two other boarders at the dining table. But unlike the lost way she'd left church and walked into the house, she sat there beaming. She could almost feel herself sparkling, like Moses fresh off Mount Sinai after talking with God.

A once-enslaved servant who now worked for pay at the boardinghouse brought in the food. The diners gave thanks. Sunday suppers in the house were usually an easy-going, refreshing time, but no one seemed to know what to say. Each person looked to another.

Lottie dug into her plate of chicken pot pie. "It's been a joyous Sunday, hasn't it?"

"Indeed." The man who owned the boardinghouse spoke almost as if it were a question.

"You may have noticed I haven't been downstairs," Lottie said between bites. "I was blessed to spend the afternoon in prayer."

"Oh?" The man's wife casually spread butter over her cornbread.

"My heart has been divided and troubled lately. It's good to go to God with these things."

"Amen," said one of the other boarders.

"And you don't feel so divided and troubled now?" Anna asked carefully.

"I feel completely clear and united in my focus." Lottie set her fork down and dabbed her mouth with a napkin. "I'm confident God is calling me to China."

Anna dropped her fork and clasped her hands together. "Oh Lottie, that's wonderful! And you're sure? After that passionate sermon today, I imagine lots of people are questioning a call to missions."

"It was as clear as a bell." Lottie grinned from ear to ear. "I don't know how God will provide the funds, but I know he's called me to go."

Lottie's announcement broke the awkward tension in the room, clearing the way for a restful and happy evening in the house for everyone.

The following day after school, Lottie had lots of work to do. She went straight to the writing desk in her room to draft letters to Mrs. Crawford and

Eddie, telling them about her calling and her intentions to join them in China as soon as she could. Of course, she needed to write to Mr. Tupper, asking about the process and what all would be required of her to be officially appointed as a Southern Baptist missionary. But first, Lottie took out a sheet of writing paper and scratched her pen across the top.

Dear Helen.

It certainly wasn't Helen's sweet demeanor that made Lottie so nervous to send that letter. It was the consequences of whatever Helen's response would be. If Helen released Lottie from her promise, Lottie would be completely untethered to America and free to go to China. If Helen held her to it ... could Lottie abandon a vow?

Thankfully, Helen replied quickly, so Lottie wasn't walking around with her stomach in knots for too long. Her reply was gracious and affirming of Lottie's decision to follow God's leading. Helen wrote that Lottie's generous promise to care for Tom had always filled her heart with affection for the Moon family and had often given her peace and comfort in dark moments, especially after her second husband died. Helen expressed faith that the God who so clearly wanted Lottie to go to China would also care for her and her children in America. She released Lottie from her promise. Lottie clutched the letter to her heaving chest. Her head fell back in relief, and she whispered many thanks to God.

After Lottie got Helen's blessing, she received the other missionaries' enthusiastic support and Mr. Tupper's assurance that she could be appointed by the Foreign Mission Board as soon as June that year. It was all happening so fast.

In the flurry of writing letters, gathering references and information for the mission board, and working at the Cartersville school, Lottie was glad for Anna's invitation to share a simple afternoon tea in the last week of March.

Lottie eased into a wicker chair behind the boardinghouse next to Anna. As she leaned forward to select a cookie from the tray, the chair creaked as if it had helped many busy people relax throughout the years. Lottie nibbled her cookie and suspected this might not be a simple social tea. It seemed that behind Anna's smile was something she was eager to let out. When she finally did, Lottie's eyes popped open along with a wide smile.

"When did this happen?" Lottie asked.

"Nearly the same time as you. The more I tried to subtly convince you to go, I seemed to have convinced myself too."

Lottie laughed and set her plate down so she could wrap her friend in a hug. "Well, I wouldn't call it subtle, but I'm glad for you. And they're sending you to China too?"

"Yes, but in a city farther south to yours. I can't pronounce it yet. It's written on a paper upstairs. It's where many other Presbyterian Mission Board people are. How strange that we'll be in the same foreign country but not roommates or even neighbors."

Lottie nodded her head solemnly. Even if they got to travel on the same steamer and see each other every once in a while in China, she would miss Anna terribly. If it weren't for her, Lottie might not have had the courage to take the teaching opportunity in Georgia, much less one in China.

Thankfully, she didn't have to tell the families at the school alone. When she and Anna announced they were leaving to pursue foreign missions, most families expressed their hearty congratulations and thanks for all that the two principals had poured into their daughters' lives. Some even said so while wiping a tear.

But one Sunday shortly before the church service started, a well-known woman made a beeline across the lawn to speak with Lottie, the feathers on her hat bouncing wildly.

"Some of the families—not many, mind you," she said, slightly out of breath, "they just feel it's a bit wasteful for two highly educated and competent women such as you and Miss Safford to leave their fellow Southerners to go off and teach foreign girls in China."

Lottie might have been discouraged if she wasn't so resolved and if so many others hadn't already given her so much support. She just smiled and went into the building after the woman with the feathered hat.

Lottie made her way to a seat more toward the back than her usual pew. She wasn't embarrassed by her choices, but she didn't want to be a distraction during the pastor's sermon—not on her last Sunday at Cartersville Baptist Church. Some people were bound to not understand what she was doing. Whether they supported Anna and her or not, it seemed that everyone was talking about them. Lottie had hoped she was just being paranoid or proud, but her suspicions had been confirmed when the town's newspaper had printed an article about them. Yes, the back row was the best place to enjoy the service without being noticed. Except, of course, it was rare to not be noticed and greeted by at least one member at Cartersville Baptist.

When Pastor Headdon got to the pulpit and started preaching on missions, half of the congregation subtly peeked over their shoulders at Lottie, while the other half craned their necks to get a good look at her as she stared straight ahead and smiled at her pastor.

Dr. Headdon led the congregation to consider God's passion for the nations to know him and worship him. His sermon started with God's promise to Abraham to make his people a blessing to the world, and he went all the way to God's promise in Revelation, the fulfillment of which God showed to John—people from every nation and language worshiping God in heaven.

"God's desire is for the world to know him. When he calls a Christian to cross borders and boundaries to reach the lost, we should celebrate that and support them. It won't be easy for this woman who is sent out by God," he said, looking at Lottie, causing a fresh wave of craning necks. "But God will be with her. Let us be like the wind at her back, sending her out by generously giving of our prayers and our purses."

Dr. Headdon's eldest daughter made her way to the piano, and everyone stood. Lottie shared a hymnal with another woman on the back row. Lottie's voice cracked, and her hands weakened under the book's spine as the crowd filled the sanctuary with singing as well as a special offering plate with fifty dollars for the Foreign Mission Board. The woman next to Lottie offered her a spare handkerchief and gently took the hymnal to hold for both of them.

Lottie dabbed her eyes and nose, watching people add coins and paper bills to the plate before passing it along. God had sparked a passion for missions in this church, and a tinge of sadness rose at the thought of leaving before she got to see it grow and bear fruit. What beautiful things would God do in this congregation after she left?

Chapter Thirty-Three

1873

O rie returned from the yard to her front porch rocking chair of her Alabama home. "When does your steamer leave?"

"September 1." Lottie reached for her fan on the small table between them.

"Boys!" Orie yelled across the front yard. She didn't get up this time. "Didn't I just tell you? Don't let your little brother wander toward the river!"

Lottie's nephews sent a murmuring of "yes ma'ams" up to the porch.

Holding the fan, Lottie flicked her wrist, trying to make something of a breeze. She took a sip of iced tea with her free hand.

"After an August in Alabama, I'm sure you'll be plenty ready to leave the heat," Orie laughed as she snapped peas into a bowl in her lap. Her face clouded. "I'm getting more ready each day."

Lottie turned to her with raised brows. "But you all moved here not long ago."

"John thinks moving back to Albemarle County will bring more opportunities for paying work." Orie's heavy tone hinted that the thought made her tired. "He just hasn't been able to establish a steady practice here. We might stay till next year."

Alabama was Lottie's last stop before catching the train to San Francisco. After the Foreign Mission Board appointed her in June, Lottie spent time with her family in Virginia and then visited the Baptist women in Maryland. Mr. Tupper had told Lottie that they had been organizing women's groups in churches all around the South that raise support for missionaries, and she should meet them for herself. When she listened to the women talk about their plans, there was a sense in the air that something powerful and holy was brewing in that nearly Northern state. They weren't a large group, but they were focused on raising funds for foreign missions, especially for women missionaries. They seemed to have a friendly rivalry with the Presbyterians, who led the country in sending and supporting missionaries. These Baptist women told Lottie about small groups of women across the South that met regularly and advocated passionately for their fellow church members to support missions. Even if they couldn't give more than the biblical widow's mite, they would give it freely and joyfully. The trip had been a worthwhile detour from visiting family.

Orie turned to Lottie. "And your friend, Anna? She's going on the same boat, right?"

"Yes." Lottie smiled. God was so generous to send her to China with a friend. "But when we get to China, she will be south with the Presbyterians. I'll head up north with Eddie and the Baptists."

Orie laughed and shook her head. "Even in China, the Presbyterians and Baptists are separated."

"Only by location," Lottie said in their defense. "From what I gather, they're more united in heart than we are here. The mission keeps them focused on what's really important." She couldn't help a sly smile from spreading across her face. "But really, what's the harm in a little friendly competition?"

"Yes, right." Orie nodded as she stood and walked over to scoop up her littlest son, who was toddling over to her, crying, apparently hungry. She stepped inside to feed him.

Lottie refilled her glass with iced tea from the pitcher and continued watching her other nephews run and play. It felt good to rest after the whirlwind of the summer. The Foreign Mission Board had been ready to send her right away, even if she didn't have her financial support completely lined up. Lottie was as eager to go as they were to send her, but she wanted to spend her last few months in America wisely, inquiring about support and enjoying her family.

At Viewmont, Ike and Meg were still running the plantation, although it was more like a small farm, growing smaller each time Lottie visited. Mollie and her husband, Dr. Shepherd, were in Virginia, too, so they came to visit. Sallie was reportedly in a Catholic convent somewhere, but Lottie left a goodbye letter for her.

Lottie hadn't visited Georgia since she left the school, but she kept up correspondence with the Cartersville Baptists. She even sent them the photo-

graph that she'd had taken while she lived there, which wasn't difficult for her
to finally part with, once and for all.

The evening before Lottie would make her way west, she and Orie stayed
up late in the parlor, squeezing as much time out of the day as they could. The
boys had gone to bed, and John left Lottie and her sister on the sofa with
their tea.

Under the sofa near her foot, Lottie found one of the marbles that the
boys had left behind. She picked it up and admired the white swirl frozen in
the middle of the glass ball.

Orie smiled. "You've always liked those."

Lottie twirled it around her palm. "They're beautiful. Especially this
shooter."

"They're a hazard is what they are, especially when the boys forget to pick
them up." Orie pointed out a couple more on the floor. "No, you don't have
to—I didn't mean—"

But Lottie had already moved to the floor to pick them up. Orie grabbed a
small leather pouch and held it open, something neither of them ever did as
children, preferring to let the chaos roll all around them.

Lottie brushed her hands together. "Now it's safe to walk."

Orie laid the bag atop a side table, then plopped back down onto the sofa.
"It's nice to have the option, but I'd rather sit."

Lottie laughed. "It's been a real gift, seeing so many people I love before
tomorrow. I can hardly believe I got to visit with Mr. Tupper and the board,
the women in Maryland, Ike and Meg, and even Cary Ann and Mary in
Albemarle."

"That first leg of your tour must have been exhausting."

"The time here has been very settling," Lottie said.

"Well, I'm glad you got to visit all of us." Orie squished around for a more
comfy spot. "I haven't seen Mary since before the war. What about your other
friend? The sister of that handsome fellow—Mr. Toy." Her eyebrows bounced
at Lottie.

"That 'handsome fellow' is married now." Lottie was resigned to having
lost that opportunity. "His sister, Julie, seems to be doing very well. She and
her husband didn't go to Japan as they'd planned, but I have a hunch Julie
isn't done with missions. Her husband's a minister now, preaching in a few
Southern Baptist churches in Virginia. I think they'll be great allies in raising
funds and support for missions."

Lottie slapped her knee. "I almost forgot to tell you. When I was at Viewmont, Fannie shared some news about Peggy."

Orie smiled and took a sip of tea. "Good news, I hope."

Lottie beamed and nodded. "She and Matthew settled south of Chicago.

He got a good job, working some fields. Fannie told me they're saving up for a home with their own farm. Until then, Peggy has four children to keep her busy."

"Four babies." Orie lifted her face and closed her eyes as if imagining it. "That's wonderful. I'm happy they're settled."

"So am I." Lottie gave a soft sigh and frowned. "I don't think many of the freedmen had anywhere in particular to go after the war. They just left. I wonder if many of them settled into good jobs as Matthew did."

Orie shook her head as a quiet moment passed by. She swirled the dregs at the bottom of her teacup. "Are you nervous about tomorrow?"

"In some ways," Lottie admitted. "I'm not excited to spend a day on a train and then a month on a boat. But I'm completely thrilled to go. My heart is already there on the mission field. I'm just crossing the ocean to catch up with it. Mostly, I feel grateful, so deeply grateful for the chance to do the work that God has put in my heart."

Orie smiled at her with what looked like a mix of pride and awe. "Two of my little sisters—missionaries to China. Mother and Father would have boasted about that at every church missions meeting and prayer meeting."

Lottie laughed.

"Remember when we were young and in love with freedom and adventure?" Orie laid her free arm over a needlepointed pillow beside her.

"Of course. It was all we ever talked about—all I ever wanted," Lottie said. "I've enjoyed a few adventures in my time. But I suspect this next one will be really something."

"Yes, I reckon so." Orie nodded, her eyes growing wide.

Lottie sipped her tea and smiled into her cup. It seemed like yesterday that they'd been girls. "Back then, sneaking books by Grandmother Harris and getting as much education as we possibly could felt so rebellious and fun. It felt like freedom, and in a way, it was," Lottie said as she flipped through memories like a stack of postcards. "Going away to school and then teaching in different states—those turned out to be such fun and challenging adventures. And I *loved* leading the Georgia school and teaching those girls and supporting missions. For a while, I thought that's how the rest of my life was going to be. It was a dream job—a dream life, really. But now it's as if my little dreams are waking up to God's dreams for me, which are turning out to be even bigger and more exciting and wonderful than my own."

"It's good to see you so in love with him."

"It's so good to know him. Some days, I can't believe it. I can't believe he spent so much time coming after me when I was his enemy. I used to hate him —after Father and Tom and seeing you struggle so much after you graduated. You were so sad at home when no one here would hire you. I blamed God for every bad thing and worshiped every good thing he ever gave me instead of worshiping him for it." Lottie shook her head. "He is a merciful God to save a wicked sinner like me."

Orie swirled the tea in her cup, looking at her as if mulling over something she wasn't sure how to say. "True, you were his enemy," she finally said. "I was his enemy, too, choosing sin day after day instead of choosing him. But Lottie, I hope you know that you were also his prize."

Just where was Orie going with this?

"It's not as if God saved you because he felt sorry for you or because he needed you," Orie said. "He loved you. He saved you so that you could be together. That's what you're going to tell the Chinese, right? The God who made them wants to share his presence with them, but as they are now in their sin, that can't be. They need to know that Jesus made a way for them to be cleansed of sin so that they can be with God and know him and know his love."

"Now that's a sermon." Lottie raised her eyebrows. "The longer I'm here, the more I feel as though I want to stay with you and learn what you've learned about God. It's good to know you this way—my older, wiser sister who knows God so well."

"I'll miss you when you leave." Sadness clouded some of the pride in Orie's face. She reached across the sofa and laid a hand on top of Lottie's. "I miss you even now. So much of our time together at home was when we were far away from God. Now that we're both Christians ... it's just good to be together again."

"It's hard to leave good things for the better things God has planned next," Lottie said. Then she added with a laugh, "It'd be easier to leave if you were a mean, awful sister."

The lamplight was just bright enough to reveal Orie's pained expression.

"Orie?" Lottie said, concerned for her sister's sudden silence.

"I *was* an awful sister. I didn't know ..." Orie's voice broke. She struggled to continue. "Back then... I didn't know that *God* is the greatest adventure. Following him is the greatest freedom. Aunt Julia tried to tell me once, but it all sounded like a foreign language at the time."

"A lot of those things that she said—and Mother and Father and everyone at Scottsville Baptist—it just took some time for it to translate and work its way into our hearts," Lottie said in a comforting voice. "If I hadn't been so hard-headed and just surrendered to him earlier in life, I'd probably already be in China now like Eddie."

"You mean, if you didn't have a hard-hearted big sister, leading you astray for years." Orie broke down into tears. "I'm so sorry, Lottie," she sobbed. "You might have known Jesus much sooner if I were a better sister."

Lottie rose from her seat and knelt in front of Orie, taking her hands. "We were both so lost," she said, looking up at Orie. "But when you found Jesus, you told me right away."

Tears fell uncontrollably down Orie's face as she listened. She hung her head low and to the side as if she couldn't meet Lottie's eyes, which were now brimming with tears.

"When I was in school and got the news of your salvation ..." Lottie's voice began to shake. "It shocked me like an earthquake." She steadied her voice. "It made cracks in my stone-cold hard heart for God's love to finally find a way in. He used you to bring me to himself."

Orie's head collapsed into her hands, her shoulders heaving.

Lottie let her cry for a while and gently patted her head, whispering a verse like a blessing. "'And we know that all things work together for good to them that love God, to them who are the called according to his purpose.'"

Orie lifted herself up, heaved a great sigh, and let her shoulders relax as if they had been relieved from carrying a very heavy burden for a very long time.

The next morning, it was time for Lottie to pack her bags and board the train to San Francisco. The whole family had given her the wonderful gift of one last normal breakfast, behaving as if she wasn't going away for who knew how many years.

John loaded up the carriage, and when Lottie was settled on the bench, signaled for the horse to go. Tears fell on either side of her wide-stretched smile as she waved goodbye until her sister and nephews were out of sight.

When they reached the train, it steamed and whistled like a braying horse eager to run. Lottie's brother-in-law took her bags all the way inside to Lottie's compartment. He left her with an uncharacteristically hearty hug, as if he had just realized that he was the last family member she'd see on American soil for a long time.

Butterflies fluttered in Lottie's stomach as she took her seat. She looked around for something to distract her from the gravity of what she was doing. She was leaving everything and everyone she ever knew to live among the Chinese, who, from what Lottie understood of Eddie's letters, didn't particularly want missionaries there. She wanted to pray and sit quietly with God, but she felt exhausted with praying for herself and all that was going on in her life.

But wait ... While she was at Viewmont, Ike and Meg had told her that George and Fannie would be traveling at the end of August too. Possibly at that same moment, they were boarding a train to Illinois to see their daughter, Peggy, and her growing family. Lottie smiled, rested her head against her seat, and prayed for them. Thinking about someone else calmed her down.

Once Lottie finally arrived in San Francisco the next morning, she had the whole day ahead before her steamer departed the next morning. Anna was arriving later that day.

"Not late, just later," Anna had said when she and Lottie were planning the trip.

Lottie had warned Anna that the ship wouldn't wait for her.

San Francisco was so different from any city Lottie had known, she felt as though she was already traveling to foreign lands! Walking through a market, she slowed by a stall selling vibrant flowers, some of which she had never seen before. She took a deep breath to carry the scent with her, then immediately regretted it. Right next to the flowers were buckets and boxes of all sorts of fish for sale! Lottie scrunched her nose as the odor from San Francisco's bay mixed terribly with that of the scent from its flower fields. She scurried farther down the street.

All of the city's sounds were louder than she was used to. Bells rang on streetcars, alerting pedestrians who were trying to cross the road. Men roared with laughter as they stumbled out of saloons. Music that Lottie had never heard before poured out the swinging doors with them. She couldn't tell if people on the street were angry as they yelled at each other in incoherent languages or were simply trying to be heard above all the noise.

As Lottie explored the city, her butterflies fluttered again, this time about what she was doing. She searched for signs of Chinese culture. She had heard that many people had emigrated from China to California over the past several years. After attempting to walk up one of the city's many hills only once, she paid to ride the streetcars.

Lottie's heart leapt when she found Chinatown. She hopped off the streetcar and walked into one of the Chinese stores. It sold groceries that looked familiar—eggs and vegetables, but they were all of different sizes and colors than the ones back home. Among the fish, Lottie even saw what looked like shark fins. Since the labels were all in Chinese, she couldn't say for sure. She purchased a few items to investigate further back at her hotel room, including a handful of beans that had sprouted long white tails and a few dumplings, which looked like perfect little pastry purses. Anna would want to see these! With her groceries in tow, Lottie continued wandering through Chinatown, listening carefully as people spoke to each other in their language from home.

Late in the afternoon, she headed back toward her hotel to meet Anna.

Lottie turned a corner and froze. A shining gold cross atop a large building in the Chinese style stopped her in her tracks. Was it a Chinese church? What else could it be? She lifted a smile. The good news of Jesus had spread across America, coast to coast. Even Chinese immigrants had an opportunity to hear the gospel in their language. Her heart swelled with pride for her country.

She hadn't secured funding yet. Maybe she didn't need to waste the Foreign Mission Board's money on a steamer ticket if she was only going to be called home because they couldn't afford to keep her out there. Perhaps she could stay in San Francisco until she raised enough funding. Lottie could learn Chinese culture right here. She could visit Chinatown every day, listening to the language and eventually interacting with the Chinese. She could minister among them here in her own country. Then she could visit Viewmont a bit more often and grow in relationship with Orie again.

But the moment Lottie reached her room and started praying over her new plan, she remembered the prayers she had poured out for the people in China who didn't know God and had little opportunity to learn the truth about him. God had called her and provided for her all the way up to this point. How could she turn back now? She shook the idea out of her head. Anna better arrive at the hotel soon. Lottie needed to get on that ship as soon as possible.

Anna arrived in time to rest for the night, even though she was later than she'd said she would be.

Lottie gripped her friend in a bear hug. "I'm glad you're here."

Anna laughed. "Were you that bored, waiting for me?"

"I wandered all around the city. I think I saw a church in Chinatown."

Anna sucked in a quick breath and smiled. "Yes! A pastor back home told me about it. It's one of ours."

"Presbyterian?"

Anna nodded with a proud smile.

The Chinese in California needed a Baptist church. But that would be an adventure for someone else.

There was a knock at the door. Lottie and Anna turned. Anna started unbuckling her bag, so Lottie got the door. It was a telegram—for her. Mr. Tupper had written to encourage her that the women's missions group at Cartersville Baptist Church had decided to financially support Lottie.

Lottie closed the door, staring at the paper with a gaping mouth. If that wasn't confirmation to go, she didn't know what was.

The next morning. Lottie took quick strides down the street and determined steps up the gangway to the ship's deck. Most of the passengers gathered at the coast-facing side to wave goodbye, but Lottie didn't. She made her way to the other side of the ship and set her face toward where she was going.

Salt-tinged wind whipped her hair wildly as she looked out over the ocean. Tears swelled like the sea in front of her as she imagined the faces of millions of Chinese who were living their lives without knowledge of their creator who loved them. For almost half of her life, she had followed rebellious paths to empty destinations. Now at nearly thirty-three years old, she was embarking on an adventure more grand than she had ever imagined as a girl. Following Jesus brought her here. She felt the urge to hold his hand as they crossed the ocean together. But on this side of heaven, she gripped the railing instead.

The wooden gangway knocked on the port side of the steamer as the crew pulled it up and readied the ship for departure. Lottie closed her eyes and listened. Passengers shouted goodbyes to the cheering crowd ashore who were offering hearty farewells. The ship joined in, releasing a steaming whistle. As it started to move away from the dock, Lottie lifted her face into the wind and sang to God, who was going with her, "'There is a happy land far, far away, where saints in glory stand bright, bright as day. Oh how they sweetly sing 'Worth is our Savior King.' Loud let his praises ring, praise, praise for aye.'"

Author's Note

Lottie Moon is a big deal to Southern Baptists and to their missionary sending entity, the International Mission Board (IMB). And rightly so. She was instrumental in galvanizing Southern Baptists, particularly women, to give generously as well as to go and spread the gospel, whether they were married or not. After her death in 1912, the Women's Missionary Union of the Southern Baptist Convention made Lottie Moon the namesake of their annual missions offering that has raised over $1 billion.

The more I discovered about this missionary legend, the more I became interested in how she became one. Lottie was raised on a Virginia plantation by a Baptist family of slave owners, and her biographies paint her as a rebellious girl who thought church was a waste of time. How does someone like that grow up to travel across the world to preach the gospel of freedom in Jesus Christ? I spent several years researching Lottie's life, letters, and the world around her, determined to find out.

Becoming Lottie Moon explores how Lottie might have grown from a rebellious six-year-old on a Virginia plantation in 1847, doing whatever she could to avoid another church service, to a thirty-three-year-old single woman following God on a missionary adventure in 1873. I drew from a well of wide-ranging sources while researching and writing this novel.

Without Catherine B. Allen's diligent work in her biography, *The New Lottie Moon Story*, this book would not have been possible. Regina Sullivan's *Lottie Moon: A Southern Baptist Missionary to China in History and Legend* also enhanced the historical accuracy of this book.

I am indebted to the excellent staff at the Library of Virginia as well as that of the Virginia Baptist Historical Society, who generously helped me track down census data, church minutes, and other primary sources.

I also owe a great deal to Jennifer Oast's scholarship in *Institutional Slavery: Slaveholding Churches, Schools, Colleges, and Businesses in Virginia, 1680–1860* as well as to Ethel Morgan Smith's work in *From Whence Cometh My Help: The African American Community at Hollins College*. These two books revealed to me the true story of Ann Scott and were crucial to my understanding of the lives of enslaved people at Hollins.

The Civil War as a Theological Crisis by Mark A. Noll and *Reconstructing the Gospel: Finding Freedom from Slaveholder Religion* by Jonathan Wilson-Hartgrove were indispensable in my research about what Christians in the Civil War-era preached and believed about slavery.

While there is no record of Lottie's direct views on slavery, I found no evidence of Lottie pining for the Southern "Lost Cause" or bemoaning the loss of her family's personal fortune, which depended on the work of generations of enslaved people. Based on Lottie's writing and the influences in her life, I deduce that Lottie likely recognized that the gospel of Jesus Christ should radically change not only individual lives, but also social systems— changes which could be disruptive and costly. I became convinced of this when I read one of her letters from China in 1878, in which Lottie wrote about "the wickedness of the practice" of binding young girls' feet. Footbinding was a system in China that degraded God's image bearers and carried economic consequences for families. As Lottie described it, it was "utterly inconsistent with the gospel of Jesus."

Becoming Lottie Moon is a work of historical fiction, not a biography, but it is grounded in extensive research and obsessively strives for historical accuracy. Researching and writing this book has impacted me greatly as a writer and a follower of Jesus. Now, I am thrilled to share Lottie's story of how trusting and following God is the greatest adventure and the way to true freedom. My prayer is that this novel blesses readers and, above all, glorifies God.

Visit **EmilyHallBooks.com** for a collection of FAQs to discover what was fact and fiction in this novel. And don't miss the thought-provoking discussion starters to help you or your book club go deeper with Lottie's story.

About the Author

Emily Hall writes stories with nuance and grace about everyday people who have become extraordinary legends. She is fueled by cookie dough, kickboxing, and library visits. Whether it's the Library of Virginia, historical society libraries, or story time with her little one, Emily loves spending time in libraries. She lives in Richmond, Virginia with her family.

**Visit Emily online and sign up for her newsletter at
EmilyHallBooks.com.**